ORAL LITERATURE AND MORAL EDUCATION AMONG THE LAKESIDE TONGA OF NORTHERN MALAWI

I0593048

Published by
Mzuni Press
P/Bag 201
Luwinga, Mzuzu 2

ISBN 978-99908-0244-3

Mzuni Press is represented outside Africa by:

African Books Collective Oxford (orders@africanbookscollective.com)

Printed in Malawi by Baptist Publications, P.O. Box 444, Lilongwe

Oral Literature and Moral Education among the Lakeside Tonga of Northern Malawi

David Kapenyela Mphande

MZUNI PRESS

Mzuni Books no. 13

Mzuzu

2014

Contents

Foreword 10

Chapter One.. 12

Oral Traditional Literature: A Survey 12
    Oral Traditional Literature in Malawi.................................... 12
    Oral Traditional Literature outside Malawi 24
    Oral Transmission in Biblical and Traditional Texts 30
    Myth and other Genres in Folk Tradition 43

Chapter Two 53

The Tonga People and their Culture 53
    Kinship and Locality.. 56

Chapter Three 78

Forms and Nature of Tonga Oral Literature 78
    Introduction 78
    Tonga Artistic Expression... 78
    Classification of Tales 79
    Stories about Animals 82
    Stories about People and their Ecology............................. 83
    Stories about Chiuta and Origins 83
    The Concept of *Nthanu* 84
    Thematic Analysis of the Stories... 85
    The Oral Tale Performance.. 86

Chapter Four... 93

Tonga Rituals and their Influence on Moral Education........... 93
    The Cycle of Life 93

Chapter Five.. 107

Influence of Christianty and Islam on Tonga Culture........... 107
    Christianity and Tonga Customs 107
    Islam and Tonga Traditional Values 131

Chapter Six.. 141

Anthology of Tonga Myths and Folktales................................ 141
    Introduction 141
    The Narratives and their Use in Moral Instruction 141
    (1) A Legend about the Origin of the Tonga People....... 144

(2) Origin of Death (Chameleon and Lizard) 154
(3) Cursing the Birds 158
(4) The Role of the Aged 160
(5) Quality of Friendship 165
(6) The Orphaned Millipede 171
(7) The Head (*Chimutu*) 175
(8) Hare and the Well 182
(9) The Three Brothers 192
(10) The Blind and the Hunchback 197
(11) Why Monkeys Live in Trees 206
(12) Why Hyena does not Look at Wild Cat 206
(13) The Dumb Maiden 208
(14) Why the Hyena has Ugly Spots 209
(15) The Wild Cat and the Rooster 210
(16) Courage 211
(17) Who had performed the best? 212
(18) The Five Helpers 213
(19) The Three Wives 214
(20) Breaking the Promise 215
(21) An Eye for an Eye 217
(22) Rich Man and Poor Man 218
(23) Finders Keepers 220
(24) Kindness Pays 221
(25) Friendship 223
(26) Friends for a time 225
(27) An Old Woman who did not Heed Advice 226
(28) The Lion and the Sparrow 228
(29) Tupa and his Children 229
(30) The Roan Antelope and the Lion 230
(31) Dishonesty 232
(32) The Beautiful Proud Girl 233
(33) Someday someone may be better than you 234
(34) The Wisdom of the Spider 236
(35) The Fox who Cost the Life of his Wife 238
(36) The Lions and the Hare 241
(37) Evil Returns to the One who Does it 243
(38) The Greedy Hyena 244
(39) The Warning that Went Unheeded 246
(40) The Two Hunters 247

General Comments on Tonga Myths and Folktales 249

Chapter Seven... 252

An Anthology of Tonga Proverbs 252
   Sources and Authority of Proverbs 252

An Anthology of Tonga Proverbs 257
   1 Abaya chiwanda 257
   2 Abaya soro cha 257
   3 Amunkhwele asekana viphata 258
   4 Boza liwele mweneko 258
   5 Changa epa wamko ku mchira wataya 259
   6 Charu mbanthu 259
   7 Chigau ndi ku mupozwa 260
   8 Chikumbu chimoza chituswa nyinda cha 260
   9 Chingana nyoko wawi ndi nyivu ndi nyoko mbwenu 261
   10 Chiuta wamto 262
   11 Chiwele vuli chingubaya Tungwa 262
   12 Cho chingukwezga Pusi, chingukwezga Munkhwere 262
   13 Cho chituza chitumba ng'oma cha 263
   14 Cho utanja ndichu chipunduwa 264
   15 Garu yiruma mbuyake 264
   16 Jenda-yija wangukukurwa ndi maji 265
   17 Juwani lapa mchenga nkhwambiya pamoza 266
   18 Kanda apa nani ndi kandepo 266
   19 Kanthu kekose kendi nyengo yaki 267
   20 Kayuni ko kaja pauta kalasika cha 268
   21 Kufumba nkhuwona nthowa 268
   22 Kujikama uryengi kanthu ndi wala, kusoka uwengi waka 269
   23 Kukana kwa mutu wa garu 269
   24 Kukanda pa moto 270
   25 Kakuza kija kasikuwa 270
   26 Kulinda malinda-linda 271
   27 Kumuzi waku ndi kumuzi waku 272
   28 Kupaska nkhusunga 272
   29 Kusewe ndi chirwani mbuzereza 273
   30 Kusewe ndi lezara la uyi kosekose 274
   31 Kuwezga janja or, Kase ruta kase weku 274
   32 Kuyambiriya nkhugona pakati 274
   33 Kwambiriya maji gheche mugongono 275

34 Kwawiyako Chiuta 276
35 Kwe karakato 277
36 Likhwechu lamunyako payika, mawamle pako 277
37 Lilime lenge moto 278
38 Limphezi liweliyamo cha mu chimiti 278
39 Maliro nkhuliyana 279
40 Malo gho utanja kusambapo ndigho patachikukole mng'ona 279
41 Manda ghawole pa khomo 280
42 Mata gha mula ghatuwa pasi cha 280
43 Matako ghawi ghaleka cha ku kwenthana 281
44 Maungu tikumwa, matali tikurya, kwajanji so? 282
45 Mawala ghatuswa vyaka 282
46 Mazua ghasintha 283
47 Mazua nganande, weya wang'ombe ngumana 284
48 Mbawa kume masengwe nkhuwambala lisito 284
49 Mlamba ndiyo watunga 285
50 Mlendo ndi dungwi 286
51 Mlendo ndiyo wabaya njoka 286
52 Mnthenkhu waryiya pa chipando 287
53 Moto walimbuni utocha lisuwa likuru 288
54 Mtiti ungamugolore cha pa mazila ghake 288
55 Mtonga nchigumbuli 289
56 Mu moyo ndi sitolo 289
57 Mukucha nkhazunguliyanga chulu 290
58 Munthu wambura kuvvwa wabuchira mbavi ye mu mutu
waki 291
59 Munthu wamtimba kuwi 291
60 Munthukazi wakuja pa khonde watuba vyaweni, po anyaki
alima yiyu cha   292
61 Mwana kopa kazimu nkhumuluma 292
62 Mwana mranda wasambira vyo wanthu wakamba pa
mphara 293
63 Mwana ndi chola 293
64 Mwana wakuti kaya kuti wachila cha 294
65 Mwana wambula kuvvwa wangume masengwe ku masu 294
66 Mwana wamunyako ndi samba m'manja, wako ndi ryangako
295
67 Mwana wangu wakana marangu yiku yimulange ndi Njovu 296
68 Mzimu ndirinde 296

69 Mzinda unyenga 297

70 Mazu gha wala ghawe pawaka cha 298

71 Ndakana Chiuta mkali 298

72 Ndakukambiyanga kuti ndi nyanga cha kwene mheni ndi
   tiringanenge   299

73 Ng'ombe yo yadanjiya yitumwa maji ghakutowa 300

74 Njifwa ye pose 300

75 Njovu yitufwa ndi mivwi yinande 300

76 Nkhombo atamba kusuka mkati 301

77 Nozga kapasi mwakuti kapachanya kasike 302

78 Nyoko ndi nyoko chingana wapunduki 302

79 Nyoli yizirwa ndi mavungwa 303

80 Palima mphamoyo 303

81 Po pe josi pe moto 304

82 Pundu waruwa cha po wangurya chiwanga 304

83 Pusi wakukota atimuliska wana wake 305

84 Somba yakuvunda pamumphika yiziwa kuvundiska zonse 306

85 Sonu awiya ose pa msana pe, ndikuti manja pu! pu! Pepa,
   pepa! 306

86 Sunga khose mukanda wazamuvwara 307

87 Ubwezi wa mbavi wanbura kurumba mbuyaki 307

88 Uchiwinda ukamba wako 308

89 Uku-vyanowa, uku-vyanowa, Pusi wanguwa chagada 309

90 Ulemu ubaya 309

91 Uyu ndi Chimbwi 310

92 Vimiti vyo vyepamoza vileka cha kuchita ng'wema 311

93 Vitotoka vigona mu chikutu chimoza cha 311

94 Vya mzinga 312

95 Vyotikamba vya mng'ombe 313

96 Wabila pa chandi mutu uwoneka 313

97 Wakozga kwa wiske 314

98 Wakuya ku muzi ukuru 314

99 Wamuchontha muguto 315

100 Wavituta 315

101 Wawona masu gha chulu ghatema 316

102. Wazamukumana ndi aweya wa mujino, mumphunu ulimu
    kale 317

103 Wendi jisu la nkwazi 317

104 Wendi mzimu uheni 318

105 Wendi mzimu wamampha 318
106 Yo pamuko pa moyo ndiyo wajura kukhomo 319
107 Yo waswela mviheni wariyengi 320
108 Yo watenda ndi mnkhungu nayo wawengi mnkhungu 320
109 Yo watondo wasunga, yo wataya waliya 321
110 Zeru yimoza yibayiska 321
111 Zeru zakuwija zibayiska 322
112 Ziulikanga zikumpoka mahomwa 322
113 Zua limoza kuti liwozga nyama ya Njovu cha 323
114 Zunguliyane, ine ndizunguliyengi uku tikumanenge
kurweka 323

Conclusion 325

Recommendations for Application 327
On the Use of Folklore in the School Curriculum 327
Creation of Tales and Proverbs 327
Status of Tonga Oral Literature in School 328
Story-telling and its Alternatives 329
Recreation of Venues for Moral Instruction 330
Inculturation of the Gospel 331

Additional Tonga Proverbs for Study and Reflection 333

Bibliography 339

FOREWORD

For a number of years I have had an interest in oral traditions and related problems, although I am not a specialist. In October 1994 I was fortunate enough to receive some grants to support my research in this area. Support came from the Pew Charitable Trust in Philadelphia which was associated with the African Proverbs Project. The title of the research was "*On the Use of Tonga Myths, Folktales and Proverbs in Moral Education.*"

The purpose of the research was to investigate the use of Tonga myths, folktales, proverbs and rituals for their role in Moral Education and assess and evaluate their contribution towards value formation for the youth.

A basic proposition of modern sociology shows that cultural sciences are concerned with values and meaning, developing concepts and interpretations relevant to the society in which they take shape. In this book we shall see that Tonga oral literature relates to the beliefs and values of their society and on the ideal community they seek. The concern is that the oral traditions, myths, folktales, proverbs and customs of the Tonga people, are constantly endangered. If a people's culture is endangered, the consequences are that the community loses its identity, dignity, unity, security and continuity. Of late we have seen a political will to promote our Malawi cultural heritage.

The Tonga culture has not influenced other cultures except in the areas of Western Education and the spread of the Christian Gospel in and outside Malawi. But the Tonga Community has no cultural values to contribute to other communities. Therefore, this book seeks to promote and preserve the Tonga oral traditions. The youths as future Malawian leaders should be culturally, socially, linguistically, and ideologically equipped in under-standing and appreciating their cultural values.

The author of this book expects the reader to learn from the wealth of insight and knowledge carried on by the older people of any community as indispensable. On occasion an older person may even learn from a younger person. A wider concept is that a nation evolves through the passing on of knowledge, values and skills. Successive generations thereby acquire knowledge and skills with which a better life and a strong nation can be built. I encourage the youth and any reader of this book that all of us together we must learn from those who have already walked the path.

Each chapter in this book aims to discuss some ideas in the anthropology of religion and to illustrate them with specific case studies formed primarily through conversation with friends, both young and old, over some years since I first went for field studies In 1994. The author understands that culture is dynamic and that some of the cultural elements discussed in this book have since been changing; for example the "Malipenga dance" has been overtaken by the "Chilimika dance."

Chapter 1 of this book provides a general survey of oral traditional literature within and outside Malawi. This provides a relevant Introduction to the chapters that follow. Chapters 2 and 3 focus on the Tonga people and their culture, also examining forms and nature of their oral literature. Chapter 4 discusses Tonga rituals and their influence on Moral Education.

Chapter 5 deals with the interventions of Christianity and Islam into Tonga culture. This intervention shows that both Christianity and Islam did not seriously consider the inculturation of Tonga culture into their religious teachings.

Chapter 6 gives case studies showing how Tonga legends, myths, folktales that can be used for Moral Education. Chapter 7 is a collection of Tonga proverbs with annotations for Preaching and Teaching.

Finally I dedicate this book to Mary, my wife who tirelessly typed the original manuscripts. Also to my late father and mother for their unceasing love and care during my boyhood, who, through the filter of folktales, legends and proverbs helped to lay the foundation for my endeavour to explore our African way of life.

It has been a pleasure to work with Mzuzu University und Mzuni Press, because it provided an opportunity to work with Professor Klaus Fiedler, with whom I have collaborated on various publishing projects over the past 15 years.

If something has been done in a hurry or omitted from this book, it is my fault. May you enjoy the challenge of always asking "Why?"

David Mphande, January 2014

CHAPTER ONE

ORAL TRADITIONAL LITERATURE: A SURVEY

Since time immemorial, African peoples have been expressing their experiences, their concerns in bringing up the next generation, their wisdom and vice to master life's challenges, and their total worldview in stories and myths, riddles and songs, proverbs and sayings and other forms of oral literature. Therefore, a good way to know a people is to study its oral literature, and this is what this book attempts.

This is a book about the Tonga of Northern Malawi, sometimes called the Lakeshore Tonga to distinguish them from other ethnic groups with the same name further west in Central Africa. The Lakeshore Tonga were the first ethnic group to identify themselves with the Christian faith the Free Church of Scotland missionaries under the leadership of Dr Robert Laws brought, with their strong emphasis on Western style education.

Being a Tonga myself, an educationist and a minister of religion, as well as a politician, I intend to inquire how the rich oral heritage of the Tonga can be utilized for a better understanding of Tonga culture and for the education of future generations. To do this I first want to place Tonga oral literature into a Malawian and generally African context.

Oral Traditional Literature in Malawi

Cultural studies in print based on Malawian oral traditions are probably scattered in academic theses and inaccessible private collections of interested sympathizers all over the world. Steve Chimombo discusses trends of oral literature in Malawi by summarizing first the work done from the earliest in print. He has also made evaluations of the works of this period.[1] He has stated the factors giving rise to the interest in this area, the nature, quality, and quantity of the work, and the overall significance of the

---

[1] Chimombo discusses Cullen Young's work on the Tumbuka-Nkhamanga people in: *Malawian Oral Literature: The Aesthetic of Indigenous Arts*, Zomba: Centre for Social Research, 1988, p. 15.

material, by focusing mainly on Chewa and Yao oral literature and not on Tumbuka and Tonga early works.

The Pre-Colonial Period

Steve Chimombo's study shows that most of the early sources available have come from the pen of foreign missionaries, traders, administrators, explorers and anthropologists. The earliest collection of texts in Malawi is that of Duff MacDonald, who studied some traditional oral literature among the Yao, publishing fifty-eight Yao narratives in 1882. He observes that there are four distinct forms of oral traditional literature. The first form is the *Ndawi* or conundrum, as where the *"house without a door"* stands for an "egg." There are also conundrums in the form of a little story. The second group consists of *Ndano* or tales also called *Ndawi*. Duff observes that *Ndano* were often recited in this form on public occasions after sunset.[2] However, the purpose of these early collections was to learn the local language, reduce it to writing and then teach the people in their own language. In other words, the reasons were purely anthropological, religious, linguistic, and literary.

The Colonial Period

The colonial period saw the publication of more collections of Yao narratives. These collectors saw the narratives as a way of analyzing and learning the language.[3] The most useful collection is that of R.S. Rattray, who worked as a trader in the Central Region. He claims that

> Quite apart from their ethnological value, any stories from the mouth of a native ... are of value, as being the very best way of gaining a colloquial knowledge of the language, showing as they do its idioms, syntax and grammar, in their purest and most natural form in a way that halting replies to single questions put by an interlocutor could never do, and occasionally giving one glimpses into native humor and character that could not otherwise have been obtained.[4]

---

2   Duff MacDonald*Africana or the Heart of Heathen Africa*, vol 1, London: Dawson, 1882, pp. 48, 122.

3   Steve Chimombo, "Oral Literature Research in Malawi," in Bernth Lindfors (ed), *Research in African Literature*, vol. 1, no. 1, University of Texas Press, 1987, p. 488.

4   R.S. Rattray, *Some Folklore Stories and Songs in Chinyanja*, London: SPCK, 1907, p. 213.

Rattray was, therefore, interested in collecting folk stories as reflectors of linguistic stylistic features and of the personality of the people.

In 1905 Alexander MacAlpine set about the task of familiarizing himself with village life among the Lakeside Tonga of Nkhata Bay. He produced some ethnographic material in article form in the Livingstonia periodical, *The Aurora*, starting in 1905. The articles were remarkably devoid of sensationalism, and could be seen as the first really systematic study of Tonga culture and religion. MacAlpine paid particular attention to Tonga religious beliefs and customs, and he provided a full account of Tonga mortuary rituals.[5]

In 1929 Cullen T. Young produced his first vernacular text, *Makuliro gha Mahara Mkati mu Wanthu* (*The Growth of Wisdom in People*). In 1931 he wrote *Notes on Customs and Folklore of the Tumbuka-Nkhamanga People*. Young classifies their oral literature as consisting of fables, sayings, and proverbs. He notes that several of these were heard in a village school at different dates, being taught by an old African teacher during the weekly period set apart for moral lessons. Young, unlike MacDonald, recognizes the existence of proverbs, although he does not give the vernacular terms. He puts it this way:

> The proverbial wisdom of this federation of early people as well as the language in which many of these proverbs are couched, presents points of interest ... I shall let these African aphorisms speak for themselves.[6]

In speaking about "sayings" for the same forms, Young observes that "the great bulk of sayings recorded here - some witty, all wise sayings, have already appeared ... these aphorisms naturally use a slang, rather than a 'cultured' form wherever a choice of that sort offers."[7] Another work was the combined effort of Hastings Kamuzu Banda and T. Cullen Young, *Our African Way of Life* (1946), which was written from a distance. This work consists of three short stories translated from Chichewa. Banda and Young wrote a short introduction, explaining the story of the examination room

---

[5]   A.G. MacAlpine, "Tonga Religious Beliefs and Customs," *Aurora*, 1905, pp. 182-190, 257-268.

[6]   T. Cullen Young, "Notes on the Customs and Folklore of the Tumbuka-Nkhamanga Peoples of the Northern Province in Nyasaland (Livingstonia)," *Africa* 4 (1931), p. 179.

[7]   T. Cullen Young, "Some Proverbs of the Tumbuka-Nkhamanga Peoples of the Northern Province in Nyasaland," *Africa* 4 (1931), pp. 345-351.

and the subsequent re-acquaintance in Edinburgh. *Our African Way of Life* is an exposition of Chewa virtues.[8]

Ernest Gray made a collection of 400 proverbs between 1930 and 1940, chiefly from Nyanja and Ngoni living in Zomba and Ntcheu districts. Gray identifies three distinct types of proverbs. The first type is proverbs in which no metaphor is used and no attempt made to conceal the meaning as in *kupatsa ndi kuika* (giving away is keeping on one side). The second group is those proverbs that contain metaphors. The meaning is not so obviously clear, e.g. *fodya ndi yemwe ali pa mphuno* (snuff is that which is at the nose). The third group is proverbs, which depend for their meaning on some underlying *nthanu* (folktale), e.g. *Chisoni chinapha nkhwali* (Pity killed the francolin).[9]

Gray classifies oral literature as consisting of riddles, proverbs, witty sayings, customs handed down, traditional songs and folk stories. For Gray, these do not appear to have been clearly differentiated in the minds of the Nyanja people as the terms used to denote these are loosely and vaguely used with varying connotation due to the admixture of tribes and languages. However, on collecting the proverbs Gray observes:

> They are not commonly on the tongues of young people neither are they used for amusement or as a pastime. The ideal way therefore - though it is a very slow one - is to be constantly in conversation, when the circumstances in which they are used can also be noted. The ideal place to collect proverbs is in the courtyard, where ecclesiastical or secular meetings take place. If proverbs are solicited care must be taken to ask other reliable informants if the proverbs so collected are known to them and recognized as such.[10]

Gray further categorizes the proverbs according to the particular moral value commented upon, the lesson taught, or the rule of conduct inculcated in each proverb. Some of these proverbs are varied, some go straight to the point, and others use some animal or inanimate object as a symbol. Others are spoken in an abbreviated form. All these early works were intended for linguistic purposes, communication, and for evangelization.

---

8   T. Cullen Young and Hastings Kamuzu Banda (eds), *Our African Way of Life*, London: Lutterworth, 1946, p. 152. (Dr Hastings Banda was the first President of the Republic of Malawi. He met T. Cullen Young in Britain in his early days).

9   Ernest Gray, "Some Proverbs of the Nyanja," *African Studies* 3, (1944), p. 102f.

10   Ibid., p. 101.

Studies by Malawians between 1900 and 1960 show scanty interest in this field. The earliest publication in Nyanja was by Stevenson Kumakanga, *Nzeru za Kale*, in 1934;[11] S.Y. Nthara published *Mbiri ya Achewa* (The History of the Chewa) at Nkhoma in 1944-5. A revised edition appeared in 1949, and it has subsequently been translated into English (1973). However, most of the published versions of this period show errors in collection, translation and presentation. There is duplication of other people's works or absence of comparative notes or comments across ethnic groups. In the case of some translations, foreigners could not do full justice to the text. Furthermore, since the collectors were not oral literature scholars, aspects of style, aesthetic, and performance tended to be ignored. Also, the materials suffered from an imbalance of genres. Genres like songs or riddles suffered as a consequence. A related problem is one of classification of genres of the oral literature rather than understanding the indigenous terms.

The Post-Colonial Period

This period witnessed a revival of interest in oral literature. Independence and the establishment of the University of Malawi encouraged this. The museums of Malawi, as well as the National Archives, ensured support at high levels. The University of Malawi also placed research into Malawian culture on a respectable footing. However, most of the literature of this period was heavily censored before publication. This also restricted some writers to come up openly with their research.

In the area of oral historical research in Malawi, Kings Phiri cites several works done during this period. His article surveys a contribution which oral historical research has made in Malawi by looking at specific research projects, as well as the methodological tradition to which researchers subscribed.[12]

Phiri first cites the work of Harry Langworthy who conducted research on the oral traditions of the Chewa in eastern Zambia and central Malawi between 1964 and 1965. Langworthy made the assumption that an understanding of contemporary Chewa political and social structure is a

---

[11] Stevenson Kumakanga, *Nzeru za Kale*, Blantyre: Dzuka, 1934.

[12] Kings M. Phiri, "Oral Historical Research in Malawi: A Review of Contemporary Methodology and Projects," *Kalulu: Bulletin of Malawian Oral Literature and Culture Studies*, vol. 1, no. 1, (June 1976), pp. 86-93.

prerequisite for discerning Chewa history.[13] Leroy Vail and Landeg White conducted a research on Tumbuka oral history between 1969-1971. Vail has been the foremost critic of Cullen Young on some of the historical methods taken to study the history of the Tumbuka people.[14] Vail points to the absence of a centralized bureaucracy, or army, or legal system worth speaking of between the Chikulamayembe and the Balowoka, and further observes that there were strong pressures on all sides to accept the myth of a powerful empire controlled by a Chikulamayembe paramountcy.[15]

Owen Kalinga made his study of the Ngonde traditional history in 1971 and 1972. His work is based on oral traditions.[16] Kalinga recognizes the value of the contribution of the Ngonde spokesmen in Young's historical work and also praises Young's classification of all clans in the main Tumbuka speaking zone according to their area of origin. Rangeley and Marwick underlined the importance of oral tradition for the understanding of Chewa migrations into Malawi, early settlement formation, and the growth as well as the spread of chieftainships.[17]

Mtthew Schoffeleers in "*The History and Political Role of the Mbona Cult among the Mang'anja*," has managed to outline the dynamic process by which political power in the Lower Shire Valley shifted from one ruling family to another over a long period of time. The aim in doing so, however, was to show that the shift of political power that took place had a direct bearing on the control of the Central Mang'anja religious system created by Mbona, the religious hero.[18] Schoffeleers' work is on the influence of the Mbona Cult on the Lundu dynasty.

---

[13] Ibid., p. 89.

[14] T. Cullen Young, "*Notes on the Speech and History of the Tumbuka-Henga Peoples*," Livingstonia: Mission Press, 1923, p. 223.

[15] Leroy Vail, "Review of 1970 'Republication of Notes on History'," *African Studies*, 30, (1971), p. 67.

[16] Owen Kalinga, *A History of the Ngonde Kingdom of Malawi*, Berlin: Mouton, 1985, pp. 27-45.

[17] Kings M. Phiri, "Oral Historical Research," *Kalulu*, p. 91. Also see Rangeley, "Notes on Chewa Tribal Law," *Nyasaland Journal*, vol. 1, no. 3 [1948], pp. 5-8.

[18] Ibid., p. 92.

Another important work is that of the anthropologist, Jan van Velsen, who did his study on the Lakeside Tonga of Nkhata Bay.[19] As a result of his field investigation, van Velsen published a monograph on the Tonga. The main focus of van Velsen's study are the Tonga clans. He observes that Kabunduli and his party, including Kanyenda, initially settled in Tongaland. The political rivalry between the Phiri (Kabunduli) clan and the Kapunda Banda is central to van Velsen's analysis. As an anthropologist, he stresses the importance of considering such traditions in light of present day knowledge of the society in question. He sees myths as charters for existing social relationships. He shows that legends can validate present social and political relations in terms of the past; thus caution is needed in treating them as historical evidence.[20]

Some Major Contemporary Studies on Oral Literature in Malawi

The foregoing discussion on the development of oral literature and oral history research in Malawi necessitates the examination of some contemporary works of some artists, folklorists and researchers.[21]

Again Chimombo attempts to put together some views of other Malawian artists, folklorists, novelists and researchers, who have tried to explore some of the definitional problems encountered when discussing the major Malawian folklore items. In his attempt to reclassify some verbal arts: *mwambi, mwambo, nthanu, chifanizo, nthabwala, mbiri, nkhani* or *chisomo* and *chitagi*, he defines each of these folklore items.

Chimombo also makes a broad investigation into the current usage of some of the Chichewa folklore terms. He claims that thirty-one usages were examined from twenty-seven published sources by nineteen different Chinyanja authors.[22] He further lists problems encountered in the collection of oral literature. These problems include collecting tales out of context,

---

19 Jan van Velsen, "The Missionary Factor among the Lakeside Tonga of Nyasaland," *Rhodes-Livingstone Journal*, 26, (1960), p. 1-22. Van Velsen uses the term 'Lakeside Tonga' to distinguish them from the Tonga of Lower Shire and those of Zambia.

20 Jan van Velsen, *The Politics of Kinship: A Study in Social Manipulation among the Lakeside Tonga of Nyasaland*, Manchester University Press, 1964.

21 Steve Chimombo, *Malawian Oral Literature: The Aesthetics of Indigenous Arts*, Domasi: Malawi Institute of Education, 1988.

22 Ibid., p. 20.

cross-cultural perspectives on form and context, dubious sources of information, crude methods of collection resulting in distortion of the texts and the fluidity of the verbal arts themselves. He sees that these problems are related to the collector's unfamiliarity with conventions and due to the collector's unfamiliarity with narrative performance.[23]

Another field report on Chewa folk narrative is that of Enock Timpunza Mvula. The study is important in that it relates in some ways to my work, although his work is for linguistic purposes. Mvula describes the performance of *nthanu* as *kuyimba nthanu*, and *nthanu* means "folk narrative" (*vidokoni* in Tumbuka).[24] Mvula, like Duff MacDonald, observes that folktales are told in the evenings. It is considered a taboo for *nthanu* to be told during the day. Children are warned that if they tell stories during the day their mother will die or become an anthill.

Mvula locates many places where the Chewa exchange stories, for example, in the *mphala* (unmarried boys' dormitory), around the fire, during moonlit nights in an open space, or in the house of the parents after supper. The common place is the *kuka*, around grandmother's house. Mvula observes that the folktales are used for different purposes: for settling a disagreement at the *bwalo* (village court), the elaboration of a biblical passage in church; the imparting of traditional histories, customs and beliefs to boys or girls during an initiation rite; and the explanation of a proverb to a child in or outside the classroom. He observes that in Chichewa the women are the best story-tellers. Various story-telling events and functions influence the style of individual narrators. At the same time, the content of the folk narrative is affected by the occasion as well as the function of the particular performance.

In speaking about oral narrative performance, Mvula observes that songs, chants, and sayings are the most stable elements in the oral tradition:

> Among the same audience there is the smaller group of people who are able to judge the correctness of the folk narrative and the style of singing the songs. These people who are well versed in the folk narratives and techniques of story-telling comment as the story is being told. A narrator

---

23 Ibid., p. 55.
24 Enock Timpunza Mvula, "Chewa Folk Narrative Performance," *Kalulu* 3 (1982). Mvula also discusses similar concepts in his "Some Chewa Folkstories from Central Malawi," MA, University of Leeds, 1978, pp. 22-24.

who substitutes details in some stories with those from other narratives is corrected.[25]

Mvula notes that the Chewa story-tellers, though non-professionals, are good narrators and respected for their imagination. Some story-tellers have inherited their talents through the father's or the mother's line.

In discussing what happens at the time of performance, Mvula states that the stylistic devices among Chewa story-tellers are: audience participation and the song, the opening formula, characterization, idiophones, repetition, suspense, stringing folk narrative together and the closing formula. Story telling is seen as a joint activity by both narrator and audience, the story-teller leading and the audience receiving the message, and supporting by giving immediate feed-back. The audience reacts to some funny words, exaggerations, mimicry or gestures, which have dramatic effects. Mvula observes that the story-teller is sensitive to word and melody to achieve a structured rhythmic pattern. After the opening formula: *Padangotero* or *adangotero* (They told it this way), the audience response is *Tili tonse* (We are ready to listen to your story), and as long as the audience keeps on assuring the story-teller each time, he/she advances in the narrative. For Mvula, stories are made lively and dramatic by the narrator's ability to play on words, phrases and sentences, which he calls "idiophones." He puts it in this way:

> You can hear the sound of a person walking on the dry leaves (*tswa-tswa-tswa*), a child walking in water (*chuwa-chuwa*); the frying of maize (*weye-weye*, and *the-the-the*); the hunter chasing an antelope (*suyo-suyo-suyo*) and the thunder storming and flashing (*gu-gu-lulue*) and (*ng'ani-ng'ani*).[26]

By using ideophones the narrator is creating images. This serves as a process of remembering traditional elements. The images also help the audience to see, hear, feel, smell, laugh, and enjoy the narrative.

In his classification of the Chewa oral narratives Mvula observes that the Chewa traditional prose narrative consists mostly of *nthano* (tales), *ndagi* or *zilape* (riddles), *miyambi* (Prov) and *nthanthi* (jokes). He notes that the "genres of verbal verse are *ndakatulo* (poems), and *nyimbo* (songs). The

---

[25] Enock Timpunza Mvula, "Chewa Folk Narrative Performance," pp. 35-36.
[26] Ibid., p. 39.

basic oral drama is the Nyau performance, *Gule wamkulu* (the big dance)."[27] Mvula also thinks that proverbs deal with human intercourse and that they reflect the forms of feeling and imagination that are ingrained in the people's culture. Proverbs cover subjects such as hospltallty, treatment of strangers, marriage and family life, cooperation, gratitude, difficulties in community life, or keeping secrets.

Another important work in this development is that of Matthew Schoffeleers and A.A. Roscoe.[28] Their work has accommodated some comparative classification of stories, the tracing of the history, their plots, and enumeration. The material is divided into seven chapters, each containing texts that deal with major aspects of a person, his/her society and culture. The material is a wide collection of traditional concepts of creation, matriliny, polygamy, religion, disease and chieftaincy. The aim of the book has been to provide both text and context. The texts originate from across societies, as stated by the authors themselves:

> The texts studied here have all been collected in the Republic of Malawi, and in particular from the Sena, Chewa, Lomwe, Mang'anja and Tumbuka people, all members of the Bantu-speaking group who live in fairly close proximity to one another.[29]

Schoffeleers and Roscoe have also identified certain recurring "themes" or "motifs." The themes include: fear of famine and draught, fire and rain, tension caused by various strategies used for social and family organization, and so on. From these themes one can make a statement about the nature of oral literature and its function, contentment and polarity underlying the structure of texts. The nature of oral literature is depicted as "brilliantly symbolic and ploddingly literal, ingeniously fantastic, and mundanely realistic. Usually optimistic, they can also prove bitterly fatalistic, able to catch and exploit comic mode, they sound well to the haunting note elegy. The tales can be seen as recital dramas or lyrics, satire poems, fantasies and sentiments."[30]

---

[27] Enock Timpunza Mvula, "Some Chewa Folkstories from Central Malawi," pp. 22-23.

[28] Matthew Schoffeleers and A.A. Roscoe, *Land of Fire: Oral Literature from Malawi*, Limbe: Montfort Press, 1985.

[29] Ibid., p. 7.

[30] Ibid., p. 11.

In certain cases the structure of the stories is confused, maybe due to the way they have been transmitted. Since retelling nearly always involves a change, it is likely that details of emphasis might change, yet there is remarkable identity of aim and outline in most of these versions. There is frequency of change during transmission, which can be viewed as verbal variability. Some stories can be classified as stories about people. Then there are myths about the beginning of life and causes of eternal death and *Chiuta/Chauta* (God) as the creator of human beings, animals and rain. Then one meets in other folktales talking animals, snakes, birds, chameleons, and so on. However, Schoffeleers and Roscoe have not indicated how these stories are performed, and when they are performed.[31] In any case comments show the origins of these stories, and it can be indicated that some of these were connected with rituals of birth, marriage, funerals, religious activities, and chieftaincy.

Since those studies, major efforts have been made to safeguard Malawian oral literature. J.C. Chakanza did pioneer work with his comprehensive collection of 2000 Chewa proverbs.[32] After him Ian Dicks published a collection and interpretation of 203 Yawo proverbs. New in his approach was that he also recorded, where appropriate, the stories that are closely attached to a specific proverb.[33] This book was part of a wider research on the Yawo worldview,[34] which was largely based on an interpretation of various forms of Yawo oral literature. While the main body is dedicated to understand and interpret the Yawo worldview, eight appendices give the recorded oral literature that is the basis for this study,[35] containing proverbs

---

[31] After this research Tito Banda published *Old Nyaviyuyi in Performance. Seven Tales from Northern Malawi as Told by a Master Performer of the Oral Narrative* (Musical notation by Mjura Mkandaŵire and Andrea Matthews), Mzuzu: Mzuni Press, 2006.

[32] J.C. Chakanza, *Wisdom of the People. 2000 Chinyanja Proverbs*, Blantyre: CLAIM-Kachere, 2000.

[33] Ian Dicks, *Wisdom of the Yawo People. Under the Elephant's Belly, you can't Pass Twice*, (*Lunda lwa Ŵandu ŵa Ciyawo. Kusi kwa Lutumbo kwa Ndembo, Kwangapita Kawiri*), Zomba: Kachere, 2006.

[34] The PhD research, done with the University of Malawi, was ultimately published as: Ian Dicks, *An African Worldview. The Muslim Amachinga Yawo of Southern Malawi*, Zomba: Kachere, 2012.

[35] For the appendices see: Ibid., pp. 398-490.

(*yitagu*) with the adisi (stories) linked to them,[36] stories (*adisi*) without associated proverbs, Yawo myths (ngani sya kalakala), initiation advice songs (*misyungu*) and traditional prayers (*mapopelo*).

Before the publication of this book I contributed a collection of 200 Tonga proverbs, attempting to find out how these traditional proverbs can be used for teaching and preaching.[37] Further Tonga oral literature was made available by republishing the Tonga folk stories of Filemon Chirwa.[38] It is hoped that this book will considerably increase the available corpus of Tonga oral literature.[39]

A new branch of recording oral literature is the collection of initiation songs. The first publication was by Rachel NyaGondwe Fiedler, who recorded all the 92 songs sung and performed at the occasion of one initiation in Southern Malawi together with the standard prose explanation going with each song, and any drama, where appropriate.[40] Years later Ian Dicks incorporated initiation songs in his study of the Yawo worldview.[41] Ian Dicks and later researchers did not restrict themselves to one initiation process, but collected songs from various camps. Their research has not yet resulted in further books, but much of it has been made available in simple format as Mzuni Documents.[42]

---

36 These are in general contained in Ian Dicks, *Wisdom of the Yawo People.*

37 David Mphande, *Nthanthi za Chitonga za Kusambizgiya ndi Kutauliya*, Blantyre: CLAIM-Kachere, 2000. The English version is: *Tonga Proverbs for Preaching and Teaching*, Zomba: Kachere, 2006.

38 Filemon Kamunkhwara Chirwa, *Nthanu za Chitonga*, Zomba: Kachere, 2007.

39 The process of collecting and interpreting Malawian proverbs is continuing. There are, still unpublished and in the process, collections of Sena, Tumbuka and Ngonde Proverbs.

40 Rachel NyaGondwe Fiedler, *Coming of Age. A Christianized Initiation among Women in Southern Malawi*, Zomba: Kachere, 2005.

41 He recorded 122 songs, of these 76 of *Jando*, 24 of *Msondo*, 5 of *Litiwo*, and 17 of *Ucimwene*. Ian Dicks, *An African Worldview. The Muslim Amachinga Yawo of Southern Malawi*, Zomba: Kachere, 2012.

42 The most comprehensive of such collections are: Edward Jeffrey, The Impact of Jando Initiation on its Initiates in the Area of Kasamba Village in Nkhotakota, BA, Mzuzu University, 2012; Macduff Kapito, The Impact of Yao Traditional Initiation Teachings on Women: A Case Study of Traditional Authority Malemia, Zomba

Recently Mzuzu University produced two works that deal with Tumbuka oral literature. The first book is a collection of 23 stories,[43] while the second portrays one lady, Mrs Nyaviyuyi, a famous story teller. Here new ground is broken in that for Old Nyaviyuyi not only the texts are recorded, but for the first time also the intonation and the style of performance.[44]

Though over the last 10 years much Malawian oral literature has been secured, there is still much more to be collected and appreciated.

Oral Traditional Literature outside Malawi

It would be absurd to have the impression that the Malawian culture has no share in the cultural unity of the African traditional societies. I shall look at four folklorists who have done their field studies in Africa, outside Malawi. Their works further reveal some problems faced in studying the body of stories and myths, how these are created and handled by oral narrators at the scene of performance.

The first work to consider is that of Ruth Finnegan on *Oral Literature in Africa*. Ruth Finnegan complains about the state of oral literary scholarship. She mentions "a dearth of detailed studies in depth of the literary and social significance of the various stories in any one society," suggesting that these aspects merit greater treatment than "the comparative classification of stories, the tracing of the history of their plots, or the enumeration, however impressive in itself, of the quantities of texts that have so far been collected."[45] Her book is an attempt to bring together and review the scholarly material of oral literature in various parts of Africa. In speaking of composition and transmission, Finnegan indicates the wide range of possibilities reflected in respect of African literature. She sums up the situation this way:

> It is clear that the process is by no means the same in all non-literate cultures or all types of oral literature, and between the extremes of totally

---

District, BA, Mzuzu University, 2010; Dennis Luka, Christian Boys' Initiation Rites at Sitima Catholic Parish in Zomba, Mzuzu: Mzuni Documents, 2010.

[43] Boston Soko and Brian Shaŵa, *Tumbuka Folk Tales. Moral and Didactic Lessons from Malaŵi*, Mzuzu: Mzuni Press, 2007.

[44] Tito Banda, *Old Nyaviyuyi in Performance. Seven Tales from Northern Malawi as Told by a Master Performer of the Oral Narrative*, Mzuzu: Mzuni Press, 2006.

[45] Ruth Finnegan, *Oral Literature in Africa*, London: Clarendon Press, 1967.

new creation and memorized reproduction of set pieces there is scope for many different theories and practices of composition.[46]

Finnegan is struck by the frequency of change during transmission and so she lists verbal variability as a notable characteristic of oral literature. In Finnegan's discussion of prose materials, she observes that contrary to the assumptions of many writers, the likelihood of stories having been handed down from generation to generation in a word-perfect form is in practice very remote. One of the main characteristics of oral literature is its verbal flexibility.

Finnegan regards variation due to creative change as a major feature of oral literature. In her study of the Limba of Northern Sierra Leone, Finnegan employs a three-fold classification. First, there are stories about people, these being the most common and most elaborate. They have a number of stock leading figures. Then there are stories about the god, *Kanu*, and origins. Last, there are stories about animals. Finnegan claims that all stories to a greater or lesser extent, according to circumstances, can contain some or all of several elements—moralizing and generalization; explanation; comparison, whether implicit or stated as an explicit dilemma; and finally, an intention to amuse and entertain by an interesting plot, a shocking episode or character and a vivid style and delivery.[47]

Finnegan observes that Limba stories are usually told during the evening in informal groups or gatherings. Narrators tell stories in turns. Some narrators are recognized as better than others. Finnegan is prepared to believe that Limba story-telling is a living art and the traditional themes and motifs find their realization in the actual performance, embellished on each separate occasion with differing dramatic devices, emphases, and wording or with episodes or references peculiar to the occasion. Even the "same" story told by the same story-teller may vary from narration to narration in wording as well as enactment.[48]

Finnegan notes that there are two ways in which a narrator can expand or compress a story. The first is by increasing or decreasing the number of

---

[46] Ibid., p. 7-8.

[47] Ruth Finnegan, *Limba Stories and Story-telling*, Oxford Library of African Literature; London: Clarendon Press, 1967, p. 31.

[48] Ibid., p. vii.

parallel or repeated incidents; the second is by elaboration. She puts it this way:

> There is what might be called a common fund of standard events, turns, or runs which occur in many stories not so much as part of the basic plot or form but as a potential elaboration of it. These include such common episodes as the trapping of an enemy up a tree ... girl running away from a man who marries her if he can catch her ... Someone dying, then being revived by leaf medicine.[49]

The kind of transmission process described by Finnegan for the Limba story shows the role traditional elements have in building and elaborating stories.

Another field study is that of Harold Scheub. He presents a very detailed analysis of a story called the *Ntsomi* from the Xhosa of South Africa. A selection of 114 texts, mostly from a single district, was chosen for analysis in the dissertation. Scheub prefers to avoid the use of the term "text" when referring to the items he recorded, because his contention is that the objects of his study are dramatic performances in which gesture and voice play significant roles. Instead of speaking of *Ntsomi* texts he uses terms like *Ntsomi-image*, *Ntsomi-performance* and *Ntsomi-production*. The term image is used very frequently, meaning the dramatic performance, the finished production. Scheub resorts to more familiar language describing the *Ntsomi* as a fabulous story, unbelievable, a fairy tale, and a seemingly insignificant piece of fantasy, endlessly repetitious.[50]

Scheub observes that one meets in these stories talking animals, birds, and monsters. A woman normally performs the *Ntsomi*. The performances occur before members of the family, neighbours and friends. The primary purpose of such performance is private entertainment.

> Entertainment is one of the chief aims of both story-teller and performer. The story-teller seeks to entertain mainly by producing little more than an objectification of the core-image, allied with relatively unsophisticated stylistic devices. The performer goes beyond that, but in her efforts to do more than merely entertain the members of her audience, the fact remains

---

49 Ibid., p. 90.

50 Harold Scheub, "The Ntsomi: A Xhosa Performing Art," PhD, University of Wisconsin, 1969. [Some articles appeared in 1970 and 1972]. See also "Parallel Image Sets of African Oral Narrative Performances," *Review of National Literature*, 2, 1969, pp. 119.

that she still entertains them. She seeks to externalize the core-image, to evoke it, to give it a pleasing form. We can deduce certain structural patterns of the tradition from the productions of both story-teller and performer, but aesthetic principles, while they do exist in rudimentary form in the works of the story-tellers, can be found fully realized only in the works of the performers.[51]

Scheub makes a distinction between an ordinary story-teller who lacks artistic sophistication in the narration of a tale and a performer who shows a certain professional expertise in the control of central ideas and images around which the tale is built.

The stories are traditional and well known, yet the artists do not memorize fixed texts. On the one hand, there are certain traditional elements, which the artist knows and works with. These provide stability. On the other hand, the artist is free to select and choose, expanding and contracting the story at will, all of which indicates a good measure of flexibility. In speaking of the performance of these stories, like Finnegan, Scheub, observes that:

The constant process of arrangement and rearrangement of details and episodes is a part of the creative process and is deeply involved in the aesthetics of *Ntsomi* production. The artist has inherited kaleidoscopic possibilities for *Ntsomi* creation and she is free within the limit of the thematic image and within the bounds of logic and cohesiveness, to deal with them as she chooses.[52]

In the 114 texts, which form the basis of Scheub's study, he is able to identify seventy-eight core-images, which recur in these texts. Thus, it seems that the core-images, each involving a core-plot with one or more episodes are building blocks of traditional stories discussed in the field studies of Finnegan, referred to variously as motifs, stock scenes, and episodes. Scheub's remarks are worth noting, that the core-plots are among the first things youthful artists learn. Both Finnegan and Scheub mention traditional elements, which are used by narrators in their stories during performance. In Finnegan's study stock incidents and episodes are certainly an important device used to fill plot outlines.

In analyzing oral poetry of Angolan tales, Albert Lord observes repetition of incidents, use of larger blocks of material, and patterns of incidents, which he calls "themes." These themes are defined as "repeated incidents" and

---

51 Harold Scheub, "The Ntsomi: A Xhosa Performing Art," p. 165.
52 Ibid., p. 192.

descriptions, which are the narrative building blocks of any story tradition.[53] With themes, the repetition is rarely exact. The wording usually varies. The repetition here is of elements of content like scenes, incidents, and descriptions, which recur with variable wording. Lord calls clusters or groupings of themes "patterns."

Repetition in the Angolan stories, according to Lord, is internal repetition or "repetition of similar incidents" within the same story. Lord calls the various kinds of repetitions, "the theme of repetition itself,"[54] meaning that the structure of repetition itself functions as compositional device in constructing tales. Lord also observes that repetition occurs when incidents appear in more than one tale. As an example of this, Lord calls it theme of distraction. He puts it this way:

> The theme of distraction is found especially, it would seem, in those tales in which a series of people (or more frequently and perhaps, significantly, animals) attempt to do something but are distracted there from; only the hero steps in finally and does not yield to distraction.[55]

Lord refers to multiforms of a single idea, either "thunder" or "dance," as distraction. Lord further distinguishes groups or clusters of themes, which often amount to story patterns or plots.

Lord also speaks of mythic patterns rather than compositional devices. Finally, Lord introduces a further refinement with the use of the word "motif" when referring to another kind of pattern. In order to bridge the gap between orally composed prose and written prose, Lord applies terms like transitional or mixed poems.

Lastly, a major recent study on African oral literature is that of Isidore Okpewho. In his book, Okpewho examines in some detail contexts in which African oral literature operates. He puts considerable emphasis on the oral artist and the artist's personal circumstances as a principal factor in the achievement of any levels of excellence in the art: "Oral literature may be communal property, but without the individual recreation given it by one

---

[53] Albert B. Lord, "A Comparative Analysis" in Merlin Ennis, compiler and translator, *Embundu Folktales from Angola*, Boston: Beacon Press, 1962, p. xvi.

[54] Ibid.

[55] Ibid., p. xix.

artist after another its appeal or its performance can hardly be granted."[56] He gives full attention to factors operating at the scene of performance and the visible effects of these factors on the verbal text of the performance. Okpewho further examines the wider social or cultural millieu within which oral literature is set so as to understand the usefulness or relevance of it that partly explains its continued appeal.

On the function of African folktales, Okpewho observes that the characters and events contained in them are fundamentally symbols illustrating various moral issues relating to people. In many cases a specific message is given at the end of the story, which confirms that the various elements operating in the tale have simply been used as symbols to illustrate that message. Okpewho contends that as in written literature, therefore, "symbols are widely employed in various forms of African oral literature for probing deep philosophical, moral and spiritual matters. They are a mark of high artistic sophistication in oral culture."[57]

Okpewho also observes that the artist's personality implies everything that the artist brings as an individual to the performance of the literature, personal artistic inclinations, family background, and personal experiences as well as training received and the circumstances in which the artist has frequently worked, that may be said to have contributed to the formation of a personal style. Okpewho puts it this way:

> By the scene of performance is meant the totality of factors surrounding the text that comes from the mouth of the artist: the resources of movement and music and the effigies used for enhancing the text; the presence and actual impact of the various persons surrounding the performer (accompanist, audience, and recorder), and other factors which immediately influence the success or failure of each performance.[58]

Like Mvula on Chewa folktales, Okpewho further observes that the audience may be hostile one time but absolutely co-operative the next time. Like Scheub, Okpewho also suggests that oral literature offers entertainment and relaxation. He notes that frequently oral literature provides relief after a day's work is over. In many African communities it is common to find families (whether immediate or extended) gathered

---

[56] Isidore Okpewho, *African Oral Literature*, Bloomington: Indiana University Press, 1992, p. 104.

[57] Ibid.

[58] Ibid.

together in the open compound at night, especially during periods of moonlight.[59]

Broadly speaking, all the field studies describe the oral composition of narrative in similar terms. Traditional stories were passed on in an unfixed form in which a loyalty to tradition and therefore a certain stability was combined with a creative retelling, and therefore show a certain flexibility.

Oral Transmission in Biblical and Traditional Texts

The aim of this section is to examine some examples of parallel accounts in both Biblical and Malawian narratives in light of the preceeding discussion on oral narrative transmission, and particularly the stock scene or episode as a device of narrative construction used by oral narrators. In reference to the biblical narrative it is also significant for one to consider to what extent it is legitimate and relevant to use information gained from studies from oral literature to make statements about Biblical texts.

The most possible applicable means of such structural analysis which comes to mind are those of Robert Culley's *Studies in the Structure of Hebrew Narrative*,[60] and that of J.M. Schoffeleers and A.A. Roscoe on *Oral Literature from Malawi*.[61] The parallels from both sources to be used are well known and fairly few in number. This survey will allow further discussion on the nature of similarities and differences in terms of content, function, and structure of traditional material.

(A) A Patriarch, his Wife, and a Foreign Ruler

These three stories bear a marked resemblance to each other. For purposes of comparison, the main features of the three stories may be summarized in the following chart:

---

[59] Ibid.

[60] Robert C. Culley, *Studies in the Structure of Hebrew Narrative*, Philadelphia Fortress Press, 1976, pp. 33-68. (Also, my lectures at McGill University 1978-79).

[61] Matthew Schoffeleers and A.A. Roscoe, *Land of Fire: Oral Literature from Malawi*, pp. 17-20, 183-185.

Genesis 12:10-20	Genesis 20	Genesis 26:1-14*
Abram and Sarai	Abraham and Sarah	Isaac and Rebeccah
Famine		Famine
Egypt	Gerard	Gerar
		Speech
Fear of life because of his wife	Deception (no reason given)	Deception (no reason given)
Proposes a deception		Fear of life because of his wife
Wife taken by Pharaoh (because of her beauty)	Wife taken by Abimelech (no reason given)	Wife not taken
Yahweh intervened with punishment	Elohim intervened in a dream: "Give wife back."	Abimelech accidentally discovered the truth
Pharaoh called Abram and said: "What then have you done to me?"	Abimelech called Abraham and said: "What have you done to us?"	Abimelech called Isaac and said: "What then have you done to us?"
	Abraham gave reason for his deception: Fear of life	
Abraham sent off with escort protection	Abimelech gave presents and wife	Abimelech gave orders of protection
	Abraham prayed and Elohim healed	Isaac did well and Elohim healed him

In these stories similarities can be reviewed very readily by looking at the characters, settings, and actions. The characters are not the same in all three stories. Abraham (Abram) and Sarah (Sarai) feature in two stories. Isaac and Rebeccah appear in the other. The ruler is Pharaoh in one story but Abimelech in the other two. Though the names change, the roles remain much the same. The hero is a patriarch who enters foreign territory with his beautiful wife. The setting varies also, being Egypt or Gerar.

The main actions and events common to the three stories are alike. The patriarch enters a foreign land and employs a deception, which is essentially the same in each case: he lets on that his wife is his sister. After the discovery of the truth, the foreign ruler summons the patriarch and reproaches him for his action. Nevertheless, one action, crucial to the plot, has taken a different form in one of the stories. In Genesis 12 and 20, the foreign ruler becomes aware of the patriarch's deception because of divine intervention, although even this takes two forms, punishment in the first story and a dream in the second. In contrast, the foreign ruler of Genesis 26 becomes aware of the deception accidentally when he sees something he was not supposed to see, namely Isaac wooing Rebeccah.

The story about Abraham and Sarai in Genesis 12 is remarkably concise. Famine is given as the reason for the move into foreign territory. The deception is presented in the form of a proposal made by Abram to Sarai that she pose as his sister. This was necessary, because her beauty would put his life in danger. This was well predicted by Abram, as seen later, Pharaoh takes her as his wife because of her great beauty. The story forms a kind of episode in itself: danger/deception/danger averted. In the end Abram prospers. At this point Yahweh intervenes and strikes Pharaoh with various afflictions. The outline of the story of Genesis 12 might be like this:

> On entering a foreign country, a patriarch fears he will be in danger of his life because of his beautiful wife (problem).
>
> The Patriarch pretends that his wife is his sister (deception).
>
> The foreign ruler takes the patriarch's wife but the patriarch remains alive and well (problem solved).
>
> This situation is not normal and cannot continue (new problem).
>
> The divinity intervenes with punishment so that the truth is revealed (divine intervention).

The second account (Genesis 20) runs differently at a number of points. No explanation, such as famine, is offered for entry into foreign territory. Then too, Abraham tells an apparent lie, yet no reason is given for this until the end of the narrative. Similarly, the bare statement that Abimelech took Sarah is left without further explanation. Thus the deception, along with the explanation for it, and the taking of the wife, both of which appeared to be significant steps in the narrative of Genesis 12, seem to be reduced to background information leading up to the intervention of Elohim in a dream to Abimelech. In the dream itself the following pattern can be seen:

> Abimelech's crime is revealed and a punishment is announced.
>
> Abimelech makes an appeal.
>
> Yahweh accepts it and gives instruction as to how the situation can be restored to normal.

Looking at Genesis 12 and 20 from the point of how the individual elements are patterned or arranged, the two versions are rather different, even though they have many elements in common. Genesis 12 has two episodes with a *problem/problem solved* structure in which the first problem was solved by the cleverness and resourcefulness of the hero and the second was solved by divine intervention. But the outline given in Genesis 12 cannot be used for Genesis 20. Here the matter of deception appears to be little more than background information with the result that the story seems to focus on the one episode consisting of the taking of the woman, the divine intervention, and her restoration to her husband.

Like in Genesis 12, the story of Genesis 26 uses famine as the reason for the move into foreign territory. A speech of Yahweh at the beginning tells Isaac not to go to Egypt, a comment which seems to show an awareness of the Abram story of Genesis 12. In Genesis 26, the deception element is developed in a similar way to the Genesis 12 story. Isaac tells people that his wife is his sister. The reason given is that he fears for his life because of his wife's beauty. However, the story of Genesis 26 differs from the other two in that the foreign ruler does not take the patriarch's wife. Even so, the deception is discovered, although by a simple accident rather than by divine intervention. This leads to the summoning of the patriarch and the reproach by the foreign king.

The story is curious for a number of reasons. The patriarch fears for his life and performs a deception, but his wife was not taken. In any case, the *problem/problem solved* tension which was very strong in Genesis 12, being repeated in two episodes there, is considerably weaker in Genesis 26 due to the apparent lack of any real danger. One can still discern two story movements in a shadowy way as follows:

> The patriarch thinks he faces danger (a first problem).
>
> He performs a deception, but what he fears does not come true.
>
> The deception exists, maintaining an abnormal situation (second problem).
>
> When the truth is revealed to the foreign ruler, he restores the situation to normal, bestowing his protection, so that all ends well.

It has been argued that the outline set out for Genesis 12 does not prove adequate to reflect the key movements and tensions of Genesis 20 and 26.

The relationship of these stories to each other can be explained in many ways. One can see the three stories as oral variants. The one seeks to explain the existence of three versions in terms of a literary process of redaction. In our earlier discussion, it was observed that versions of stories multiply in oral tradition, it is then in order to entertain the possibility that the three stories found in Genesis 12, 20, and 26 are three versions which developed in oral tradition. In the kind of transmission studied above there is no original version. There exists a remarkable flexibility. Culley thinks that the variations can be explained in terms of expansion, reduction, restatement, and rearrangement of these common elements.[62] This is also true of the variant Tonga stories discussed in Chapter Six (see Tales 4-10).

(B) Welcome of Strangers

These two scenes are now connected in a series of events culminating in the destruction of Sodom and the deliverance of Lot. Of the three figures mentioned in the first account, two continue on to Sodom to save Lot.

Genesis 18:1-8	Genesis 19:1-3
	Two men come to Sodom
Abraham was sitting at the door of the tent	Lot was sitting at the gate of Sodom
Abraham saw and ran to meet the three, bowed to the ground	Lot saw and rose to meet them, bowed to the ground
Offered hospitality (He said: My Lord(s) ... wash your feet, rest and eat). They accepted	Offered hospitality (He said ... my Lords ... wash your feet ... to spend the night) They refused but Lot urged
Abraham prepared food and they ate	Lot prepared food, and the ate

These two stories seem to represent a recognizable segment or stage in the narrative: The strangers appear/an invitation is issued/and it is accepted. The visitors are brought together with the main character. What follows in each case is a new segment of the narrative. In the Abraham story, there is the announcement of a son to Sarah and her response to this news. In the Lot story, the men of Sodom appear with their demand. The scenes in question both appear to perform a definite function in the larger narrative since they set the stage for a more important action.

One might argue that the action portrayed here was the sort of thing, which happened, time after time, in real life, and so it would be perfectly natural for narratives to reflect what usually happened when strangers were invited. Thus, there is some justification for entertaining the possibility that this is a case of a stock scene or episode used in oral narrative composition. One can point to both stability and flexibility. On the one hand, the similarity is close, even in wording, which is almost identical. On the other

---

[62] Robert C.A. Culley, *Studies in the Structure of Hebrew Narratives*, p. 40.

hand, the scene is adapted to different settings involving invitations of a different kind. Nevertheless, these two scenes are in such close proximity that the possibility of a deliberate repetition for artistic purposes of oral composition is very real.

(C) The Beginning of Life and the Cause of Eternal Death

The following three stories are selected from Malawi oral traditional texts:[63] These stories could be good example of mythos.

Variant 1: Horned Chameleon and the Origin of Life (Chewa)

Long ago, the horned Chameleon was the only living creature on earth. He was happy at first, walking from place to place and changing his skin colour whenever he found some beautiful leaf or flower. But as time went on he grew lonely and longed for a companion. He searched in the hills and he searched in the valleys, but found none; and in the evenings he would sit in a tree and call, hoping forlornly that someone would hear his voice.

One day he saw a fine tree, taller than all its companions. He climbed to the top where the fruit was delicious, and he ate to his heart's content before falling into a deep sleep. In the middle of the night the wind began to blow and it blew into a great storm. The branches, which had swayed lightly in the breeze, danced madly in the grip of the storm, but Chameleon was so fast asleep that he did not notice. Suddenly, however, a mighty gust shook him from his branch and he fell onto a rock, where he burst open and died.

Something very surprising now happened. Out of the Chameleon's stomach came all manner of animals and insects - things that swim, things that fly, and things that walk on the earth. Creatures great and small came from Chameleon's body in an endless stream. And last of all came man. Now of all these creatures man was the cleverest. And as soon as he discovered this he wanted to subject all the others to his will. The best way to start, he summoned the animal closest to him and told him to go out, name the others and return when he had finished. The animal went out and gave every creature a name. But he forgot to name himself. When the naming was finished, man arranged a feast with plenty of food and invited all the animals. He called the roll and each rose proudly in answer to his name. But the animal that had named the other was not called because he had forgotten to name himself. When the animals realized this they laughed

---

63   Matthew Schoffeleers and A.A. Roscoe, *Land of Fire: Oral Literature from Malawi*, pp. 17-20.

out loud. They thought it funny that the one who had taken so much trouble to name them should have forgotten to name himself. Angry and ashamed, this animal cried out, 'What are you laughing at?' And from that day everybody called him by that name. Now among the animals gathered at this feast was a small horned Chameleon, son of the first one who had died. When he saw that man had taken authority away from the Chameleons he was angry. He wanted to protest and called for silence. But nobody took any notice. When he tried to speak he was shouted down. And so he walked out and went back to the forest, there to live lonely again like his parent. And that is why we find the horned Chameleon singing sadly in the trees to this day.

Variant 2: Chameleon and the First Man and Woman (Yao)

In the beginning there was only God and the animals on the earth. Man had not yet appeared. The creatures went peacefully about their task and there was great contentment. Now Chameleon was a fisherman in those days. He sewed wickerwork traps, which he made with great skill from bamboo strips. Each day he would go out to inspect his traps and collect the fish, which he sold for a living. One morning, however, a surprise was awaiting him. In one of his traps, instead of fish, he found two strange creatures that had blundered into it during the night. They begged Chameleon not to kill them but to set them free on the land.

Chameleon was unsure what to do. He thought it wise to ask advice and went to see God. He was told to let them live. "Place them on the land," said God, "and you will see that they will grow." So Chameleon placed the two human beings (for that is what they were) on the land and soon they grew to their full size. But now they started doing things unknown to the animals. For example, one day the male of the pair began twirling a hard stick on a piece of soft wood. The animals watched, wondering what it was all about. When they saw smoke rising from the wood they were afraid. But their curiosity was greater than their prudence for presently a flame appeared and immediately all the grass around was set alight. The animals fled in terror to the forest and across the rivers while behind them a roaring fire leapt to the sky. The Chameleon escaped by climbing the highest tree he could find. But God could not climb because he was too old. Nor could he run like others. At last an idea came to him and he called spider. Spider climbed the tree, spinning a ladder as he went, and then came down to fetch God, who went up with him on high. When he was safely above the fire, God said, "When those human beings die let them come up." And behold, when men die now they go up on high to be slaves of God because they destroyed his creatures here below.

36

Variant 3: The Kaphirintiwa Myth (Chewa)

In the beginning there was Chiuta (God) and the earth, waterless and lifeless. One day dark clouds built up and covered the sky. Lightning flashed and claps of thunder rent the air. The sky opened and, in a great shower of rain, down came Chiuta, the first man and woman, and all the animals. They landed on Kaphirintiwa, a flat-topped hill in the mountains of Dzalanyama. Afterwards the ground where they landed turned into rock, and the footprints and the tracks of many animals can be seen to this day. The man's footprints are larger than the woman's and you can see also the imprints of a hoe, a winnowing basket, and a mortar. Plants and trees grew on the earth yielding abundant food, and God, man and the animals lived together in happiness and peace. One day man was playing with two sticks, a soft one and a hard one. He twirled them together and, by accident, invented fire. Everyone warned him to stop, but he would not listen. The grassland was set alight and there was great confusion.

Among the animals the Dog and the Goat ran to man for protection. But the Elephant, the Lion, and their companions ran away full of rage against man. The Chameleon escaped by climbing to the top of a tree. He called to God to follow him, but God (Chiuta) answered that he was too old to climb. When the spider heard this he spun a fine thread and thus lifted God to safety. So God was driven from the earth by the wickedness of man, and as he ascended into the sky he pronounced that henceforth man must die and join him in heaven.

Similarities and Differences in Three Stories

The similarities and differences in the three stories can be analyzed: The stories show some of the ways in which the questions about origin of life and death have been answered. The first story portrays a lonely Chameleon roaming in search of a companion with whom to enjoy earth's beauty. The second Chewa text, on the other hand, shows God, man and the animals descending to a waterless world in a cataclysmic storm. Like the first story, the Yao account shows man appearing after the beasts, but from a fishing trap at dawn rather than from a Chameleon's stomach. The Chameleon features in all three narratives. In the first he is a figure of compelling solitude, anxious to share his good fortune with others. In the Yao story the Chameleon is a fisherman. When the first human pair emerges from his fish-trap, Chameleon kindly refrains from killing them.

In the Chewa account, pinpointing Kaphirintiwa in the mountains of Dzalanyama, Chameleon plays but a minor role. Here too the Chameleon escapes from the flames by climbing a tree, as he did in the first Chewa account. It is striking also that the two last stories depict the closeness of the Chameleon to God as a symbolic manifestation of the divine. A close association between the Chameleon and the deity is a feature of all three accounts. In the first Chewa account God instrumentally uses the Chameleon for creation of all other beings when he falls from the tree. In the Yao account the Chameleon gets the first pair of human beings from his trap. He decides to consult God, who is living nearby as an earthly neighbour. Again in the last two stories man's finding of fire is as traumatic as his arrival. Man simply rubs two sticks together and fire is lit. In both stories the discovery results in serious confusion. God is depicted as old and ageless, a walking figure of eternity. In the two last versions the Chameleon uses the spider to spin a ladder for God to come up safely above the fire.

(D) Parents and Children

The following twin stories portray the relationship between parents and children:[64]

Variant 1: Kalikalanje I (Yao)

There was once a woman who was widowed when she was only six months pregnant. During her pregnancy she had a craving to eat human flesh and this food she got from a certain sorcerer, Lisimu. She also promised to repay Lisimu with the child when it was a year old. When the boy was born he was named Ambungo. Now one day while his mother was away drawing water, he accidentally fried himself in a pan, which his mother had put on the fire to cook some groundnuts in. When she returned he told her that his name was no longer Ambungo but Kalikalanje (The Fried One) because he had fried himself in the pan. He was at the time still under a year old.

Lisimu waited patiently for his flesh to be repaid. But three years passed and nothing happened. One day he approached Kalikalanje's mother and reminded her of her promise. The woman loved her son and grew sad, but she told Lisimu that she would fulfil her promise. Now to hand the boy over to the wizard was not easy. On the first day she put food for the boy on a shelf and hid the wizard so that he could kill the boy when he approached. But the boy turned into a cockroach and ate the food that way. So this plan failed.

Next day the mother bought a red piece of a cloth for her son so that the wizard could identify him among his friends. But the boy tore up the cloth and shared it among his playmates. On the third day the mother went to

---

[64] Ibid., pp. 183-185.

her garden to cut some grass, and tied Lisimu inside a bundle of it. She then told the boy to take it to the garden. Once there, Kalikalanje said, "I cannot carry your bundle, unless you stand up and dance." The bundle therefore stood up and began to dance. The boy said, "This is strange. I have never before heard of grass dancing. I am sure there is somebody inside this bundle." And so he returned home.

Finally he was instructed to collect honey from a big tree far away. While he was up the tree, Lisimu arrived and began to hack away at the trunk; but his dog, Maliranyenje, which attacked the wizard and killed him, saved the boy. The boy took the evil man's intestines to his mother and she ate them greedily, not knowing their origin. When Kalikalanje revealed the truth she was sorry for Lisimu but rejoiced because her son would live.

Variant 2: Kalikalanje II (Nyanja)

There was once a woman who went with her husband to hoe in the garden. While there the woman sneezed and the man said, "What do you want?" The woman said, "I want the eggs of an ostrich." And the man said, "Well, I want water from where frogs do not croak." So they struck a bargain. The man went to find the eggs of an Ostrich, brought back five, and gave them to his wife. The woman set off to find water where frogs do not croak. But alas she found that a wizard called Namzimu was guarding the water.

She told him that she wanted some, and he asked, "What will you give me in exchange for it?" The woman bargained with Namzimu saying, "I am with child. When the child is born, I will give it to you." Namzimu then said, "Draw water."

So she drew a large pot of water, went to her village, and gave it to her husband. The husband said, "My wife, this is very good." Sometime later Namzimu came to the woman and said, "Give me the child to eat." She replied, "No, the child is not yet born." And Namzimu went away. Three days passed and the child was born. It was still tiny when, one day, while the woman was roasting castor-oil beans, it leapt on a potsherd and said, "I am Kalikalanje" and then jumped off the potsherd with a bow, a spear, and four dogs.

When Namzimu came a second time to ask the child, the woman said, "The child has been born but he is very clever. If you want to catch him, you must devise a trick. Go and hide on the roof when the sun sets." This Namzimu did. At dusk she told Kalikalanje that there were strange noises on the roof and that he should go up and see what was causing them. While Kalikalanje went searching for his arrows, the woman called up to Namzimu, saying, "Dance on the roof."

When Namzimu danced, however, Kalikalanje stood at the door and said, "Ho! What's dancing up there? I don't want to climb onto a roof where there is dancing." So Kalikalanje ran away and Namzimu did not catch him that night. Next day the woman took Namzimu to the garden and hid him in the grass, saying, "Stay here. Tonight I'm sending Kalikalanje to come and burn the grass. You will see a youth with his head shaved on one side and wearing a black loincloth. That is Kalikalanje."

When they came to a parting in the paths, his mother shaved Kalikalanje on one side of his head, put on him a black cloth, and sent him to the garden, saying, "Go and burn the grass in the garden." So Kalikalanje took his shaving knife and black cloth, and his dogs and his spear, and called his companions. "Come to my mother's garden to play."

When they came to a parting in the paths, Kalikalanje said to his friends, "Come, let me shave your hair on one side so we can play properly." When he had shaved his companions' heads, he put on them pieces of black cloth and said, "You are all now Kalikalanje. When we reach the garden and start to burn the grass remembers that everyone is called Kalikalanje." His comrades readily agreed to fall in with the play.

They came to the garden and burned the grass, meanwhile constantly calling one another Kalikalanje. When they came to one especially large bundle of grass Kalikalanje said, "Let us burn this grass through and through and let us hold our bows in our hands." Quickly Namzimu leapt out of the bundle and Kalikalanje shouted to his comrades saying, "Come on, let us kill him." So they killed Namzimu with their bows and arrows.

Then Kalikalanje returned to the village. Here he met his mother and spoke to her, saying, "Mother, you wanted a wild beast to eat me. For that I am going to kill you." So Kalikalanje killed his mother.

These twin stories concentrate on the relationship between parents and children, that fathers and mothers are often less than ideally paternal and maternal; equally, that children are often less than ideally filial. The texts have striking similarities as summarized in the following chart.

Kalikalanje I	Kalikalanje II
Woman craving to eat human flesh	Wife craves eggs of an ostrich
Boy changes his name to Kalikalanje after cooking himself in a pan	Boy changes his name to Kalikalanje after his mother burns him with castor oil beans
Woman makes a bargain with the wizard (Lisimu) to repay him the child	Woman bargains with the wizard (Namzimu) to give him the child after birth
Lisimu reminds her of her promise	Namzimu comes to the woman and says, "Give me the child to eat"
Proposes the sign of a red piece of cloth on her son so that the wizard can identify him	Boy is shaved on one side of his head and wearing a black loincloth for identification
Boy tares the cloth, shares it among his playmates	Shaves his companions' heads on one side (deception) and puts on them pieces of black cloth (deception)
Scene takes place in the garden	Scene takes place in the garden
Wizard dancing inside	Namzimu dances on the grass roof with the bundle of grass
Dog (Maliranyenje) attacks the wizard and kills him	The boy shouts to his comrades (i.e. four dogs, a bow, a spear) "Come let us kill him," and they kill Namzimu
Punishment inflicted (Boy takes the evil man's intestines and mother eats them greedily)	Punishment inflicted (Boy kills his mother because of planning his death)

The texts are about a mother prepared to let a sorcerer kill her son, after a father who willfully causes the death of his son which is morally bad. The two narratives display a four-phase structure as outlined below:

41

A woman, who is pregnant, meets a sorcerer who renders a service in exchange.

The child is born, but leaps from birth to initiation age by virtue of emerging by cooking himself.

The mother conspires with the sorcerer in an attempt to keep her part of the bargain and they work out a series of tricks to catch the boy.

The boy makes virtue triumph by killing the sorcerer and sitting in judgement on his mother, with a different punishment inflicted in each story.

The stories can be analyzed as follows: In the first text the mother is allowed to survive but only by eating the sorcerer's intestines. In the second, her son kills her. At the most literal level they can be read as tales about women prepared to barter an unborn son for a favour rendered by a sorcerer not necessarily through a complete lack of love, for in each case there is evidence that they try to save their children. Both texts show an approach based on features of the kinship system. Here in the Yao culture the people appear to be attending to the relationship problems of the father and son. Both the Yao and Nyanja (Chewa), have a kinship system that is both matrilineal and uxorilocal, in which children trace their descent through their mother and belong to her kin-group; and youth upon marriage must live at the wife's village.

The texts, in a concealed way, reflect the basic principle of social organization. Stated simply then one can say that Yao sons must be trained to distance themselves from their fathers. The woman's husband plays an insignificant role in both stories. In the first one he dies before the child is born. In the second, he only appears in the opening stage of the plot and then vanishes without explanation. In both texts the sorcerer is symbolically portrayed as a father. This is suggested by his intimate connection with the woman's pregnancy. In the first story he gives her human flesh to eat (i.e. he causes the foetus to form in her womb). In the second, he gives her water in which frogs do not croak (i.e. semen). Thus in the first story, she was sorry for Lisimu (the sorcerer) but she rejoiced because her son would live. It can be argued that the mother felt sorry for the sorcerer, because he was someone very dear to her.

Lastly, the fate of the mother is different in both cases, and shows the effects of two different attitudes on her part. Firstly, she finally decides in favour of her kin-group by acquiescing in the killing of the sorcerer through eating his innards. Secondly, she is unable to distance herself from her husband and is therefore killed. Like in other texts described, the degree of likeness in these twin stories is interesting and forces one to the conclusion that a necessary connection exists. It is possible that the stories use a stock scene, which is a traditional element in oral composition, which is adaptable to both Yao and Nyanja ethnic groups. Here too, it seems difficult to rule out the possibility that oral variants may be the basic reason for two rather similar stories. This does not exclude creativity on the part of the narrator.

Examples from the Biblical texts and Malawian traditional texts show similar episodes and stories which give an opportunity to consider the phenomenon of repeated elements of narrative in the light of oral traditional literature and give light to inquire further about similarity of stories and stock scenes during the field study. The examination of the four examples produced a varied picture. In some cases, the parallel stories had items of content in common, that is the same or very similar actors, actions and other details, but no common framework (e.g. wife-sister-motif). Others had both items of content and framework in common (e.g. Kalikalanje I and II). Many of the examples cited could be stock or traditional material. They also reflect the stability and flexibility to be expected in the field studies in that the material appears to be adapted to different narrators. Apart from the question of oral tradition, the comparison of parallel stories permits a few observations relevant to the problem of structure to be considered later in this study.

Myth and other Genres in Folk Tradition

Myths and folktales are oral narratives. However, definitional problems have been noted from field studies to relate myth and other genres of oral literature. Linda D'egh, who concentrates in her study on what she calls either "folktale," or Märchen as the most important in her investigation, also makes a general observation that the same motifs are widely shared by Märchen, myth, and legend.[65] In each case their functions have also been questioned. Thus, several theories have been suggested as to their interrelationship and functions. In his definition of a myth, Carl Jung says:

---

[65] Linda D'egh, *Folktales and Society*: *Story-telling in Hungarian Peasant Community*, Bloomington: Indiana University Press, 1969, p. vii.

43

Myth is the natural and indispensable intermediate stage between unconscious cognition. True the unconscious does, but it is knowledge of a special knowledge in eternity usually without reference to here and now, but couched in language of the intellect. Only when we let its statements amplify themselves ... does it come within the range of our understanding, only then does a new aspect become perceptible to us.[66]

The world, as Jung notes, is full of unconscious knowledge, which contains "primeval images."[67] These images rise into man's consciousness through dreams and into man's social order through ritual. These images serve as solutions to practical problems confronting a person in his/her particular cultural and social situation. J. Petersen notes that the primeval images, even though they represent the collective unconscious of mankind, are manifested to consciousness in symbolic representations familiar to the dreamer.[68] A myth becomes a sign that translates human experience into concrete symbolic representation. H. and H.A. Frankfort observe that myth is a form of poetry, which transcends poetry in that it claims a truth. In the Frankforts' view a myth is a form of poetic language, which tells symbolically the truth as perceived by a people.[69]

One of the categories of biblical literature identified by Rudolf Bultmann is called "myth." Bultmann observes that the Greek word *mythos* covers a wide range of literary types, fairy-tale, fable, legend etc. Bultmann uses the word "myth" in a quite technical sense. According to Bultmann, a myth is a story about the gods or divine beings without any reference to history as such, though it may have the appearance of a historical narrative. It is a

---

[66] Carl Jung, *Memories, Dreams, Reflection*, New York: Vintage, 1963, p. 311.

[67] Ibid., p. 392: The term "primeval images" is equivalent to "archetypes." Jung defines archetype as follows: "The concept archetype ... is derived from the repeated observation that ... the myths and fairy-tales of worked literature contain definite motifs, which crop up everywhere. We meet these same motifs in the fantasies, dreams, deliria, and delusions of individuals living today. These typical images and associations fascinate us. They originate in the archetype, which is an irrepresentable, unconscious, pre-existent form that seems to be part of the inherent structure of the psyche and can manifest itself spontaneously anywhere, anytime."

[68] J. Petersen, "Lessons from the Indian Saul: A Conversation with Frank Waters" in *Psychology Today*, vol. 6, no. 2, (1973), p. 72.

[69] H. and H.A. Frankfort (eds), "Myth and Duality" in *Before Philosophy*, Baltimore: Penguin, 1966, p. 62.

story set in the world of the gods for the purpose of expressing a profound truth about the world inhabited by human beings.[70]

Mircea Eliade has a notion of myth similar to that of Bultmann. Eliade observes that religious people tell stories in the form of myths describing how the original, formless, unstructured, chaotic and hence homogeneous space became formed, structured, ordered and non-homogeneous with fixed centres. For Mircea Eliade "myth narrates a sacred history; it relates an event that took place in Primordial Time, the babe time of the beginning."[71] Ninian Smart says that a myth is a moving picture of the sacred, which is depicted in the form of a story. He notes that, for a story to qualify as a myth, it must have two components: it must tell of the relationship between the sacred and the world. Like Bultmann, Smart defines myth as "stories concerning divinities, typically in relationship to men and the world."[72] Lord employs the word "myth" often describing story patterns in terms of myths about the dying and the rising also.[73]

James Cox specified six features of myths, which are apparently shared by several scholars: In the first place, Cox says that a myth tells a sacred manifestation (hierophany); secondly, myths relate stories of the origin of structures, the making of the homogeneous and non-homogeneous through the founding of sacred space and time; thirdly, myths provide for believers a picture of the sacred; fourthly, myths contain stories of divine beings and their interactions with humans and the world. In the fifth place, myths are local stories and events, which point towards a universal reality. Finally, myths are true if they are true for the believer, both in religions that stress the historicity of the sacred and those, that do not.[74]

Joseph Campbell also finds four functions of myths: First, myths have the mythological or metaphysical function of linking up regular waking consciousness with the vast mystery and wonder of the universe. Secondly, they provide the cosmological function of presenting some intelligible

[70] R. Bultmann, *Jesus Christ and Mythology*, New York: Scribner's: 1958, p. 19.

[71] Mircea Eliade, *The Sacred and the Profane*, New York: Harcourt Brace, 1959, p. 1930.

[72] Ninian Smart, *The Phenomenon of Religion*, New York, 1973, pp. 79-80.

[73] Albert Lord, *The Singer of Tales*, pp. 175, 186.

[74] James L. Cox., *Expressing the Sacred: An Introduction to the Phenomenology of Religion*, Harare: University of Zimbabwe Publications, 1992, p. 85.

image or picture of nature. In primitive culture the relationship between man-woman is frequently seen as a mirror of nature: the universe is created as a union of Father Sky and Mother Earth. Thirdly, they provide the sociological function of validating and enforcing a specific social and moral order. Myths act as a poetic check and balance system in ethical social behaviour. And fourthly, they have the psychological function of providing a marked pathway to carry the individual through the stages of life: dependency of childhood, the responsibility of adulthood, the wisdom of old age. [75]

Myths describe us all. They open up a new horizon, which reveals an unexpected turning. For example, Amos Tutuola's work shows the role of myth in creative writing. In his novel Tutuola gives illustration to the point. When people at the King's residence rejected Tutuola and his wife, they were able to use one of the sources of the world. This is what he says:

> As me and my wife did not talk a single word by that time, they thought that we were unable to talk, then their king gave one of them a sharp stick to stab us, perhaps we might talk or feel pain; he did as their king told him to do. So as he mercilessly stabbed us with that stick, we felt pain and talked out, but at the same time that all of them heard our voice, they laughed at us as bombs exploded, and we knew 'laugh' personally on that night, because as every one of them stopped laughing at us, 'laugh' did not stop for two hours. As 'laugh' was laughing at us on that night, my wife and myself forgot our pains and laughed with him, because he was laughing with curious voices that we never heard before in our life. We did not know the time we fell into his laugh, but we were only laughing at 'laugh's laugh'.[76]

On his journey with his wife, Tutuola reports the incidents when he sold his "fear" and his "death" to people. About to leave the home of the faithful mother who hosted them for one year and two weeks he says:

> We took our 'fear' back from the borrower and he paid us the last interest on it. Then we found the one who had bought our 'death' and told him go bring it, but he told us that he could not return it again, because he bought

---

[75] Sam Kern, 'Man and Myth': 'A Conversation with Joseph Campbell," *Psychology Today*, (1971), p. 35.

[76] Amos Tutuola, *The Palm-Wine Drunkard*, New York: Grove Press, 1988, p. 71.

it for us and had paid for it already, so we left our 'death' for the buyer, so we took only our 'fear'.[77]

As they continued their trip with fear accompanying them, they entered "Dead's Town," which was neither the abode of a human being nor a spirit. They were confused. But knowing that beside "fear," the world had also "courage," Tutuola's wife said, "This is only fear for the heart but not dangerous to the heart."[78] This mythical illustration shows that the world of things has meaning, is personal, and inanimate as a means of dynamic and continuous connection between man-woman and the primeval experience. For Tutuola the world is never impersonal. Each component of it can be personified, because it is a force, immaterial perhaps as it appears to man or woman, but it is also material; it can talk, walk, protect, harm or heal.

Myths and Rituals

There are various theories of myth, and the most debatable is the "ritual theory of myth." This is a view shared by some scholars that all literature and folktale influenced by myth ultimately derive from antecedent ritual performance. James Frazer concluded that many of the gods found in traditional myths were once kings and priests who died ritual deaths and whose careers were later turned into the stuff of imaginative fancy. He further argues that myth was the idea of "dogma" that started off first the rite and later the text.[79] This view was adopted by many scholars, for instance Bronislaw Malinowski. He had observed that myths are chapters for customs, institutions or beliefs. Malinowski points out that rituals, ceremonies, customs and social organizations contain at times direct references to myth, and they are regarded as the result of mythical thinking.[80]

Mircea Eliade, who states that myths and rituals operate within sacred space and time and hold a central place in the life of the religious person, has propounded Malinowski's idea again. Religious people tell the sacred cosmogonic myths over and over again. As they do so, they create a sacred time, ritual time, when the myth comes to life as it is re-enacted, and thus transforms the lives of the believers. In ritual, the people are able to go

---

[77] Ibid.

[78] Ibid.

[79] James G. Frazer, *The Golden Bough*, vol. 1; London: McMillan, 1911, p. 374.

[80] Bronislaw Malinowski, *Myth in Primitive Psychology*, New York: Norton, 1926, p. 291.

back to the origin of the world, to experience the creation of order out of chaos, and to find themselves renewed.

Ninian Smart also argues that the primary context of myth is ritual. He says that "in ritual one time is represented in another time."[81]

In the study of ritual lies the key to an understanding of the essential constitution of human societies; it also opens the door toward an understanding of people's concepts of their customs. This view is popular with anthropologists including Mtthew Schoffeleers, who occasionally analyses Malawian oral texts in this light.[82] For instance, in Malawian oral literature this theory fits in well with the Chewa creation myth and the symbolism of the Nyau secret society dance, the *Gule Wamkulu*. James Cox observes three points on the interaction between myths and rituals. The first is that telling a myth itself constitutes a ritual. The second is that a myth is a myth only if it is employed in ritual. Thirdly, the combination of myth and ritual transforms the believing community by making its space and time non-homogeneous.[83]

Myth and Folktale

Many attempts have been made to distinguish myths from other forms of oral prose narrative, like folktales and legends. This section will sample out some of the findings from field studies. In discussing Limba stories, Finnegan refers to some stories as historical narratives. She points out that these stories are both like and unlike the kinds of folktales, which were the main object of the study in her book. *Occasion*al stories about the great figures of the past were similar in many ways to the folktales. The more or less official stories transmitted in the families of chiefs were much less like folktales. In her closing sentence of her discussion of the topic, Finnegan notes that much more research needs to be done on the indigenous contexts, tone, and classifications of historical narratives before we can make assertions about them.[84]

---

[81] Ninian Smart, *The Phenomenon of Religion*, New York, 1983, pp. 81-87.

[82] Matthew Schoffeleers, "Myths and Legends of Creation," *Vision of Malawi*, vol 3, no 4. (1972), p. 24.

[83] James Cox, *An Introduction to the Phenomenology of Religion, Harare: University of Zimbabwe Publications, 1992*, p. 86.

[84] Ruth Finnegan, *Oral Literature in Africa*, p. 373.

Henry Murry has suggested six classes of myths that are often treated exclusively. First are the myths, which portray firmly held beliefs as to the origins of things that are "aetiological" myths. The second class consists of the "unusual event" myths, which are supposedly true descriptions of momentous occurrences, such as the story of the "Great Flood." The third class is the "interpretive myths," representing beliefs as to the supernatural agents responsible for recurrent natural processes. Fourthly are the "heroical historical" myths, which recount the life and exploits of a man-god or culture-hero, the charismatic possessor of pre-natural energy which once upon a time enabled him to contribute in some remarkable way to the foundation, survival, or development of his society.[85] Here, the Mbona stories of Malawi, are a good example. Mbona is the protagonist in a number of legendary chronicles, which purport to describe the genesis of a widely known earth cult in Southern Malawi, particularly in Nsanje district.[86] The fifth and sixth classes relate to psychoanalytical thought, which is in line with Jung's observations. In her understanding of legends, Linda D'egh sums up that the legend's essential characteristics are looseness of form and content, oscillating around a stable nucleus, and its attachment to real life and belief.[87]

It appears that the main kind of legend studied is the belief legend, which has to do with experiences of the supernatural like dealings with witches. She could tell legends of a historical type as well as Märchen (folktales). D'egh observes that the narrator could show the difference in telling legends and telling folktales. She notes that as a teller of legends he exhibited a different attitude from that of the story-teller; his texts tried to be realistic and he treated them differently than a Märchen (folktale), yet, the motifs are widely shared by folktales.

Levi-Strauss' "structural and functional theory" recognizes that native distinctions present a great interest for the ethnographer. Levi-Strauss considers a separation between myth and folktale, yet they are binary. He puts his observation this way:

---

[85] Henry A. Murry, "The Possible Nature of a Mythology to Come," in Murry, H.A. (ed), *Myth and Myth Making*, Boston: Beacon Press, 1968, pp. 300-353.

[86] Matthew Schoffeleers, *River of Blood: the Genesis of a Martyr Cult in Southern Malawi c. AD 1600*, Madison: University of Wisconsin Press, 1992, pp. 1-14.

[87] Linda D'egh, *Folktales of the World*. (ed Richard M. Dorson), Chicago: The University of Chicago Press, 1965, p. 78.

In the first instance, the tales are constructed on weaker oppositions than those found in myths. Tales are not cosmological, metaphysical or natural but more frequently, local, social and moral. The tale is a weakened transposition of a myth. A myth is more strictly subjected than the tale to the triple consideration of logical coherence.... The tale offers more possibility of play, its permutations are comparatively freer, and they progressively acquire a certain arbitrary character. Tales are of course difficult to identify.[88]

The basic assumption in all these statements is that myth is a type of a tale, which stands midway between history and fiction, and it is characterized by being based on a firm structure of binary oppositions, which is progressively lost to either of those other genres.

Roy Wills and Aylward Shorter demonstrate the kinship between history and myth. Willis has uncovered the fundamental structure of binary opposi-tions between symbolic units in African historical characters. Willis thinks that these units, as they appear in aesthetic, are an expression of language, which is literature.[89] Thus, Shorter concurs with Willis and calls them "simple forms" of literature and gives them the following designations as "saga," "myth," "riddle," "proverb," "memoir," "folktale," and "joke."[90]

Lastly, Isidore Okpewho attempts to formulate a flexible theory of myth. He starts by narrowing down the various approaches to the study of oral narratives. Okpewho suggests "a qualitative approach" of defining oral narrative. In his view, he qualifies every tale, whether in prose or verse, whether in a sacred or secular environment, in manner of belief it is held in its indigenous setting by recognizing the relative weights of fact and fiction in it. Consequently, the main guideline becomes fluidity between "history" and "poetry."[91] In this new light Okpewho suggests a distinction between "historical" and "romantic" legend, depending on the relative tendency toward fact and fiction. He accepts the potential of fiction in the legend. For Okpewho, the mythical force of literary work, which uses tradition, depends on the degree to which it embraces the spirit of fanciful play. This

[88] Claude Levi-Strauss, *Structural Anthropology*, vol 1 London: Allen, 1968, p. 95.

[89] R.G. Willis, "Traditional History and Social Structure in Ufipa," *Africa*, 34, (1968), p. 95.

[90] Aylward Shorter, "Religious Values in the Kimbu Historical Charter," *Africa*, 39, (1969), pp. 227-237.

[91] Isidore Okpewho, *Myth in Africa*, Cambridge University Press: 1983, pp. 59-71.

consideration leads Okpewho to conclude that besides time, the creative or poetic temperament of the narrator is an important feature in the determination of categories of oral narratives.[92]

In conclusion this chapter has explored the development, nature, and form of oral traditional literature in Malawi. It has examined oral traditional literature outside Malawi; how it is composed and transmitted. In the Malawian situation, the type of oral traditional literature described in the field study has shown that there is a common fund of plots, formula of opening and closing, actions, and characters. Repetition of incidents, retelling, and repeated patterns are characteristic compositional devices of oral style found in all field studies. There is a general clue discussed in the field studies that something like stock scenes and episodes are characteristic of orally composed narrative. Many of the examples cited could be stock or traditional material. They reflect stability and flexibility. The categories discussed were *nthanu* (folktale); *mwambi* (proverb); *ndagi* (riddles); *mbiri* (history or legend) etc. Performance was a crucial issue because it is the occasion when the story-teller demonstrates his/her abilities to make the audience participate in the story.

The four field studies outside Malawi reaffirmed what many folklorists have observed for a long time: oral transmission of stories is a very flexible process in which narrators recompose traditional stories during performance. There appears to be both stability and flexibility in creation and transmission. The stability resides to a large part in the traditional elements, which are so much a part of the process of story telling. In the field studies, it was seen that something described variously as stock incident, episode, or core-plot was identified as a building block for the construction of narrative. Such traditional elements appear to be very flexible in that they can be expanded, adapted, elaborated, and linked together in many different ways. Thus, some similarities in all field studies show cultural unity reflected in these oral traditions.

As for the relationship between myth and other genres of oral tradition, the line adopted here is that taken by anthropologists and folklorists working in Africa, whose researches have shown that there is no real distinction, for example between myths and folktales. As in the case of the various theories

---

[92] Isodore Okpewho, "Rethinking Myth," *African Literature Today*, no 11: *Myth and History*, Eldred D. Jones (ed), London: Heinemann, 1990, p. 13.

of myth, the qualitative approach has been identified for a theory, which sufficiently accounts for the common features between oral literary genres without blurring the basic differences.

What is seen in the foregoing examination of field studies is that there is interplay between oral narratives, yet, their differences are clear. The various theories from field studies also suggest that is what "myth" in one community could be "legend" or folktale in another. Also, myth and ritual belong together. Myth explains ritual, depicts or embodies myth. A myth is more than a story, or, at least it possesses a strange power beyond mere entertainment when it is rooted properly in the culture to which it belongs.

Despite the fact that even in common themes (motifs), there is an enormous difference between tale and legend, there is nevertheless close relationship between the two. However different, tale and legend interpret the world and its secular and moral laws, both assume the same fundamental attitude as far as the world and its order is concerned. Genres in oral traditions seem to serve the same human purpose. The discussion on myth and other genres of oral narrative is also a clue to considering Tonga oral literature in the forthcoming chapters.

CHAPTER TWO

THE TONGA PEOPLE AND THEIR CULTURE

The Lakeside Tonga people of Malawi, in Nkhata Bay district, share in the Bantu history to which their ancestors belonged.[1] History is dominated by change. It is marked at times by slow expansion and at other by rapid migration. Their great ingenuity is shown in the ways they learned to adapt to different environments, modifying life-style and culture accordingly. The account of their creativity and enterprise is extraordinary. Most historians would see the Tonga people as of heterogeneous origin.

Jan van Velsen has noted that the genesis of the Tonga nation probably lies in the later decades of the 18th century. This was the period of the penetration of ivory trading groups from across the north-eastern shores of Lake Nyasa and the tribal movements in the northern part of what is now Malawi, when some groups settled in Tongaland.[2] As noted earlier, some believe that the Tonga came from the same place as the Chewa and Tumbuka, and point to Chewa and Tumbuka names found in Chitonga (*Phiri, Banda, Mwale, Nkhoma*), and to the presence of many similar words.[3]

Chichewa	Chitumbuka	Chitonga
nthanu	chidokoni	nthanu
mayi/mama	mama	ama
atate/tate	adada/dada	ada
nkhoswe	nkhoswe	nkhoswe
kuitana	kuchema	kudana
mwamuna	mwanarume	munthurume
mwana	mwana	mwana
fodya	foja/hona	foja
nsima	sima	sima

---

[1]   Jan van Velsen, *The Politics of Kinship: A Study in Social Manipulation among the Lakeside Tonga of Nyasaland*, Manchester University Press, 1964.
[2]   Jan van Velsen, *The Politics of Kinship*, p. 15.
[3]   Leroy Vail produced a comprehensive dictionary of the Tonga language. As he died before putting the final touches on it, it still awaits publication.

What seems to be most likely is that the Tonga had good relationships with Tumbuka and Chewa with whom they intermarried.

Historical evidence on certain aspects of the nineteenth century Tonga history is also provided in an excerpt from a letter written by the Tonga teacher, minister of religion, politician and historian who was baptized at Bandawe, the Rev. Yesaya Zerenji Mwase. He wrote to the Rev. A.G. MacAlpine on 7th April 1924:

> I am so absorbed in Tonga History. This is rather a passion to one ... both you Europeans and most of the natives will be much startled to find out that Wiza, Ng'oma, Rungu, Tawa, Bemoa are blood related or are of the same family with a Tonga; that Banda and Phiri are real landowners of Nkhamanga; that Banda on the mother's side and Phiri on the father's side are certainly of one family and I am sure almost all principal men or headmen are identified in a way I did not know before in Tongaland and elsewhere. Now let me state briefly about this relation.[4]

Yesaya Zerenji Mwase pursues the argument of origins and connections which serves to illustrate the relationship of the Tonga people with other members traceable to the Banda and Phiri clans; and also that this can be pushed to the narrow limits of the present boundaries of Tongaland and centuries before the nineteen century. These connections had some cultural impact upon the people.

It appears that the Tonga people of old spread out beyond the limits now defined as Tongaland for various reasons such as internal or external disturbance, land shortage and a desire to return to old sites or to other localities of later choice.[5] Later on these clusters amalgamated into at least four different groups: the Nyaliwanga Tonga, whose home area is *Timbiri's* area around Mpamba and Chikwina, and who may be the oldest inhabitants of Tongaland. They were also the people who earlier fought the Ngoni at 'Uliwone aTonga' hill, (You will see your fate, Tongas). Kabunduli with his followers the 'Phiri' is another group who are found mainly in the hill region

---

[4]   Quoted from Church documents at Bandawe, 13th October 1994.

[5]   I am greatly indebted to my informant, Mr 'Chiŵiŵi Kabunduli Mwase, the grandson of Karonga Mzizi. He states that Karonga Mzizi went as far as across the Zambezi and some of his people came back to claim the lands around Chintheche (Chiteche), which means the 'freshlands.' 'Chiŵiŵi has provided a legend for the Tonga people which is recorded under the collection of Tonga myth and folktales in chapter 6 of this book.

westwards, around the upper reaches of the Luweya river; the *Kapunda Banda* who settled by the lakeshore, south of Luweya, and who may have been a Chewa off shoot entering their present habitat from the south; and the *Mankhambira* and *Kang'oma* who are said to have come from across the lake with guns.

The process of amalgamation may have been speeded up in the third quarter of the nineteenth century through the external pressure of the Ngoni under Mbelwa. Raided by these Ngoni from the 1850s, the Tonga had retained a tenuous independence by retiring into a number of large, fortified villages instead of living in small scattered villages. The four 'stockades' (*Malinga*), known from tradition and from travellers' accounts are: the *linga* of *Mankhambira* and *Kang'oma* by the Chintheche River; *Malenga Mzom'sa linga* by Bandawe; *Chavula's* in Mtete valley just south of Bandawe; and *Chenyentha linga*, just south of the Luweya.[6]

During the frequent Ngoni raids some of the Tonga subjects were taken as captives. In 1881, however, the Ngoni experienced a temporary resurgence of power. Many of their earlier difficulties appear to have arisen from the rapid accumulation of these captives, and their failure to assimilate them fully within their society. According to tradition several Tonga captives distinguished themselves as captains in the Ngoni armies. The state of bondage in which the Tonga lived in Ngoniland did not last long. In the middle of the 1870s the Tonga rose in revolt and decamped to the lakeshore where they were received in the *malinga* and elsewhere. The pursuing Ngoni were routed in the battle of the Lueya River around Chintheche by *Mankhambira's* stockade. This is confirmed in the words of John McCracken.[7] He puts it this way:

> The escape of Tonga refugees from Ngoniland in 1875 and the devastating defeat of the regiment sent in pursuit marked the beginning of a troubled period in Ngoni history during which few raids on Tongaland took place.[8]

No doubt, this early interaction between Ngoni and Tonga had an important impact on the Tonga culture. Those Tonga who were under Ngoni captivity

---

6   Jan van Velsen, *The Politics of Kinship: A Study in Social Manipulation among the Lakeside Tonga of Nyasaland*, Manchester University Press, 1964, p. 17.

7   John McCracken, *Politics and Christianity in Malawi, 1875-1940*, London: Longman, 1977, Zomba: Kachere, [3]2009.

8   Ibid. p. 76.

for about twenty-five years, obviously intermarried.[9] This explains why names like Chirwa, Kamanga, Phiri, Mphande, and so on, are common in Ngoniland. By living in the stockades, the Tonga learnt to live together in harmony. Here family relations and marriages were strengthened, chiefships were expanded to clans and so on.

Kinship and Locality

The Tonga live in small clusters of houses scattered all over the dambos, the hillsides and by the lakeshore. Most villages are small, often 50-80 houses. These grouped compact clusters of thatched huts and some iron-roofed houses constitute Tonga villages. The villages are the most common settings for the various stories told by the men and women as they sit relaxed by their hamlets in the evenings. It is therefore important to understand something of their appearance and significance.

The distribution of the population is determined by the geographical features of Tongaland. Along parts of the lakeshore the population is more concentrated than in the hill regions. As one gets farther inland from the lakeshore plains, the population becomes less concentrated, and the distance between one group of hamlets and another may be greater. The villages are reached by steep winding paths up which both visitors and residents must negotiate to reach their settled community at the top, and which the women travel many times daily with their water containers balanced on their heads from a well, a running stream or a borehole below the hill. Kabunduli and Timbiri areas are typical for such features.[10]

The staple food of the Tonga is cassava. The cultivation of cassava requires comparatively little hard labour and can be done entirely by women. Cassava is normally served as a thick porridge (*sima*) together with a side dish of relish (*dende*). The favourite relish consists of chicken meat, beef or fish, and this is the kind of relish which every hostess or host strives to offer her/his visitors. The Tonga also raise cattle, goats and sheep. There are some cash crops of minor importance such as rice, groundnuts, bananas, maize, tobacco, millet, coffee and tea. Most of the millet, coffee and tea are cultivated in the hills. The lake area is better supplied with fish, some of

---

[9]   The Nyaliwanga Tonga have been directly affected by this interaction from the Tonga spoken along the Lakeshore.

[10]   In recent times social development projects have provided boreholes in some areas.

56

which finds its market in the hill area, and as far as the city of Mzuzu. Roads are few in the district, and most of the hill area cannot be reached by car. In the 1980s a tarmac road has been built which passes through the lakeshore of Tongaland. The road cuts across most of he big villages which once formed one hamlet and now line the road side by side. Small markets and stores line the sides of the main road or a crossroad along which many people travel each day. Some settlements are easily reached by vehicles. The main towns are Nkhata Bay and Chintheche.

Recent economic developments have led some people to abandon their original villages and start new villages on the edge of the hills. These have begun to live a new life altogether. The rainforest has a variety of plants. Birds and insects fill it with sounds of all kinds. Monkeys and baboons live in the trees where they find their food in plenty. This explains why many Tonga myths and folktales depict common topics about talking birds, snakes and animals. There are also stories about hunters.

The Tonga call all settlements *muzi* (pl. *mizi*). The expression for 'hamlet leader' and 'village headman' show the same flexibility. For instance, *fumu or fumukazi* (pl. *mafumu*) can refer to either office. The word *fumu* or its abstract counter *ufumu* (headmanship or chieftainship) is sometimes used as synonymous with *munangwa* (freeman), as opposed to *kaporo* (slave). Many of the *mizi* which together form the village are set apart as distinct local units. Most houses have adjacent cassava gardens although many people may have gardens elsewhere in the village as well. And in between the hamlets there may occur a clump of trees, a mango grove, high grass or a deep gully with a stream. Some of the trees are symbolizing names of the villages (eg. Mtaŵa or Kachere). Between some compounds, there are high fences of dry reeds or cane grass which dwarf the children as they run between them. All these features tend to give the hamlets an appearance of independence. It is in these villages that family values are shared. Today, most valleys and dambos are being cultivated with rice, vegetables and sugar cane.

Chieftaincy

In the centre of the village is usually built a bigger house, perhaps with a square roof, for the Chief who is the head of the clan, called the Traditional Authority (T/A) or Group Village Headman (GVH). The small groups attached in various ways to the group village headman (*fumu or fumukazi*) may claim a direct or primary link with him or her, either as his or her

57

children or through membership of the headman's matrilineage. The category can be further divided into patrilocal residents whose ties with the village are patrilateral throughout, that is, the headman's children and his sons' children, and those villagers whose links with the village do not follow either line. This interaction has an influence on moral attitudes to their close neighbours.

Chieftainship is of great significance, and the theme plays an important role in Tonga stories. It is the centre of social activities in the village. A stranger is always first directed to the house of the local chief. He or she looks up to the large sub-chief who controls the area in which the village lies, and they in turn are bound to the Traditional Authority (TA) who controls the chiefdom. The position of chiefs is not simple. There are several grades of chiefs and their duties. The honour given to the chief by his/her subjects are embedded in the words, *Fumu Yidu*, or *Fumukazi Yidu* meaning 'Our Chief'. A Chief is expected to be generous and hospitable. This can be seen in everyday practice as it can be seen in some of the Tonga oral literature.[11]

Sources for Moral Instruction

Along the takeshore area the Tonga word for a net-shelter is *khumbi*, but this refers only to the structure, if the net-shelter is also the place where men sit together, they will call it *mphara*. But also *padowoko* (at the shore) is *mphara*. The community life of the Tonga revolves round the *mphara*. In most cases the *mphara* is the men's open place in a village, or at the shore. *Mphara* also means a court or any other *ad hoc* meeting of men trying to decide on a specific problem, for example, discussions at funerals or of divorce. It is a place where men live together, where they share jokes, sing songs, weave baskets, make mats and hoe handles, play *nchuwa* (drafts), *mbela* (teatotums), *mangolongondo* (wooden musical instruments) and games, while young men sit there to learn various arts and crafts and run errands. The *mphara* life is a source of disciplining the young. Here, young people acquire general or collective basic information concerning themselves. Here again children would listen to songs, narratives, proverbs, riddles and related Tonga values containing the dynamic of the society to absorb the ideas that will guide them through life. At the women's open

---

[11] I am indebted to several Chiefs, Group Village Headmen (or Women), Sub Traditional Authorities and Traditional Authorities who were the primary sources for some of the stories collected.

place (*paduli*) or pounding place or *kukati* the women likewise play their games, sing songs, gossip, hear and settle disputes, pound cassava for flour prepare food, and work on arts and crafts, such as making pots, *visaku* (fish traps used by women) and so on. When night falls young women sleep in the *nthanganene* (girls' dormitory), while young men sleep in the *mphara* (the young unmarried men's quarters). In other communities girls between 6 and 12 years used to play their games around *visenga* (the young girls' shelter). Here they learn to pound, cook, imitate weddings and are initiated into womanhood. *Chinamwali* is only a once off event. It must be emphasized here that the *mphara*, *nthanganene* and *visenga* are the early settings for moral development in the young people's rites of passage, although these are now phasing away because of mixing of cultures.

In speaking about the *mphara* as a venue for moral instruction, Rev. Wesley Manda claims:

> The *mphara* is a place where boys would receive moral teaching from the elders: to respect the elder, to be obedient, to be punctual, and acquire several skills. Likewise, *nthanganene* for girls. The Tonga society is losing this way of life because of modern life and western education.[12]

Every individual knows his or her rightful place and role in the village, and sex and age are determining factors for a person's social participation. All the members of each hamlet know each other well. There is good understanding, co-operation and group dependence, so much that they scorn individualism. Anybody's problems are everybody's and anybody's joy is everybody's. At funerals, births, weddings, building a house, and entertainments, the society co-operates and works as a team. The Tonga philosophy of community life is reflected in the following proverbs: *Muti wamphara ngwakukoleyanako* (You need to help your friend by carrying a log for the fire at the *mphara*). *Uchembere nkhurgherana*, meaning solidarity is when you eat from the same plate. Likewise, it is expressed in stories such as: "*The Hare and the Well*." This story illustrates co-operation in the community and portrays the idea of working together. There are few homes in which the *mphara* concept is still in use, and it would be shared by one or two families only, unlike in the past when the whole hamlet would participate in one *mphara*. This used to be the main centre for moral education to the youth.

---

[12] I am greatly indebted to Rev Wesley Manda. He was one of the main sources of primary information.

Marriage Customs

Marriage is an important topic as much in day to day conversation as in Tonga oral literature. Many Tonga stories, as will be seen, depict the theme of marriage. For a young man, the marriage to his first wife marks a major step forward in his social and economic status within the village, comparable in importance only to his initiation into manhood. Marriage is the most important factor integrating otherwise independent groups of kinsmen. Marriage serves not only the ends of ordered procreation, but it has also emotional, domestic, economic and political functions. Van Velsen observes that the integrative role of marriage is of great political importance, because the Tonga political system is basically a system of overlapping networks of kin groups and kin interests.[13] The men await marriage with great expectancy. Especially for the first marriage the arrangements are hard, expensive and protracted. The difficulties of wooing and marrying a wife are very common. The marriage negotiations are sometimes long and involved. Marriages are usually not prearranged, except in rare cases perhaps in intra-village marriages. In such circumstances girls are betrothed to their cousins or close relatives in childhood. A young man may have to wait many years for the wife that is promised to him. He many see her gradually growing up over long years, and then comes at last the occasion when, between about fifteen years old or above, she is initiated into womanhood. In formal circumstances a man woes a wife when he feels he has reached the stage of proposing a girl for marriage. The transactions which precede a formal marriage should fulfil several stages that are connected with Tonga marriage customs, such as:

Chijula mlomo (mouth opener) - the initial stage of "opening the mouth" cost not less than K5000.

Chikole (betrothal payment), which varies from K20,000 to K30,000 these days. This does not establish any legal rights. It is handed over directly through her grandmother or female cousin.

Chiziya pamuzi (home coming) involves a payment of K5000.

Chimanga matumbo (tying the intestines), a payment that is given to the mother of the girl as a token for giving him her daughter (eg. giving a blanket).

---

[13]   Jan van Velsen, *The Politics of Kinship: A Study in Social Manipulation among the Lakeside Tonga of Nyasaland*, Manchester University Press, 1964, p. 79.

Chisinkha pamuzi (protecting the home) is the idea of appeasement or security of home that the ancestors should be also happy that the granddaughter is getting married (eg. a token as determined).

Chilowola (bridewealth) - the legal payment in a formal marriage. The general rule is that there should be a go-between (*thenga*), who comes from the village where the suitor is resident. The Tonga people see a connection between the go-between's starting-point, the village which is the source of the bridewealth, and the place of residence of the married man. The *thenga* is symbolically a binding figure. If there is dispute as to whether a case of cohabitation is a formal or informal marriage, the first and often decisive question is: Who was the *thenga* and who received him? The attorney (*nkhoswe*) is the one who sends the go-between.[14] In recent years the amount of chilowola (bridewealth) has gone up from about K10,000 to K50,000 or even more. This includes the initial payment 'to open the mouth' (*chijuliya mlomo*). The existence of a go-between and the payment and acceptance of the 'mouth opening' money are proof of public marriage negotiations, and they establish a formal marital relationship.

In the case where the bridegroom has duly paid bridewealth to his wife's attorney, there is still a debt involved in his relationship with his wife's people. It rarely happens that the man pays the whole *chimalo* or *chilowola* at once, he gives a 'promissory note' (*kalata*) for about half, which he will pay another day when he has found the money. Thus *chimalo/chilowola* seems also to be a binding factor between husband and wife. For instance, if the girl was just given to the man for marriage, as in the case of informal marriages, or inter-relation marriages, and no bridewealth was demanded, when conflicts arise, the woman will often say to her husband, "Did you pay *chimalo* to my parents?" This is reflected in a story, '*Mwali wa mbuwu*' (The dumb woman), who challenges her husband for not having paid any bridewealth to her parents. Then, she may go back to her parents freely.

The Tonga kinship pattern puts stress on the bond between men and women within the same patrilineage. They distinguish two primary categories of kinsmen; *kuchinthurumi* (on the man's side), and *kuchinthukazi* (on the woman's side) and call their daughter-in-law

---

14   Interview: Information supplied by Mr Amon Karren Kamanga of Chituka village. He feels that these stages can vary accordingly. He also suggests that *chiziya pamuzi* (coming home) and *kupempha mwali* (asking for the bride) can be combined. The amounts have been updated to the year 2012.

mkumwana. Tonga wives live virilocally, unlike the matrilineal Chewa where husbands live uxorilocally.

In a patrilineal group every adult male member is a guardian or responsible relative (*nkhoswe*) to the women members of his patriclan. The guardian or *mweneku wa mbumba* calls the patriclan women members *mbumba*.[15] A man's *mbumba* is composed of his sisters, his mother, his mother's sisters and daughters of his mother's sisters. The *nkhoswe* is responsible for the well-being and good conduct of his sorority group at all times. He appears in court and pays fines for his sorority group. The story about *Urghargha waku Kalulu* (The Crafty Hare) reflects this responsibility. The Hare is depicted as one who looks after the welfare of his *mbumba*. The Hare takes things on credit from the Elephant in order to support his *mbumba*. At the funeral of any of them, the *nkhoswe* is the chief mourner and he consults a diviner (*ng'anga*) as to the cause of death. In a legal contract, if there are sureties, one for each party, usually the *nkhoswe* is one of the sureties and has one or two assistants, in most cases a brother of the contracting parties. It is the responsibility of the *nkhoswe* to hear and settle all disputes.

Marriage in Tongaland creates bonds which extend beyond village or other geographical boundaries, it creates a common focus for individuals or groups who may be spread over a wide area. Marriage rituals are powerful. A wedding is an occasion, which attracts the inhabitants within the neighbourhood of the village. A big wedding with its attractions of girls, gambling, beef (*bevu*) and dancing is an event all like to attend. *Ndelitha* is a dancing enterinment, which is sinking into oblivion. A wedding draws not only the people from a wider area around the bridegroom's village, but also many people from the bride's village attend.

A wedding is important in that it brings together people from many differ-ent localities and may thus produce lasting contracts or friendships among the Tonga, also wedding may beget wedding. Wedding songs are created and reflect how joyful the people are joined together in a marriage ceremony.[16] During the vigil night the young couple is initiated into these events and mysteries through rituals that symbolize their union. The old women give them moral instructions to live together happily.

---

[15] J. Clyde Mitchell, *The Yao Village*, Manchester, 1956, pp. 25, 138.

[16] I had a chance to attend a wedding ceremony on 8th Oct. 1994 at Munkhokwe village. Both *nkhoswe* from *akuchinthurumi* and *akuchinthukazi* were called in turns to give gifts and *moral instructions* to the new couple.

Informal marriages often involve cases of fornication. When an unmarried woman finds she is pregnant, her attorney (*nkhoswe*) will be informed of the fact. He will go and see the relatives of the man whom the woman has named to present him with his wife. The man may deny the responsibility of the case. But if the case is taken to the local chief court the alleged lover does not stand much chance, the law's legal presumptions are weighted heavily against the man. Outside the court the woman's *nkhoswe* has no means of enforcing damages. If the man accepts responsibility, the woman may go and live with him as his wife or she may stay in her own village, in which case the man will still be expected to accept the normal economic and other duties of a father and husband. Sometimes there is no way the *nkhoswe* can force her to do so. In Tonga society, informal marriages which involve fornication or abduction, though commonly practised by people, are not pleasing to most of the families. In Christian families such marriages are condemned altogether.

Some Tonga clans practice polygamy. Among the Muslim families, polygamy is generally accepted as something the Quran accepts. In other families it is simply part of the tradition. The Christian families condemn polygamy. Usually, chiefs or village elders have more wives. There could be different motives for this option. Some of the reasons are to have more children or more wives in order to provide more labour in the gardens. Again, children are the heirs and continue the family tree. Like in Chewa, Yao and Tumbuka societies, for the Tonga children are an essential part of a successful marriage, for not only is a prosperous garden likely to result from their co-operative labour, but after the father's death, he with the other ancestors, will be remembered in prayer and sacrifice.

Special rituals may be performed so that the wife may bear children, and wives are intimately concerned with the rights of their own children against those of their co-wives. However, the eldest wife should be most respected by other wives, though in practice this is not so. Orphaned children are quite common in Tonga society. This is illustrated in the story about *Ŵabongolo ŵawi* (The two millipedes). The orphaned millipede listened to what the mother of his friend was saying. He heeded the advice. When the rains came the orphaned millipede dug a hole to hide in. His friend did not, for he thought he would always be with his mother. He died during winter, when he could not find a hole to hide in.

Though marriage is assumed to be the necessary aim for both men and women for mutual interdependence of husband and wife, they also see it at times as involving conflict. Sometimes sex has been abused in marriage. Sex intensity has been seen as a contradiction to stable marriages in many families. Many of the cases that are heard in local courts (or magistrate courts) before elders or chiefs are concerned with quarrels between husband and wife, or cases where a wife has been abducted by another man, and a refund of the bridewealth (*chilowola*) is therefore demanded. Stories about greedy or cunning characters will reflect this theme, such as that of the *Greedy Hyena*.

Fishing

Apart from marriage, fishing is a provider of local association and kinship bonds. Most fishing activities are centered on the village, whose men folk share one net-shelter (*khumbi*) which is also their *mphara* (men's gathering-place). It is also a place for moral instructions to the boys and also for learning how to be kind or share with others. Individuals who live inland may be regular visitors to some *khumbi*, as the basis for friendship with one of the members of the lakeshore village. Here, they exchange with one another stories that take place within their related hamlets or villages. Fishing songs are often composed and reflect Tonga creativity.

Dances

Dances bring the people together socially. The main Tonga dances include: *chioda* (for women), *kamchoma* (for both men and women) *mangolongondo* (for men), *chilimika* (for men and women, boys and girls), *visekese* (for women), *mtangala* (for girls and women), *ndelitha* or *kordioni* (for men and women), *maskawe* (for men and women, usually possessed by a spirit) and *malipenga* (for men). Perhaps *chioda* and *malipenga* are the most popular Tonga dances. *Chioda* and *ndelitha* are performed during weddings and political rallies. Women dance *chioda* accompanied by songs throughout the wedding night, while the bridegroom and the bride rest somewhere within the village. *Ndelitha*, often accompanied by the *honara* (accordion), is the activity of the wedding day. These dances are meant to entertain those who have come to attend the wedding. *Gulutu, mchoma* and *gule wakawole* are Tonga dances which have sunk into oblivion. "These

64

dances have died a natural death, yet they were meant to preserve our cultural identity," one informant remarked.[17]

The *malipenga* dance is, however, quite unique. It is clearly organized on a territorial basis. Each dance group, called a *boma*, comprises the men (mostly young) of a number of villages which are often separated by a river from the group of villages comprising another *boma*. This territorial division is rigidly maintained: if a boy lives in the area of one *boma,* but would prefer to dance for a neighbouring *boma*, he is told: "Either you come and live here and you can dance in our *boma*, or you stay where you are and you help your own village in their *boma*." The villages constituting a *boma* may be from the Nyaliwanga Tonga and other *bomas* from the Mankhambira Kang'oma Tonga or Kapunda Banda Tonga, and so on. The villages constituting one *boma* may be strongly opposed to one another in other respects. The *malipenga* dance may be a reconciling factor. *Malipenga* or *mganda* dances are for men only, imitating infantry drill,. Dance groups enter into competition with both neighbouring and distant groups.

The *malipenga* dance plays an important role in Tonga society, because of its function in male initiation. The in-charge of the *boma* is called captain. Each *boma* has a 'King' or 'Queen'.[18] The members initiated in the *boma* must be disciplined people. They must attend all the practices and must be punctual. Those who disobey can be punished very severely. In cases of indiscipline appeal can be made to the Queen or King. The King or Queen inspects the band (*boma*) at the time of performance. During performance the dancers wear white or khaki shorts and a white T-shirt. They also wear hats with ostrich plumes. The drums are modelled on the European military drum, with a skin on either side. They use trumpets (*malipenga*) made of gourds with holes covered by membranes made from spiders' nests. Songs often depict historical or political events. Some of the choruses praise their King/Queen or chiefs, to which the *boma* belongs. The songs carry moral instructions, advocating cleanliness, obedience and respect for the elders or the authority.

The *malipenga* dance is performed during the dry season and within school holidays. It functions as entertainment drama, yet, through *malipenga* the

---

[17] Information given by Mr Jamson of Chituka village.
[18] The idea of King and Queen is a western element. It appears as if some foreign ideas in the dance were brought in by people who went to fight in the world wars.

65

individual person or the group is taught Tonga moral codes: obedience, respect for elders, honesty, community life, modesty, friendship, unselfishness etc. In short, the *malipenga* dance covers the virtues the people esteem, the vices they condemn and the follies they ridicule.

The rules are administered through categories of people: the adjucate gives orders and makes sure that discipline is observed. The sergeant major also gives orders but he mostly commands the band. The King or Queen gives moral support and a sense of belonging or solidarity. On the other hand *malipenga* songs have important moral messages, including self-praise, praising their chief, praising their political leader, praising heroes/heroines, or recite in songs some historic or legendary events. In this case the *malipenga* dance functions to validate both culture and origin of the Tonga people.[19] The missionaries to Tongaland condemned *malipenga* as sinister and unholy. Christian families have been reluctant to allow their children to join *malipenga*. However, *malipenga* as a traditional dance has survived such foreign opposition, while some of the Tonga customs such as offering sacrifices to ancestral spirits seem to sink into oblivion.

Ubwezi

Friendship (*ubwezi*), in Tonga society, is another aspect that creates bonds which extend beyond village or other geographical boundaries. This happens when there is lack of relatives at strategic points which may sometimes be overcome by institutionalized friendship or *ubwezi*, but never friendship is entered into solely for economic or political reasons. For instance, two Tonga who meet for the first time abroad may seal their casual friendship with *ubwezi*. Friendship is a common theme in Tonga oral literature. Stories convey moral messages which warn young people from being dishonest, selfish, irresponsible and so on. In Tonga society, however, *ubwezi* is inferior to relationships that exist through kinship bonds. The story about *ubwezi* (friendship) reflects this point. In the story, the chief spends his riches on his friend and ignores his kinsmen. Then the chief tests his friend, if the friend can care for him at death, and he discovers that his friend shuns away. Later on the chief discovers that his kinsmen, those once rejected, prepare for his burial. The *fumu* discovers that "friendship can be entered upon temporarily and is unlike the kinship bond." Thus, the moral

---

[19] This information was given by Mr Austin Banda, a teacher trainer, who, throughout his youth, was a *malipenga* dance champion (12.10.1994).

66

advice goes: *Ubwezi umala, ubali umala cha*, meaning friendship can end, but not kinship.[20] The theme of friendship is very common in Tonga folktales, as shall be reflected from time to time in this book. This is also linked with the theme of twinship and asymmetry in society as reflected in some of the tales.

Beliefs in Mystical Powers

The cosmology of the Tonga people is the medium in which the interplay of forces is at the root of every person's health, illness and death. It has dynamic beings, the living and the dead; space and time are unlimited; its past is always present and can influence the events of the day. These characteristics of Tonga society are but generalizations, which may not present themselves exactly in all Malawian cultures as they are presented in this book.

Witchcraft

Witchcraft is historically known to be universal. The belief has to do with a theory that the witch devours the spiritual life of an individual which eventually causes physical death. In Tonga society the belief in witchcraft and magic is very common. Magic may be defined as positive acts performed with a view toward manipulating supernatural powers or supernatural beings.

The Tonga people believe that certain men and women have the power to injure their fellows through the magical means of witchcraft. A witch is thought to go out secretly at night to hunt those of whom he/she is jealous, and by witchcraft can cause death or illness by mystically 'eating the heart' - the life of the enemy. The belief in witchcraft is common in Tonga traditional society in day to day life, and after death, divination is normally used to discover if it was due to a witch. If so, there are set means by which the one considered responsible can be sought out and punished, or a similar attempt in the future frustrated. Any early death of a person is attributed to witchcraft. Tonga believe that a witch turns into a peculiar creature (*ndondochi*) to travel in disguise at night or even during the day.

In Tonga communities witchcraft is considered a peculiarly dreadful crime, in that it is, in the normal way, impossible to detect. Witches are believed to

---

[20] Filemon K. Chirwa, *Nthanu za Chitonga*, Livingstonia Mission, printed by Mission Press, Blantyre, 1933, pp. 80-83.

be conscious of their meetings, and to know and recognize their fellow witches.[21] A person may smile and laugh with you by day, and greet you well, concealing the jealousy of the heart, but at night he or she goes out to try and kill you by witchcraft. Those suspected as witches or wizards (*afwiti*) are often discovered by 'witchhunts' (*seketera*) or by the spirit-possessed in the community, usually called *mchimi* (diviner). The theme of witchcraft is frequent in Tonga oral literature, as in the stories: 'A witch burnt alive', and 'A witch and the girls'. Also, some of the Tonga names like *Nyamazawo* (Their meat), *Mwatimara* or *Tamara* (You have wiped us) portray the evils of witchcraft. Tonga society has condemned witchcraft practices as morally bad. Black magic, which is deemed as harmful, is totally condemned in Tonga society. This can be illustrated in an incident I experienced: 'A certain man died. He was much feared in the community as possessing dreadful magic. At the time of his death it was feared that the magical concoction that was mixed with his blood would enable him to turn into a leopard, a lion or a snake. At his death his face was blindfolded with a piece of cloth. His son was assigned by some diviners to keep continuous watch at his father's grave and was ordered to kill any animal that emerged either at the head or feet of his dead father's grave. In so doing, for such a period, it was certified that the son had really controlled the spirit of his father.'[22] This kind of magic also illustrates the Tonga concept of incarnation of the spirit. The purging of witchcraft by witch-hunts is a sign that the Tonga people would like to promote a morally good society. Witchcraft is considered as immoral because it breeds fear, envy, jealousy and mistrust among people.

Spirit Possession

Bourguignon defines spirit possession as "possession trance" that manifests itself in an alteration of the consciousness, personality or will of the individual.[23] This is in line with Tonga beliefs that intercourse between the living and the dead is sometimes believed possible in certain individuals by spirit possession of some dead relative or acquaintance. In the land of the living, spirits are believed most commonly to take human forms or other forms. This is in line with the view of Wiese on some of the Ngoni beliefs:

---

[21] E.G. Parrinder, *African Traditional Religion*, London: SPCK, 1968, p. 125.

[22] Rev D.K. Mphande, "Memories" from the Diary - Bandawe (1977).

[23] E. Bourguignon (ed), *Religion, Altered States of Consciousness and Social Change*, Columbus: Ohio State University Press, 1973, pp. 3-35.

They believe that certain souls come to reside temporarily in the body of other human beings. When this happens, the individual who is that soul's host, feels desires which he at once recognizes as being the spirit's; for instance, to possess nice clothes, a fine weapon or any other expensive article. If he is not able to satisfy the spirit's demands at once, he begins to fall ill and does not feel well until he has granted what the intruder wants. Very often a big dance is what the spirit desires and he manifests it by dancing the possessed person down to prostration. It is always after great suffering or prostration and incoherent monologues that the spirit departs from the body.[24]

On the other hand, spirits might visit their haunts either in form of snakes, lions, leopards, crocodiles, or other animals and by such transmigrations either express their wishes regarding the living or work on them their revenge. If some few days after the burial of a man or woman a snake is seen to haunt the house of the deceased, the relatives have no doubts about its being the deceased relative in this spirit form. To kill such a snake is believed to kill the spirit (*kubaya mzimu*). There are many tales about snakes in Tonga oral literature as reflected later in this book.

The Tonga, like the Tumbuka, believe that the *mchimi* or *mneneri* (diviner or soothsayer) receives his messagees from the spirits, and his word is seldom called into question, claiming, as it does, such supernatural origin. The spirit might choose a dream in which to make its communication, or it might come on the soothsayer during his waking hours. The deliverance of the message is usually preceded by sickness, real or feigned, or by the prophet falling into a trance. These physical disturbances are sure indications to the villagers that some prediction will shortly be forthcoming, and when the soothsayer begins his heeheeing (*kuchima*) and inarticulate mumbling, several would be ready to support him in their arms while he delivers his message. Possession by a spirit does not always lead to prophetic utterance. There is a very interesting and complicated type of supposed possession, under the influence of which an individual might be drawn to the burial enclosure of the dead. The people may think that the dead have called her and she begins heeheeing. This is the belief that the *azimu* or *viŵanda* (spirits) possessed her.

It is not resolved whether *maskaŵi'* (*viŵanda*) is treated as a special disease, or a possession of ancestral spirits. Boston Soko observes:

---

24 Matthew Schoffeleers (ed), *Guardians of the Land*, Gweru: Mambo, 1967, p. 139.

Described as a special "disease," the 'Vimbuza' requires special "treatment," since Western medicine cannot combat it. It is believed in certain quarters that spirits are those of defunct ancestors. It should be recalled, however, that the Vimbuza spirits come under different groups of families with their proper denomination, and that these spirits are likely to meet the dead ancestors' spirits at the Msoro tree.[25]

The spirit-possessed person always names the spirits whose communication he or she has to give, either by saying so and so had talked with him/her in a dream or by identifying himself with the spirits, "I, so and so (naming the spirit), have to tell you." My late mother used to do this once possessed by the spirits. She used to identify the spirits tormenting her as: *M'Bemba, M'Biza, Mhalure, Mngoma, Senga*. Sometimes the spirit of her late father was mentioned, ARobert *andikoma* (Robert is tormenting me). Some of these names are associated with tribes (e.g. 'Senga' in Zambia) or, some disguised persons.[26]

Other symptoms of the possessed are: changes in language and accent, or speaking in tongues, showing aspects of supernatural power—that it takes several strong men to hold a woman, causing severe torment on the possessed person. The spirit may drive him away from his home so that he lives in the forest (or graveyard). It may cause him/her to jump into a fire and get burnt, to torture the body with sharp instruments or even do harm to other people, eat raw flesh or bitter herbs, drink filthy water from the ponds, eat human waste. Gradually, the possessed may lose his/her own personality and act in the context of the personality of the spirit possessing him/her. The possessed person becomes restless, may fail to sleep properly, and if the possession lasts a long period it results in damage to health. In Tonga society, women are more prone to spirit possession than men.

Certain medicine men called 'exorcists' perform various rites to calm down the spirits bothering the possessed. These rites involve offering food and other articles, or the pouring of libations of beer, milk, water, blood from an animal, like a goat or a chicken. Through the songs, mimics and gestures the victim gives the portrait of these dominant spirits which inhibit her. The

---

[25] Boston Soko, "The Vimbuza Possession Cult: The Onset of the Disease," in *Religion in Malawi*, Nov. 1987, no. 2, p. 14.

[26] For comparison refer to Boston Soko, *Vimbuza. The Healing Dance*, Zomba: Imabili, 2014.

musical instruments often used include a drum and a calabash. The chief exorcist sings, calling names of the spirits in the person and the loud orchestra accompanies the singing.[27] The high volume of music attracts not only the current possessor into dancing, but also neighbouring women. After dancing for about two hours, the possessed falls down as if dead, apparently from exhaustion. She lies for a while, then gets up renewed, she or he will eat or drink something that the spirit had chosen to eat or drink like blood of a goat, sheep or cattle or even of a chicken. From that time on the spirit either leaves the possessed or no further hardship would be inflicted on her/him.

The moral function of spirit possession in Tonga society is that it consolidates the belief in the reality of the spirits. It also strengthens the hope and security of the people with the work of ancestral spirits. Thus, the understanding of spirit possession helps the people see the bond of relationship between the living and the dead. Spirit possession also helps people to determine their origin and boundary relationships like in the case of territorial spirits. *Maskawe* (spirit possession) can also become an entertainment dance. There are Tonga spirit-possessed who have become professionals. In this case spirit possession may not be considered as a disease.

Beliefs in Supernatural Powers

The ancestral spirits are believed to be the custodians of morality. They passed it to the elders and the elders to the young. In the life of the Tonga, this belief is regarded very highly. Motives connected to it being alternately love, fear, gratitude or need. The objects of their worship are *Chiuta* and the *azimu* (*mizimu*), that is God and the spirits. Some prayers addressed to ancestral spirits like, *Muyane ndi Chiuta* (Be of one mind with God) seem to point to the belief that there was intercommunication of some sort, and that the dead were acquainted with the intentions of the Supreme Spirit (God) regarding the living suppliant. This is in line with what Silas Ncozana

---

[27] I observed the scene live at Maula in Chintheche on 9.10.1994, when a group of exorcists and singers had gathered at a home to drive away the spirits which possessed a certain woman. The choruses, the drumming and the whole intercourse were converted into therapeutic practices with symbols familiar in Tonga society.

has indicated when he notes that ancestors occupy an intermediate position between God and the living.[28]

Likewise Tonga worship of the spirits in the sense of prayers to the dead was an attempt to reach the Supreme Spirit through them. In other words the worship could be best referred to as accredited to the dead over the fortunes of the living, and it was accordingly in the interest of the living to see that they kept on good terms with those who had gone to the spirit world, the world of the *departed* or the *living dead*.

In their own times of need the living went out to or yearned after the unseen powers they knew best, and who, being related to them, would be most willing to help. Gratitude had its share in the acts of worship practised by individuals, in offering the first-fruits to God or in the setting apart of some portion of game or fish caught in a successful hunt or haul to the favourable spirit, whose good offices were understood to have brought them their good fortune. Veneration of the *mzimu* or *chiŵanda* (spirits of the dead) would begin at the time of burial and the first offerings are made as the funeral party is on its way to the graves.

In the past the order would be: first the players on pipes (*malipenga*) and drums (*ng'oma*), then the corpse carried, head foremost, by the *azukulu*, behind it the party carrying the flour, grain or beer to be poured out to the departed spirit along the route to the grave and lastly the general company of mourners. At the grave further sacrifice was made, the offerings being either placed in the grave along with the body, or arranged on top at the head of the grave after the soil had been filled in. Before that they clapped their hands as a gesture of salutation and homage to the dead, using the word so frequently repeated throughout their acts of worship: *Pepa, pepa*, (Be appeased, be appeased). Even to this day, the meaning of these words has not changed. They are the common words used at funerals or when one is sick or had an accident.

After the interment, the *chibwi* or chief of the *azukulu* conducting the funeral rites and solemnities offered prayer, its requests being mostly that the spirit should go away and that it might work only for the good of its

---

[28] His concern is particularly with the work of the ancestral spirits. Silas Ncozana, Spirit Possession and Tumbuka Christians, PhD, Aberdeen University, 1985, published as Silas Ncozana, *The Spirit Dimension in African Christianity. A Pastoral Study among the Tumbuka People of Northern Malawi*, Blantyre: CLAIM-Kachere, 2002.

friends, and provide them with abundance of the desirable things of life: *Sonu awiya ose pa msana pe, ndikuti manja pu, pu; pepa, pepa* (Then all fell over on to their backs, assenting by clapping their hands and saying: Be appeased!). Subsequently to the burial sacrifices and prayers might be offered at any time either at the grave, or at the *makunthu* (the house in which the dead relative had died). The taboo for a *makunthu* is that it should be pulled down or left to fall of itself.

There is a site at *nkhorosa* for Chief Malenga-Mzoma, at Chituka village. Sometimes worship or prayer was conducted around the *chiriza/kavuwa* (shrine) which was especially erected for the worship of one spirit, and was either an enclosure made by planting a circle of trees round the house of the dead, or an enclosure of reeds with a sort of model hut built inside it. On the top of this little hut was often placed a piece of fancy cloth as a gift to the spirit, while food and beer were placed inside or splashed against its small door. I was able to visit the *chiriza* or *nkhorosa* for Chief Malenga Mzoma. What now remains is a thick forest. The offering was mostly flour, beer, fish, meat of game or cloth, usually of some uncommon colour or pattern. The *chimbwi* or his counterpart was generally called to officiate. The shrines were dedicated to their ancestral spirits and not to *Chiuta* (God). Perhaps this is why the Tonga have few myths about God, unlike the Chewa who dedicated their shrines to *Chisumphi* (God) at Msinja or Kaphirintiwa in the Dzalanyama range.

Veneration of ancestral spirits is a common practice, even today, though many of them would claim allegiance to Christianity.[29] The idea is to seek peace and reconciliation, and that they may have good luck in the community of the living. A prayer rendered at a gathering around the graveyard would go like this:

Tafika pamalo ghano. Wana awa	We have come to this place with
waziya kuti mukumane nawo	these children so that they can see
nawo, amuwonene mukugona apa.	where you are laid to sleep.
Ndipo achituwa pano muwapaske	We pray that as they leave this place,
chimango. Nthenda zose mutuzgepo.	they would find peace in their hearts.
Mwawi muwapaske,	Protect them from all diseases and
mwakuti kumuzi aje amampha.	give them good luck so that they live
	abundant life in the village.

---

29   Int. Rev W. Manda, Gordon Nyirenda and Zgawowa Mphande.

There are stories which show that the Tonga believe in the reincarnation of the spirits of the dead. This is reflected in the story of the *three brothers*, in a later chapter.

In the past, favourite places for it were at *nthowa-ndekano* (crossroads), the supposed meeting places of spirits as well as men and women or under the *msoro* tree, which was believed to possess very strongly the power of attracting to itself men or women and things. *Kusoro* means to draw, attract. The Tonga call the honey-bird *Soro* because it has the power to draw man after it. We see this idea in the story about *Tupa and the Snake*, where *Soro* (Honey-bird) comes and attracts the children so that later on *Tupa*'s wife has to go to a pool where they would be swallowed by the big Snake. Later on, *Tupa* comes to rescue his family. So the *msoro* tree was believed to have the virtue of drawing to it all on whom its influence was directed. Chiefs and others kept pieces of it among their medicines and charms that they might draw to them, and to their village, people from other districts. Here also is a good example where ecology was well preserved.

It should be stressed here that the moral aspect in the concept of ancestral veneration is to train the young to respect the living-dead—those still remembered in the family. It is to show their continued love to those who are departed. By offering the best sacrifices the young are trained to share things unsparingly. Another moral aspect in the veneration of ancestors is that the ancestors are generally seen as benevolent. Punishment by the ancestors is only to remind the living of their obligations. There are also special occasions when graveyards are cleared and protected from being destroyed by bush fires. The whole community comes together in obedience and submission to do this noble task. T/A Malengamzoma told me that her people did this so that "the ancestors should feel happy that their home is cared for."[30]

Through these rituals the young develop a sense of responsibility and learn that they have an obligation in the community to participate in the activities of the elders. In many Tonga clans the people prepare *sadaka*, where they gather ceremoniously so as to remember and appease the dead.

---

[30] Information given by T/A Malenga Mzoma of Chituka. She showed me the shrine (*chiriza*) of her ancestors at *Nkhorosa* (10.10.1994).

In this sense the ancestors are the foundation of morality. The ancestors passed on their moral principles to the living elders and the living elders pass them on to the youth. Moral goodness can be understood only in relation to our ancestors. The departed are considered the helpers and protectors of the clans.

Belief in the Supreme Being

As in all Malawian societies, the spiritual life of the Tonga community plays a central and vital role. This is reflected in some of the Tonga myths, stories, proverbs and rituals which portray God as the Creator, source of life, cause of death and giver of rain. The Tonga have several names of God, common are, *Chiuta, Leza, Mlengi, Chata, Mulungu*. These names also indicate that God is the Spirit Supreme.

The Tonga moral attributes of God include: *Chiuta wa Wezi* (The Gracious God); *Chiuta wa Lisungu* (The Merciful God); *Chiuta wa Kwanja* (the Loving God) etc.[31] Thus, like the Chewa people, the Tonga speak of God as *Chiuta* as Giver of Rain, and Creator of the World. This is in line with the observations made by both Cullen Young and J.C. Chakanza. Young notes that:

> The name *Chiuta/Chauta* is intimately connected with the Chewa national cult. *Chauta* is the Chewa version which has *Chiuta* as its equivalent in the Tumbuka language.[32]

J.C. Chakanza advances this idea by observing that besides the Tumbuka, "the Tonga and Nkhamanga peoples use the same name. The prefix 'Chi' is for size and greatness. Hence, *Chi-uta* means the Great Bow in the Heavens."[33]

MacAlpine thinks that the name *Chiuta* for the Tonga people means that God is the "Wonderful" and the "Wonder-worker." The name is a word very difficult to derive with certainty, but whatever its root may be, it now denotes one who inspires wonder and awe, and in consequence the word is particularly applicable to Him to whom all things are believed to be possible.[34] While Chiuta is thought of as a Spirit and not a man, he is not a

---

[31] These names are known across the Tonga people. However, most of the young informants, were most familiar with names like, *Chiuta, Mulungu* and *Mlengi*.

[32] T. Cullen Young, "The Idea of God in Northern Nyasaland" in E.W. Smith (ed), *African Ideas of God*, London: Edinburgh House Press, 1950, p. 50.

[33] J.C. Chakanza (ed), *Religion in Malawi*, 1987, p. 7.

[34] A.G. MacAlpine, "Tonga Religious Beliefs and Customs" in *Aurora*, p. 377.

mzimu in the ordinary sense—not a departed spirit, but the Spirit Supreme, the self-existent one, the Creator and the Sustainer of Life, the God of Heavens (*Chiuta wa ku Chanya*).[35]

The name *Leza* is also connected with God, frequently associated with lightning as in the curse: *Lipambi likurghe* (May lightning eat you). But *Leza* also means, He who Nurtures or Rears (*kulera*). Here again, J.C. Chakanza thinks that "Leza, from the verb, *kulera* in Chewa and Tonga, means one who rules or rears." *Leza* then refers to God as the one who nurtures, rears or rules the creation. In certain Chewa and Tonga dialects *kaleza* means 'lightning.'[36] For Chakanza, another rare Tonga name for God is *Chisumphi* which leans heavily on Spirit. Hence, it refers to God as Chief among spirits and provider of rain, or it may mean 'wind spirit'.[37] Thus, the name also connotes "powerful God." *Mphambi*, like *Leza*, means God. The name is also associated with lightning and rain.

In Tonga oral literature the names *Mulungu* and *Chiuta* are used regularly. *Mulungu* also means the High Spirit associated with the sky, rain, thunder and lightning. In Tonga, *Mulungu* gives the picture of one who creates or moulds. This view could agree with Cullen Young's suggestion on the origin of *Mulungu*. He observes that the suffix *-lunga* means to put together, smoothening surfaces of an earthen pot (*nkhulungu*).[38] Other rare Tonga names of God are *Nyangoyi*, associated with God of the mountains and rain, and *Chamjili*, associated with storms. The Tonga people have many other attributes applied to God. These include: *Chandu* (Beginner), *Mlengacharu* (World-maker); *Mlimiriya, Msungi* (Preserver or Keeper); *Mlengavuwa* (Rainmaker); *Mhiwa, Mlerawana* (Nourisher). The Tonga people believe that God can have intercourse with people on earth. This concept is reflected in the tale "Origin of Death" (Tale 2, Chapter 6).

Frequently names of *Chiuta, Leza* or *Mphambi* are used in swearing and in cursing as in, *Ndakana Chiuta mkali, Ndakana Leza* or *Mphambi (*with an implied challenge to God or lightning). So in the heat of anger they may sometimes say, *Leza likurghe* (may lightning eat you). Here is also implied that the Tonga see "lightning" as God's manifestation, as also might be a

---

[35] Ibid.

[36] J.C. Chakanza (ed), *Religion in Malawi*, 1987, p. 4.

[37] Ibid., p. 4.

[38] T. Cullen Young, *African Ideas of God*, p. 50.

heavy thundercloud, or another terrifying phenomeon in nature. Also, the Tonga people believe that God is the source of good. He cares for his people. He provides them with rain and a good harvest. He provides them with good health and saves them from death. He is to be worshipped. God needs good people in the society. God loves, but also punishes. Quite frequently the works of *Chiuta* are called by his name, especially when they are such as to bear out his character as awe-inspiring. Thus, disease is frequently spoken of as judgement of God. The area of an epidemic disease is referred to as *Kwawiyako Chiuta* (God has fallen on them there), meaning that smallpox has wiped out the inhabitants. God should feared. People should be obedient to God. God is the source of morality. He revealed Himself to their ancestors as a kind God, loving, merciful and gracious. So people should be kind to others, care for others and respect one another.

CHAPTER THREE

FORMS AND NATURE OF TONGA ORAL LITERATURE

Introduction

So far very has been written and printed on Tonga oral literature. Moreover, everyday situations arise in which the Tonga employ stories, proverbs, riddles, aphorisms, songs, rituals and taboos. The most important form of Tonga oral traditional literature is the *nthanu* (tale/myth). This is the most significant narrative literary form. Other forms include: *nthanthi* (Proverb); *vindawi* (riddles); *ndakatulo* (poems); *sumu* (songs); *gule* (dances); *mwambu* (rituals) and *vinguzgu* (taboos). The basic oral drama is the *malipenga* dance for boys and young men, and *chioda* for women.

Tonga Artistic Expression

The Tonga word *nthanu,* usually translated as story, is common in Tonga life. This is followed by *sumu* and *gule* (song and dance). All such artistic expression and inspiration, whether of singers, storytellers, dancers or drummers is thought to come essentially from the ancestors and the old people as founders of the Tonga culture. It is a cultural heritage passed on orally to the younger generation. Drumming as an activity is usually learnt from those who are experts. It has a specialist aspect. The Tonga people have always called to their minds a man called "Konimo Muhone," who was a unique drummer of the *chioda* dance. He was a widely recognized expert, who received honours and gifts for the exercise of his skills.[39] Much the same applies to dancing, which also has its own specialists who perform on certain prescribed occasions - whether it is at *malipenga, chioda, ndelitha, mchoma* or *maskawe* dances.

The master-drummer, for instance, must dominate through his playing, and compel the attentive response of the other drummers joining him. He does this not only through the vigour and subtlety of his playing, his laying down the beat, but also by his introduction of variations to which the others must

---

[39] Information supplied by village Group Headman Jiriki of Chintheche on 8th Oct. 1994. Konimo Muhone made *chioda* a success during the wedding ceremonies.

respond. In Tonga drumming one does not only have to attend to variation in meters and timbres, but one can also feel the meter of the master-drummer pulling against and away from that of the others. These skills should be passed on to the younger generation.

Beside dances performed on ceremonial occasions, dances and rhythmic movement run all through Tonga work and leisure. People are likely to break into steps of a dance or into a song on any occasion, sometimes apparently quite unconsciously. This is typical of young men and women who are used to dancing *malipenga* or *chioda*, respectively. Therefore, in discussing Tonga literature, it is important to realize that the stories represent in fact only one facet of Tonga culture. Indeed, in the sphere of music and dance the Tonga use a more specialized and differentiated vocabulary and lay more explicit emphasis on expert skill than they do in respect of the stories.

This brief reference to Tonga music and dance illustrates the way artistic expression becomes a dramatic activity into which individual performers and the audience join in a manner very similar to the dramatic activity of both telling and listening to the stories. The Tonga themselves are quite conscious that these stories form an important definable part of their cultural heritage and one of which they are proud. Mr John Bright Chikuse Chirwa, a retired politician, observed:

> Definitely, the Tonga culture seems to be getting out of the way. Much of the intermarriage, inter-crossing of the people and the bringing in what we might call 'Western Civilization', have brought an end to most of the cultural situation of our people. Today you can hardly find what we call *mphara*, where people came together in the evenings, warming themselves around the fire and so on, singing or dancing of little kids when elderly people do some talks of stories, proverbs or riddles and so on ... As a result the Tonga culture has gone down.[40]

Classification of Tales

A close analysis of the Tonga narratives shows that the environment and the characters in the Tonga narrative are real, both to the performer and the audience. The distinction between myth and legend poses some

---

40   I am indebted to now late Mr John Chikuse Chirwa, of Chituka Village, for this information which was recorded on 9th October 1994. He died just five months after I had interviewed him.

problems in the classification of Tonga folktales. It is not easy to separate a "myth" that is a tale having to do with an imaginary world existing before the present order was created, and a "legend" that is a tale regarded as true or told as if true or unauthenticated narrative folk-embroidered stories from historical material, sometimes popularly deemed historical.

Every classification approach using tale categories has its own merits and demerits. The motifs once found do not necessarily imply that the tales have a one to one relationship with others in the same category. The thematic approach has some pitfalls too. It is possible for one tale to have more than one theme. Ruth Finnegan is correct when she observes that the stories in Limba tales can address several themes or topics, which are primarily intended to communicate.[41]

Within the broad class of *nthanu* (story), the Tonga themselves do not make any further clear distinction between myth and folktales. There are also shorter forms such as proverbs and riddles, as well as what could be called *mbiri* (myth/history or legend). *Mbiri* as legend or history functions to help people trace their origin or claim boundaries or claim property like land. The Tonga proverbs deal with human interaction and reflect powerful forms of feeling and imagination that are in the grain of the people's culture. The proverbs cover subjects such as hospitality, treatment of strangers, marriage and family life, cooperation, gratitude, difficulties in community life and keeping secrets. They address family values and norms.

The proverbs play an important role in the inculturation of the morals of the society. They also act as regulators of behaviour, because they are a result of long human experience. The proverbs function as a store house of Tonga wisdom and philosophy. Tonga proverbs are used by adults in many situations: in the home, at work, in court etc, for they are considered a mark of eloquence and wit. For example, on generosity towards one another, they may say, *Kase ruta kase weku*, meaning "What a good neighbour has done to you, do the same" or "do what you expect your friend to do for you"; on co-operation, *Kamuti kapa mphara nkhakukoleyanako*, meaning "Take the burden of your friend"; on hospitality - *Kwenda ndisima yakubikabika*, meaning "If you are kind to others, wherever you go, people will be kind to you also"; on secrets, *Wakamba wataya, kaja mumoyo wasunga*, meaning, if a secret is revealed to one person it is no longer a

---

41   Ruth Finnegan, *Limba Stories and Story-telling*, Oxford, 1967, p. 62.

secret. It becomes a secret if it is kept in the heart. And on obedience, *Kuwa ndi masengwe gha kuwurongo ghambula kuvwiya* (To have horns in the forehead which don't become controlled), meaning "a disobedient person who does whatever pleases him/her." (Proverb no. 56). Thus, *nthanthI* (pithy sayings or proverbs) are frequently used in the context of persuasion, as in *Kuwika mphoro nkhudanga charya ku mlenji.* (To keep some food, one must first eat something in the morning), meaning, "Do not blame someone before you have a solution for him/her."

Proverbs may be used according to situations. This is seen when they are used contradictorily. At other times they become mere figures of speech or brief analogies. Informal analogies are common in arguments, oratory or joking, and are a form of speech, which is admired. Analogies and similes are also frequently introduced to convey to a listener some point that seems to be peculiar to him/her as in *Kuja nge umoyo waku chigwangwala*, meaning "Being proud in the manner a of a mouse called '*chigwangwala*'" or, *Kukana nge ndi pusi yo wangukana kusele pa zenje* ("One who refuses to be sent, is like a monkey which does not go into a hole even if it is in danger," meaning "One is hard-hearted," and so on.

Other *nthanu* are in the form of historical narratives. These could be referred to as "legends" (*mkoka* or *mbiri*). These historical narratives are often referred to by a periphrasis like "speaking about old days" or "about the old people." The delivery differs from stories proper in that there are no songs. It is sometimes rather more serious in tone, but it may portray amusing or exciting incidents or details and include many of the characteristics of style and delivery so evident in the stories, such as dramatic dialogue, imitation, swift narrative, and vehement diction. The legend about the "origin" of the Tonga people recorded in this book is a good example (Tale 1 in Chapter 6). They function in order to preserve property of things or validate culture and boundaries.

In classifying oral narrative forms, the basic distinction rests on the extent to which a narrative is or is not based upon objectively determinable facts. Some are pragmatic and relativistic, relying on local distinctions made by members of the societies in which the tales are told, between narratives regarded as fiction and narratives regarded as true by the narrator and his/her audience.

Of the Tonga stories (*nthanu*), some are about people, some about animals and a few about God and origins. For instance, in the myth about "Origin of

Death" recorded in Chapter 6 (Tale 2), the actors include animals, people and *Chiuta*. The myth ends with an explanation of the present relations between man and the Chameleon or man and the Tortoise—whichever character is to blame in the story, and so on. To settle whether a story is intended to be basically an explanatory or aetiological tale, a dilemma or a moralizing story might be seen on the basis of the form of the story. Stories often end with an explanation, question or moral making the classification a straightforward one.

The kind of ending adopted in the case of a particular narration seems to depend on the storyteller or the occasion rather than to be a defining mark of a special fixed type of story. Similarly with dilemmas; in some plots certainly a concluding dilemma is stated and seems to be a matter of choice for the teller rather than an inherent characteristic of the story itself (Tales 5, 16 and 18 in Chapter 6). A story is told to "give someone conscience" (*kupaska njuwi*), showing a person through a parable either that he/she has acted wrongly, or that he/she and others should try to act in a certain way in the future.

In any case, some stories are told on formal occasions with a primarily moral purpose. Some discussion in chapter one on oral transmission here make sense that all stories to a greater or lesser degree, according to circumstances, can contain some or all of several elements: moralizing and generalization, explanation, comparison, whether implicit or stated as an explicit dilemma; and finally, an intention to amuse and entertain by an interesting plot, a shocking episode or character, and a vivid style of delivery. For instance, generalization might lead to a pattern or structure, as seen in the example on structure like: problem/response/problem solved. This is also seen in stories in which a deception rather than a miracle solves the problem.

Stories about Animals

There are tales about ridiculous creatures. They are perhaps the most common type of tale in the Tonga repertoire. Most important for understanding the place of this tale in Tonga village life, whenever a trickster emerges, everyone begins to laugh, for the very idea of his/her existence is ridiculous. His antics represent just what sane and mature people do not do, as in "The Fox who Cost the Life of his Wife" (Tale 35).

These stories about animals are liable to be rather shorter than tales about people. The most common characters in this category of tales are: *Kalulu* (hare) is mostly represented as shrewd or crafty; the *hyena* is represented as stupid and gluttonous; the *snake* is represented as clever and dangerous; the *chameleon* is represented as stupid; the *hare* or *rabbit* is represented as clever and able to out-wit even the lion; the *spider* is represented as intelligent and so on. Many of the animal stories end with the statement of a moral or with account of the origin of some characteristic or habit of a bird or animal, or the present distribution of animals: some in the bush, some in the village, or why there is hatred between certain animals and birds etc. Some function as aetiologies (see Tales 2, 3, 11, 14 and 15).

Stories about People and their Ecology

These are stories about moral aspects of behaving told to initiate deep discussion on important themes, for example, how to live within the family and the community, how to make friendship etc. They focus closely on the fundamental and recurrent problems of social relations: the qualities of love, the nature of obedience, the ethics of choice under stress conditions. But in spite of the fact that they deal with everyday problems, these are among the most fanciful and even ridiculous tales. These stories in some ways relate to the ecology of the Tonga society and help to sound a note on how this ecology can be cared for and preserved.

On the whole, stories primarily about people seem to be the most popular and often the most elaborate. There are a few stock heroes, as in the story of "*Tupa and the Children* (Tale 29). It is he who rescues his two sons when he almost swallowed the big snake and drank all the water from the pool, leaving the snake on bare ground. These stories are all marked by their light-hearted tone and rather far-fetched and shocking character; they are always greatly enjoyed by the listeners. Other Tonga stories are about unnamed characters and commonly begin with such phrases as, "Long ago, a man came out," "A man married a wife," "Three children were born," "Kindness pays," and so on. However, even within this anonymity there are some stock characters.

Stories about Chiuta and Origins

Stories about God or far-off origins are commonly referred to as myths. These also fall in the category of *nthanu*. They share the same motifs as legends and function in a similar way. I have not been able to identify as many myths as one could expect. The Tonga dedicated the shrines to their ancestors. This should perhaps be the reason why they do not have many myths about gods.[42]

The tales cannot be accorded the title of "myths" for they do not form part of any systematic theology, philosophy or mythology. Common to Tonga myths is that of the "Origin of Death" (*Kuza kwa Nyifwa*), which is also known in various Chewa and Sena versions. The chameleon, who brought the wrong message to people, is blamed for the fact that the dead must stay for ever. Some myths are concerned with historical progenitors and their heroic accomplishments like the Karonga Mzizi stories. These deeds involve such supernatural powers and abilities that even allegedly historical narratives read like myths (Tale 1 and 2 in Chapter 6).

The Concept of *Nthanu*

As seen, the word *nthanu* (story or myth) is used in a wide sense, and a *nthanu* may, on different occasions, be used for varying purposes: for amusement, description, generalization, tactful means of persuasion or advice, dramatic and artistic expression related to song and dance, ritual or for many or all of these at once. The ending of many stories includes reference to some moral truth connected with the subject matter. Here a general comment is being introduced, in analogy with the events depicted in the story, for example, "*ahurwa a zeru alingana ndi kalulu, akupusa ayana ndi fu, yuwa wanguwozga mbutu*, (wise boys are like hare, who sowed seeds in time, the foolish ones are like tortoise who just kept seeds to rot), or, *mlimu wamampha ndi wakukomdweska wendi marumbo ghamampha* (good works deserve high praise).

Most frequently in the shorter animal stories, the plot is simple in that there is little switch of scene throughout and successive actions of protagonists are simply followed. The stories are in the main about individuals. The main characters that appear in the tales are either humans, named or unmamed; and talking animals or birds. The hero is often described as "a man," "an orphan," or "a chief" (*fumu*).==

---

[42] The Chewa dedicated their Kaphirintiwa shrine to Chauta/Chiuta, the High God, while there was nothing of this approach to the High God (Chiuta) in the Tonga society. The Tonga people developed ancestral shrines. This could have been the main reason for the absence of myths about God in Tonga society (see Matthew Schoffeleers and A.A. Roscoe, *Land of Fire*, p. 19).

Thematic Analysis of the Stories

A thematic examination of the stories shows that they are mainly didactic rather than merely entertaining. There is a tendency in some tales of moving from tragedy to comedy or vice-versa. The suggestion of a thematic approach is supported by the nature of the progression of the stories. Perhaps the most common situation described is that of marriage or of love. This theme comes into tales of all kinds, whether about humans, animals or origins. It is one of those themes that centre on human relationships. Thus, the main characters all portray these human relationships such as family, friendship and other relationships. It is, for example, normally assumed in the stories that, as in real life, men must work to win a wife. Marriage is assumed to be a man's aim. And yet, as will be shown in several stories in chapter 6, marriage too has its drawbacks. For instance, the problem of widowhood is very common in Tonga society.[43] Other stories touch on similar relationships, though often without asserting such an emphatic generalization. The relationship of mother and child is often illustrated. So there are situations when parents can approve a certain marriage, if faced with a serious personal crisis. This is the case in *Mwali Wambuwu* (The Dumb Virgin), or in the story of *Chimutu* (The Head), recorded in Chapter Six (Tales 7 and 13).

The position and fortunes of an orphan is also a popular theme. His lot is one that is expected to elicit pity, so that his triumphs, whether in recalling his mother or father or in gaining of a chiefdom and riches have a particular meaning through their paradoxical nature—that a child, beginning from such well-known disadvantages, should yet achieve success, as in the story of *Kajikazinge* (the Fried One).

An orphan shows this progression from tragedy to comedy in a more subtle way: an orphan is on a pilgrimage of triumphs and oppressions. Thus, again in the story about *Chimutu* (The Head)—the child, who was nothing more than a head, is the protagonist and this mystery is intensified, rather than mitigated, when he performs superhuman tasks. These feats help the rejected suitor to fulfil his ambitions.

---

43   See on this: Howard M. Nkhoma and Moira Kirwan, "Social Change and Widowhood: the Experience of the Tonga People of Northern Malawi," *Religion in Malawi* no. 7 (1997), pp. 13-18.

These tales further serve to illustrate the marriage motif discussed earlier. In the *Chimutu* story there is the inevitable misfortune of a handicap in being refused marriage by girls. When a humble girl accepts him, she later discovers that she is married to a man worth admiring. She is extremely delighted and the girls, who had refused, regret their earlier decision. Friendship and co-operation or their absence, forms another common motif. This is treated most obviously in the plot about friendship (*ubwezi*). Here *ubwezi* is seen as not superceeding kinship. In this story friendship is something very temporal, though useful. The chieftaincy is another motif in the stories as it is in real life. The Chief is represented in many ways. He may appear as a judge or as a kind and sympathetic father, more often he is represented as powerful and wealthy. Thus, the Chief offers his pretty daughter and land to anyone who will kill the fierce lions (Tale 10). The theme of chieftaincy is also closely linked with the theme of justice. This is illustrated in the story "An Eye for an Eye," from this saying, which portrays the triumph of justice (Chapter 6).

Cunning is another common motif in the tales. The most frequent word is *uryarya*, which means not only cunning, but also special powers, irresponsibility, and the capacity for extreme and far-fetched actions. Other kinds of shrewdness are also depicted as in *zeru za duwiwuwi* (the wisdom of the spider), in Tale 34; Lion and Hare (Tale 36); or in the ingenious reversals in some of the stories. Another significant theme in Tonga tales is the reward of obedience and the penalty of disobedience, as in the survival from a drought, when the orphan follows the advice of her stepmother. In many stories the obedient ones are saved from certain calamities, while the disobedient lose their lives. Here the story about the Orphaned Millipede is a good example (Tale 6).

The Oral Tale Performance

The picture gained from the field study shows that oral narrative provides an especially rich focus for the investigation of the relationship between oral literature and social life, because part of the special nature of the narrative is to be doubly anchored in human events. That is, narratives are keyed both to the events in which they are told and to events that they recount, toward narrative events and narrated events. The storyteller takes what he or she tells from experience: his/her own or that reported by others. And he or she in turn makes it the experience of those who are listening to the tale. Oral performance, like all human activity, is situated, its form, meaning and function rooted in culturally defined scenes or events—bounded segments of the flow of behaviour and experience that constitute meaningful contexts for action, interpretation, and evaluation.

By performance in this sense is meant a mode of communication, a way of speaking, the essence of which resides in the assumption of responsibility to an audience for a display of communicative skill, highlighting the way in which communication is carried out, above and beyond its referential content. From the point of view of the audience, the act of expression on the part of the performer is thus laid open to evaluation for the way it is done, for the relative skill and effectiveness of the performer's display. Performance, thus, calls forth special attention to and heightened awareness of the act of expression and the performer.

In speaking about the Tonga myths and folktales collected in the course of a field study during which performances were recorded on tapes in various parts of Tonga society, observations can be made that the constant process of arrangement and rearrangement of details and episodes is part of the creative process and is deeply involved in the aesthetics of *nthanu* production. Artists vary in the manner they perform, though the Tonga storytellers are not professionals. The performer would be free within the limits of the thematic-image and within the bounds of logic and cohesiveness, to deal with them as he/she chooses. Core clichés (songs, chants and sayings) would be repeated several times during a performance of a given story, (see Tales 31 and 35), thus enabling the audience to recall core images, the traditional elements out of which the stories are built by the narrator.[44]

During my field study at the scene of performance, each artist's personality implied everything that the artist brings as an individual to the performance of the literature. These elements of the artist's total personality provided a context for the oral literature in the sense that together they shape the material that ultimately emerges in performance. Each scene of performance thus provided the totality of factors surrounding the text that came from the mouth of the story-teller. These would include the resources of movements, gestures, music and the presence and actual impact of the various persons surrounding the perfomer.

---

[44] This confirms the earlier observation made by A. Lord about themes and patterns in oral narratives (A. Lord, "Comparative Analysis," p. xix).

87

One observes that each performance differs from others precisely because these physical factors are never quite the same, even for the same material or the same story. The audience may be hostile one time, but absolutely cooperative the next time. The musicians may be inspired on one occasion but drowsy on another. No two performances are ever quite the same, because these physical conditions are never really duplicated. This would easily be seen from storytellers who show a certain professional expertise in the control of the central ideas and images around which the tale is built. Lack of professionalism is mostly seen in school pupils. However, as they watch and listen to the performance, the younger ones rather unconsciously absorb the skills shown by those who perform better.

Tonga stories are most frequently told in the evenings, after the sun has set. There is no explicit rule that stories should not be told during the daylight hours, but in practice people are then normally occupied. At these performances members of the audience have the much-needed opportunity of relaxing not only their bodies after a hard day of work but even more importantly their minds. Psychological relief is not the least of the functions performed by oral literature. The minds of both performer and audience are relieved of various problems that have been pressing on them throughout the day. In schools stories are told by teachers and pupils in classroom situations during day time.

Through these occasions the tales are not only jointly enjoyed and performed, but they also bring wisdom to the members of the group and publicly carry the story forward so that others too may know it. The nature of the audience of the stories varies somewhat according to circumstances. I observed that riddles and short stories were told by one child to another, in pairs, or larger groups, and were often preliminary to longer narratives. Proverbs, analogies and parables are often used in small informal groups or, occasionally, introduced into a formal speech, perhaps at a law case in an official chiefdom court or to a classroom situation of 60 or more pupils.

One observes that the audience is very much a part of the whole situation and activity of story telling. It resembles the related activities of speech-making, dancing, and singing. The audience may be asked to clap at certain points during the story and at the end, showing honour to the narrator. In most cases the group of listeners takes up the chorus of a song. The narrator sings the first line, which is then repeated or added to by the rest. It is during singing that the artist more openly demonstrates his or her grievances, or pours his/her heart out in a song. The story teller can be anyone of whatever age or status. The anthology in Chapter Six is drawn from a cross-section of the Tonga narrators: pupils, men and women

Two of the narrators among the people visited were men who could tell legends of a historical type of their clan, as well as stories. A difference could be seen between telling a legend and telling a tale. As tellers of legends they exhibited a different attitude from that of the storyteller: their texts were realist and they were treated differently from a tale.[45] The vocabulary of the stories is much the same as that of ordinary speech used in day-to-day conversation, reporting some special event, or the formal speaking at law cases or funerals. In this respect, again, spoken narrative is in contrast to songs, both those interpolated into the stories, and, even more, most of those sung independently.

Repetition in stories is commonly observed. This involves the repetition of incidents and repeated patterns of events, which are characteristic compositional devices of oral style. The repetition here is repetition of elements of content like scenes, incidents and descriptions or elaborations, which recur with variable wording. The repetition can also be of similar incidents within the same story. Repetition also occurs when incidents appear in more than one tale. Repetition often serves to bring out some point in the story more dramatically. In a much less elaborate way, and one that commonly occurs in every kind of speech, single words are themselves often reduplicated.

Besides repetition of words or phrases, constant use is also made of parallel phrasing. This also involves repetition of a sort, but with variation of certain key elements. A certain amount of imitation or mimicry is also used to make the narration more vivid. This may involve direct imitation of what is understood to be the sound of animals speaking. Mimicry is also employed in the sense of imitative gestures or expressions. The storyteller also employs ideophones to embellish the narration.[46] This in part overlaps with the imitations mentioned earlier. Thus, there are certain words in Tonga,

---

[45] I am greatly indebted to my informants, 'Chiŵiŵi Kabunduli Mwase and Richard Zilakoma Phiri who narrated the legends about the origin of Tonga people: how titles like Karonga Mzizi or 'Chiŵiŵi had started and how some names like, Manda, Phiri or Banda began.

[46] For a detailed discussion of ideophones in Tumbuka see: Boston Soko, *Vimbuza. The Healing Dance*, Zomba: Imabili, 2014, pp. 139-160.

which always represent some particular sound. In the story, "Kindness pays" the sound of the ants is conveyed as, 'Waa! Waa! (Tale 24), and that of the sparrow is, 'Ti, ti, ti, ti' (Tale 28), and the movement of some animals is conveyed as 'Swayu-swayu-swayu.'

Tone or pitch is another device the storyteller employs in special and exaggerated ways to retain the attention of the audience. Variety is produced by exaggeration or alteration in the tempo or rhythm. The storyteller usually alters his/her pace of delivery to mark a change in tempo of the action in a story. The use of direct speech is popular in the stories and is a means by which the action can be advanced and presented through a quick exchange of greetings or questions.

The voice, character, and bearing of the protagonists can be dramatically represented, and effective use made of the common exclamations of surprise, shock or admiration. Songs, as mentioned earlier, are to be taken up and repeated by the listeners. Sometimes the songs take up the major part of the story; more often songs occur only at certain points in the narration. The exact meaning of the words often seems to be obscure, even to the singers themselves, and sometimes to be without any clear sense at all. Suspense is therefore another technique the narrator employs in order to retain the attention of the listeners. The suspense is created by delaying the climax or the crucial moment of the prose narrative.

The openings and conclusions of most stories are marked by certain formulae or stock phrases. In most cases the story is presented as a unit with beginning and end clearly marked by these conventional phrases. The common openings often rendered is 'Nthanu, nthanu mkuti mukuti asala nyanda' (Here is an old story, as old as the days when our ancestors used to wear bark clothes), or 'Boza buli nthanu buli' (Here comes a lie and a story, for you). Very often there is no formal title and the storyteller either plunges directly into a sentence about one of the characters, or opens formally with the announcement that she or he is going to tell the story.

Again, the story usually opens directly with a sentence about one or two of the characters, usually the heroes or heroines. For example, Mwaka (or Kalekale) kwenga wachiburumutiya ndi wagonyo (Long, long ago there were a blind man and a hunchback), or, Muwinga nyama (a hunter); Munthurumi and munthikazi (A man and a woman) without any more exact name. These include such situations as: 'Winning a wife', as in Kalulu ndi Pundu (Hare and Hyena), or in 'returning home': 'eating or being left hungry', 'announcing', 'outdoing each other in cunning or revenge'. These are often accompanied by a generalizing moral comment, an ascription of origin or a dilemma. The storyteller may simply end his/her story with the announcement: *Nthanu boza yamaliya penipo* (Here ends the story and a lie). The basic form may be similar in many stories or performances, yet the treatment and content may be very different.

Sometimes the good storyteller may string two or three tales together during one rendition. The story teller selects stories which have common characters or a common tricksters like the hare. The tale of the hare who tricked the hyena (or the elephant) is told as two separate narratives in some areas, but the man who narrated at the scene rendered it as one.

In conclusion this chapter attempted to explore Tonga artistic expression as a dramatic activity into which the performer and the audience join in a manner very similar to the dramatic activities of both telling and listening to the stories. In classification of the Tonga tales, the term *nthanu* (story) is a broader term, which does not make any distinction between myth and folktale. However, words like *mkoka* or *mbiri* have to do with "legend" or "history." These functions help people trace their origin or how things happen to be like they are. In addition, proverbs, riddles and rituals also belong to the corpus of Tonga oral literature. The folktales have three categories: stories about animals; stories about people and ecology and those about Chiuta and origins. The stories carry important themes such as marriage, unity (cooperation), obedience, respect, honesty, good and evil, famine and drought and so on. Tricksters in the stories are portrayed in various ways. The analysis and comparisons of the first ten stories in Chapter Six show much symbolism in the stories. The characters are analogous to human behaviours.

The discussion of conventional topics or favourite themes, and standard conclusions has been introduced not only to clarify certain general tenden-cies in the tales, but also to illustrate that no one moral is being put for-ward, explicitly or implicitly, in the stories as a whole, nor is it possible to draw up any simple philosophy of life from the stories. Even the very popu-lar and common motifs such as marriage, family relations, obedience and disobedience or chieftaincy are not treated from just one point of view. It would be misleading to say of Tonga tales that there is any one message or purpose conveyed. And one principal appeal of these tales is that they reflect closely the fundamental ways of life of the average member of society, and for this reason they bear such a close relationship to life.

There are lessons contained in these texts of oral literature on the consequences of breaking the accepted rules of conduct. For instance, if a tale assures us that patience will triumph over oppression, or that the small can overcome the mighty (Tale 36), it also implies that both the oppressor and the mighty should beware, for their unjust ways can only lead them to disgrace if not death. But it would be foolish to expect that everyone in the society would heed these lessons. It would also be unsafe for society to leave its moral health solely in the hands of tales, and proverbs, which in many cases tell how to conduct oneself only by implication.

At the scene of performance, the general process of narration depends on the narrator, who seems to take two central roles: that of medium, externalizing the core-images of the past and that of the artist, imaginatively selecting, controlling and arranging the materials and sources of the past, and giving them new life and freshness. The variations can be explained in terms of expansion, reduction, restatement, and rearrangement of the common elements.

The area within which the individual creation is possible is clearly two-fold, covering both style of delivery and content. Though it is impossible strictly to separate these two, it is clear that each occasion is, almost by definition, a unique artistic creation. The teller enacts the tale, depicts the action with more or less characterization, mimicry, exaggeration and effect through the use of tones, length, speed or singing, in order to make the narrative vivid, attractive and amusing to the audience. The characteristics in the performance and delivery of the story vary from narration to narration, in wording as well as enactment. The next chapter covers a discussion on Tonga rituals and taboos, with the understanding that myths and folktales are linked with rituals and taboos. Some of these are used for moral teaching.

CHAPTER FOUR

TONGA RITUALS AND THEIR INFLUENCE ON MORAL EDUCATION

The Cycle of Life

This chapter examines Tonga rituals and taboos that are linked with the life cycle of a person, and how these have an impact on moral behaviour. Attention is devoted to rituals of birth, adolescence and marriage and mortuary rituals and taboos. Rituals are rites of passage commonly conducted to mark stages in the life of an individual passing from one stage to another through a sacred event. Thus, rituals are intended for individual blessings and for communal participation. In Chapter One, it was observed that a myth is a myth only if it is employed in ritual, and some Tonga stories are also linked with ritual.

Birth Rituals

The Tonga people have a great reverence for human life. Rituals of birth concern the parents, especially the mother, as well as the baby. There is a significant morality behind rituals of birth in order to ensure that there is no contamination to the lives of family and relatives.

There is a great desire to have children, no wife feels her marriage secure till she has borne a child, and no man feels that his family can be continued till a child is born. Barrenness is one of the commonest causes of divorce and the desire for more children is a frequent reason for polygamy. If a young woman is barren, the parents try hard to find a medicine person to assist the young couple. Both the young man and his wife take herbs through water, tea or porridge. The young woman may wear amulets *mphiyu* to 'open up her womb' (*kujula mphapu*). Expectant mothers may wear protective amulets and avoid taboo foods, they may be advised not to eat some fish like *milamba* (mud-fish). They are forbidden to go around anybody's house, and so on. The husband of an expectant woman may be advised not to touch a corpse or participate in digging a grave.

At delivery prayers are made, and if it is difficult, the woman is told to confess sins against purity. This is to avoid *mapinga* (difficulties met at delivery). She must tell the *azamba* (midwives) if she met any man outside her wedlock, in order to save her life. Thus, honesty is a prerequisite or a condition to life.[1] The cutting of the umbilical cord is done carefully by an elderly woman, and the cord may be buried at the foot of a tree. Common trees used for this purpose are *msoro, mutawa* and *muwanga*. At the birth of a child whose delivery may be done by traditional midwives (*azamba*), normally elderly women, the bringers of the good news come ululating and dancing. People bring gifts like money, clothes and food.[2]

The young mother is kept *muchisachi* (in seclusion) with the baby until the umbilical cord falls off. This is done in order to observe rules of purity. Name giving ceremonies are popular and several names are bestowed on the infant at a family festival. They call this occasion *kudumuliya mwana* (naming the child).[3] Libations are poured on the ground. The traditional names depend on circumstances of birth, likeness to parents and ancestors. For example, the name *Masuzgo* (suffering) may symbolically remind how the mother suffered at the time of delivery. Sickly children are loaded with charms to drive evil away. This then also marks the coming out ceremony for mother and child from *muchisachi*. The young mother is schooled on how to care for the child and for her husband. She is advised to keep away from sexual intercourse with her husband for a time up to six months to avoid *mudulu* (sudden illness of the child).[4] These taboos are there to enhance cleanliness. The implication is that there are values to be adhered to by young mothers and fathers for them to succeed in bringing up children. Carelessness may result in the early death of a child. These birth rituals serve as lessons to guide them in areas of responsibilities.

Adolescence Rituals

The Tonga people have a long tradition of initiation rites. Through these initiation rites the youth are born anew into their society and their

---

[1]   If she has nothing to confess, even after being pressed, her difficulties can be ascribed to the husband's infidelity.

[2]   Today the traditional *azamba* are prohibited to carry out these deliveries outside a health centre.

[3]   After *kudumuliya mwana* she is allowed to start cooking again.

[4]   For a detailed treatment of the whole mdulo complex among the Chewa see: Joe DeGabriele, "When Pills don't Work—African Illnesses, Misfortune and Mdulo," *Religion in Malawi*, 1999, pp. 9-28.

manhood or womanhood is clearly defined. Mother or father fixation is prevented. Initiation rites are also practised by, among others, the Chewa, Lomwe, Ngoni, Nyakyusa, Tumbuka, the Yao, and so on. Variations in these initiation rites are common, just as in the case of circumcision. The Tonga do not go through communal rites like the Yao ceremonies of *Jando* and *Litiwo*, or *Msondo*, except those who are Islamised. But the Tonga boys and girls would undergo private ceremonies, where ritual experts take turns in giving instructions. After that, the boys or girls are no longer regarded as boys or girls, but as men and women of the village.[5]

These instructions are given during storytelling sessions in the *mphara* (unmarried boys' quarters); in the *nthanganene* (unmarried girls' quarters), or *paduli* (open space for pounding cassava or any grain), or in *vihewelo* (unmarried boy's shelters made of dry elephant grass), by elderly men and women (*madoda or zinchembele*).[6] When parents think their boy or girl is ready for initiation they sent them to join others in the *mphara* or *nthanganene*, respectively. These in a way would serve as initiation camps. Unlike in Yao ceremonies, among the Tonga preparations are very informal. The candidates or novices do not bring food, clothing, entertainment and payment for those who would look after the boys and girls in these initiation ceremonies.

The *nchembele*[7] (a woman who has reached motherhood), who is the first to discover the girl's first menstruation, or to whom the girl reports her first menstruation, becomes responsible to give instructions to the candidate. The *nchembele* should be experienced in married life. The girl is instructed to stay in the house for 7 days. Within this period, she has to wash her body every morning and evening from a nearby stream or in a water pot without being noticed by men or boys around the village.

She is advised not to cook or salt relish, until the menstruation period is over, and when menstruating, even in marriage, she has to abstain from

---

5   For a detailed study of the girls' initiation see Esha Fikilini, Umwali. Umwali Initiation among the Tonga in Kasitu in Nkhotakota District, Mzuni Press, 2013 (Mzuni Documents no 48) [BA, Mzuzu University, 2012].

6   A reader commented: "Since in *mphara* boys who are still young also sleep there, it is difficult to give instruction to both. Girls are instructed only in seclusion and not in *nthanganeni* because in *nthanganeni* different girls of different ages sleep there."

7   The equivalent Chewa word for *nchembele* is *namkungwi*. She should be a mother.

sexual intercourse and therefore has to sleep on a separate mat. The belief is that, if this is not observed, the husband will have swollen legs and a swollen face (*thayu*).

On the last day the girl's pubic hair is shaved completely or trimmed. This is done to avoid contamination. The instruction given includes the general etiquette of the Tonga, respect for parents and elders and also for agemates, general behaviour expected from a mature Tonga woman, behaviour in the presence of men, the handling of menstruation and correct conduct towards others in the community.

Likewise, the boy's adolescence stage is recognized by a change of voice or growing of hair in the boy's armpits. Thus, at the *mphara* the adolescent boys are subjected to rigorous discipline and instructed in various skills and tribal lore. Apart from sex education, they are given instructions by the *madoda* (elderly men) on how to live in society with respect for themselves as well as for elders, relatives and friends. The Tonga proverb brings out this idea clearly when it is cited to young people; "*Wanthu akuziza kuti aziwa cha kukambiya ahurwa wa vibwetu makani ghaku ubendi,*" meaning; "Wise people do not reveal secrets to foolish children." At the end of these instructions the boys involved are no longer regarded as boys, but as men of the village.

Marriage Rituals

The puberty initiation ceremony is to prepare the young women for married life and all that goes with adulthood in general. Thus a great deal of time is spent on tutoring about sexual education so that the young woman would be able to handle married life. This is of paramount importance, particularly since she has to employ such tips when she gets married. Furthermore, the young woman is given instructions on how to keep her premises clean and presentable, including the general management of her household. Usually, her parents and relatives express their happiness by throwing money in the plates as a gesture to the *nchembele* for a job well concluded.[8]

The stages noted earlier in Chapter two have in a way to do with marriage rituals. The stages were: *chijula mlomo* (mouth opener); *chikole* (betrothal payment); *chiziya pa muzi* (home coming freely); *chimanga matumbu*

---

[8]   For details see: Esha Fikilini, Umwali Initiation among the Tonga in Kasitu in Nkhotakota District, Mzuzu: Mzuni Press, 2013 (Mzuni Documents no 48).

(arresting the intestines); *chisinkha muzi* (protecting the home); and *chilowola* (bridewealth). The mere existence of a go-between and the payment and acceptance of the mouth opening money and finally the payment of *chilowola* are proofs of public marriage negotiations.

Chikole is used by the woman for buying utensils like pots, baskets and plates which will be used in the household. That is why the payment of *chikole* used to be a little more than *chilowola*. Usually *chilowola* is received by the woman's attorney, which can be "eaten" (used) by him to show that he has *nthazi* (strength, power or authority) over the woman and over her marriage. *Chilowola* is returnable if the marriage breaks down.

During the impending marriage a group of female relatives of the bride take food, including baskets with cassava flour, pots with *dendi* (relish) and a young goat (usually led by the boys) to the bridegroom's village. On a formal wedding (*zowara*) day the bride and bridegroom sit at their own table. Three or four men at the other table note down the gifts which friends and relatives of either side hand to the *spikara* (the speaker or master of ceremonies). After this activity comes the time when elderly people will give some moral instructions to the newly married couple. This is done on by *nchembele* standing for both the bride and the bridegroom.

This takes place in the early evening hours before they go to bed. The instructions are very important, because they involve sex eduction and advice on matters of purity. For instance, she will be advised not to salt the relish unless the period of menstruation is over. This is to avoid contamination, which is believed to affect the people who will eat the food.

In sum, although marriage is a rite of passage leading from one state to another, its religious side is not distinctive. It is regarded as the normal sequel to rites of adolescence, whose purpose was to prepare for this state.

Enthronement Rituals

Since the chief's office brings moral obligations, there are also enthronement rituals in the Tonga society. Where there is chieftaincy, the accession of the chief has been marked with ceremonies, which of course differ between different Tonga groups. For instance, among the *Kabunduli/Phiri* Tonga, the heir to the throne may not be made known until the ruling Chief is dead. A man or woman is chosen to be the successor. Sometimes there is an *interregnum* during which councillors (*nduna*) become partisans of possible candidates for the succession. The claimants are kept in the house. The elderly people call upon the spirit of the deceased chief to decide which is to reign. This is sometimes done through tricks or magic.[9] The young man or woman, once chosen or identified, is kept for a period in seclusion, with family and those close to the royal line, for seven or more days before he or she is publicly installed. During this time the candidate will receive instructions on how to behave with people. Sometimes a *mutawa* tree is planted during the period of seclusion. Once the shoots appear, then the new chief will be shown to the people.[10]

It should be noted that the choice of a Chief is a crucial one. The chosen Chief should assume all good qualities of a leader, such as kindness, tolerance, responsibility and so on. During the day of coronation, the people assemble outside in an open space under the trees. Dances like *malipenga, chioda, gule wakawoli*, have been on since the last seven or more days, when the new Chief was under seclusion. The new Chief is ceremoniously taken from the house to the public by the councillors who present the chief to the people with the words: "Here is your Chief." He/she receives royal emblems, which are few. For the *Phiri/Kabunduli,* the Chief receives *nkhazu yifipa* (a black crown), which symbolically stands for the 'Black continent of Africa.' On the other hand, the *Akapunda Banda* Tonga use *nkhazu yiyera* (a red crown), symbolising that they are warriors.[11] Some of the emblems given to the new Chief include *mpando* (a throne), *mkondo* (a spear), sometimes *goza* (an ivory bracelet), *nthonga* (a staff) and *mukhanjo* (black or red gown).

Meanwhile, one of the councillors is chosen to be the master of ceremonies, who leads the new Chief to the throne, and says to the people, 'This is your *Fumu* (Chief), hear him, honour him, obey him, fight for him'. Then he/she is clothed in a new black or red gown and a crown like those worn by the original ancestor. He/she is exhorted to look kindly on the people, to deal justly and honour everyone of his/her subjects. The Chief's office brings privileges but also responsibilities. The subjects too are told to

---

9   Information provided by Zilakoma Richard Phiri. A man called Bomba used to do such tricks at the installation of chief 'Chiŵiŵi II Kabunduli. This was part of the entertainment during the ceremony.

10   For a comparable chief's initiation among the Yawo see Ian Dicks, "It Takes an Initiation to Make a Yawo Chief, " *Religion in Malawi* no. 16 (2011), pp. 3-11.

11   Information provided by Ex-Chief 'Chiŵiŵi II.

honour their new Chief. Thus, the Tonga Chief is ritualized by special blood ties between himself/herself and chosen subjects.

Taboos

In Tonga society taboos are practices forbidden by custom because they are believed to bring evil. Taboos address the theme of obedience. These include: whistling at night, because it is believed that it invites witches; sitting on a mortar, because the mother-in-law also uses it; some think that narrating stories during the day might be a bad omen; wrapping oneself in a mat, is a sign of inviting death. Beating someone with reeds is believed to make the beaten person lose weight and may eventually lead to death.

Pounding in the mortar without foodstuff is regarded as a sign of inviting death or famine. It is a taboo for a daughter or any woman to put salt in relish when she is menstruating, because it is believed to cause the legs to swell (*nthaka*). It is a taboo for a daughter to go into her fathers bedroom or vice-versa. The value is self-respect. The fear is that the father may be sexually attracted to the daughter. It is a taboo for the children to see a corpse or a coffin, and it is a taboo to cook on *moto wa kwanguzga* (forbidden fire) prepared at the funeral. The value is that death must be respected.

Young people should abide by these norms of the society, because it is believed that breaking these rules may invite trouble upon the whole community or the individual. Here again the idea of pollution comes in. Thus, the obligation to observe purity is one of the prerequisitions in Tonga society.

The Tonga people have no written code of their rites of passage and taboos, so the method employed is that of oral transmission. The practices are conveyed through imitation by seeing what elders do - the way they talk, dress, pound, hoe, cook, mourn, laugh and so on; through initiation rites, when the young are initiated into new stages of life by special elderly people at special times and places; and through judgement of cases - by listening to court cases one gains wisdom and knowledge from the sages of the Tonga community. Through these initiation rites and taboos the youth are born anew into their society, and are aso oriented to family values.

In a way, these are initiation schools. The emphasis is on moulding and developing the moral character of the young. The knowledge, understanding and practices of Tonga traditions, norms, values and ethics are transmitted through their myths, folk stories, rituals and taboos. These customs and taboos are geared at training pupils in proper manners, behaviour and habits conforming to the accepted standards of Tonga society. By participating in these rituals and by observing the taboos, the youths become acceptable members of the community in which they live. In so doing they preserve the Tonga culture that has been established by their ancestors. In this way, values and beliefs are preserved and passed on to the next generation. These values include self-respect, self-control, and respect for life.

However, some Tonga taboos, beliefs, practices and related values can have some discriminatory effects against some people. Two taboos illustrate this point:

Taboo	Belief	Practices	Value
Sex outside marriage.	Women have no self control.	Varie	Virginity and faith-fullness in marriage
	She will be unfaithful to her husband.	Some give axe and handle separately as gifts symbol-izing virginity	

The implication in this taboo is discrimination against women because the hymen can be ruptured by causes other than sexual relations, for example by certain diseases. The Tonga society should come up with solutions to maintain the value without discrimination.

Taboo	Belief	Practices	Value
Women not to eat eggs	Women may find difficulty at delivery.	Pregnant women were not allowed to clean chicken runs or any place where there were animal droppings.	To preserve chickens in the village
	Baby will be born with no hair		
	Child will be epileptic		

The implication is about discrimination against women, because eggs are a good form of food, especially for pregnant women. The Tonga themselves should find solutions to maintain this value without discrimination.

Mortuary Rituals

The Tonga people conceive of the *mvuchi* (breath) of man as man's 'soul' or 'life' (*uzima umoyo*). As long as there is *mvuchi* in a person and as long as a person *watuta* (breathes), that person still 'lives' (*ngwamoyo or ngwa uzima*). When he ceases to breathe, *ngwakufwa* (he/she is dead). As death is seen to be near, someone from the kinsmen comes out of the house to *fwifwinthiya* (weeping silently as a sign that the end is very near, and thereafter the wailing begins). The wailing is joined in by all the relatives and friends of the deceased.

The corpse, meanwhile, is probably held up in the arms of the wife or mother. When this first mourning has been carried out, the corpse is laid on a mat and covered with a sheet or a blanket. As the *azukuru*[12] (those who wash the corpse or those who prepare the burial) bid the mourners rise, a fresh wailing breaks forth as the wife or mother cries. In their cries they utter their views on the cause of the death, the effect of the death on the bereaved family or on the society. In some parts this requires professional skills.

The *azukuru* might come from the village or from a neighbouring village, and relatives of the dead might always call them *abale* (brothers or relatives). The *chimbwi*[13] is the chief *mzukuru* because he first had approached the dead body, thus showing that he had no fear. The first person to whom the death would be formally announced is the Chief of the village while messengers are also on their way to tell distant relatives and other chiefs. Proverb 55, in Chapter 7, C*ho chingukwezga pusi ndichu chingukwezga m'nkhwele*: ("what made the monkey to climb up a tree made the baboon also to climb up a tree"), shows how kin groups are interlinked by death. Griffin Manda, who observes what happens at a traditional funeral ceremony in Tonga society, puts it this way:

---

[12]   The term *azukuru* covers several areas. If connected with funeral these are the people who prepare the burial or dig the grave. They also wash and dress the corpse. *Azukuru* can also be the grand-children in a family. The term used in Chichewa is *zizukulu*.

[13]   Information given by Richard Zilakoma Phiri on 7th Oct. 1994, at his home in Tukombo. *Chimbwi* (a hyena) is used metaphorically or symbolically to refer to one who first detects death signs.

Odi, Odi is a familiar expression calling for attention at funeral services in Nkhata Bay District. It is this expression that arouses the attention of visitors to Nkhata Bay at funeral services.[14]

The phrase, *Odi! Odi!* is a formal approach to powers beyond. The man in charge of sending messages to concerned people has to be very careful he does not leave anyone out. Should he miss or ignore someone, he will be questioned. To avoid mishap, usually it is an elder in the bereaved family who sends messages from his knowledge of *mkoka* (history or relations) aided by other elders. Messengers are advised to use techniques in breaking funeral news. The best approach is one that gives little shock. They may say to a son in the garden whose father has passed away at home that his brother from abroad has come. In fact approaches are as varied as are the causes of death. Normally when a person dies he/she will be buried the following day, especially if the person is an elder. A delay is usually caused by the idea that key people in the family should be present when the burial takes place.

When the friends or relatives come to a funeral, a present for condolence should be given to the bereaved family. This demonstrates communal responsibility. As is common in Tonga culture, the kitchen (*kukati*) activities are primary performed by women. Each woman is bound by cultural norms that, when attending a funeral, she should either carry flour (*ufwa*), relish (*dendi*) or firewood (*nkhuni*). Meanwhile, the funeral room is full of people, usually close relatives, especially women. Men will gather at the *mphara* (council of elders). A little way in front of the door of the funeral house, and around the *mphara* is burning the *moto wakunguzga* (forbidden fire). It is called forbidden because no one can cook on that fire, or take a light for a pipe or a cigarette or put it to any ordinary use. Fires for this purpose must be brought from the house of the living. This fire is prepared if a night has passed since the person died, and the mourners have already lain one night on the mats.

Dressing and mode of behaviour at such times should indicate sorrow and respect. Interesting again is the way women spit, talk and walk at the funeral. In both Christian and non-Christian families, a group of young people stay full time in the room or on the verandah consoling the

---

[14] Griffin Manda, "Funeral Conduct in Nkatha Bay," *The Society of Malawi Journal*, 18, (2), (1965), pp. 30-35. This was also confirmed during my field study when I attended some funeral gatherings.

bereaved by their songs. Children under 12 years are usually kept away from the funeral place. It is taboo for children to view the corpse. This is perhaps to prevent children from having bad dreams at night, and for the respect of death.

At the funeral, elderly people from *kawulu-ka-unkhaka* (a gathering council of the elders) discuss how the funeral ceremony should be conducted. The council announces its views through a speaker. The speaker is chosen for his knowledge of the Tonga funeral customs and for the fluency of his speech. The council's duties include briefing those who come about the authenticity of the message received about the death, arrangements of the coffin, arrangements where the deceased is to be buried and settling differences when misunderstanding occurs at a funeral.

After the *azukuru* have completed their graveyard chore, they come home to report to the elders. In carrying the corpse out to burial, the *azukuru* enter the house. The body may be in a coffin or wrapped in a mat tied firmly to carry it between two poles *(kasalasala)*. In rare cases, taking the body out of the house, the door does not make exit. So they break down the back wall of the house, opposite the door to let out the corpse. The procession to the grave is orderly. In the forefront are those who bear the coffin, secondly, close relatives, then everyone else. Those who bear the coffin to the grave are also called *azukuru*.

The burial rituals honour the moral behaviour of a person. The procession to the grave has much to say about the character of the deceased and, perhaps, his family, at least in some places. If the deceased and his family members are perceived as good according to the Tonga cultural norms, the coffin is carried gently to the graveyard. On the other hand, if the deceased was considered to have been a witch or wizard or sorcerer, the coffin or bier *(mtembo)* is carried carelessly and hurriedly to the grave, and the funeral is not dignified. This shows that only good people are accepted in Tonga society. Sometimes the *azukuru* go to the extent of just throwing the bier into the grave. There have been cases where a dead body has been not buried so that vultures or wild animals should feed on them. This was to avoid the contamination of the land if the person had lived an evil life, as the sin of one person is believed to affect the whole community.

As the procession reaches the grave, elders take control again. After some conferring they authorize the *azukuru* to lower the coffin into the grave gently, then bury it. When the grave is half-way filled, the closest relatives there, after kneeling down, do homage to the dead and push or throw earth into the grave. After a little while, the *azukuru* continue, filling up the grave. After all has been filled in, the poles on which the corpse was carried are driven into the ground, one at the head and the other at the feet, the body of course being always interred with the feet to the east, and facing the head up. On top of the grave other articles belonging to the dead are disposed. In returning to the village after the funeral, the whole party goes to wash in running water, the men at some point up the stream and the women lower down. As contact with the dead renders the person unclean, none of them would be allowed to re-enter their village without this ceremonial cleansing. The *azukuru* may wash their hands with medicine (*chilopolo*) to neutralize the influence of the dead that may befall them. This process of washing hands is called *kukawuwa*. I recently learnt from a brother's burial ceremony in Nkhata Bay that the reason for washing face, hands and feet is to ensure that purity rules are observed. It is also from fear that the spirit of the dead might come to haunt those still living.

In the evening, all mourners gather at the house again, in front of which they are now to sleep on the mats while the mourning lasts.[15] Until they leave the mats each mourner wears a badge of sorrow round the head or chest or wrist. The sign is of black or white cloth, which was used for wrapping the dead body and had been left over, usually called *mulaza*. This is a symbol to identify the direct relatives to the deceased.

A dead body is seen as impure in Tonga society. This is symbolized by washing of hands or bodies of the bereaved. It is a purification ritual that symbolizes removal of the death contamination. At the elders' council, they announce the day of *chimeta*. This is an event when they shave the bereaved people to get rid of bad spirits and bad fortune. It is also an occasion to school people in the discipline of constructive living. Between burial and *chimeta* there is *chivumbi*, when close relatives stay behind to comfort the bereaved. In ancient days *chivumbi* would last up to three months and *chimeta* would take place after one lunar month. Sometimes drinking and dancing would take place to relieve the tedium of their mourning. One of the dances commonly engaged in was *gule wa kawole*. Today this dance is gone into oblivion.

---

[15] In olden days, they would sleep on leaves, 'no one of them may use a mat to sleep on during that time, nor may they use salt in their food, or wash themselves.'

If the relatives are satisfied with the settlement that has been made by the husband over the death of his wife, supposing a woman is the person mourned, they give permission at the end of a longer or shorter time to bring these rites to a close. The *moto wakwanguzga* is also put out, and thus the long season of public mourning is brought to a close.[16]

Other Categories of Death

The funeral activities described here may be modified to suit the rank of the deceased. The death of a Chief may have its modifications accordingly. There may be the salutation of a gun, or a *malipenga* dance—the common traditional dance among the lakeside Tonga of Nkhata Bay. The women of the village bury infants of about a few days old alone, and these are not publicly mourned. If one of twin children dies, no audible weeping is allowed. It is believed this would affect the one alive. If possible parents should have joyful expression on their faces despite the sorrow. A daughter-in-law who dies at her home, if *chilowola* (bridewealth) has been paid, may be buried at her own village, but they bring all the children to her husband's home. This is called *kupinga chitenje* or *chiliro* (transferring the funeral). However, in the case of a daughter-in-law dying without *chilowola*, the husband, along with his parents, will be forced to pay the *chilowola*. Otherwise the dead will not be buried. Such payments are referred to as *mutupa* (payments effected after a daughter-in-law dies). The death may be due to complications, which in many cases could be *mapinga* (difficulties at delivery). *Mapinga* is believed to be caused by the immorality of the woman or of her husband during or before the period of pregnancy. Husbands are strictly advised to observe purity when their wives are pregnant.

In case of death caused by abortion or infant death, women only organize the whole funeral service. Burial of little babies is often under *msoro* or *muwanga* trees. Again, parents feel it unsafe for the bereaved couple to have sexual intercourse until the woman has resumed her monthly period known as *kusauwa*. To protect the couple, the lady usually goes to her home until she resumes menstruation, usually after two to three months. Lepers in Tongaland are buried on the other side of the graveyard not to

---

[16] Information was given by village headwoman Wachaza on the 9th Oct. 1994, at Chifira village.

105

mix them with the normal deaths. The reason was to avoid contamination with those who died with other diseases and are considered clean.

In sum, the discussion on various death rituals shows that the Tonga people respect the dead in various ways. Since dead bodies are believed to be impure, the obligation to observe purity is everywhere in the Tonga society. These obligations are for every member of the society, young and old. Rituals, which have to do with purity, should be strictly adhered to so an to sustain a healthy society. Doing so means to get rid of contamination. The observation of ritual purity in some food acquires a special moral dimension and significance in daily life for maintaining the ritual purity of food at all times, and eating the meals in ritual purity. This is for fear of transgressing through impure food to erect social barriers between themselves and neighbouring ethnic groups, who may not be so scrupulous in observing the purity of food.

To conclude, this chapter has attempted to discuss the main rites of passage within the context of Tonga oral literature. Here the concern was to examine the cycle of life, which the average citizen is recognized by Tonga society to cover as he/she moves from birth to death. Each of the five stages in this journey—birth, adolescence, marriage, title-taking and death—are traditionally marked by a ritualized observance which is itself captured in Tonga oral literature. Thus, rituals re-enact stories of chiefs, heroes and ancestors. Death rituals occupy an important place since these are observed in a cross section of Tonga society. Rituals that are linked with the ancestors are also common. As a matter of fact, these ceremonies are parts of the socialization process. They have been handed down through inter-generational communication.

CHAPTER FIVE

INFLUENCE OF CHRISTIANTY AND ISLAM ON TONGA CULTURE

This chapter is devoted to the planting of Christianity and Islam in Tongaland: the way in which early missionaries and Muslims interacted with Tonga culture, the role they played in suppressing Tonga customs and the effect of this attitude on moral education. The first part looks at how Christianity spread into Tonga land focusing on the observations Christian missionaries made on the Tonga people with whom they interacted. Of particular interest is their general perception of traditional rites of passage and the effect they appeared to have on the progress of mission work and especially on the educational and evangelical aspects of it. The second part looks at the impact of Islam on Tonga initiation rites, with particular reference to *jando* (circumcision) for boys, and *msondo* for girls, as religious rites.

Christianity and Tonga Customs

It was after their difficult experience at Cape Maclear, in the Central Region, that Dr Robert Laws decided to find a new place for the mission. Dr Laws and his party went on reconnoitering journeys as early as 1875, though the first observation post near present Chintheche was established only in 1878. The Livingstonia Mission was officially transferred from Cape Maclear to Bandawe in 1881. At Bandawe, rapid progress was made with the extension of the mission's work inland to pacify and convert the Ngoni from their activities, which included frequent attacks upon the Tonga people.[1] This led Robert Laws to try and bring about a truce between the Ngoni and Tonga to be sealed by the establishment of a mission in Ngoniland.[2] This

---

[1] For a collection of essays on the Ngoni Mission see: Jack Thompson, *Ngoni, Xhosa and Scott. Religious and Cultural Interaction in Malawi*, Zomba: Kachere, 2007. For the early development of written literature, see pp. 152-165.

[2] The first mission station, an "observation post" at Kaning'ina, now an eastern suburb of Mzuzu, was established in 1899 by William Koyi, a Xhosa missionary from South Africa (Jack Thompson, *Touching the Heart. Xhosa Missionaries to Malawi, 1876-1888*, Pretoria: UNISA, 2000). See also Jack Thompson, "Xhosa

was one of the main factors the Tonga allied themselves with the newly established mission, because when the Ngoni raided them, the Tonga chiefs like Malenga, Mankhambira, Kang'oma, Chimbano and Chikuru frequently appealed to the missionaries for protection.[3]

The growth of Tonga stockaded villages may well have increased internal political rivalry, for each village remained an autonomous political unit in which the authority of the stockade Chief was frequently challenged by the heads of smaller villages who had taken refuge for protection. The alliance between the Tonga chiefs and the missionaries at Bandawe had an impact on the Tonga cultures.The Tonga sent their children to school, and it was the strategy of the missionaries to win a good number of converts to Christianity. Culture conflicts were frequent. The church sessions were empowered to discipline such people by suspending them. This meant that once suspended, an individual's case would be reviewed from time to time until such a time the session was convinced that he/she could be reinstated. Those who committed adultery or were charged with beer drinking faced suspension. At adult baptism the candidates were also requested to renounce traditional customs like engaging in polygamy, witchcraft, sooth-saying, participating in the *mwavi* ordeal; marrying by way of abduction, consulting the dead spirits and the mediums, wearing *njirizi* (amulets) etc.

The missionaries and their preachers agreed that they should speak more on these evils and emphasize to their audiences the message that Jesus Christ had conquered the powers of darkness. As church leaders, they themselves were also supposed to be firm in their own lives, thereby demonstrating that they had abandoned all evil doings. In other words, what was being emphasized was exemplary behaviour, which could win respect and admiration among their followers.

The expectations aroused in the early stages of Fraser's reforms were thus never fully realized. Many church members remained puritan zealots, loud in their condemnation of idleness, beer-drinking and dancing, and fierce in their denunciation of the playing of games, the love of high wages or the

---

Missionaries in Late Nineteenth Century Malawi: Strangers or Fellow Countrymen?" *Religion in Malawi*, 2008, pp. 8-16.

[3]   For a good description of the relationship see John McCracken, *Politics and Christianity in Malawi, 1875-1940. The Impact of the Livingstonia Mission in the Northern Province*, Zomba: Kachere, [2]2008, pp. 89-120.

desire for fine clothes. Several people, however, turned against the mission's policies as being intolerably confining.

African dances, condemned outright by most missionaries for fear that the harmless would lead to the obscene, had their African supporters. In 1902 Charles Domingo read a paper at a mission conference in Blantyre praising some aspects of them, and later Charles Chinula of Loudon Mission, then a teacher, was a strong believer in purifying rather than destroying customs.[4]

Education was one of the potential advantages. Tongaland rapidly became the scene of extraordinary educational enthusiasm. Chief Marenga had asked that a school be established at his village as early as August 1879, but this request was not followed up till 1883 owing to the missionaries' insistence that he must build the school himself without payment. Mankhambira specifically asked for a European teacher to reside with him and rejected the African offered instead.

In the pioneer years the attraction of education for the Tonga may well have lain primarily in the opportunities it gave them to strengthen the alliance with the mission. New schools were opened in 1888 at Marenga's, Chikuru's and Fuka's and later three further schools were started at Chintheche, at Dwambazi and Mtete. By 1890 the average attendance in Nkhata Bay district was 2,279. In 1894, eighteen schools were open with 1,000 pupils regularly attending.[5] However, despite their readiness to accept education and employment from the British, the Tonga were reluctant to take the final step of religious conversion. In 1890, the total number of communicants in the whole mission was fifty-three.

Tonga religious institutions were less of a barrier to Christian influence than the village-based Nyau cult of the Chewa and Mang'anja, but they provided the Tonga with satisfactory answers to many of the social and spiritual problems confronting them. As noted earlier, the Tonga believed in a high God, *Chiuta*, creator and sustainer of life, but concerned themselves more frequently with the spirits of the dead, who had power over the future of the living, and sometimes possessed mediums or soothsayers (*mchimi*),

---

4   Bandawe Station entries for 14 and 22 January 1879. Quoted by John McCracken (1977) in *Politics and Christianity in Malawi 1875-1940: The Impact of the Livingstonia Mission in the Northern Province*, p. 62.

5   *FCSMR*, June 1890; Livingstonia Mission Report, 1894, p. 3.

men of influence whatever their rank. In comparison with the *mchimi*, the missionaries, must have appeared disturbingly alien.

Some Tonga agents held village services regularly throughout the 1880s. Hymns were sung at these services to Scottish tunes, and simple biblical addresses were delivered, most of them dealing with redemption and sin. Early cases of imorality have also been reported. During the 1880s several incidents occurred in which pupils or agents seized supposed wrong-doers and otherwise acted violently towards neighbours, and were themselves attacked by aggrieved Tonga in turn. In August 1885, for instance, parties of schoolboys who had seized a man from Chifira, Chief Chikuru's village, for ill-treating a woman, and were bringing him bound to the Station were attacked by an armed band of villagers who fired at them and stole their loads. Later in January 1887, Chief Chimbano brought what Dr Laws believed to be an entirely baseless accusation of adultery against one of the elders, which resulted in the headman placing a boycott on the sale of all food to the station when satisfaction was not granted to him. The case was not settled till the chiefs around Marenga's area had intervened and Dr Laws had threatened to depart from Bandawe. These incidents are just a few reflections on how the missionaries were confronted with some moral issues in Tonga society.

The waves of religious enthusiasm, which swept Tongaland, were marked between 1895 to 1898 and again from 1903. Dr Boxer behaved as one of the richest times of spiritual harvest at Bandawe. African Christians held weekend services in all the principal villages, and the sound of hymns was said to have replaced that of dancing.[6] At village after village the attendance and interest gradually increased until the people were coming according to their houses. By 1906 Sunday services were being held in ninety-eight village centres attended each week by more than 14,000 hearers.[7] Vast and emotional audiences flocked to the mass conventions, which Rev. Fraser had started. Hundreds of Tonga sought comfort and stability in a changing world in the certainties, which appeared to lie in baptism.[8]

---

6   Livingstonia Mission Report 1903, p. 23.

7   Ibid. 1906, p. 32.

8   For details see: John McCracken, *Politics and Christianity in Malawi, 1875-1940: The Impact of the Livingstonia Mission in the Northern Province*, Zomba: Kachere, [3]2008, pp. 159-161.

An extract from a document titled, "The Story of the Building of the Church at Thipula," 1929-1931, shows how young people accepted to follow the Christian faith:

> You Tonga people probably already know from your stories that in 1929, there was a spontaneous Evangelical Revival going on. I am including some that Jack wrote because I like to think of this entire renewal happening while the Church was being built. 'On 17-08-29. I do not think people at home can believe that we have seen today. Today was the climax of the third series of meetings. There has been an atmosphere of expectation and when Charles Chinura asked those who wished to confess their faith in Christ to wait behind, 150 did so. In the evening we met for prayers, and a large number of the new people rose and prayed, and gave thanks. One quite young boy rose and said, "I am ignorant, I don't know anything, but I want to follow Christ, God help me." A lot of women prayed too, and one elder asked to be forgiven for his past slackness and for strength to be more energetic in his work for God. It was really wonderful. There was no excitement but just a red-hot glow of happiness. It convinces me that the Church of Central Africa is now of age.[9]

If moral and religious education was properly to be imparted to people, they were to be thoroughly instructed in their beliefs. Baptism, they believed, should be not granted unless the candidate has been under definite religious instruction throughout a period of at least two years, during which the missionary had had means of ascertaining his life and character, and that instruction should include as a minimum a course of teaching on the Lord's Prayer, the Ten Commandments, the Sacraments and the Apostles' Creed with the relevant passages of Scripture.[10] Missionaries also believed that if church members were to be properly instructed in their faith it was necessary, A.G. MacAlpine decided, that they should receive education. In 1899 he gave orders that no candidate for the baptism class should be recognized who was not attending school.

---

9   Rev Jack Martin: A letter written to his daughter, Margaret Sinclair, extract from page 3. The Church building is dedicated to Mrs M.E. Martin *Nyankhutowa yo wangwanja Atonga*. The Tonga people nicknamed Mrs Martin as the Beautiful one who loved the Tonga. The document was referred to me by Mr Alick Phiri, a retired school teacher, at his home, Mgode, on 20th Oct. 1994. Many of the Martins' letters have since been published as: Margaret Sinclair, *Salt and Light. The Letters of Jack and Mamie Martin in Malawi 1921-28*, Blantyre: CLAIM-Kachere, 2002.

10   Proceedings of the Nyasaland Missionary Conference. 1900, 67.

Many new classes for Catechumens and Hearers were set up, with extra grades being inserted through which the candidates had to pass, and the task of watching the behaviour of candidates devolved on African deacons and elders, none of whom had the power to baptize. The inevitable consequence was that long delays took place before classes were examined. The missionaries were strongly convinced that to a very large extent the success of their work depended upon educating the youth. By educating the youth a link would be easily formed with the adult population, to the benefit of missionary work in general. In line with this strategy the missionaries made sure that wherever they opened a station or built a church, there was also a school. Very often they also used the same churches as classrooms.

One symptom of the tension was the differing attitudes that developed between certain white men and black people towards some African institutions and customs. Despite the lip service they paid to the creation of a genuinely indigenous Church, the early missionaries of Laws' and Elmslie's generation had sufficient confidence in the virtues of Western society to reject any major compromise with habits or beliefs which ran counter to their own. This is a clear indication that the moral values they wanted to impart were to be western.

Even MacAlpine, while he acknowledged 'the large use which the Apostles made of popular customs and institutions in the organization of the Christian Church', argued that it was often so difficult to separate the good from the bad that 'sometimes ... the best way is simply to cut the Gordian knot and make a clean sweep altogether'.[11] Under his influence, Church members in Tongaland in 1895 banned beer drinking in any form, along with slavery and polygamy, however defined.

So, the expansion of missionary work in terms of opening sub-stations, like Kaning'ina, Kasangazi and Chisangawe and church schools was no easy affair. These social problems had to be overcome if at all their work was to succeed. Among these social problems were Tonga rites of passage (rituals) and traditional dances such as *chioda, malipenga, gule wakawole, mchoma* etc. Also the Tonga beliefs in their ancestors were all condemned as heathenism. The following quotation from a letter by Donald Fraser illustrates the point:

---

[11] Source: Proceedings of the Nyasaland Missionary Conference, 1900, pp. 17-20.

Often I heard Dr Elmslie speak of the awful customs of the Tonga Tumbuka, but the actual sight of some of these gave a shock and horror that will not leave one. The atmosphere seems charged with vice. It is the only theme that runs through songs, and games, and dances. Here sure is the seat of Satan .... You turn out to the village square to see the lads and girls at play. They are dancing; but every act is awful in its shamelessness and an old grandmother, bent and withered has entered the circle to incite the boys and girls to more loathsome dancing. You go back to your tent bowed with an awful shame, to hide yourself .... The next morning the village is gathered together to see your carriers at the worship, and to hear the news of the white stranger. You improve the occasion, and stand; ashamed to speak of what you saw. The same boys and girls are there, the same old grandmothers... and when you are gone, the same horror is practised under the same clear moon."[12]

Here, the problem of the Tonga people still clinging to traditions in spite of the preaching of the Gospel to which they were exposed was a common thing throughout Malawi and wherever the missionaries ventured. That was equally true with other parts of Africa. Thus, in Fraser's experience, the same people, including some converts to Christianity, would spend the night dancing in their different types of ceremonies regarded by the missionaries as evil and then turn up the following morning to listen to the Word of God. The Tonga had their customs for generations and it was not possible for them to break away from such overnight.

Of course the missionaries did not just sit back and watch their converts changing colours like chameleons. They took disciplinary measures against their converts who, among other things, participated in initiation or in dances at the school house unknown to the resident missionary. Polygamous marriages were also disciplinied.[13]

Rise of Independent Churches in Nkhata Bay

As a result of the early missionary activities in Nkhata Bay district, the area also witnessed a proliferation of Independent Churches. Since the Presbyterians were very much opposed to traditional customs like rituals and dances, it was obvious that the local people got attracted to such Independent Churches, which may not have seriously denounced the local

---

12 Source: *Life and Work*, no. 1881, April 1904, p. 6.
13 Source: Reports on Native Christian Conference at Livingstonia, in *Livingstonia News*, April 1908, pp. 11-14.

customs, or may have found it difficult to accept all the activities of the missionaries. However, before narrowing this rise of Independent churches to Nkhata Bay, a brief historical survey should be made in the connection with the activities of Joseph Booth's mission foundations.

J.C. Chakanza suggests four main periods of historical development in the independent church movement in Malawi.[14] The first period falls between 1900-1915. This period saw the Native controlled missions, which were proscribed in the aftermath of John Chilembwe's rising of 1915, as a result of the interactions blacks had with Booth. The second period is from around 1922-1945, which was dominated by Livingstonia secessionists, such as Eliot Kamwana and Yesaya Zerenji Mwasi on which the present study will focus. The third period is from around 1945 to 1964. This was the period dominated by secessionists in Southern Malawi Independent churches. Fourthly, the post-independent period from 1964, to the present day. This period has witnessed the mushrooming of many independent charismatic type of sectarianism and fellowships, with their teachings emphasizing the work of the Holy Spirit e.g. Pentecostals etc. and their emphasis on spiritual morality, focused on purity of the individual through the "born again" process.

Joseph Booth arrived in Blantyre, southern Malawi on 11th August 1892, from Australia as an independent missionary.[15] Shepperson has observed that Booth had "remained constant in the belief that salvation of Africa, political, economical and social would have to be undertaken by the African himself."[16] Booth set models for autonomous congregations. He was prepared to enter into partnership with Africans like John Chilembwe and others to form the African Industrial Mission.[17] He also introduced to the outside world people like John Chilembwe to the United States of America

---

[14] J.C. Chakanza: "Religious Independency in Southern Malawi Sectarianism in Joseph Booth's Mission Foundations 1925-1965, and the Response of the Mainstream Churches," in *Ministry of Missions to African Independent Churches* (1987), by David A. Shank (ed), Mennonite Board of Missions, pp. 134-151.

[15] For his background and early career see: Klaus Fiedler, *The Making of a Maverick Missionary. Joseph Booth in Australasia*, Zomba: Kachere, 2008.

[16] Quoted by J.C. Chakanza in *Ministry of Missions to African Independent Churches*, 1987, p. 35.

[17] For his full biography see: Harry Langworthy, *"Africa for the African." The Life of Joseph Booth*, Blantyre: CLAIM-Kachere, 1996.

in 1897,[18] and Peter Nyambo to South Africa in 1904. He also kept in contact with some Livingstonia-trained men such as Charles Domingo and Elliot Kamwana. It has been suggested that Booth had taken advantage of a general movement in Africa South of the Zambezi called "Ethiopianism," which encouraged a process of African reaction to European culture.[19] However, it would not be correct to attribute to Booth the whole process of religious independency in southern Malawi, as the origin of some churches has no clear association with Booth. For the purpose of this study it is important to show how the secessionist movement from Booth's mission foundations has connections with Livingstonia.

Here again, it should be noted from the outset that the section, which follows, will show that the secessions from Livingstonia Mission arose out of criticism centered on the mission policies. However, schisms in the southern independent churches centred on leadership for both African and European, on some relatively issues of ritual and doctrine.

Elliot Kamwana and Watch-Tower Church

The first to challenge the activities of the missionaries at Bandawe was Elliot Kamwana Chirwa who has gone down into history as the father of Independent Churches in Nkhata Bay.[20] He was born around 1882.[21] After completing his Junior Primary education at Bandawe he went to Livingstonia together with some of his schoolmates, among whom were Yesaya Zerenji Mwasi, Yoramu Mphande, Edward Boti Manda and Filemon Kamunkhwara Chirwa in 1894. In 1901 Elliot Kamwana left the Livingstonia Institution as a protest against the introduction of fees,[22] and others have said that he left the mission because of ill-health, but this is all wrong. Mr. Rabbi Munkwakwata at one time the General Secretary and Treasurer and also the right hand man of the late Kamwana says that Kamwana left

18   There he published "*Africa for the African*" (Lynchburg 1897), reprinted as Laura Perry (ed), Joseph Booth, *Africa for the African*, Zomba: Kachere, 2008.

19   George Shepperson and Thomas Price, *Independent African*, Edinburgh University Press, 1958.

20   For the life of Elliot Kamwana see: J.C. Chakanza, *Voices of Preachers in Protest. The Ministry of Two Malawian Prophets: Elliot Kamwana and Wilfred Gudu*, Blantyre: CLAIM-Kachere, 1998.

21   Ibid, p. 14. Footnote 15 there also shows other opinions.

22   Ibid, p. 15.

Livingstonia because he was disappointed by the way the teachers were answering his questions during question time. It is said that Kamwana was fond of asking questions about God and the Bible, so much so that both teachers and students did not like him and as a result of which Kamwana was so disgusted that he decided to leave Livingstonia.[23]

After leaving Livingstonia in 1901, Kamwana left for the present day Southern Region. He went to the Shire Highlands where he came into contact with Joseph Booth in 1902, and thereafter he was baptized at Malamulo by Thomas Branch as a Seventh-day Adventist.[24] before he went to Zimbabwe where he worked for a time at a hospital as a medical assistant in Bulawayo. While in Bulawayo he read in a newspaper about the Watchtower Church in South Africa and he sent in his application for training as a preacher of the Word of God. Joseph Booth, who had known and met Kamwana in Thyolo, called him to South Africa.

Kamwana worked for a time in Johannesburg and then visited Durban, Pretoria, and finally went to meet Booth in Cape Town. There he was trained as a Watchtower preacher. Finally in 1908, Kamwana returned to Nyasaland to establish a new Church. If Booth from afar supplied the literature on the Watch Tower Bibles with Millennial Dawn, and the initial inspiration for this oral method, the director on the spot was Elliot Kamwana. He began his teachings in the South, but soon proceeded to his home district Chintheche in mid 1908.

He went about preaching true baptism of total immersion in water as John the Baptist had done. He told his listeners that the dead are buried here on earth and therefore they do not go to heaven. Kamwana also preached against immorality and the introduction of hut tax. The 1909 increase of hut tax with its hated labour rebate had already produced much African criticism and discontent throughout the protectorate.[25] It is worth noting

---

[23] Bentley Martin Ndonde Phiri, Independent African Churches in Nkhata Bay, History Seminar Paper, 1969/70, Soche Hill College.

[24] J.C. Chakanza, *Voices of Voices of Preachers in Protest*, p. 15. See also: Yonah Matemba, *Aspects of the Centenary History of Malamulo Seventh-day Adventist Mission, Makwasa, Malawi*, 1902-2002, Zomba: Kachere, 2008 (Kachere Documents no. 53), p. 4. - At Malamulo he was given the prestigious position of Standard One English teacher by Mabel Branch.

[25] George Shepperson and Thomas Price, *Independent African*, Edinburgh University Press, 1958, p. 156.

that in 1902 the people at Nkhata Bay had organized a mass demonstration outside Nkhata Bay Government Station to voice their opposition to the new tax regulation and this led to a dispatch of a company of the King's African Rifles to quell the demonstrations.

Kamwana preached about the abolition of tax and he also talked about the coming of a New Age in 1914, when all Europeans would have to leave the country and there would be no more oppression from the tax collector. He promised his followers free education for all and quick baptism. The response to Kamwana's revolutionary teaching was dramatic. He conducted his prayer meetings in open-air and baptized by total immersion. When he found that he had a large number of followers he settled down at Mdyaka where he established his headquarters. It is here at Msuli (Mdyaka) in Chief Longwe's area that he inflamed the minds of the people by prophesying the coming of the war in 1914, which he said would be followed by influenza and other illnesses.[26]

While at Mdyaka Kamwana was visited by Rev. A.G. MacAlpine who was in charge of Bandawe Mission. Rev MacAlpine went to see Kamwana in order to persuade him to rejoin the Church of Scotland so that he could fill the vacuum created by the resignation of Y.Z. Mwasi. But Kamwana refused to rejoin the Church of Scotland. However, Mwasi was persuaded to go back to his work as an evangelist and was posted to Mdyaka to act as a counter-veiling power to Kamwana. Within a year Kamwana baptised well over a thousand people in his Church.

How far the Watch-Tower movement drew upon indigenous traditions among societies west of the Lake and how far it arose from a situation created specifically by Livingstonia are difficult questions to answer. However, Watch-Tower with its emphasis on the imminence of the second coming and the limited numbers to be saved, were ideologically distinct. There was no attempt to expose witches or to destroy anti-witchcraft devices, and neither was there any attempt to use traditional culture to enhance moral teaching or the life of church in general. Many of the 9,000 baptised within his six-month preaching tour may have believed that the act of immersion cleansed them for all sin. And such an act of communal purification, one may argue, would involve an attempt to eradicate

---

[26] For all of Kamwana's activities in that period see: J.C. Chakanza, *Voices of Preachers in Protest. The Ministry of Two Malawian Prophets*: *Elliot Kamwana and Wilfred Gudu*, Blantyre: CLAIM-Kachere, 1998, p. 16-27.

witchcraft. It can be argued that the act of speeding up baptism helped to safeguard morality of those who needed immediate entry into the Church.

His preaching about what was to happen in 1914 landed him into trouble. His open air meetings and instantaneous baptisms also caused him trouble. There were cases where the Christians from the Church of Scotland deserted and joined Kamwana's new Church and thus the missionaries of the Church of Scotland instigated his arrest. Kamwana was arrested sometime in March 1909 together with his first wife Annie Nyamanda whom he had married in 1908. The arrest of Kamwana in 1909 resulted in an uprising. This uprising among his followers has gone into history as the "Kamwana Revolt of 1909." The government of the day had to deploy its police to Sanga and Mdyaka where the uprising was felt most. Soon after the arrest, Kamwana was sent to Zomba where it is believed that John Chilembwe visited him.[27]

Thereafter, Kamwana was exiled by the government of the day to the Seychelles Islands and on his way to the Seychelles, together with his wife Annie Nyamanda, he passed through Chinde where he was later joined by Yohane Chandaka Chirwa and his wife Nyalongwe, and by William Mwenda and his Yao wife, both of whom had been arrested while they were in Limbe. Kamwana's deportation obviously marked the beginnings of a new phase of religious independency in the Malawi. Deprived of its prophet the Watch-Tower movement in the West Nyasa district (i.e. Nkhata Bay) experienced a crisis of leadership.

When Kamwana and his friends went to the Seychelles they were no longer detained but were only restricted within the Islands. Kamwana was not allowed to preach, neither was he allowed to attend any church service. Nevertheless, he used to have secret services. While here Kamwana lived happily with his wife until her untimely death in 1934.[28] While in the Seychelles, Kamwana was visited by ministers of the Anglican Church and others from Likoma Island who tried to persuade him to join UMCA. And that if they joined they would be released and then be made "Bishops" when they returned to Nyasaland. Kamwana and Yohane Chandaka Chirwa refused to join UMCA. However, it did not take long before Kamwana and

---

[27] For a play on the Chilembwe Rising see: D.D. Phiri, *Let us Fight for Africa*, Zomba: Kachere, 2007.

[28] Cf J.C. Chakanza, *Voices of Preachers in Protest. The Ministries of Elliot Kamwana and Wilfred Gudu*, Blantyre: CLAIM-Kachere, 1998, p. 26.

his followers were released. They arrived at Chintheche on 16th October 1937.

When Kamwana reached Chintheche, both members of Watch-Tower and Jehovah's Witnesses gave him a tremendous welcome. Members of both churches were anxious to know which church Kamwana was to join, and he eventually chose to join the Jehovah's Witnesses and so he was made its leader. But before long he disagreed with other members of the Church and denounced both churches as having been founded by Europeans. He said that it was high time that Africans started their own churches. It was with this in mind that he founded his own church, which he called Watchman Healing Mission, on 16th December 1937. Kamwana's moral message to his followers was abstinence. If people wanted to serve God, they should not indulge in earthly things. He also advised them to refrain from taking any kind of medicine. He forbade women from using cosmetics and any other ornaments. He forbade members of his Church to overcharge *lobola*, the bride price. He strongly recommended that the highest *lobola* that they could demand from the suitors of their daughters, should be £10 for non mebers, and for a fellow member £6. They composed their own hymns, though they still used the Nyanja Bible version. Members of the Watchman Healing Mission do not refer to Jesus Christ but to God the Father, and Michael the Angel (usually they refer to *Yehova ndi Mikael*). They do not believe in Christmas Day - 25th December. They maintain that Jesus Christ was born on 25th October and not December, but what is note-worthy is that they do not observe 25th October as Christmas Day. It should be noted that the idea of composing their own hymns was an attempt to contextualize the Gospel into Tonga culture.

Kamwana set up the Headquarters for his Church at Chiwanga-Lumwi, in Msuli, Longwe Village near Mdyaka, not far from where he had established his headquarters in 1908. He chose his disciples and taught them the study of the Bible. These people were chosen soon after the founding of the Church and Phiri and Mukhwakwata had their training in Bible study for 15 years with Kamwana Chirwa himself, and Bestine Phiri was chosen to succeed him after his death as the President of the Church; but it turned out that he never succeeded him and this was the cause of the schisms which occurred within the Church. The people in Nkhata Bay refused to recognize Mr. Bestine Phiri as the President of the Church because by then he was staying at his home in Chiradzulu and they did not want someone to rule them in absentia. In fact Phiri furthered the teaching of Watchman Healing

Mission. Here, it should be noted that even in the Northern Region secessionist churchs internal clashes on leadership were still felt although the main ones were those affecting policies of the established churches.

Kamwana died on 31st July 1956, at his home and Headquarters - Chiwanga-Lumwi aged about eighty-years. His Church is still going on and is still growing and one can see its members even in Chiradzulu put on badges labelled *Ine wa Yehova nda Amikaeli*. Before Kamwana died in 1956, the distribution of the membership in the Watch-Tower Church was as follows:

In Malawi	*Northern Region*	823
	Southern Region	711
Zambia		687
Zimbabwe		353
South Africa		755
Tanzania		698

These statistics show the impact of Kamwana's Church on the people. Since then the number of the followers of Kamwana has risen sharply particularly in Nkhata Bay. Kamwana himself can be seen as a man of courage and tenacity whose readiness to stand up to Europeans made him in the eyes of many of his compatriots a symbol of African independence. It was in this guise that he entered the pantheon of saints and martyrs of Independent Watch-Tower Churches in Zambia and Zimbabwe during the 1920s.[29] Thus, one cannot forget Kamwana's moral message of hope as quoted by McMinn; although his prophecy did not realize:

> The advent of Christ was to take place at the end of 1914. The whites were all to leave the country. There would be no more oppression from the tax gatherers. 'These people there' (indicating the Residency on the hill) 'you soon will see no more; for the government will go. In the meantime do not let your hearts be troubled; for the white men I represent will not only educate you freely, but will provide money for taxes. We shall build our own ships, make our own powder and make or import our own guns etc, i.e when the revenue is in our hands.[30]

---

[29] Taylor and Lehmann, *Christians of the Copperbelt*, pp. 238-246.

[30] McMinn, 'The First Wave of Ethiopianism in Central Africa', in *Livingstonia News*, August 1909, pp. 56-59.

Kamwana's courage represents an indigenous missionary heroism ready to suffer for his people. He criticized the morality of the Church of his day and safe-guarded this morality in his own way of understanding. However apart from attacking western religious ideologics and government administrators, it seems Kamwana did not embrace much of Tonga culture, except in the achievement of creating their own hymns. Again, the moral message of Kamwana was dominated by threats of the coming of the new Kingdom. The pure person will inherit the Kingdom of God. For Kamwana, unlike his counterparts, the Livingstonia Mission, hurried baptism was a means of safe-guarding morality for the new converts.

Yesaya Zerenji Mwasi and the Blackman's Church

The second secessionist from Livingstonia Mission was Yesaya Zerenji Mwasi. One cannot say with clarity when Yesaya Zerenji Mwasi was born but it is quite certain that it was during the time of the Angoni wars before the advent of the white men in Nkhata Bay in particular and in the northern province in general. Yesaya Mwasi was about six years old when the Tonga broke away from the Ngoni and when the Ngoni suffered a humiliating defeat at the hands of the Tonga in 1875.

Mwasi was born at a place called Chunji near Chipaika about 10 km away from Chintheche Station. It was while at Chipaika that Mwasi first went to a village school, and later to Bandawe school. He was baptised in 1895. The European missionaries at Bandawe were so impressed with Mwasi's performance that they decided to send him to Overtoun Institution at Khondowe after Livingstonia Mission had been transferred there. Mwasi went to Livingstonia in 1897 together with some of his colleagues, men like Samuel Longwe and Philemon Chirwa. Mwasi was sent for Teacher Training course but while he was there he changed his mind and took to studying theology. He became a great friend of Dr Robert Laws who heaped on him responsibilities so as to prepare him for the future. The basic aim of Livingstonia, constantly repeated, was to create a "self-supporting, self-governing, and self-extending Native Church,"[31] and therefore, the African clergy-to-be were given the highest training available in the Normal and Theological classes at the Institution; yet again and again their ordination was postponed on the grounds that congregations could not be found

---

[31] Terence O. Ranger, *Dance and Society in East Africa*, London: Heinemann, 1975, p. 195.

which would support them financially. This meant that Mwasi who had completed his theological training in 1902 could not be ordained until after many years. The way Mwasi was handled by missionaries at Bandawe is reflected in this quotation from his own document.[32]

> I have served the mission for up to now the period of 45 years, from January 1888 to 1891. I have served as a pupil: from 1892 up to 1897, as a monitor: from 1898 up to 1905, as both certificated school master as well as a divinity student from 1906 up to 1913 as both licentiated preacher and school master - at the expense of the native fund alone: from 1914 up to 1916 as an ordained minister: from 1917 up to date as placed minister over the Sanga Congregation: in 1930 the Limphasa Congregation was added by induction to the former charge: and from 1907 up to date I have been working alone from the mission station - at a distance of more than 20 or 30 miles according to the respective areas of the congregations - *Without a help of a newspaper, medicine or school teacher from the mission*. Children around me grow wild yearly my own children go into the Bandawe area in search of central school. (p. 6).

Mwasi was appointed as an evangelist in 1902 and was stationed at Bandawe Mission. The missionary-in-charge was A.G. MacAlpine and at first the relations between them were friendly, but before long they became strained. Mwasi as an evangelist could be sent anywhere and thus in 1906 he was sent to Zambia to preach the Word of God there. He remained in there for a year and returned in 1907. In May 1908 he was asked to go back to Zambia but this time he said that he was prepared to go provided they gave him porters to carry his luggage. Porters were provided to the white missionaries travelling on duty, but MacAlpine did not give Mwasi porters and Mwasi refused to go to Zambia. Here Mwasi saw that there was no justice in the Church.

In 1909 Mwasi wrote a report against MacAlpine accusing him of harsh and discriminatory behaviour against Africans in general, which he sent to Dr Elmslie who was acting on the behalf of Dr Laws at Livingstonia. However, Dr Elmslie advised MacAlpine to normalize relations with Mwasi and make

---

[32]   Rev Yesaya Zerenji Mwasi, *My Essential and Paramount Reasons for Working Independently*, 1933. I am indebted to Rev Flywel Chimwembe Mwale, Synod Moderator of Blackman's Church at Ching'oma for releasing the Document to me on 9th Oct. 1994 during my field study. Since then Mwasi's text has been published, with a thorough introduction by Kenneth Ross: Yesaya Zerenji Mwasi, *My Essential and Paramount Reasons for Working Independently*, Blantyre: CLAIM-Kachere, 1999.

any reconciliation, which might help to bridge the differences between them. Dr Elmslie was afraid lest a similar situation might develop as that of Elliot Kamwana who had started a new Church in Nkhata Bay. At the beginning of 1909, Mwasi resigned his post as an evangelist and was only persuaded to return after pleas made by the Scottish missionaries. Dr Turner, was also a missionary at Bandawe pressed for an immediate ordination of Mwasi for fear that he might break away from the Church and form a Church of his own like Kamwana had done earlier. Thus Mwasi was eventually ordained in May 1914 together with two ordinands, Jonathan Chirwa of Loudon and Ezekiya Tweya of Ekwendeni.

Soon after the ordination Rev. Mwasi was given his own congregation of Mdyaka, an area that had been affected most during the Kamwana rising of 1909. Mwasi played an important role within the Church of Scotland during the presbytery meetings. Whenever he was called upon to speak, he always spoke sense and both European and African ministers admired him.

Mwasi and the Policy of the Church

Although Mwasi was ordained as a minister, it did not mean that he was happy with the status within the Church. There were many underlying reasons, which made him unhappy. He quarreled not only with European missionaries but also African church elders of his Mdyaka congregation. At one time, being in charge of his own congregation, he suspended a church elder whose daughter had eloped with a polygamist. When Mdyaka church elders took this case to the Presbytery at Livingstonia, the Presbytery disapproved the strong steps taken by Mwasi and this was more than Mwasi could take. He considered the Presbytery's action as improper and blasphemous because the Church had always suspended the parents of children who had misbehaved in oneway or another. This was a deliberate attempt to undermine the good name of Mwasi.

The other matter of concern to Mwasi was the way the European mission-aries handled reports on Church matters and schools. Africans prepared these reports, but the European missionaries handled these reports as if they effected the fruits of their own labour. Worse still, the European missionaries announced these reports during congregations, instead of the Africans who had prepared the reports and this meant that all credit went to European missionaries and not to African missionaries. Furthermore, when these reports were being sent to Livingstonia the European missionaries signed them and in most cases they did not let the Africans know the results of the reports, which they had sent to Livingstonia. Rev. Mwasi also discovered that the European missionaries discriminated against African church ministers. He proved his case by saying that when he was given his own congregation at Mdyaka, he had no vessels of his own to use during the times of Holy Communion and he had to ask for them from Bandawe, which were church property.

But the missionaries at Bandawe used to ask Mwasi to pay for the vessels after use. This was really discriminatory because as a church minister Mwasi was not supposed to pay for these vessels and perhaps if it were any other man apart from Mwasi he would not have paid for the use of these vessels during Holy Communion. The other point was that he discovered that any white man who came to Bandawe could be empowered to baptise Africans even if he had not studied theology. He also observed that while white ministers baptised African children, African ministers could not baptize a white man's child. This was, to him, a clear manifestation of discrimination. The other point was that the young white missionaries had no respect for the Africans in general and for Mwasi to be treated as if he were a child just because he happened to have been born an African was a thing he could not condone. Mwasi had great respect for Dr Laws and this respect was mutual. But the young white missionaries lacked tact.

The other point of interest is that when Dr Laws was on leave in Scotland he sent a book of *Christianity and the Nation* to Mwasi through MacAlpine at Bandawe. MacAlpine did not give the book to Mwasi until after six years in 1914 at the time of his departure from Bandawe. He gave a lame excuse that he had forgotten that Dr Laws had sent him the book. But in actual fact MacAlpine was afraid that had he given the book to Mwasi it would perhaps have inflamed him more because at this time Mwasi was already politically minded. After reading the book Mwasi became more aware that the white missionaries came to Africa to teach Africans the Word of God and that the church itself should belong to the Africans. He requested therefore that the Africans should run the church and not the whites.

Moreover, his meeting with Dr Aggrey in 1924 at Livingstonia and Mvera Missions contributed greatly to Mwasi's independence of mind. That kind of cold war went on until 1932, when Rev Mwasi convened a meeting at Bandawe during which he asked white missionaries to tell him and explain more fully why there were such great differences between white ministers and African ministers. This meeting was adjourned to a later date when another meeting was held at Livingstonia. At this meeting Mwasi repeated his charge against the white missionaries though his fellow Africans did not want to take sides, partly because they were afraid to lose their jobs.

When Mwasi thought of separation from denominationalism he put some of his concerns this way:

> The whole Christendom, Nature and God approve what I am able to undertake. If I succeed God succeeds in me and if I fail God fails in me. The time has now come for the Native Church to take up its responsibilities alone as the individual churches planted by the Apostle Paul did without fear that absence of mission is death of the Christianity of the soil. God alone is the essentially vital factor here. It is impossible for the Head to leave this body: "I am in the midst of them." He says. [33]

On 12th July 1933 he declared his six essential and paramount reasons for working independently. Here is an extract from his document:[34]

> I wish to avoid unjust persecution by my fellow country men that I am proclaiming strange Gods to them: that I am a preacher employed by foreigner for the sake of money to uproot native customs and traditions, hence I am exposed to this that I am traitor to my country.

> I wish to prove God and demonstrate to my native race as to what God can would do in, within, with ,by and through me - black African: that success does not depend upon money or human wisdom or institutions whatever,v but upon and by the power of God.

> I wish to save my fellow natives from or to detract their mind from erroneous idea that God is more in foreign missionaries, lands, language, institutions, thoughts, words and actions but is less or not in the native Christianity, languages, institutions, thoughts, words and actions that God loves White colour and hates black colour. In short that what man on account of his good surroundings is nearer God than a black man who lacks such environments. That is, another man's God, faith, thoughts or actions have no personal appeal to me.... Christianity of the soil shall begin in members of the churches when they believe in an indigenous and personal God...

> I wish to save my people from the identification of the State, Mission with Christianity of the soil. They are of opinion that missionaries because are out of the nationalities of the Ruling States and as the natives are subjects

---

[33] Ibid., p. 5.

[34] Source: Rev Y.Z. Mwasi, *My Essential and Paramount Reasons for Working Independently*, Sanga, Chintheche: West Nyasa, 12th July 1933. pp. 1-5.

to those ruling states therefore the native churches are subjects to the missionaries.

I wish to save missionaries from merely trading upon the works of the agents of the native church.... Constantly, therefore we see missionaries demanding urgent and early supply of statistics from native ministers subject to the statement. "If you fail to supply us early with the reports of your works the home Church will never send us money."

I wish to naturalize and nationalize God, Christ, Faith - in short Christianity. There is no say that object and goal of the missionary enterprise is to naturalize and nationalize Christianity, to grow out of its own soil, having its own customs and traditions purified by the Gospel of Christ, an exotic Christianity will never take vital coat in the life of the natives. It is a mistaken view to think that the missionaries themselves shall do the measures of introducing initiative force of indigenous Church.... (pp. 1-5).

Mwase saw that the idea of the pure native Church was being pushed far from its destined realization, and was being gradually sinking into oblivion. This is what he thought:

I strongly protest dissent and cease to be a member of that an organization. It is not the divinely ordained orders I cease from - orders of Church Government by "Presbers" or "elders," but I cease from the abuses of denaturalisation and denationalisation of the native Church. I claim for a purely indigenous Church to be wholly independent from exotic predomi-nance and traditions. My paramount reason or purpose therefore is to have the merit of having introduced the Initiative Measures of purely Native Church in or out of this presbytery.[35]

The time really came when in 1933 the desire to break away from the Free Church of Scotland became stronger in him. Mwasi turned to his congre-gation and told his faithfuls that he was leaving the Free Church to found his own Church, which could be run by Africans only. He wrote a letter to Livingstonia threatening them that if things did not improve within the Church he would have no option but to quit their Church. However, the Presbytery at Livingstonia sent two ministers - Rev. Turner and Gordon to discuss matters with Mwasi and a meeting was held at Phiri - just a few km from Nkhata Bay proper, along the road to Chintheche. Rev Gordon presided over the meeting. Mwasi arrived late at the meeting and he found that the Church in which the meeting was taking place was filled to capacity with people. Among other things he accused the white missionaries of

---

[35] Ibid., p. 5.

hating male Africans while remaining on intimate terms with African females. He also accused them of coming to Nyasaland not as missionaries but as rulers. After reading his letter of resignation he walked out of the room and those who were behind him followed. This happened in June 1933.

Establishment of Blackman's Church of Africa

Mwasi was given support not only by his former supporters but also by some chiefs among who were Malenga Mzoma, Chiweyo, Chimbano, Chenyentha, Thuli, Thowolo, Fukamalaza, N.A. Kabunduli, Fukamapiri, Mkumbira, Timbiri, Mg'ona and Gawaza. He named his newly founded Church *Mpingo wa Afipa wa Africa* (Blackman's Church of Africa). He established his headquarters at a place called Ching'oma, Parankhanga Hill, south of Nkhata Bay. He trained and ordained his own ministers and established churches at various places in Nkhata Bay district. He was later joined by Rev. Charles Chinula of Mzimba district and Rev. Yafeti Mponda Mkandawire of Deep Bay (Chitimba) both of whom had been dismissed by Livingstonia Mission.

The first meeting between them took place in 1939 at Kamwala near Sanga, and it was here that they were officially welcomed into the new Church as ministers. Thus, the Church had branches both in Mzimba and Karonga Districts.

His church continues to grow to the present day and in 1968 the Church had 5,410 members in Nkhata Bay alone and it had branches in Zimbabwe, South Africa, Zambia and Tanzania. Here in Malawi the Church is represented in Mzimba, Karonga and North of Nkhotakota.[36]

Mwasi did not confine himself to religious matters alone. He took an active part in political affairs of his day. He was a members of the West Nyasa Native Association of which he had been secretary since its inception. This Association was formed in 1920 but a European missionary J. Riddell Henderson stationed at Bandawe opposed its formation.

In 1930, the then governor Thomas Shenton Whiteledge was delighted with the activities of the West Nyasa Native Association so that when he came to Nkhata Bay he made it a point to meet Mwasi. All principal chiefs were

---

[36] For the wider history see: Devlin Chirwa, *The History of the African Methodist Church in Malawi*, Zomba: Kachere Documents, 2003.

members of the Association. Because of misunderstanding, which developed between Mwasi and some of the chiefs, the Association was dissolved in 1933, and soon thereafter the "Atonga Tribal Council" was founded which consisted of thirty-two chiefs and a few educated people. Mwasi was among the few educated men. Mwasi advocated the creation of independent schools directly under African control, which could act as alternative means of improvement to those offered by the Europeans. In 1933, Mwasi formed the West Nyasa Blackman's Educational Society with the avowed aim of promoting the establishment of a University in the then Nyasaland.[37] The idea of the society was "to improve or develop the impoverished conditions of the Blackman religiously, morally, economically, physically and intellectually, by starting a purely native controlled High School or College,"[38] so wrote Mwasi. Had Mwasi lived longer he would have been delighted with the establishment of the University of Malawi in 1965, and Mzuzu University in 1998.

It is noteworthy that Mwasi fought against the morality of the day. Mwasi was not only against the malpractices of the missionaries but also of the government of the day. He knew too well that education was necessary for the betterment of his fellow Africans and if only he had funds presumably he might have started a higher institution in his day. Of course, there were problems here for Africans were not offered higher education yet to do the jobs. His death in July 1955, at the age of 87 was a great loss to the Tonga people. Today, the Church that Mwasi founded is still a growing and a missionary Church. Its members are all over Central Africa including South Africa. Sometimes African missionaries from the Republic of South Africa come to attend Blackman's Church Synodical meeting in Malawi. They also give some financial support and training to the Church in Malawi. I had a chance to talk to Rev Flywel Mwale and Rev. Henry Chikhowe Banda who agreed that the Blackman's Church has spread to many parts in Nkhata Bay. The membership was estimated at 3,500 Christians in Nkhata Bay district alone: "There are many congregations with established in Nkhata Bay

---

[37] That had been the desire and plan of Dr Laws, which his successors considered inappropriate (John McCracken, *Politics and Christianity in Malawi 1875-1940. The Impact of the Livingstonia Mission in the Northern Province*, Zomba: Kachere, ²2008, pp. 277-288.)

[38] Terence O. Ranger, *Dance and Society in East Africa*, London: Heinemann, 1975, p. 201.

District. The youth is taught to be disciplined, show good behaviour and demonstrate good Christian living."[39]

Mean while, the Blackman's Church or African Church as was known at the time of my study has changed its name to "Church of Africa Presbyterian CAP." It is also a member of the National Christian Council in Malawi.

The missionaries came to realize how difficult it was to suppress the rites of passage. Even among their converts, many of them had one foot placed in Christianity and the other one in traditional beliefs and rites of passage. The rise of Independent Churches in Nkhata Bay has shown that some leadership in the church was dissatisfied with the approach of uprooting all the Tonga traditional values. Whatever Mwasi meant by his 'wish to naturalize, God, Christ, or Christianity' seems to imply that he wanted to embrace some native 'customs and traditions purified by the Gospel of Christ'. In other words he would welcome the idea of Christianizing some of the Tonga rites of passage.

Anglicans and Roman Catholics tried to solve the problem by instituting Christianization of some of the rites. This would seem to have been some kind of compromise. For instance, the Roman Catholics tried hard to introduce or develop Christian initiation for girls in some communities. This was particularly true with *chinamwali* initiation among the Chewa people, which was similar to traditional practices in *nthanganene* for girls, in a Tonga setting. Just as Bishop Marthurin Guilleme of the Roman Catholic Church admitted:

> *Chinamwali* will have to be tolerated, as it is impossible to suppress it. However, missionaries should recommend to their Christians that they suppress anything immodest in the ceremony.

This was a good compromise, unlike the Scottish missionaries, who were fighting for the total suppression of the rites of passage. Thus, the Catholics appointed their matrons, the *alangizi* (or *aphungu* in Tonga), who assisted the girls in passing through these rites. Anglicans and Catholics also realized how deeply rooted in their customs the Tonga were. The Anglican Church (UMCA), which had spread from Likoma Island to Nkhata Bay, thought of

---

39   Interview: Rev Flywel Chimwembe Mwale and Rev Henry Chikhowe Banda at Ching'oma, the Headquarters of Blackman's Church on 9th Oct. 1994. Rev Mwale is the General Secretary of the Synod, while Rev Chikhowe is the Moderator. These ministers are not relatives of late Rev Yesaya Zerenji Mwasi.

Christianizing beer drinking, but totally condemned drunkenness. So too did the Catholics. This was undoubtedly the best compromise if ever they were going to win some converts among the Tonga.

In some mission schools, especially at Bandawe, where *Mabuto* (Girls' Boarding School) was established, the main concern was in the Christianization of the local rites for girls' sexual education and their necessary preparation for marriage. The lady Christians (or the lady in charge of *Mabuto*), were encouraged to counsel the girls. The whole idea was to discourage the girls and their parents from participating in or associating with the rites of passage, and to ensure that they were properly prepared for Christian marriage and life. But even among these missionaries there is not much evidence showing how they went about christianizing Tonga rites of passage apart from Christian counselling for the girls. Tonga culture on the whole was a neglected discipline. This is because too much emphasis was put on imparting the Christian faith to the Tonga people, thus suppressing all Tonga cultural heritage.

On the other hand it is difficult to tell how much influence indigenous churches had upon moral education in Tonga society. Both Kamwana and Mwasi seemed to have embraced western religious and moral values. Although Kamwana might have encouraged that the pattern of his Church should address the African way of life, his approach on spiritual morality was confused with his visions of a new age. His morality focussed on purity, and transition to the new life was through immediate baptism. There is no indication that Kamwana encouraged Tonga customs or religious beliefs. Likewise, Mwasi simply adopted the whole liturgy of the Scottish people without making any consideration for Tonga customs. He accepted the rituals and doctrines taught by the Free Church Mission at Bandawe and Livingstonia. This is supported by the fact that his Church continues to use the Tonga Presbyterian hymns. This also explains why the missionaries did not excommunicate Mwasi after his secession. They recognized his Church until after his death. Mwasi did not actually achieve what Dr Laws thought would become of a future Church. It appears that both Kamwana and Mwasi thought more of African leadership in the Church than of inculturation of the Gospel to adapt to Tonga culture. It is not known how much Kamwana and Mwasi used Tonga folktales and proverbs in their homiletics. What is clear is that Mwasi was a dynamic preacher and a miracle worker. It was believed that when Mwasi had organized an open air evangelical meeting during rainy season, the rains would not disturb his services, even if they threatened to come. During his preaching some of his listeners would fall into trance, or become spirit-possessed and immediately confess repentance.[40]

The charismatic independent churches, which profess a 'born again' theology, also seem not to have not contributed new moral teachings to Tonga society. In fact, with their demand for purity, they have rejected the Tonga traditional religious and moral values. They are using the same western religious and moral values by simply emphasizing the influence of the Holy Spirit. Their doctrines are rigid. Much emphasis is on prayer and healing. They are quite radical and look at a moral society, which can change through confrontation, using western religious ideologies and values. This is a new approach, but they equally condemn Tonga rituals and ancestral beliefs. Thus, the 'Born Agains' are negative to African customs. The source of their morality is the way the West has interpreted the Bible. However, their approach is that they are driven by the Holy Spirit to follow that morality, other than the laws followed by the mainstream churches. Thus they believe that the authority of that morality is the Holy Spirit. In this case I argue that, since Independent Churches are continuously adopting Western forms of Christianity and Western religious and moral values, they have done very little on imparting moral education among the Tonga youth. Their teachings do not bring a new moral dimension. The mainstream churches too have made no policy statement on the inculturation of the Gospel. At the same time the institutionalized churches have not made a policy in the way they can interact with the indigenous churches. With this lack of dialogue, what is often experienced, is a cold war waged on the pulpit, when they attack one another on doctrinal, ritual or moral issues. The end result has been misleading the people.

Islam and Tonga Traditional Values

Historical Development

Islam, which means submission to Allah, also came to have some influence on Tonga society, but less so than Christianity. The prophet Muhammad succeeded between AD 570 and 632 in giving the Arabs a new dynamic moral code. Through the Indian Ocean trade, Islam spread. The incoming

---

[40] I am indebted to my late father, David Jestory Mphande, who witnessed some of Mwasi's evangelical meetings in the early 1930s before his secession from the Free Church Mission.

Arab traders brought with them the Islamic faith and way of life. What is more, on the East African Coast they intermarried with local African people to produce a hybrid nation called *Swahili*, the majority of whose members also became Muslim.

Islam first arrived in the area now known as Malawi about 180 years ago, brought initially by traders from the Swahili Coast of Africa. It has been adopted with enthusiasm by a large proportion of one of the country's main tribal groups, the Yao, who form the majority of Malawian Muslims.[41]

At least three places in Malawi had received early Islamic influence before the advent of Christianity in 1875. The first of these was Nkhotakota on the central west coast of Lake Malawi where originally the long-distance traders of Swahili Arab origins, established their dynasty from the 1840s onwards.[42] The second was established by Mlozi, an Arab ivory trader at Mpata in present-day Karonga at the north-end of the lake around 1880. Mlozi was related to the Jumbes through marriage. The third was the Mangochi area at the southern end of Lake Malawi. Here too Islam found fertile ground in the areas of chiefs Mponda, Makanjira and Jalasi.

Muslims and Education in Malawi

Malawi has recently experienced a resurgence of Islam. It has been estimated that there are over 800 Friday Mosques in Malawi, and at least one or two are to be found in almost every town.

The last government census indicates the Muslim population as about 13%. Islam has gained much in public presence and self-esteem, and this has revived the Islamic faith in all parts of Malawi, including the Muslim communities in Tongaland. Though Islam is a missionary religion, its percentage of the population is not growing significantly. Until the mid 1970s Malawi was very much cut off from the mainstream of the Islamic world with few contacts with the wider Umma. This is now rapidly changing. Significant numbers of young Malawians are going abroad for advanced Islamic studies and some of the richer Muslim countries have given generous support to educational and mosque building projects within Malawi.

---

[41] See David Bone (ed), *Malawi's Muslims. Historical Perspectives*, Blantyre: CLAIM-Kachere, 2002.

[42] George Shepperson, "The Jumbe of Kota-kota" in I.M. Lewis (ed), *Islam in Tropical Africa*, London, Oxford: Oxford University Press, 1966, p. 196.

Traditional Islamic education antedates western style schooling in Malawi. The caravans of the traders through whom Islam arrived in the region were conspicuous for the boards they carried for the teaching of the Quran. One of the attractions of Islam for the first Malawian chiefs to be converted was the literacy in Swahili that its missionaries offered. By the time of their entry to Malawi in the last quarter of the 19th Century, pioneer Christian missionaries found the Quran being taught in *madrassas* in towns like Mangochi, Nkhotakota, Mponda, etc. The setting up of a system for *madrassa* education was a feature of the spread and consolidation of Islam among the Yao.

When the Christian missionaries established themselves in Malawi, the education system that they set up offered skills of a very different nature. Basic as their schooling generally was, it offered literacy, numeracy and skills in technical subjects. This education offered people even white-collar jobs. As a result the western system of schooling came to dominate the educational scene in all except the Muslim areas of this country. In the pre-independence era the Christian missions heavily dominated western education, which they actively used as a means of proselytization. It is not surprising that the reaction of the Islamic communities was negative.

In the mid 1920s the Colonial Government decided to take some measure of control of the education system and in 1926 a Department of Education was created. During this time there were small-scale attempts by some Muslims, particularly Muslim chiefs, to have provision made for western education free from Christian influence and bias. From the late 1940s attempts were made, first by individual Muslims then by Muslim Associations, to set up community schools providing both western style secular education and Quranic instruction. However, these efforts were beset by many difficulties.[43]

When Malawi became independent in 1964 its government, through the Ministry of Education, made it a priority to rid the education system of denominationalism.[44] As a result, though the various Christian churches

---

[43] See more in: Alfred J. Matiki, "Problems of Islamic Education in Malawi," *Religion in Malawi* 1994, pp. 18-22.

[44] The 1961 Manifesto of the Malawi Congress Party made the pledge: "The party, when in power, will pay special attention to those parts of the country like the Muslim areas where education has been deplorably neglected," *Malawi Congress Party Manifesto*, 1961, p. 7.

remained the proprietors of the majority of schools throughout the country, control of education policy and control of schools passed firmly into the hands of the Ministry. Muslim religious leaders are given access within the schools to pupils of their own faith at some time during each week. With the increased endorsement of western schooling from some sectors of the Muslim leadership and with larger numbers of Muslims attending school, pupils are nowadays less likely to give up their Islamic identity as they progress through the education system.

The present situation for Islamic education has never been better since the 1985-1995 Educational Development Plan for Malawi. The Ministry of Education had directed to revise the Primary Education curriculum. The Ministry further recommended a conceptual approach of Religious Education with an emphasis on concepts, skills and attitudes involved in understanding religion. The result of this has been that Religious Education has developed an integrated syllabus, which includes Malawian Traditional Religion, Christianity and Islam. This has been an attempt to accommodate Muslim pupils much easier into the primary school system. [45]

Spread of Islam in Tongaland

During the reign of Kanyenda Manyenya of Nkhotakota, about 1831-1861, through a combination of his tactful diplomacy with local chiefs and the distribution of gifts: cloth, beads, salt etc, Salim bin Abdallah was able to consolidate his position to establish a powerful dynasty in Nkhotakota. According to Tonga cultural history, Kanyenda is believed to be the grandson of Karonga Mzizi and cousin of Chief Kabunduli of Nkhata Bay.[46] This link also brought about inter-marriages between some of the Kanyenda people and those of Kabunduli.

It is therefore believed that the influence of Islam on the Tonga spread from Nkhotakota through trade in ivory and slaves. It is quite possible that the

---

[45] For a critical study of the new syllabus see Jessica Olausson Jarhall, *A Look at Changes in Primary Religious Education*, Linköping: Linköping University Electronic Press, 2001. Also available on the web under swepub:oai:DiVA.org:liv-62973 for free download. – Her observations are two: (1) Traditional culture is wrongly identified with African Traditional Religion, and (2) The picture painted of Christianity and Islam is in no way Malawian, but European/Near Eastern.

[46] I am again indebted to ex-chief 'Chiŵiŵi II. (Mr Kanyama 'Chiŵiŵi Mwasi of Mgodi village who dictated to me some aspects of Tonga cultural history, on 8th Oct. 1994).

predecessors of Tonga chiefs and their followers began to deal with Swahili-Arabs and were exposed to Islamic influences.

There is also evidence that the spread of Islam was assisted by the immigration and settlement of Indian traders, most of whom were professed Muslims. These established their shops around Nkhata Bay *boma*, Chintheche etc. This is confirmed by Sheikhs Admad bin Ali, Palera and Willie, of Chintheche Islamic Centre who have observed that, "the consolidation of Islamic religion around Chintheche and Nkhata Bay *boma* began from the time Indian traders began to establish themselves in these areas. Today there are several mosques in Tongaland."[47]

Islamic itinerants were important in spreading the faith. Having won the chiefs and headmen and other leading figures in the society, it was easier for the Islamic faith to spread to other areas either peacefully or by way of imposition. The itinerating teachers, the Mwalimu, set up a *madrassa* or school. The method of instruction the Mwalimu employed was the same in all the societies where they planted their religion. A typical scene of what went on was reported in 1903:

> Often outside a native house on the sort of space that is a kind of verandah may be seen sitting one of the teachers of Mohammedanism with his wooden board, on which are Arabic portions of the Koran. Around him may be several, or perhaps only one, who repeat after him, word by word, that is before them, thus gradually are sentences learnt. The words are more or less intoned in a loud monotonous voice, which can be heard at some distance. One notices the great earnestness and eagerness with which what is given is learnt.[48]

> The Mwalimu has not much to teach: a few prayers in Swahili to be learnt by rote and certain customs to be remembered for future observance. Within a couple of months the pupil is ready to be initiated as a follower of Muhammad. At this time he pays his final fee to his teacher, having already paid a similar fee when he entered upon his course of instruction. Some documentary evidence also suggests that the Mwalimu also took advantage of their pupils and exploited them by engaging them in some other works in addition to paying fees:

---

[47] Source: Sheikhs: Admad bin Ali, Palera and Willie, interviewed on 7th Oct. 1994 at their Mosque, Chintheche Islamic Centre.

[48] A.L. Hofmeyr, "Islam in Nyasaland," *The Moslem World*, p. 7.

Their disciples have to pay substantial fees, when they have finished their course of training, and, in the intervals of learning, the pupils have to do a good deal of work of all kinds for their teachers.[49]

It is evident from such citations that it was much easier to be converted to Islam and rise through its ranks than to become a Christian, but still Islam remained a minority.

Much of what was taught in these *madrassas* was very elementary. Pupils are taught Islamic practices, including the ability to transliterate and recite the Quran. Although elementary, the system provides a spiritual and moral orientation in their lives and give them a distinct identity which is most pronounced in their mode of dress.

In Tonga society, like in other societies in Malawi, Islam as a faith and way of life did not interfere much with the traditional beliefs and customs of the Tonga people. If anything, it merely made slight changes to some of the local customs, thus integrating, assimilating and preserving vital indigenous elements. This very policy of retaining traditional customs and beliefs proved extremely useful in the spread of Islam. Some of the customs Islamized were polygamy and birth and funeral rituals. Boys and girls who have accepted the Islamic faith undergo initiation rites - *jando* for boys and *msondo* for girls.

Jando in Yao, and *mchinjo* in Tonga, has two meanings. In the first place, it means circumcision of males. In this case it is an initiation rite, which marks the transition of a boy from childhood to adulthood. The word also means a place, usually in the barn, where circumcised boys stay during their convalescent period. This is because it includes all the *moral instructions* given to the boys during their period of seclusion at the *jando*. In Tonga society *jando* came with the introduction of Islam among the Yao. The Muslims believe that circumcision is a very important and necessary prerequisite for any entry into Islam. Thus, *jando* is a religious rite. It would mean that any Tonga boy, who participates in it, first and foremost accepts the Islamic faith, because no one can be regarded as a Muslim without it.[50]

Since the practice of Islam, as that of other religions, requires one who has reached a stage of maturity and understanding, circumcision came to be

---

[49] H. Machell Cox, "A Debasing Influence," *Central Africa*, vol. 27, no. 313, 1909, p. 96.

[50] This is accepted practice all over East Africa, but neither the Qur'an nor orthodox Islamic theology demand circumcision.

regarded also as an entry into adulthood. Originally *jando* (*mchinjo*) was allowed to those who were about to get married. However, in these days, age no longer matters. Sheikh Admad bin Ali observed, "even today adults can undergo *jando* through a minor operation by any medical doctor so long there is some arrangement between the candidate and the Sheikh."[51] The *jando* ceremony has to wait for the schools to close, so that the boys have time to attend. The greatest event during their stay at the *jando* is circumcision, which marks the boys' Muslim baptism. The actual descriptions of the process disclose little of what exactly happens inside the *jando* school, so Johnston's brief description may suffice:

> Usually towards the end of the dance the old man (the *ngaliba*) who is to circumcise takes the boys aside one by one; arrangements are then made for their circumcision and they are suddenly told to look at a strange figure in the sky; whilst their gaze is thus diverted the act is smartly performed. 'The boys cry a great deal.' I was informed, but a few days rest in the grass hut and the application of certain astringent remedies soon heals the wound. Much good advice is said to be given to the boys by these elderly instructors, but there is also much loose talk and the boys are thoroughly enlightened as to sexual relations. They are given (by their guardian or sponsor, generally, who usually sees them through the ceremonies) a new name and the appellation they have hitherto borne is absolutely discarded. It must never be again used and to call a youth who has been initiated by the name of the childhood is an unpardonable offence.[52]

What Johnston wrote is still the practice today. The loose talk he referred to has to do with sexual education. This includes not only sexual techniques, but also instructions to be followed for example when the woman is menstruating. Apart from marking the boys' entrance into adulthood, the ceremony also prepares them for marriage. The pains mentioned by Johnston during these moments of crisis undoubtedly make them feel that they are adults and brave men. During the *jando* school the boys are subjected to rigorous discipline and instructed in various skills and tribal

---

51 Interview: Sheikh Admad bin Ali on 7th Oct. 1994 at Chintheche Islamic Centre.

52 Sir H. Johnston, *British Central Africa: An Attempt to Give Some Account of a Portion of the Territories under the British Influence North of Zambezi*, London: Methuen, 1897, p. 409.

lore, how to maintain a family, duties to their chief and community, religious beliefs, warning against selfishness and so on.[53]

On the same principles the girls undergo the *msondo* (*mchinjo*) initiation rite. The girls should have attained puberty. This too is a religious rite. It is conducted for girls of about ten years of age. After the *msondo* initiation ceremony is over, the girls are initiated and during the period of the ceremony some religious practices are passed on to the candidates. On this last day the girls are given new clothes by their parents and relatives. This is a day of celebrations and feasting. The instructor (*nyamkungwi*) and other people responsible for the girls' ceremony are given some money and food. Plenty of food is also consumed there to mark the end of the ceremony. The *msondo* initiation ceremony is similar to Tonga girl's initiation rites, which are practiced in the *nthanganene* or *visenga* setting. During the seclusion period girls are instructed to prepare for their future married life and all that goes with adulthood in general: respect for their parents, elders and chiefs of the community, how to look after a husband and how to keep their homes clean and presentable.

It is clear from the discussion that the Islamic faith proved readily compatible with crucial elements of Tonga culture. This was because; among other reasons, the Islamic faith flexibly accommodated itself to the general tone of Tonga life. Unlike Christianity, for example, it did not interfere with Tonga traditional customs like circumcision or with social institutions such as polygamy. The cultural contacts with Swahili-Arabs and Yao influenced some aspects of the Tonga rites of passage: birth, adolescence, marriage as well as funerals, and to some extent even dietary habits as well.

However, it can be still argued that Islamic moral education has not been effective among the youth in Tonga society. One reason for this is that those who go through Islamic religious rites are very few, and only those who have accepted Islam. Another reason involves the teaching methods. An observation of classes in session in a *madrassa* showed that *Amwalimu* are continually in problems because their lessons lack direction, stimuli and

---

[53] For contemporary studies of *jando* see Edward Jeffrey, The Impact of Jando Initiation on its Initiates in the Area of Kasamba Village in Nkhotakota, Mzuzu: Mzuni Documents no. 49, 2012; Harold Mdoka, The Impact of Jando and Msondo on Boys and Girls: A Case Study of Ntaja, Machinga, Mzuzu: Mzuni Documents no. 137, 2012; Dennis Luka, Christian Boys' Initiation Rites at Sitima Catholic Parish in Zomba, Mzuzu: Mzuni Documents no. 88.

motivation.[54] These problems arise because most *Amwalimu* have had no formal training in methods. The most common method of teaching is rote-learning, particularly in the teaching of the Quran and Hadith as Islamic literature.

The teaching essentially involves memorizing the Quran by heart. What is most objectionable about this method is that the pupils learn to recite the Quran or Hadith without understanding its meaning. The problem is compounded by the fact that many of the *Amwalimu* neither understand Arabic nor speak it. Another handicap to effective classroom instruction is the Mwalimu's inability to use appropriate teaching aids to reinforce what is taught. The instructional materials are either from the Quran or the Hadith and nothing from Tonga traditional folktales, which could complement stories from the Hadith. The observation Mtiki has made seems to apply to the Tonga situation:

> While it may be accepted that some students have responded positively to Islamic education, there is a general discontent among the Muslims in Malawi about the behaviour of the young Muslims in general and those who have been to the madrassa in particular. The behaviour of these graduates falls short of levels expected of spiritual training. It is not uncommon, for instance, to find students using foul language even in the *madrassa*.[55]

Some of the causes of this spiritual torpor and lack of moral commitment are as stated earlier: lack of moral instruction and the use of questionable teaching methods. The Muslims in Tonga society are exposed to three cultures—Islamic, Christian and Traditional Tonga. The differences between these cultures are vewry big and the socio-economic and linguistic demands of this triple heritage can be conflicting at times. For instance, when the behaviours that brought good results at home are deemed improper at the *madrassa*, a youth becomes a victim of negative transfer of training. It is highly probable therefore that the bad behaviour that the youths show is in part caused by sheer copying of foreign values and their inability to discriminate between the traditional rules of the homes and the demands of Islam on the individual.

---

[54] I observed a lesson at Chintheche Madrassa on 9th Oct. 1994 conducted by a Mwalimu for the youth to be initiated into the Islamic Faith.

[55] A.J. Matiki, in *Journal Institute of Muslim Minority Affairs*, p. 133.

In the *madrassa*, the emphasis is on the teaching of the Qur'an and Hadith as the only sources of Moral Education. The Muslims too have not taken any initative to use Tonga oral literature in their preaching and teaching. Even the Hadiths are in Chichewa.

Unlike the Scottish missionaries, the Muslims did not suppress some of the Tonga rites of passage; instead they introduced *msondo* and *jando* initiation ceremonies as vehicles of Islamization. However, these rites have become hopelessly confused with their religion.

CHAPTER SIX

ANTHOLOGY OF TONGA MYTHS AND FOLKTALES

Introduction

The purpose of this chapter is to serve as a case study for the preceding chapters, which form a preparation for the oral literature that follows. The chapter attempts to put together a small representative sample of the innumerable Tonga tales. The Tonga tales have their own literary conventions about the kinds of characters, topics, forms, and conclusions that are acceptable. They embody the inherited wisdom, social, personal and moral, of the Tonga people, whose world is seen through the filter of their folklore.

In some cases, each group of stories is introduced by a general explanation of the cultural context of the tales and of their background. I have attempted to analyse critically each of the first ten folktales, sometimes reflecting on their themes and categories. In some cases I have identified those myths and folktales which have parallels in other collections of myths and folktales found among the Chewa, Lomwe, Sena, Yao and Tumbuka. This approach has helped me to make useful comparisons and appreciate how the Malawian cultural unity manifests itself through these folktales. The last thirty folktales close with a moral lesson at the end of each tale to fulfill an important function, in the light of this book.[1]

The Narratives and their Use in Moral Instruction

I have found out that there are very few myths and legends in Tonga society about the origin of things, people and gods. This is because the Tonga did not build shrines to the High God/Chiuta, rather shrines were built to the ancestors. I have made a selection of 40 texts. In some tales the deeds involve such supernatural powers and abilities that even allegedly historical narrative reads like myth. The first narrative of this section depicts the origin of the Tonga people. Karonga Mzizi and Chiŵiŵi are the heroes. The

---

[1] See Tales 11-40.

Tonga themselves see this legend as portraying the genesis of some Tonga groups of people.

The other mythical narratives in this anthology show how things were in the beginning. This state is referred to only for dramatic contrast to the chaos. In these stories the punchline may be the explanatory statement commonly found at the end of these tales, for example, *"and that is why to this day the monkey lives in the tree and will not stay on the ground* (see Tales 11, 12, 14 and 15).

The other folktales are directly about the moral aspects of behaviour. The Tonga people tell these stories to initiate deep discussion on important themes, for example, how to live within the family and the community. They focus closely on the fundamental and recurrent problems of social relations: the quality of love, the nature of obedience, the ethics of choice and stress conditions. These stories deal with everyday problems. In appearance they are the most fanciful and sometimes even ridiculous tales. These tales are subject to the criteria of judgement. If any narrative is badly told, this will seem to the audience to compromise the continuity of group tradition.

Some of the stories in this group are dilemma tales without an end. The rest are profound moral examples: stories that explicate a lesson, or answer a central question. Virtue, in the context of Tonga story telling, resides both in the ability to argue eloquently, and in the ability to demonstrate a command of tradition. In arguments over the problems set by the stories, it cannot be stressed too strongly that it is the flow of the discussion that counts, or the finding of a solution. Through arguments, the customary practices of the community are rehearsed and celebrated when people gather around a fire, or at the *mphara,* to tell tales like these, the argument that follows the story is pursued by extended analogies with everyday activities.

Each person tries to put his/her interpretation of the situation in the best possible light. There is argument over the focus of the case, and over interpretation. Decision-making becomes something of a corporate process. Finally, the discussion comes to a halt when an influential elder expresses the concerns of the group because of his eloquent summation. These folk problems can be traced in stories like, "An Eye for an Eye" (Tale 21), "The Five Helpers" (Tale 18), and "Hare and the Well" (Tale 8).

Many of the moral stories reflect upon the conditions of the community and family stress, like how people act when they don't have enough to eat. The emphasis is placed on the sharing of food, usually illustrated by the selfishness of one character or another as in the story of "Rich Man and Poor Man" (Tale 22). The disparity between the two is instigated by a theft of food, as in "Baboon who Claims to have Found it" (Tale 23).

A related theme is that of a "do-unto-others" form of reciprocity, as in the story about "Kindness Pays" (Tale 24). The hunter is saved for releasing the Muskrat. A kind act and a long-suffering approach to life lead to eventual repayment and the ultimate triumph of virtue (Tale 10). Thus, many of the moral stories and dilemma tales alike focus on aspects of living correctly within the family. Another important theme in these stories is that of keeping one's own counsel, for example in "Breaking the Promise" (Tale 20). Another theme is that of obedience. Illustrations of the theme of disobedience are the stories: "The Orphaned Millipede" (Tale 6); "Lion and Sparrow" (Tale 28), and "Tupa and his Children" (Tale 29).

The theme of marriage is also quite common. Such stories illustrate the nature of marital or sexual relationships. Some of these stories also show how parents can approve or disapprove certain marriages (Tales 7, 32 and 33). The stories show that marriage is one of the binding human relationships. The other categories of stories specifically reflect on the conditions of the community (Tales 22-26). The last category are tales of 'Tricksters.' The Trickster is a figure who, at one and the same time, represents primal creativity and pathological destructiveness, childish innocence and self-absorption. There is a great deal of scheming with little thought of the consequences, even to the schemer. The Trickster is always a marked creature, an anomaly among animals or humans. His physical character and qualities, as well as his outrageous actions, make the audience laugh at his ridiculous antics.

In some of these tales the reader finds patterning of structures, for instance, a pattern of false friendship that leads to a contract, the violation of the contract, a series of deceptions and finally escape. On the other hand, the Rabbit or Hare explicitly represents all the other little marginal animals. It describes how Rabbit scares them away by hiding in a bag and surprising them, a device used again and again in some of the tales. Deception most commonly occurs through hiding. These undercover deceptions of tricksters can have quite grave consequences as for example, in "Hare and the Well"

(Tale 8); "The Wisdom of the Spider" (Tale 34); "Fox who Cost the Life of his Wife" (Tale 36); "The Greedy Hyena" (Tale 38); and "The Warning that Went Unheeded" (Tale 39).

(1) A Legend about the Origin of the Tonga People

This brief legendary history was collected by late Filemon Kamunkhwara Chirwa, a great Tonga sage, a teacher, Inspector of schools as well as a CCAP Church Elder. He is also the author of "*Nthanu za Chitonga*" (Tonga Fables). I have adopted it here with permission from his daughter, Mrs Annesty Kamanga.[2] Since it is a legend, the authority of it is subject to discussion.

The method adopted by Filemon Chirwa in presenting the information was more or less in a legendary way. Legends carry some historical truths and they serve to provide tribal history and boundaries of kinship. Legends are also a mixture of myths, stories and true history. Therefore we should not blame Filemon Chirwa or the author of this book for not presenting more accurate information, or blame him that some of the clans are not included in this document. The purpose of incorporating this manuscript is to stimulate the Tonga people to remember their traditional history.

The most important thing to see is that the Chewa, Tonga and Tumbuka are presented as one people in their traditional history. Their leader and Paramount Chief was Karonga Mzizi (or Karonga Mazizi). Their history is like a spider's web. I am therefore challenging the Tonga young historians, theologians or anthropologists to conduct research in order to reconstruct Tonga history. According to van Velsen the main Tonga streams are of four categories:

The Mankhambira Tonga

The Nyaliwanga Tonga

The Phiri or Kabunduli Tonga

The Akapunda Tonga[3]

It is my hope that the Tonga elders will appreciate this legend and give more information to those who would like to improve or reconstruct their

---

[2] Now republished as: Filemon Kamunkhwara Chirwa, *Nthanu za Chitonga*, Zomba: Kachere, 2007.

[3] See discussion on Jan van Velsen noted earlier in this book.

history for their generation. The Tonga version is copied word by word from the original manuscript. The translation into English is mine. The future generations will reconstruct the information which is at variance.

The Origin of the Tonga People

Before we understand this traditional history of the Tonga people, at least two questions come to our mind:

Where did the Tonga people come from?
Who were their chiefs or rulers?

In an attempt to answer the first question, we may say that the Tonga, like any other Bantu peoples in this area, came from the North. Possibly, like other Bantu, they interacted with the Nilotes and Cushites around the Upper Nile regions.

To answer the second question, we may say that the Tonga had no specific chiefs. It seems that they were headed by leaders of the clans. Tradition tells us that, when the Tonga left the Nile regions, they moved South-West in groups together with other Bantu peoples. However, the Tonga, Chewa and Tumbuka may have been one tribal group with no chief to rule them until later years.

According to Kamunkhwara Filemon Chirwa, tradition says that the clans later on were identified by their habits. Following this we see the emerging of the main clans, which form the chains of the families such as: *Aphiri; Amwali; Abanda; Ankhoma; Amanda; and Ang'oma*. These clans are found everywhere in Malawi, amongst the Chewa, Tumbuka, Nyanja, Yao, Sena.

Again, tradition has it that the Tonga came through Uganda or the Great Lakes region to Zambia. It is believed that some of the Tonga were left in Uganda. Those of us who have visited Uganda appreciate this fact. The English accent of the Buganda people is similar to that of most Malawians. Their staple food is cassava and the environment in Entebbe and Kampala is similar to the Tropical rain forest of Nkhata Bay, with its identical birds and shrubs.[4]

Tradition further tells us that in Zambia the Tonga settled in the land of "Chitimukuru of the Bemba," whose title clan was Mng'oma around lake

---

[4]   From my diary "Uganda Visit, 1993."

145

Bangweolo. Tradition further says that the Tonga people developed their title clans while in the land of Chitimukuru.

The Aphiri used to settle along the hills (*mapiri*). These groups of people were later on called *Aphiri* (people of the hills or mountains).

The Achirwa used to settle on Islands (*chirwa*). These were called the *Achirwa*. The Nyaluwanga belong also to this group.

The Abanda used to settle in flat lands (*bandawanga*), hence they were called the *Abanda*.

The Ankhoma used to catch a type of fish (*nkhoma*), so they were called *Ankhoma*. Some say this clan liked to enjoy eating *nkhomo*, a type of mushroom, and so they were nicknamed the *Nkhoma*.

The Ang'oma used to make drums (ng'oma), so they were called *Ang'oma*.

The Amiala used to grind their grain on a stone (*mwa*), they were called *Amiala*

The Amwali came as a result of a conflict among the same families separated and dispersed from each other (*akumwalarikana*), hence they were called *Amwali.*

The Amanda title was given to them because their ancestors used to collect a type of mushroom (*manda*) on their journeys.

The Asaka used to collect another type of mushroom (*msaka*) on the way, hence they were called *Asaka*. They are also related to the *Mwali* and *Ngoma*.

The Ankhata were called so because their ancestors used to have a wrapper or piece of cloth on the head (*nkhata*), to support any heavy load they carried. Thus they were called the *Ankhata*

It seems that from these clan titles gradually developed the idea of chieftaincy. The Chief from each clan would come from the elder family (*nyumba yira*) or from a related family as long as one was found responsible, caring and well behaved. In most cases a nephew would be installed as the next chief. In some cases, as today, succession to chieftaincy is taken by a son or nephew. Some clan names in Utonga include, Amuhone, Amwenda, Angwira, Akamanga, Amkorongo, Anthali, Akaunda and Amkunkha. Tradition tells us that these people were at best sons-in-law. Their ancestors were the Mwase, Longwe, Chembezi, Gumba, Kawere and Kaweche.

Tradition also tells that the people never settled at one place. The people wandered around in search of good lands or healthier places. Each clan had to choose the best land to settle on. Tradition has it that the Tonga and Chewa people came in late, perhaps around 1300 AD.

The Tonga in the Land of Chitimukuru

While in the land of Chitimukuru of the Bemba, the Tonga and the Chewa clans were subjected to the tyrannical rule of Chitimukuru to the extent that he would make them slaves. So the clans rebelled against Chitimukuru and moved eastwards in order to be free from Bemba rule.

One tradition has it that Chitimukuru was very cruel. He would punish those who broke the rules by removing their eyes or cutting off their hands and noses.

Tradition further says that when the Tonga and other clans rebelled, Chitimukuru sent an army to wipe them out from their new settlement areas. The Bemba armies attacked them mercilessly. The Atonga, Achewa and other clans fought back. The battle was fierce and lasted for many days. Some of the clans escaped as far as the east of Lake Malawi. These belonged to the *Aphiri* and *Achirwa* clans and were later on known as the Mlowoka, because they had crossed the lake.

Tradition further tells us that during this fierce battle there arose a great fighter (*Ngwazi*) among the Tonga people. His name was Mzizi, the elder brother of *Kabunduli Chiŵiŵi*. He fought to the best of his ability and encouraged other clans to fight on, until the Bemba armies were defeated. He killed so many people in battle that it was difficult to count them. Mzizi ordered the people to make baskets and pack in the heads of their victims. In that way they would easily count them.

When the baskets were being filled with human heads, Mzizi himself began dancing majestically with a song of victory: All the clans joined at the song in triumph.

> "Tondole, Kajawa, Mzira kuviona! Karonga, Wakuronga mitu ya ŵanthu muvitete!." (literally, "Tondole, Kajawa," titles of the hero, "Karonga," one who packs human heads in baskets").

That day the title of Karonga began. Mzizi was now to be called "Karonga," meaning one who would fill baskets with human heads.

Tradition does not name the place where the battle took place. There are speculations that the battle was fought before the clans crossed the river

147

Chimbezi. The Tonga, Chewa and other clans moved to the Nkhamanga range, which was already inhabited by short people, called the "Akafula."

The Akafula were fierce and dangerous people. They were hunters and tin-smiths. They were the owners of the land all over from the North to the South. The heroic fight of Karonga Mzizi during the 'Bemba war' made Mzizi to be highly respected and honoured by all the people. As a result they made him their Chief and leader.

Settlement in Nkhamanga Land

Tradition tells us that the *Aphiri, Achewa, Abanda, Aminjala, Ankhata, Ang'oma, Amwali* and others settled along the Nkhamanga hills and around the plains (Nkhamanga is what is now called Rumphi or Tumbukaland). However, the Manda clan settled in Mwazisi. The owners of the land were the 'Akafula' or 'Akusula'. Their mines (*ng'anjo*) can still be seen in some areas to this day. The mines were shallow. They melted iron from which axes, spears, knives, scissors, needles, iron-chairs and hoes were made.

Then there was a battle between the Akafula and the new inhabitants, that is the Tonga, Chewa and Tumbuka who waged war against the Akafula.

How the Akafula were Dispersed out of their Land

The tradition tells us that when the Akafula saw that foreigners settled in their lands, they began killing those around them. If a person met them and greeted them, and asked from which distance he had been recognized (*mwandione pani*?), and if the person said, 'I just saw you now', then the person would be shot and killed.

The Akafula would only spare those who recognized and respected their small stature. The Akafula caused a lot of deaths. The lesser chiefs and the elders discussed the situation with Karonga Mzizi and how they would arrest the problem. They all agreed to attack the Akafula in their homes or anywhere they would be found. Many Akafula were slaughtered like chicken.

When the Akafula saw that they were in great danger, they ran away in two groups. Some went southwards as far as Mankhamba, where Lake Malawi forms a fork. Others moved westwards and disappeared in the Congo forest, where we still find their remnants called the Pygmies.

Tradition also says that most people who moved from the Nile regions were light skinned, dark and black. This is implied by some of their names such as

Kayela, Kajesa, Kafipa and *Katuwa*. Later on children who were born light skinned or as albinos were being killed and this practice became common in all clans. This practice was later on condemned.

The Arrival of Chikulamayembe in Nkhamanga

After the Akafula were wiped out, the Tonga and Chewa enjoyed a time of peace in Nkhamangaland. One day they were surprised by the visit of a foreigner who was a great trader in cloth, salt and beads. His name was Chikulamayembe. He was received by all the clans with great respect. Chikulamayembe was not only a trader, but also a great hunter. Each time he went hunting he brought meat to the people and shared it with them. The people liked him because of his kindness. Many people gave him pieces of ivory, which gave him a lot of fortune.

Tradition has it that Chikulamayembe decided to marry some of the daughters and sisters of the Phiri and Amwali clan. They accepted him because of his good behaviour, so he became their son-in-law. Tradition says that there were other people who followed Chikulamayembe. These crossed the lake and came to Nkhamangaland. Among these were the *Uhango, Ukandawire, Unthali, Uzumara, Unkhwazi, Chavula, Unkhonjera, Usiska (Siska), Umhone, Umwenda, Ukamanga, Uharawa,* and *Ungwira*. They assimilated with those they found in Nkhamanga and intermarried with them.

Enthronement of Chikulamayembe as Chief

Tradition says that Karonga Mzizi as Paramount Chief gathered all the chiefs and told them his intention to make Chikulamayembe Chief of those who wanted to stay in Nkhamanga, since Karonga had indicated his intention to move on to other lands. All the chiefs accepted the idea. The day came when Karonga Mzizi installed Chikulamayembe as Chief. The people gave the new Chief all sorts of gifts including hoes, which were being removed from the handles. It is from here that the name "Chikulamayembe" was born. He himself did not make hoes, but he might have been bringing hoes from across the lake to exchange with ivory in Nkhamangaland.

Exploration of the South

Tradition further says that Karonga Mzizi selected some people to explore the land in the South. Among those selected were *Kanyenda Chilimanyungu*, a cousin to Karonga, and his younger brother *Kabunduli*

Chiŵiŵi as leaders. The explorers left Nkhamanga and crossed the Rukuru and Kasitu rivers. They went through Choma hills and passed between Usiska and Kaning'ina hills.

They arrived at a place called Nguli, which is located at the place where Mwambazi and Liwawa rivers meet. They crossed the Dwambazi river. They explored the lands as they wandered around. They moved on to a place called Mankhamba and found the Akafula, who had escaped from Nkhamanga.

Then the explorers went back to Nkhamanga and reported their findings to Paramount Chief Karonga. Tradition tells us that Chitimukuru M'bemba again followed the Tonga, Achewa and Tumbuka into Nkhamangaland. At this time Kanyenda had settled at Mlowe from Chirumba. This is when he heard about Chitimukuru following them again. However, the army of Chitimukuru retreated and never followed them further.

Trekking of Karonga Mzizi to Mankhamba

Tradition has it that after the explorers reported what they found, Mzizi decided to leave Nkhamanga. He went further South as far as Mankhamba, where he founded new settlements, Chikulamayembe as a son-in-law remained in Nkhamanga as chief for those clans which stayed behind.

Kanyenda Chilimanyungu, who was cousin to Karonga and *Kabunduli Chiŵiŵi* followed Karonga Mzizi. They crossed the Rukuru and Rwambaza rivers, and passed through Choma hills in between Kaning'ina. They went southwards and arrived at Mankhamba. Here they found Akafula and dispersed them. Another tradition says that the Chewa under the Banda and the Mbewe established their settlement at Msinja near the Dzalanyama mountains. Later Chewa (Proto-Chewa) came and went to Mankhamba. Some of these assumed political leadership under the titles of Karonga Mazizi, Karonga Mazuura and Karonga Chizonzi. The other Chewa who settled at Msinja committed themselves to religious activities. Tradition says that these were the Abanda and Ambewe, from which the Lundu Kingdom emerged.

Tradition also says that after escorting Karonga to Mankhamba, Kanyenda, Kabunduli and other heads of the clans came back to Nkhamanga to look after the clans which had been left behind. Karonga told Kabunduli to control the lands in the north and Kanyenda the southern part.

Among the leaders who came back from Mankhamba some decided to move to new lands. The following clans: *Kanyenda Mwali, Kabunduli Chiŵiŵi Phiri, Lazimwanda Muzali, Zighiri Mwali* (brother to Kanyenda Chilimanyungu), *Kalimanjira Banda and Chakutuwa* and others went eastwards. Later on Chakutuwa Banda and some of his families went westwards as far as Lundazi. Likewise, *Kabunduli Chiŵiŵi*, his young brother *Thula Phiri* and *Luzimwanda* also moved eastwards as far as the Rweya river. Thula went down Kakwewa river and settled at Mzuma hill.

As time went on, Luzimwanda went to join Chakutuwa Banda at Lundazi. *Zighiri Mwale*, an elder brother to Kanyenda, came to settle at Kazando and later on went back upland. The Akapunda and Marenga came to South of Nkhata Bay and joined *Zighiri* and *Chimika* at Kazando, and they were given land for settlement. *Kalizongwe Mwale* (Saka), who was a nephew to Mwasi, settled around Tundwe hill. Later on Mwasi went back to Mzuma to his uncle's place.

He was followed by his uncle's daughter and he decided to marry her. Her name was *Kanyirani* and she bore her first child who became the great grandmother of *Mseka, Chiwayo, Marenga* and *Chimbano Msinginika*.

Tradition says that *Kalizongwe Mwali Saka* inherited the land. It further says that *Munguwu M'phiri,* brother to *Kabunduli Chiŵiŵi,* and other clans who settled at a place called Bandawanda left from there and passed through Rwambaza and Liwawa Rivers and finally settled around Chombe. Many clans settled along the *dambo* and later on some clans found other lands.

Kabunduli Chiŵiŵi by this time had already settled at Rweya, ruling all other clans. This mandate had been given to him by his elder brother *Karonga Mzizi*. The Kabunduli dynasty still has its headquarters at Lueya, Mzenga, to this day.

Movement of Kanyenda and other Clans from Thete

Tradition tells us that Kanyenda Chilimanyungu Mwali and other Phiri clans also left Thete, just as his cousin Kabunduli had done earlier. The leading clans which joined Kanyenda Chilimanyungu to move southwards were *Kaluluma M'phiri* who settled north of Kasungu; *Chulu M'phiri* who settled around Mtenje, and *Chilowa Mphiri* and *Mkanda, who* found their settlement lands westwards at places now called Kasungu.

151

Zowole Mwali and *Kanyenda Mchinga* moved further and settled in a sandy region. *Kalimanjila Mwale* chose to settle in Ntchisi with other Banda clans. *Malenga Chanzi M'banda* and *Kawelama* settled in Nkhotakota. *Kanyenda Chilimanyungu* himself and some of his clans such as *Mbuna Mwali* and *Chitezi Mwali* finally settled around Bua river. They cultivated crops along the Bua valley which gave them fertile soil. In other years the Bua river came with floods. A lagoon into the lake carried part of Kanyenda's village. People found themselves on an island which was floating. The lagoon carried them to the other side of the lake, what we now call Mozambique. *Chitezi* and *Mbuna* followed their clans and settled on the other side in Mozambique. The clans which were lost in Mozambique never came back.

Knowing the danger of settling around the river, Chief Kanyenda Chilimanyangu moved to higher lands with the remaining clans. The new place was called Nkhunga.

The Sporadic Settlement of Tonga Clans

Paramount Chief Karonga Mzizi and other clans moved further south as far as Mankhamba. His brother Kabunduli Chiŵiŵi ruled the clans, which were left in the north. Those who settled at Nkhamanga were ruled by the son-in-law called Chikulamayembe Kanyenda. Chilimanyungu, who was a cousin to both Karonga Mzizi and Kabunduli Chiŵiŵi also left with other prominent Tonga and Chewa clans to settle in Kasungu, Ntchisi and other places in the central part of Malawi. Kanyenda himself finally settled at Bua and later on at Nkhunga. The Akapunda Marenga joined Zighiri and Chimika at Kazando. Zighiri Mwase was an elder brother of Kanyenda Chilimanyunga.

The settlement of the people was sporadic. They were inter-related through patrilineal systems of marriage. The title of Karonga and its chieftaincy were sustained throughout generations. The movements of the clans were gradual and in different groups. Other chieftaincies were also established such as Mankhambira, Mkumbira and M'bwana.

A Critique of the Legend

Although this history sounds like a story, it still gives us an idea about Tonga origins and relationships. It is an etiology that tells us how things have become to be as they are now.

It is not difficult to make the distinction between the unwritten and the written literature of the Tonga People. Very little is in written form, and the oral literature is still being transmitted from one generation to another. The other reason is that in the north, the missionaries of Livingstonia mission in the 1920s confirmed the status of Tumbuka as a main language by introducing school texts in the Tumbuka language. It was thought that Lakeside Tonga was a language so similar to Tumbuka that it could not readily be used as a distinctive cultural symbol for an ideology of Tonga ethnic identity.[5] I think that this was a wrong assumption. The Tumbuka people have found the Tonga language very difficult to speak and assimilate, albeit certain customs and words may be similar.

According to the categories of Tonga oral literature discussed in Chapter 3, this story is a good example of a legend. Van Velsen published a monograph based on field investigation among the Lakeside Tonga. The main critical point that van Velsen makes on Tonga oral history is that *Kabunduli,* who was *Karonga's* brother, came with his own party. *Kabunduli* initially settled in Tongaland. The rivalry between the *Phiri* and the *Kapunda/Banda* is central to van Velsen's analysis. He sees myths as charters for existing social relationships. Van Velsen shows that legends like this one can explain and validate present social and political relations in terms of the past. Caution is therefore needed in treating them as historical evidence.[6] It can be argued here that such a version of oral tradition was used to validate claims to positions for the benefit of the colonial rulers. The legend can also be seen as an aetiology, to shed light on the origins of the Tonga clans.

In speaking about the moral aspect of this legend, it can be noted that the great doings of Karonga Mzizi (Mazizi) and Chiŵiŵi give what is an allegorical discussion of morality and human frailty. It is combined with a dazzling account of Karonga's abilities to fight, endure and use his wits. Through this ability to perform as well as fight, the hero lives on as the leader of his people. Again and again his doings are associated with the genesis and flourishing of his people. The Tonga narrators claim that this legend depicts their true history. The people I interviewed on different days were very flexible and relaxed. I could see the difference between presenting a legend and an ordinary story. In narrating the legend, they were very factual.

---

5   Leroy Vail (ed), *The Creation of Tribalism in Southern Africa*, Berkeley and Los Angeles: University of California Press, 1989, pp. 157-164.

6   Jan van Velsen, "Notes on the History of the Lakeside Tonga of Nyasaland," *African Studies*, 18, (1959), pp. 105-111.

As society changes, some of the old ways of life inevitably give way to new ones. Much of the oral literature that is performed today, or that is preserved in books, reflects a life-style that may have served the earlier generations well but would be considered outmoded or even dangerous today. The contemporary generation may respond to the contents of the material with nostalgia and perhaps pride, but it is clear that things are no longer what they used to be.

However, the story of *Karonga Mzizi (Mazizi)* among the Tonga people is essentially the story of a powerful and fearless warrior, who rescued his people from the tyranny of a foreign usurper (*Chitimukuru*) and went on to consolidate the Karonga dynasty. The chieftaincy of *Kabunduli* in Nkhata Bay today is marked by a continuity with the Karonga dynasty. *Karonga Mzizi (Mazizi)* had the privilege of being a winner; his acts of courage and fortitude are still recounted even today by the *Kabunduli Phiri* Tonga. The society has a great regard for those who took great risks to achieve whatever they had in a world where might was regarded as right, a world filled with the sheer physical danger of war. Among the Tonga people such courage is upheld as a praiseworthy ideal and the most fearsome warriors are set up as the standards to be emulated. Some of these ideals may have much relevance today, disgrace is no less unattractive now than it was in the days of *Karonga Mzizi*. The Tonga youths who listen to these stories are expected to take as much from them as is relevant to their own present day situations, while, of course, avoiding reckless violent actions. War is no longer an ideal to be looked up to in present-day democratic Malawi.

(2) Origin of Death (Chameleon and Lizard)

When Chiuta had sat on his mighty chair he thought of what to do for men on earth. He planned that when men die they should come back to life and live again. Thus, after a considerable time of thought, he called the Chameleon and said, "Chameleon, I very much count on you as my messenger. Each time I send you down to the earth you carry out your mission. When I send the Lizard he spends his time thinking about women or basking in the sun. Now I would like you, Chameleon, to go down to the earth and tell men that they will not die. When they die they will come back to life again.

The Chameleon started off its journey to men on earth. You know how the Chameleon moves. Slowly, slowly and slowly the Chameleon went to the earth. Several years had passed but the Chameleon had not yet returned to

154

Chiuta. Chiuta became very worried and asked himself, "What has happened to the Chameleon? What actually has caused his delay?"

Chiuta called the Lizard and said to him, "I am very worried. I fear. I don't know what to do. I had sent out the Chameleon to the earth and years and years have elapsed. I don't know whether the message has reached men on earth. Probably he died on the way. I know that he is indeed very slow. Now, I have thought that you should follow him. Let him tell you the message. Then you carry the message down to men on earth. I know that you are the fastest animal here."

The Lizard swiftly went down to the earth. Within a short time he found the Chameleon still walking very slowly. And by this time they were a number of kilometres before the earth. The Chameleon was sweating all over. He looked as if he had just come out of a swimming pool. The Lizard felt very sorry for the Chameleon, although he (the Lizard) mocked him, "You, Chameleon, you left Chiuta's dwelling place a long time ago and you haven't yet reached men on earth! Don't you know that the life-giver is very worried? Let's not waste time, for I have been sent too. Just you tell me the message I am to tell men on earth." Since the Chameleon was very tired, he just said, "Go and tell them that they shall not die."

As the Lizard received the message while running, he heard, "People will die." So then, the Lizard hurried to deliver the message. He did not know that he had wrongly heard the Chameleon. Since then men never come back to life again.[7]

Comments on "Origin of Death"

This is another myth which is common to Tonga oral literature. It is known to a cross-section of the Tonga people. The myth is also shared by other ethnic groups in Malawi. Useful comparison with the Tonga text can be made with two similar narratives in Sena, collected by Matthew Schoffeelers:

---

[7] This myth was narrated to me by different people in several versions: Richard Chiya Phiri maintains that the characters are Lizard and Chameleon, Lile Nyachirwa maintains that the characters are Hare and Tortoise; Kanyama 'Chiŵiŵi Mwasi has it as Lizard and Chameleon, but Bright Zgawowa Mphande has it as Baboon and Chameleon. The message it carries is the same. (Recorded in October, 1994 at different occasions. The narrators were very imaginative and creative).

Lizard and the Cause of Eternal Death (Sena)

When God created everything, he told the lizard and chameleon that they could make a wish, and that whoever was the first to reach him would have his wish fulfilled. When the people heard this they suggested to Chameleon, who was, they believed, the faster of the two, that he should ask God to allow everyone to return after death and live again on earth. Lizard, who was thought to be the slower runner, was told to ask that every creature who died should stay dead.

To everyone's dismay, however, Lizard proved by far the faster runner. He reached God swiftly and told him that the people below did not want to return after death, and God agreed to grant this wish. On his way back, Lizard met Chameleon and told him the news. Sadly, Chameleon decided to return without seeing God. And from that day everyone—Africans, Asians, Europeans—and all animals and living things die and stay dead forever.

Bat as the Cause of Eternal Death (Sena)

Long ago Chameleon and Lizard were discussing death. Chameleon said, "I want people to return after they have died." But Lizard felt there was so much trouble in the world that the dead should remain in their graves forever. This resulted in a serious quarrel which lasted many days.

Now there was a wicked animal called Bat, who decided to take advantage of this quarrel and use it against Man. He approached Lizard and Chameleon and said, "Quarrels are no good, they lead to nothing. God has sent me to tell you that you must go and see him, and the one who arrives first will have his proposal accepted." Now, everyone knows that the chameleon is a slow animal: by the time he reached God, Lizard's proposal had already been accepted.

God was angry with Bat for playing this wicked trick, and he cursed it, saying, "Since you are thoroughly evil you will never again see the light of day but will only move at night." Chameleon he blessed with these words: "Because of your kindheartedness you will share my power." Lizard, however, was neither cursed nor blessed, for he is neither good nor bad.[8]

A structural model can be suggested in these myths like that treated in Chapter One, on the two Biblical texts ("*A Patriarch, his Wife and a Foreign Ruler*," and on "*Welcome to Strangers*"). The Malawian texts are "*Horned Chameleon*," the "*Origin of Life*," and "*Kalikalanje I*," and "*Kalikalanje II*." Some elements called motives stimulate us to identify a possible applicable

---

8   Matthew Schoffeleers and A.A. Roscoe, *Land of Fire*, pp. *23-25.*

structural analysis which follows that of Alan Dunde's schemata applied to American Indian tales.[9]

Luck: Chiuta wants to tell men that they should not die, or if they die they must come back to life again.

Task: Men on earth should be told by the chameleon.

Interdiction: The chameleon should not be slow to deliver the message of immortality.

Violation: The chameleon moves slowly and slowly to reach men on earth.

Consequences: Men did not receive the will of Chiuta/God.

Luck: Someone faster than the chameleon should go to earth.

Deception: Bat claims that God has sent him to tell them to see God.

Consequence: Bat is to be blind because of deceit.

Task accomplished: Lizard reaches men before the chameleon.

Luck liquidated: Men on earth have received the will of Chiuta but it is altered.

Task accomplished: Chameleon reaches men on earth too late.

Luck liquidated: Men learn that Chiuta desired them not to die.

Consequence: Men die and never come back to life again.

The Tonga and the two Sena versions all have the Lizard and the Chameleon as characters, except one Sena story that has a Bat. In one Sena story the Chameleon is blessed because of its kind-heartiness. In the Tonga and Sena versions, the Chameleon is blamed for causing eternal death. And though even here Chameleon's special favour with God and man is apparent, he is partly responsible for the visit's failure and the wrong message being delivered, with the result that the dead must stay dead. Schoffeleers observes that this is the use of symbolic doubles, a device common in oral literature and used to express negative feelings about a centrally important figure, (God himself in this case), which it would be difficult, or dangerous, to express more directly.[10]

---

[9] Alan Dundes, *Morphology of North American Indian Folktales*, Helsinki: Folklore Fellows Communications no. 195, (1964), pp. 52-60.

[10] Matthew Schoffeleers and A.A. Roscoe, *Land of Fire*, p. 28.

The details of the three versions of a myth might be due to some oral variants. It appears to be one of the travelling myths. The lizard's point of view is understandable. Its interest lies in the fact that it is a fairly isolated expression of the argument in favour of man accepting permanent death and never returning to live on earth. With chameleon very much in favour of having death made only temporary, the lizard's view adds a nice dialectical balance, which is useful for the story's structure. The intervention of the bat in the other story seems to indicate that God is sympathetic to man's desire for rebirth. His anger with the bat suggests this view-point. God blesses the chameleon who represents the rebirth view-point.

In the Tonga setting the myth is an instance of the belief that God can have an interaction with people on earth. The chameleon, however, is detested for his part in bringing death into the world.

Through such myths, the Tonga people are able to ritualize and describe the emotional and religious contents of their relationship with life and death. Death and the here-after are symbolic representations of the freedom and liberation in the here and now. The fear of death is therefore minimized as death becomes the symbol of courage, hope, and liberation. The similarities in these three myths show some cultural unity with other Malawian ethnic groups.

(3) Cursing the Birds

Long ago, Blackbird, Ringdove, and many of the other birds met together. Ringdove opened the conversation by asking, "Here, where we are all together, who is the most beautiful?" The birds answered: "Blackbird is the only beautiful one. How very black he is!" Then Ringdove said to himself: "I am going to ask Blackbird for a potion for medicine that will make me as beautiful as he is." He implored Blackbird, saying, "Change me, so that we may be alike." Blackbird promised to give him a potion the next day, when the birds of all species would be together. Ringdove was very grateful, and said: "I shall be very thankful to be like you."

The next day all the birds were gathered, feeding in the cool of the morning. Blackbird came to where they were assembled, and said: "Ringdove, you are wanting a potion?" "Yes," he replied. Blackbird said: "Come here," and putting his finger around Ringdove's neck, he made the black ring, which Ringdove still wears today. All the birds were astounded. Then another bird asked for the same, and Blackbird said: "What will you give me in return?" All the birds answered: "If only you will make us all beautiful as you, you can do whatever you want to us." Blackbird then told them: "Tomorrow I will give you all a potion, so that you will be black."

The next day, Blackbird rose early and went into the forest where he found Guinea Fowl eating termites out of the ground. He was offended that this was so unclean. "What are you eating?" he asked. Guinea Fowl answered: "Termites." Then Blackbird said: "You begged a potion from me, while you eat dirty insects. I can't help one such as you." Then she cursed the bird: "Guinea Fowl, I will give you a speckled coat, so that you resemble a leopard, and when a leopard finds you, he will devour you - all because you do not eat properly, as I do. And you, Francolin, you shall be red about the mouth and on the head, and you shall always eat the grain belonging to others. You shall be trapped by people and they will bring you trouble. All the birds who begged from me, I gave them in the same manner, things good for them or things not good for them."

Thereupon Ringdove, whose neck had been encircled, was also cursed, and told: "And you, too, Ringdove, you shall always eat the grain belonging to me, so that you may die. All the birds I condemn, because they begged for potions, saying, 'Let us be like Blackbird,' whereas in truth they do not resemble me at all, they do not act as I act, nor eat as I eat. To make you look like me is simply impossible. I refuse." So, although Ringdove has colour around its neck where Blackbird's finger encircled it, in that alone they are alike. As for the rest of the birds, they are in trouble, they are killed, they are ensnared, and they are persecuted. Some are caught in traps. And all because they were cursed by Blackbird.[11]

Comments on "Cursing the Birds"

This could be one of the travelling stories. But this is not to say that there are no stories which can be traced as having been introduced from outside. This could have come in long ago and has taken on a distingly Tonga colouring. Such Tonga folktales in this study include "The Five Helpers" (Tale 18), "An Eye for an Eye" (Tale 21), and "The Beaultiful Proud Girl" (Tale 32). It is possible that some of those tales were imported from East and South Africa. Some of the Tonga people have been adventurous to go as far as East Africa to work there. It is possible that through their interactions with other people they exchanged elements of culture.

In this story we see betrayal in "Cursing the Birds." The first thing, which strikes the listener about the story is the feature of bird-characters, or

---

[11] Source: Narrated by Lile Nyachirwa of Chiphumbulu, Dwambazi. Dictated on October 4, 1994.

159

animal characters. Although they reveal traditional people's scientific curiosity about their environment, they are, as a rule, not the most fruitful genre to explore, unless such animal behaviour explained makes a statement on the human condition as it happens in this story. The dignified Blackbird (*Mnthenku*) determines how the various other birds, all of whom wanted to change their appearance, should look. We can telescope the event in any way we feel. However, we react, at the ending of the story: "*For the rest of the birds, they are in trouble, they are killed, they are snared, they are persecuted, some are caught in traps. And all because they were cursed by Blackbird.*"

The occasion for the curse is unexplained in the story, but details of it are certainly understood by a Tonga audience. Symbolically, the curse is meant to warn people against envy. Like in Adam's curse for disobedience (Gen 3:17), where the ground is cursed, Cain is cursed from the earth for killing his brother Abel, for envy and jealousy (Gen 4:11). Thus, sustenance out of the earth is here withheld from him. In our story, there are some members of the society who are envious. These are represented by several characters such as Ringbird and Guinea Fowl.

It is vain to wish to change one's colouration simply because of envy. The Blackbird is also disgusted by those who do not eat correctly, for it is only through proper eating that culture can be manifested. The story also symbolically shows how physical or natural differences come into being and are maintained in dramatic opposition. It is, in the deepest sense, an entertainment about the way human life is. This also shows that things come apart, but never quietly and passively. The dissolution is to be discussed, argued about and entered into knowingly.

The main targets in the story as represented in the characters may be chiefs, clergy, politicians, senior civil servants, or bureaucrats of the society. Thus, the story gives us a profound insight into how society is structured. There are some members of the society who do not conform to the standards of behaviour expected of them, since their envy and greed are deadly examples for human society.

(4) The Role of the Aged

A long time ago there lived an old chief. He was bald, thin and weak. He had bad eyesight, too, because of his old age. In his village there were several other old people like him. These could not do any useful work. All the necessary work was being done by young men. One day, one of the young men said to the others, "Friends, why do we trouble ourselves by feeding these old good-for-nothing men? We don't even profit a thing when we toil for them. Why can't we just kill them all and elect a young chief of our own age?" All the young men supported his suggestion except one that loved his old father so much that he was very unwilling to kill him. At dusk he took his father away and hid him in a small hut in the bush.

The next morning, the young men killed every old person of the village, apart from the old man who was hidden in the hut. Then the young men greatly feasted over the death of the old men. They ate a lot of food, danced and drunk pots and pots of beer until they became too drank and went to sleep.

But as they woke up the next morning, they heard an alarm from the chief's home. They all flocked to the chief's village to see what had happened. As soon as they reached the chief's village they saw a huge snake with twelve heads that had coiled itself around the new chief's neck and hung its heads right above the centre of the chief's head. The young men tried all sorts of ways to remove the snake from the chief's neck but failed. At first they wanted to kill it with spears and arrows. But they were afraid of killing the chief too.

Later on, after they had failed to get rid of the snake, they started to complain, "We are now left witless. What shall we do? Our chief will die. We were fools. We killed all our old people who had the wisdom we now seriously need. They surely would have found a solution to kill the snake."

Suddenly, the young man who had hidden his old father said to them, "Listen to me. It is a pity that you killed all your old relatives. I for one did not kill my old father. He is there up in the bush. If you promise that you will not kill him, when I bring him here, I will do so. He might be able to kill the snake." All the young men desperately promised that they would not kill the old man. They implored his son to immediately go and fetch him.

As soon as the old man arrived, the young men were filled with joy and respect. The old man took a mouse, a frog and a grasshopper and tied each one of them to strings. He threw the creatures towards the snake. When the snake saw the mouse, the frog and the grasshopper, it very slowly uncoiled itself and crawled towards the creatures. The chief was set free. The young men then killed the snake. They were all full of joy and celebrated their success. They regretted that they had killed all the old folk.[12]

Comments on the "Role of the Aged"

This story is placed in the group of stories reflecting upon how things were in the beginning. As a matter of convention the scene is set for tricksters by reminding the audience at the start of a narrative that at the beginning of time everything in nature was harmonious. Everyone was friendly to everyone else. The story should be seen in the light of some Chewa versions. *"When the Young Men Seized Power"* collected by Matthew Schoffeleers. One version is fairly long. For the sake of comparison I shall adopt a shorter one here:

When the Young Men Seized Power (Chewa)

> The young people, being tired of the old King and old people in general as being opposed to "modern ways," kill them all and elect a young King. One young man, however, manages to save the life of his grandfather by taking him to the forest, where he builds a small hut for him. One evening, when the young King, after a long day's hunting, goes to sleep, a python, said to be the spirit of those murdered, coils itself around his body. Not knowing how to kill the snake without at the same time killing the Chief, the young man who saved his grandfather's life goes to him to tell him what has happened. The old man decides to come. He collects some frogs, which he put in a pouch made of squirrel skin. By-standers are terrified, thinking he is a ghost or a sorcerer. Having made the python come out from the Chief's body by means of the frogs, he kills it with a single gunshot and then turns on the bystanders challenging them to kill him, if they dare. At this point the young King interferes and warns them not to try so foolish a thing. He apologizes to the old man for the killings and asks him to come and live once again in his former village. The old man then says that the abomination of the young has to be expiated by a sacrifice to the spirits of those that have been killed, following which he is rewarded with money and many other gifts.

There are more than two versions of the same story. One aspect in the text is the qualities that people might seek in an ideal Chief and the responsibili-

---

[12] Source: This story was narrated to me by Modi Muwamba, at her home, Njasa village on October 11 1994. She also explained to me some Tonga taboos recorded in Chapter 5.

ties that go with the job. Similar features that appear in the two versions are as below.[13]

The Role of the Aged (Tonga)	When the Youth Seized Power (Chewa)
There lived an old Chief, bald, thin and weak with bad eyesight	There lived an old King
Young men had to all the work	Young people being tired of the old king
Young men revolted and killed the Chief and all old people	Young people killed the old king and old people.
One young man hid his old father in a hut in the bush.	One young man saved the life of his grandfather by taking him to the forest and hid him in a hut
Young men elected a young Chief	Young people elected a young King
A huge snake with twelve heads coiled around the new Chief's neck	A python, said to be the spirit of those murdered, coiled itself around the young King's body.
Young men tried to rescue the Chief and failed	Nobody knew how to kill snake
The young man who did not kill his old father revealed the secret and was implored to bring his father	The young man who saved his grandfather's life went and told him what had happened.
The old man took a mouse, a frog and a grasshopper.	The old man collected some frogs which he put in a bag made of squirrel skin.
When the old man arrived the young men were filled with joy and respect	Bystanders were terrified, thinking he was a ghost or a sorcerer.
He threw the creatures towards the King's body.	Having seen the frogs the snake left the Chief.
When the snake saw the frog and the grasshopper it uncoiled from the Chief's neck.	
The Chief was set free. The young killed the snake.	The old man shot the snake with a gun.

---

13   Matthew Schoffeleers and A.A. Roscoe, *Land of Fire*, pp. 64-76.

They were full of joy and celebrated their success.	
	The old man challenged the young men to kill him if they dared.
	The young King warned them not to do such a foolish thing.
They regretted that they had killed the old people	They apologized to the old man for the killing of the old people.
	The old man asked the young people to offer sacrifices to appease the spirits of the dead.
	The old man was rewarded with money and other gifts.

The similarities and differences in the two versions are clear. The Chewa story is more cultic than the Tonga tale, because of the sacrificial element in order to appease the spirits. In most cases the characters are similar. However, the Tonga version has an "old father," in the Chewa version it is the "old grandfather." The Tonga uses the title "Chief," while the Chewa version uses the title "King." The setting of the Chewa version seems to be more modern. The old grandfather uses a gun, a modern weapon, to kill the snake. The causes of the revolt are different in both versions. In the Tonga text, the cause of the revolt is that the old people could not do any useful work. In the shorter Chewa version the young people are tired with the old King and the old people as being opposed to modern ways.

The symbolism used is the snake which appears in both versions. It is a twelve-headed snake in the Tonga tale, and a python in the Chewa version. In its cultic use the snake symbolically represents the spirit of one who was murdered. The symbolism of a snake in Tonga is also linked with the spirit of the dead. In returning to the land of the living, spirits are supposed most commonly to take other than human forms. They might visit their former haunts in the form of snakes, lions, leopards, crocodiles, or birds. If some few days after the burial of a person a snake is seen to hunt around, the relatives have no doubt about its being the deceased relative risen under this form. Various snakes might be so regarded, but the one most generally believed to be a spirit-form is *Mlinga*, a short, stubby, blackish, non-poisonous snake.

The frog, the mouse (Chewa), and the grasshopper (Tonga) might be symbols of the younger generation. In the Tonga version, the young ones confess that they had been foolish by killing the elders. In the Chewa version, the old one comes back with vengeance and forces the young, once again, into submission.

The major contrast between the Tonga and Chewa versions is that in the Tonga one, the snake coils around the neck of the King while he is in his house. However, in the Chewa version, the young Chief is under the tree. Schoffeleers feels that the tree represents male symbols, the female symbols focus on the house.[14] This observation does not apply to Tonga society which is patrilineal, unless the story originated from the matrilineal Chewa. The second problem concerns the nature of conflict. In the Chewa version the charge is that the old guys do not accept the "modern ways." What are these modern ways? Are they Western values (schools, scientific ideas)? The Tonga version is implicit on this. It says, "These could not do any useful work." However, from the findings of my field studies the Tonga customs have been suppressed by Western values. Traditionally, Tonga elders are to be respected for their wisdom and guidance.

(5) Quality of Friendship

Once upon a time, there were two young men, each named Kamzunguzeni, who heard about each other, but had never seen each other, as one lived in the East and one in the West. The young man from the West went to the man who told fortunes to tell what lies ahead, and said, "I want to go over and see my friend whom I have never seen, and I want to know whether I will meet good or bad luck." The diviner looked into his mirror, and told him that if he went to see his friend, he would not find him at home, but would meet him on the path, and that when he reached the country of his friend, he must not go out at night, no matter who called, because if he did, he would surely die and never be able to return home.

Not satisfied with what the fortune-teller had said, the young man went to another, who had a similar mirror and then told him the same thing that the first fortune-teller had told him. Hearing the same words from two different fortune-tellers, he finally believed them, and said, "I will now go to see my friend, but I will keep in mind what I have been told."

He walked three days and met his friend, but, of course, he did not recognize him, and he asked the other where he was going. The young man

---

14 Ibid., p. 66.

from the East answered: "My name is Kamzunguzeni, I am going to see my friend in the West, who is also named Kamzunguzeni." The young man from the West replied, "That's me! I was going to see you." So Kamzunguzeni from the East said: "You have walked three days and I have only walked one. Come back with me to my place."

Whereupon both Kamzunguzeni went east together. On the night they arrived, a big snake swallowed Kamzunguzeni of the East. Then Kamzunguzeni cried from within the belly of the big snake until Kamzunguzeni of the West heard him and woke up. He wanted to help his friend, but he remembered that the fortune-tellers had told him that he must not go out at night. He sat down, but thought to himself, "I know I'll meet trouble if I go out, but how can I stay when my friend is in distress? And so he went outside and found that the snake had swallowed all but the head of his friend. Taking his knife, then, Kamzunguzeni from the West killed the snake by ripping his mouth open. In doing so, some of the blood from the snake flew into his eyes and he at once became blind.

Now Kamzunguzeni from the East went to find a fortune-teller. The man looked at his mirror, and told him, "You have one son; go and cut his throat, and take his blood for your friend to wash his face, and then his sight will be restored." Kamzunguzeni from the East went home and killed his son. Kamzunguzeni from the West washed his face in the blood of his friend's son, and immediately his sight was restored and his trouble was at an end.

Who was the greater friend, Kamzunguzeni of the East or Kamzunguzeni of the West?[15]

Comments on "The Quality of Friendship"

This story should be seen as a representation of twins. This is symbolized in the names "Kamzunguzeni of the East" and "Kamzunguzeni of the West." Both have the same intention of meeting each other. Also, the two fortune-tellers have similar mirrors and tell all the same things. The story should also be seen in relation to symmetrical as well as unilateral human beings. Its link to symmetry seems to symbolize lawlessness, which is provided by human twinship. Twins are therefore symmetrical. The relationship of twins to unilateral, or one-sided figures also symbolically addresses diversity of

---

[15] Source: This story was narrated to me by 'Chiŵiŵi Kanyama Mwase at his home, Mtepelela village, on 8.10.1994. He is one of the primary sources of information.

human problems, spiritual as well as social and biological. Therefore, twins, half-men and the gods can be grouped logically with another.

There are many stories told in Tonga society, which show that unilaterally mutilated people can also address a diversity of human problems, spiritual as well as social and biological. For example, there is a story about a large bird (*Chiyuni*) with a half-head, one eye, one wing, one leg and one toe which created a great river, or lake and sometimes a great mountain.

The birth of twins in a Tonga family is accompanied by several beliefs, rituals and taboos. Some parents think that to have twins is a punishment by God or ancestral spirits. In such a case they offer sacrifices or perform some rituals to appease the ancestors so that all should be well with the twins. They may attempt to make twins undergo certain rites in order to make them different from each other. For instance, if one twin-child dies, the parents and relatives are prohibited from mourning the child, because such a sound invites immediate death to the living twin. Sometimes the mother and the twins go through a kind of bath ritual so that the mother should not repeat bearing twins. Twins are also tied up with the idea of impurity.[16] When twinship is associated with rituals, the twins fit into the ideal model of social structure. This is confirmed by Turner when he states,

> One often finds in human cultures that structural contradictions, asymmetries and anomalies are overlaid by layers of myth, rituals and symbols, which stress the axiomatic value of key structural principals with regard to the very situations where these appear to be most inoperative.[17]

Turner concludes with the observation that the Ndembu, in the symbolic idiom of the twinship ritual, have elected to emphasize the aspect of opposition and complementarity, the equal but opposite aspect of duality. They think of a coincidence of opposites rather than of a doubling of similars. Turner also thinks that the Ndembu use sexual symbolism to represent the process by which social forces approximately equal in strength and opposite in quality are exhibited as working in harmony.[18] In sum, twins are held to be dangerous because they embody a set of

---

[16] The Tonga attitude towards purity and impurity has been fully discussed in Chapter Five.

[17] V.W. Turner, *The Ritual Process*, Ithaca, New York: Cornell Paperbacks, 1977, p. 47. In discussing 'ritual theory' in Chapter One, I made a reflection on Turner's view in "The Ritual Process," and its relation to myth.

[18] Ibid., p. 50.

paradoxes which run counter to the existing social, cultural and classificatory order.

Twins share the same motif with that of the unilateral beings. For the sake of similarities and differences the story of *Kansabwe* from Lomwe society is a good example:

Kansabwe (Lomwe)

Once upon a time there lived a beaultiful girl whose name was Kawala or the Shining One. Many young men came to seek her hand in marriage, but she refused them all. One day, however, she fell ill. The best herbalists were called in, but none could help and her condition grew steadily worse, her lovely body shrinking to skin and bone. Handsome young men came no longer.

In the end her father decided to call in a herbalist from a different country, who enjoyed great fame and would, so everybody said, be able to cure her. But the jouney would be dangerous. As was to be expected, nobody volunteered to go. But just when the father had decided to give up in despair, a young man presented himself who said he was prepared to go. His name was Kansabwe (Little Louse), and the name bespoke his appearance, for he was dirty and covered in rags. The father was taken aback, for, like everyone else, he had always considered the boy a disgrace to the village, but there being nobody else, he accepted the offer.

Kansabwe went on his way, crossing rivers and traversing forests. Wild beasts attacked him. He lost an eye, and one of his legs was so badly mauled by a leopard that he would have to limp for the rest of his life. Yet he arrived and was able to convey his message. Fortunately, the way back was much easier, as the herbalist had great magical powers. Streams were crossed with the greatest of ease, and before Kansabwe knew it, they had already arrived back home.

The herbalist administered the medicine and soon Kawala's health and beauty had been restored. Once again she was sought by handsome youths and wealthy nobles. All of them were told to come back on an appointed day when she would finally make her choice. When that day arrived the village was crowded with suitors. So many came that the Chief ordered them to form a queue, which soon stretched into the fields beyond the village. Kansabwe, one of the first to arrive since he lived in the village, was rudely pushed to the end of the queue, and even there he was forced to keep his distance from the others, as everyone shunned him.

The arrangement was that suitors had to present themselves one by one until Kawala made her choice. The first one went in, and then the second, but each returned after only a few minutes, the smile gone from his face. The same happened to the others. Finally, by the end of the day the last entered, delighted that he had defeated his rivals, for there could no longer be any doubt that he was the lucky one.

But unfortunately, when the door opened, it was clear from the last man's face that he wasn't the lucky one either. Not knowing what to make of this, the suitors all looked at one another in amazement. And while they were doing this, Kansabwe began to limp towards the door. Seeing him, they booed and jeered, but he ignored them. Again, eyes were fixed on the door, this time to see Kansabwe being thrown out. But nothing of the sort happened. After a while, however, the door opened and there he was with Kawala! "You may be surprised," she said, "that I have chosen this poor man to be my husband. Yet I have not done it without reason. For when I was ill, he alone did not desert me and even risked his life to save me. Therefore he alone, and nobody else, is worthy to become my husband." Kansabwe was then taken to be bathed and dressed in new clothes. And all the others went home, too ashamed to say a word.[19]

The patterns of the stories can be shown in a chart as below:

Kamzunguzeni (Twins) (Tonga)	Kansabwe (Unilateral) (Lomwe)
Two young men, of the same name Kamzunguzeni, heard about each other and intended to see each other.	
Kamzunguzeni from the West consulted two fortune-tellers how to get to Kamzunguzeni of the East	Father consulted Herbalist to cure Kawala, the beautiful girl, from her illness
Both fortune-tellers used a similar device and gave some advice that the journey would be dangerous.	Father decided to call a famous herbalist from a different country, but the journey would be dangerous.
After walking for three days	A Young man, Kamsabwe, volunteered to go.
Kamzunguzeni from the West met Kamzunguzeni from the East and they introduced each other.	He crossed rivers and traversed forests.

---

19 Mathew Schoffeleers and A.A. Roscoe, *Land of Fire*, pp. 135-137.

169

In the night a big snake swallowed all but the head of Kamzunguzeni from the East. He cried out from the belly of the snake.	On his way the wild beasts attacked him.
Kamzunguzeni from the West killed the snake by ripping its mouth open. The blood of the snake spilled into his eyes.	Kansabwe lost an eye and one of his legs. He would have to limp for the rest of his life.
A fortune-teller told Kamzunguzeni from the East to kill his son and use the son's blood to cure his friend. He did so.	Kansabwe consulted the herbalist and both went back easily through the herbalist's magic powers
Kamzunguzeni from the West washed his face in the blood of his friend's son. Immediately his sight was restored	The herbalist administered the medicine. Kawala was cured and her beauty was restored.
	Kawala was once again sought by handsome youths, but all were refused. She chose Kansabwe to be her husband. Kansabwe was taken to be bathed and dressed in new clothes.

The obvious difference is that, in the Lomwe text, *Kansabwe* was searching for a wife, while in the Tonga text *Kamzunguzeni* was searching for a twin brother. Both stories are strongly heroic and didactic. The Tonga tale is a good example of dilemma tales. The use of a mirror by fortune-tellers seems to suggest destruction of time. In the story "Who Performed the Best" (Tale 18), one of the brothers uses a mirror in order to destroy time, the others destroy distance and death. The forest through which the heroes travel is clearly the world beyond the real world, where a spiritual transformation can take place. In both accounts the "fortune-tellers" (Tonga) and the "herbalist" (Lomwe), may represent supernatural powers. The heroes find the magicians and the medicine. In the case of *Kansabwe* the sick girl is restored to life. In the Tonga tale, the blind *Kamzunguzeni* is cured.

However, each protagonist at his own initiative subjects himself to a process during which his body becomes asymmetrical (mutilated) and by this heroic act a societal crisis is solved. Similarly in Tale 17 the three boys, through the use of use of a pair of sandals, solve a death crisis. In the Tonga text there is an immoral act when one of the twins kills his son in order to cure the blindness of his friend. The father has no right to take the life of his child. Here, the act seems to demonstrate love for a friend. Abraham's story can illustrate this point when God asks him to kill his son Isaac, though this was not done (Gen 22:1-13).

In the Kansabwe story, when Kawala is restored to her great beauty, she is surrounded by a throng of potential husbands who are all rivals to each other. Schoffeleers observes that Kawala's illness symbolically suggests that the "community is in the throes of a crisis: though in principle marriageable, she is *de facto* not marriageable. At the height of the crisis a marginal character presents himself to find a solution."[20]

In both texts there is a ritual aspect. In symbolic terms, when *Kamzunguzeni* washes his face in the blood of his friends's son, the act becomes a purification ritual. Likewise, when *Kansabwe* is given a bath and new clothes, it becomes a ritual means of restoring normality at the end of transitional periods such as those connected with initiation rites like puberty or mourning.

In sum, twins and unilaterally mutilated people function as symbols of rivalry and social conflict. The morality behind the two stories is that when there are crises or conflicts in society, an attempt should be made to bring a solution. The society needs heroes or heroines who can show their love through sacrifice in order to make the society workable, when rivalry breaks through the boundaries of law and custom. When that happens moral order has to be restored and the person called upon to perfom that task must show through his or her body that he or she is not a twin or an asymmetry. The sacrificial crisis symbolized by the twins and the unilateral representative, Kansabwe, are all acts of restoring order in society.

(6) The Orphaned Millipede

There lived two young Millipedes, one of these was rich and the other was poor. The poor one was so because he had lost his father and mother. So he was raised as an orphan by the mother of his friend.

---

20 J.M. Schoffeleers, "Twins and Unilateral Figures in Central and Southern Africa: Symmetry and Asymmetry in the Symbolization of the Sacred," *Journal of Religion in Africa*, vol. 21 (1991), pp. 345-372.

The orphaned Millipede grew up in great difficulties and sorrow because all the work of the family fell upon him. It happened that one day the mother of the rich Millipede called her son indoors. She closed the door and left the orphaned Millipede outside the door. The mother said, "Be polite and hard-working. Dig a hole when the rains are coming to the end, where you could hibernate during the cold seasons." The orphaned Millipede heard the advice from where he stood outside the door, and kept it to himself. The rich Millipede did not heed the advice, for he thought that he would always be with his mother.

The Millipede, whose mother was still alive, grew up lazily, so that he would not look after himself if he were to be left alone. All he did was to spend what his mother obtained, without the slightest care. He grew up happily in luxury, but there was one snag to this, he could not do anything at all by himself. One day his mother died too. It just happened when the rains were coming to an end. Nobody bothered to train the young Millipede in anything worth knowing. He was so arrogant that all this was fine so long as there was nothing to worry him. He did not even care to dig a hole to hide in.

When the rains came to an end the orphaned Millipede started to dig a hole for himself, the rich Millipede did nothing, just weeping and regretting the loss of his mother. There was no one to make a hole for him so that he died of cold when the cold season came. But the orphaned Millipede survived.[21]

Moral lesson: It is for this tale that the elders say: *Potiwona twa moyo mu nthowa, pamwenga mumphako, pamwenga mu mphanje, tighanaghane ndi Bongolo yuwa wenga ndi nyina yo wangureka kuvwiya mazu gha anyina.* (Whenever we see small living creatures on the way or in hollow places, we should always think about that Millipede, which did not take heed of his mother's advice).

Comments on the "Orphaned Millipede"

This story shows the oral tradition reflecting and didactically attending to the problems that arise between siblings in a given family. In particular it offers a reassuringly democratic concern for the weakest members of a group. In this case the orphaned Millipede symbolically represents the weak, the poor, the marginalized or disadvantaged in society. Along with the themes of justice, obedience and disobedience goes the fact that

---

[21] Source: This story is translated by me from *Mcapu wa Chitonga*, pp. 14-15. The author is unknown.

appearances can sometimes be misleading and consequently make people resist rather than yield. Disobedience to the advice of a mother in this story is punished by a miserable life when the cold season strikes the rich Millipede. The orphaned Millipede shows a progression from tragedy to comedy in a more subtle way: an orphan is on a pilgrimage of oppressions and triumphs. The story can be compared to that of "Kaumphawi the Orphan" in Chewa.

Kaumphawi the Orphan (Chewa)

Long ago there was a boy called Kaumphawi or 'the poor one'. His father had died when he was no more than a baby and his mother when he was about ten years old. He had been brought up by his sister, Kanana, who was married to a miserly man and who was also extremely mean herself. She treated Kaumphawi not like a brother but like a slave, giving him just enough food to keep him from starving. He was never allowed to wash himself at home but had to go to a stream, even at the coldest time of the year, as if he were a leper. And he was never given soap to wash his clothes properly, instead he had to make do with maize husks, which prompted his sister to say that he always stank. Every day he had to herd the cattle they had inherited from their parents and on coming home in the evening was always told to draw water or collect firewood. He was never given time off to play with his friends or even to go to school.

One evening, unable to bear this any longer, Kaumphawi went to his mother's grave, and kneeling beside it, told her all about his miserable life. When he had finished, his mother replied, saying that she would always stand by him, but that she wanted to give her daughter one last chance to change her ways. However, matters went from bad to worse, for the sister now decided that the white maize mash or *nsima woyera* that she and her husband had for their meals was too good for her brother. As far as she was concerned, from now on he could make do with the coarse and bitter variety mixed with husks, which is known as *nsima yagaga*.

The night this happened the boy's mother appeared to him in a dream, telling him to come to the graveyard next morning. At sunrise he rose and led his cows to a safe place where there was good pasture. Then he went to his mother's grave, where he was surprised to find a large python. The creature told Kaumphawi not to be afraid as it was his mother's spirit and it asked him to guide it to his sister's house. On the way it taught him a little song in which all he had to do was to repeat the word *ndala* (python). As they came near the house—it was early afternoon and Kanana had just prepared her and her husband's meal—the two of them began to sing a song.

173

Mother:	Kanana, my daughter, Kanana!
Son:	Ndala, ndala, ndala!
Mother:	You treat your brother like a slave!
Son:	Ndala, ndala, ndala!
Mother:	Your husband gets good food!
Son:	Ndala, ndala, ndala!
Mother:	Your brother you give husks only!
Son:	Ndala, ndala, ndala!
Mother:	Kanana, you will pay for this!
Son:	Ndala, ndala, ndala!

Upon hearing this song the villagers left their huts, but, on seeing the python, fled back inside, locking their doors. Kanana, however, had no such luck. She too came out thinking someone was calling her and before she could run back to the house the snake shot forward and devoured her. Also, at the same instant, it turned into a human being and, to everyone's surprise, it was Kaumphawi's mother. Kanana's husband left secretly through the back door, while mother and son sat down to the meal prepared for him and his wife, happy to be reunited after so much hardship.[22]

The two episodes might appear at first glance to be quite different. In the orphaned Millipede both parents are dead and he stays perhaps with a stepmother. He has no freedom like that of the other friend. In the Tonga text the orphaned Millipede is mistreated by a stepmother, while in the Chewa text it is the sister who mistreats her brother. She treats Kaumphawi not like a brother but like a slave giving him just enough food to keep him from starving, just because she is the older sister. All the chores of the family fall to the orphaned Kaumphawi.

The Millipede, whose mother was still alive, believed that he would be with her always. He grew up happily in luxury. He did not want to take his mother's advice. The orphaned Millipede heard the advice from where he stood outside the door, and kept it to himself. When the rains came to an end, the orphaned Millipede started to dig a hole for himself and by doing so he saved his life. The rich arrogant Millipede died because he had made no hole to save himself. This is seen as a punishment that is administered after disobedience to mother's advice.

---

[22] J.M. Schoffeleers and A.A. Roscoe, *Land of Fire*, p. 214.

In the Chewa text disobedience is not the issue. We see that the injustices are unbearable for Kaumphawi the Orphan. His close relationship with his mother before death is what kept him going. Kaumphawi goes to his mother's grave and communes with her spirit. The vein of harsh realism is tempered by the return of the mother from the dead when virtue is rewarded and evil punished. Thus, in Kaumphawi's story, we see the supernatural power intervening in the form of the spirit of the dead mother. There is no supernatural intervention in the Tonga text.

However, what unites these two stories are the injustices which are unbearable. In both stories the orphans are ill-treated and exploited. Symbolically, in both stories the orphans represent the poor and down-trodden. Both stories develop a concept, that it is these despised and marginalized people in the society who achieve the impossible. The story about the Hunchback and the Blind Man is no exception to this idea (Tale 10). It can also be agreed that the story about Kaumphawi may symbolically involve age difference to suggest a generational difference. The story attacks the exploitation of the younger generation by the older generation in the traditional social system. It can also be noted that when injustices are unbearable, supernatural forces sometimes intervene to rectify or alleviate them. This element is missing in the Tonga story, which dwells on the theme of reward of obedience and the penalty of disobedience.

(7) The Head (*Chimutu*)

Once upon a time there lived a woman named *Chipapa-Mitu* (mother of heads). When Chipapa-Mitu gave birth to her first child, it became a living Head *Chimutu*. She decided to keep it, and cared for it. Now *Chimutu* possessed all the normal faculties: two eyes, two ears, a nose and a mouth. He could hear, see, smell and talk. The one thing he could not do, however, was to walk, for he had no legs. When he came of age he wanted to marry a wife who would be helping him. The mother put him in a basket and, together with her husband, set out on a journey to look for a girl who would be willing to become their son's wife.

They went from village to village and saw lots of girls, but none of them wanted to marry *Chimutu*. Here they were received with insults, there people chased them away or cruelly beat them. But they doggedly went on, and in the end found a girl who said she would marry *Chimutu*. The girl was called *Mtola-tola* (she who picks up anything). The girl went along with them, together with her younger brother, and they and *Chimutu* were

175

given a house of their own. The boy and *Chimutu* shared a room while the girl had one to herself.

During the night *Chimutu* changed into a European (*Mzungu*), Jee! He moved through a house suddenly ablaze with electric lights and furnished with chairs and tables and other beautiful things. The little boy, waking up one night, saw this and next morning secretly told his sister. She would not believe him and told him he had been dreaming. But the boy said he would tie a string to her ear so that when it happened again, he could wake her up by pulling it.

Night came and when the events repeated themselves the boy woke his sister, who was able to see everything for herself. *Chimutu* was still in his basket, but as long as the European moved about, it looked lifeless like a wooden mask. The girl and her brother now made a plan. They decided that on the next occasion the boy would get hold of the white man while the girl smashed the head to pieces. Night came and everything was done as planned. The white man could no longer change back into a head, and everything in the house stayed as it had been during the night. The girl too changed into a white woman, her brother into a white boy, even *Chipapa-Mitu* and her husband became white people. At daybreak, the whole village flocked to the house, everybody exclaiming in surprise. The girls who refused to marry *Chimutu* and even mocked *Chimutu's* mother were now green with envy. What would have happened if *Chipapa*-Mitu did not love and care for *Chimutu*?[23]

Comments on "Marrying the Head" (Chimutu)

This is perhaps one of the travelling stories in Malawi. For purpose of comparison there are several similar stories related to the Tonga text. For example, one appears in Chewa, another in Tumbuka, and a third one in Lomwe. The Lomwe text is very close to the Tonga text. The Chewa text is most interesting, because the marriage starts with some immorality. The Lomwe story, like the Tonga one, is fairly short. According to Schoffeleers and Roscoe, these stories are grouped under the themes of "origin of diseases" and "suitors," respectively. For a better analysis of these stories I shall adopt the Chewa version, and a summary of the Tumbuka version.

---

[23] Source: this story was narrated to me by Lilias Nyabanda of Malaza village, on October 7, 1994.

The Origin of Albinos (Chewa)

Once upon a time a boy fell in love with a beaultiful girl in his village. The parents approved and in due course the couple planned to marry. But there was one bad thing the lovers did. They had sexual intercourse before they were married and this angered the gods, who decided to punish them.

Their first-born child was a head without body or limbs. The elders said that this head-child should be thrown into the great river since it was abnormal. And this was done. But the second and third children were just heads too and were also thrown into the river to feed the crocodiles, in the hope that eventually the gods would forgive. But the fourth–born child was yet another head. This time the mother decided to keep it, and her husband agreed. They refused to throw it into the river and were therefore told to leave the village. So they built a house about a mile away on the edge of a thick jungle and took their head-child there.

The child grew rapidly and they knew from its teeth and from its deep voice and beard on its chin when it became a mature youth. The mother tended her head-son lovingly … One day the head told his mother that he wanted to marry. But the mother said that no girl would be willing to marry just a head. The head insisted, however, and finally the mother promised to take him around the villages. She washed out a large basket, cut his hair, and shaved his beard.

Next morning she washed the head, fed him, and putting him in the basket. Soon she saw that he had excreted a big heap of faeces in the nice clean basket. She called her husband to see what the head had done just as she was ready to set off. "Why are the gods punishing me so much?" She asked, forgetting that she and her husband had disobeyed the elders, first by having intercourse before they were married, and secondly by keeping this fourth head-child. She bathed the head again, washed out the basket, and was soon on her way, carrying the basket on her head.

She went from village to village interviewing girls, but could find none willing to marry the head. She was tired and longing to return home, when her head-son suggested they try one more village, and he directed his mother to follow a path leading to a tiny village at the foot of a hill on the banks of the river. It was the Bua river into which the first three heads had been thrown. Here they met a girl who had been rejected in marriage, and when asked she agreed to marry the head. The mother then put down her basket and begged the girl to take good care of the head and not harm him because, she said, she had suffered great pains bearing one head after another.

The girl prepared food and fed her head-husband, as her mother-in-law had instructed her. They slept, and at midnight the head broke open and out came an albino. When the wife saw that her husband now had a body and limbs, she rose and embraced him, and she too, turned into an albino in that instant. So they were a pair of albinos and people feared them and no one visited their house. Thus they always did everything together, just the two of them. They walked together and they ate together. This is why, down to the present day, albinos move everywhere with their wives—the wife can even go into the bathroom when the husband is bathing. When the couple started having children, the children too were albinos, and that is the origin of albinos, who are now called "*Azungu*," that is whitemen. The gods are still punishing them, flaying them while they are in their mothers' wombs, because that first pair behaved badly before they were married.[24]

Marrying a Snake (Tumbuka)

A summary of the story goes like this:

A girl called *Nyachando* joined a group of married women on a trip to gather mushrooms, though this was against the wish of the group. She got lost and ended up in a European style house, which turned out to belong to a snake. The girl and the snake were married and built a second house in the girl's village. The girl wore nice clothes, but the community was not aware of the fact that her husband was a white man in disguise. Her sister wanted to see the snake's European house, but caught in the act of visiting secretly, she was killed by the snake. *Nyachando* reported the matter to the villagers. Later on the snake was killed by the villagers and its wealth was divided.[25]

The main features of these three stories may be summarized in the following chart:

Tonga	Chewa	Tumbuka
There lived a woman called Chipapa-Mitu (Mother of the Heads)		
	A boy fell in love with a beautiful girl and had	A girl joins a mush-rooming trip though it

---

24 Ibid., pp. 106-108, (I deliberately abridged the story).
25 Ibid., pp. 141-143; 149 (Translated by Leroy Vail, and reproduced here by Matthew Schoffeleers).

178

	sex before they were married (immorality).	was against the group's wish (disobedience)
	The gods punished them for this immorality.	Because of her dis-obedience she ends up lost and comes across a modern house that belonged to a python
Chipapa-Mitu gives first birth to a living Head (Chimutu)	Their first-born child was a Head (Chimutu).	
She decided to keep the Head and cared for him	The first child is thrown into Bua River. She kept the fourth Head.	
Chimutu possessed all the faculties: eyes, ears nose, and mouth.	Child grew rapidly with its teeth, deep voice, and beard.	
When he came of age he wanted to marry a wife.	One day the Head told his mother that he wanted to marry a wife	
Mother put him in a basket and went to look for a girl who would be wiling to become their son's wife	Next morning she fed him, put him in the basket and prepared herself for the journey.	
Head excreted a big heap of feaces in the basket. She lamented why the gods were punishing her.		
She went from village to village and saw a lot of girls, but no one wanted to marry *Chimutu,* and she received insults.	She went from village to village interviewing girls but found no one to marry the Head.	After she had wandered for a long time, she came across a house with corrugated iron roofing.
In the end they found a girl called Mtola-tola who agreed to marry Chimutu.	By the Bua river-side they met a girl who agreed to marry the Head. She went with	The girl Nyachando married the Phyton.

	them together with her brother.	
	The girl prepared food and fed her husband as her mother in law had instructed her.	
The house was suddenly electrified and furnished with chairs and table and other beautiful things.	They slept and at midnight the head broke open and out came an albino	Maphindu! (Riches!) Maphindu!, and the girl pulled out a beautyful dress from the box
The boy saw this and in the morning secretly told his sister		
One night the boy got hold of the white man while the girl smashed the head-mask to pieces.	The wife rose and embraced him	
Chimutu would change into a European, the boy into a white boy. The girl too changed into a white woman.	The girl turned albino and bore children who are now called Azungu (white people).	
At day break the whole village flocked to the house. The girls who refused to marry *Chimutu* were now green with envy.		After the python was killed, the people of the village went to the python's home, they collected tables, chairs, and spoons.

The outline presents similarities and differences which can be viewed very readily by looking at the characters and actions. In the Tonga and Chewa texts the characters are almost the same. The main character in the Tumbuka text is the python. However, one can see similarities there too.

The Tonga text does not mention sex before marriage, yet, in the Chewa text this becomes an issue of immorality. Perhaps this is to show that breaking society's sexual code brings suffering. In Tonga society, as in most societies in Malawi, the deep-rooted fear all mothers have is that they will produce albinos (*afuli*) or deformed children. This is linked with the idea of guilt and punishment. In the Tumbuka story, "*Marrying the Snake*," the younger sister is killed for her pains, when she invades the snake's house secretly. However, Nyachando may be seen to be the cause of the problem because of her disobedience when she was refused to join the women on a trip to go and collect mushrooms.

The common symbolism in "*Marrying Human Heads*" (*Mitu*) in Tonga and Chewa stories, and "*Marrying a Snake*" (Tumbuka), implies that the suitors are rich and the girls who come to share their wealth are poor. The suitor's guises in each case are also surprising, for in the Tumbuka text the girl Nyachando thinks she has married a snake and in the other stories the girl allows herself to be married to a Human Head.

A thematic examination of the stories shows that they are didactic rather than merely entertaining. The Tonga and Chewa talesbegin with the tragic experience of a child who is born deformed. In the end he is transformed into a complete human being who becomes a *Mzungu* (white man), handsome and prosperous. *Chimutu,* the child who was nothing more than a head, yet with all human faculties, is the protagonist in each of the two stories. This mystery is intensified, rather than mitigated, when he transforms himself into a strange gentleman (*Mzungu*). In the Tonga story a young woman and her brother are made to discover the beauty and wealth of a husband whom everybody believes to be both repugnant and useless. The inevitable misfortune is also seen when a disabled person is being refused marriage by girls.

It is also important to note the special details in the stories. In case of the Tonga and Tumbuka texts, when the girls become wealthy, it becomes a matter of domestic production versus foreign trade, and of traditional morality being suspended because of the influence of foreign trade. In the case of the Tonga text, the girl *Mtola-tola* (one who picks up anything) may be condemned for taking initiative in courting the boys, because according to Tonga custom it is the boy who courts the girl.

The Human Head with its faculties of reasoning, and the Python, may both symbolize the category of the higher order. The Head is above in relation to the body. The Head and the Python can also present male symbols. In traditional Tonga society the male was the source of income and would go to South Africa, Zimbabwe, or Zambia, to seek wealth for his family.

It can also be suggested that the *Chimutu* (Head) stories symbolically show how reason is sometimes accepted or rejected and the inevitable consequences of such rejection. The Head biologically and psychologically is the source of reason. By insisting on having a wife, the Head shows intelligence. Similarly, when the girl(s) and the boy discover *Chimutu's* transformation, they too experience reason, for they are transformed to be the *Azungu* (white people). Also the stories of "Marrying the Head" portrays the richness in oral literature that engages itself with what are seen as contrasts of Western and traditional values. Western living has brought its own luxuries among the youth of today. European life is what appeals and the excitement of wealth has grabbed the poor societies. Poor countries are dependant on wealthy countries for economical survival.

The Tonga and Chewa texts should also be seen as a caution. The ethics of a society should not reject or despise outcasts, because these may be reputable in their own right. *Chimutu* (Head), a baby who is made an outcast because of his deformity. becomes a wealthy and reputable gentleman. The girl who agrees to marry *Chimutu* is rewarded, when her husband becomes what people had least thought of him to be.

Finally, in some cases, the Tonga and Chewa stories have items of content in common, that is, the same or very similar actors, actions and some details. The Tumbuka story has a different framework. The expansion occurs through elaboration of the elements which make up a general framework. It can be argued that the similarities are due to the use of a standard episode from a traditional stock of commonly used material in oral narration of prose with no direct dependence or imitation.[26] It should be noted that this tale advances the theme of marriage and the relationships it creates beyond boundaries.

(8) Hare and the Well

There was a great drought in the land, and Lion called together a number of animals so that they might devise a plan for gathering up water when the rains fall. The animals who attended at Lion's summons were Baboon, Leopard, Hyena, Jackal, Hare, and Tortoise.

It was agreed that they should scratch out a large hole to catch the rain, and so the next day they all set to work. Only Hare didn't help; he hovered

---

[26] What takes place in oral transmission was discussed in details in Chapter One.

nearby, muttering that he was not going to scratch his nails off in making water holes.

When the hole was finished, the rains fell and soon filled it with water, to the great delight of those who had worked so hard. The first one to come and drink there, however, was Hare, who not only drank, but also filled his clay pot with water, and then went for a swim in the waterhole, making it as muddy and dirty as he could.

This was made known to Lion, who was very angry. He ordered Baboon to guard the water the next day, armed with a huge fighting stick. Baboon concealed himself in a bush close to the water, but Hare soon became aware of his presence there and guessed the reason for it. Knowing the fondness of Baboons for honey, Hare immediately hit a plan. Marching back and forth, he every now and then dipped his fingers into his clay pot, and licked them with an expression of intense relish, saying to himself in a low voice, "I don't want any of their dirty water when I have a pot full of delicious honey." This was too much for poor Baboon, whose mouth began to water. He begged Hare to give him a little honey, as he had been guarding the water for several hours, and was incredibly hungry and tired.

At first, Hare took no notice of Tortoise. Then he looked around and said, in a patronizing manner, that he pitied such an unfortunate creature, and Tortoise would give him some honey on the condition that Baboon should give up his fighting stick and allow himself to be bound by Hare. Baboon foolishly agreed, and was soon tied in such a way that he couldn't move hand or foot.

Hare drank the water, filled his pot, and swam in front of Baboon. From time to time he chided him, pointing out how foolish he had been to be so easily duped, since he, Hare, had no honey or anything else to give him, except a good blow on the head every now and then with his own fighting stick.

The animals soon appeared and found poor Baboon in this miserable way. Lion was so exasperated that he had Baboon severely punished, and offered to catch Hare. Tortoise asked them to spread a thick coating of beeswax resin all over him. Then he went and placed himself across the path to the water hole, so that on his way to drink, Hare would have to walk on him, and would stick fast.

The next day, when Hare came, he approached very cautiously, wondering why no one was there. In order to get a better look around, he stepped on a large black stone - and at once, he was stuck fast. Hare saw that he had been tricked, for now the stone put out its head and began to move. Since Hare's hind legs were still free, he threatened to smash Tortoise with them if he didn't let him go. Tortoise answered, "Do as you like." Hare made a violent jump, and now found, to his horror, that his hind feet were also stuck fast. "Tortoise," he said, "I have still my mouth and teeth left, and will eat you alive if you don't let me go." "Do as you like," Tortoise again replied. Hare made a desperate snap at Tortoise and now found himself completely stuck, head and feet. Tortoise, feeling proud of his success, now marched quietly up to the top of the bank with Hare on his back, so that he could be seen by the other animals as they came to the water.

They were indeed astonished to find how cleverly the crafty Hare had been caught, and Tortoise was much praised for the capture. Hare was at once condemned to death by Lion, and Hyena was told to execute the sentence. Hare pleaded hard for mercy.

Lion inquired of him in what manner he wished to die. He asked that his tail be shaved and rubbed with a little fat, and that Hyena then swing him around twice and dash his brains out upon a stone. This was considered fair by Lion, and he ordered the sentence to be carried out in his presence.

When Hare's tail had been shaved and greased, Hyena caught hold of him with great force, but before he could lift him from the ground, cunning Hare had slipped away from his grasp, and was running for his life, pursued by all the animals, with Lion in the forefront.

After a long chase, Hare got under an overhanging precipice, and, standing on his hind legs with his shoulders pressed against the rock, he called loudly to Lion to help him to support it, as the rock was falling and would crush them both. Lion put his shoulders to the rock, and exerted himself to the utmost. After some little time, Hare proposed that he should creep out carefully and fetch a large pole to prop up the rock, so that Lion could escape and save his life. And so Lion, still believing the rock would fall on him, was left there by Hare to starve and die.[27]

Comments on the "Hare and the Well"

This is another example of a similar story being found in Chewa versions. Steve Chimombo has it in three versions under the title: "Kalulu the Hare in Time of Hunger," "The Well of Water and Troubles," and "The Hare and the Well." Schoffeleers has it under the title, "Rabbit, Tortoise and the Well" (Sena). In these versions the characters seem to be similar. They range from the Hare, Tortoise, Jackal, Baboon, Hyena, Bushbuck, Leopard, Lion to

---

[27] Source: The story was narrated to me by Richard Chiya Phiri at his home, Chigwira/Tukumbo village. Dictated October. 1994.

Elephant. Schoffeleers treats this story under the theme "Water symbols," I would like to treat it under the theme, "the Drought."

The stories are very similar in details, although one can also see differences. Oral variants may be the reason for the similar stories. For the sake of analysis and comparison with the Tonga text, I shall use one Chewa story collected by Chimombo and the Sena story collected by Schoffeleers and Roscoe.

Kalulu the Hare in Time of Hunger (Chewa)

Once upon a time, there was a great famine in the whole world. All the great lakes, rivers, streams, and small springs had completely dried. The King of the animals, Lion, called all the animals to come to his home for an emergency meeting. When the day had come, all the animals gathered in front of King Lion's house, except for Kalulu the Hare, who lazily stayed at his home. King Lion then said "listen friends, countrymen and all you honourable people, I am the one who called you to this meeting. You all see that many of our friends are dying of hunger and thirst and in no time this effect will face us. Would you also like to die this way?" All the animals roared, "No. No."

The Lion continued. "Then my friends, I have thought it wise that, with the effort of you all, at that big swamp which is no more a swamp, we could surely dig a pool of water. So would you all gather tomorrow morning at the big swamp." All the animals agreed to this and then left for their homes.

On the promised morning, all the animals came, but Kalulu the Hare and Tortoise did not turn up. The Lion commanded the smaller animals to start. These small animals included the monkeys, goats, sheep, antelopes and many others. The small animals jumped all about the swamp but not a trace of water was seen. When the smaller animals were completely exhausted the bigger animals were to take water. First the Buffalo jumped into the swamp and started jumping up and down trying to squeeze water out from the dry swamp with his heavy hooves, but in vain. Then the other bigger animals, rhinoceros, giraffe, and elephant took over, but still nothing came out. When all the animals were exhausted and seated resting, they saw Kalulu the Hare, and Tortoise who asked the Lion if he could get the permission to dig for water. All the animals laughed, but Tortoise pressed his request. The Lion then gave him permission to do as he wished. Tortoise jumped into the swamp, and in no time they all saw water coming up and Tortoise scampering away from the swamp. The animals all cheered for Tortoise's success.

185

King Lion roared and all the animals kept quiet. He then spoke to the animals that all the animals were free to drink the water except for Kalulu the Hare, who had missed the previous meeting and hadn't taken any part in digging for water. Kalulu the Hare laughed loudly and said they would see and ran off to his hiding place. All the animals rejoiced drinking and washing in the water. Hyena was chosen to guard the water during the night. Then all the animals parted to their various homes.

At night Kalulu the Hare came back to the swamp to drink some water. Kalulu, to his surprise, saw that the water had been put under guard. When he saw that the Hyena was on guard, he thought of a trick to play on him. Kalulu the Hare saluted the Hyena by saying, "Oh! Honourable Hyena, I wanted to bring you something at your home but since you were not present, I had to give up the idea." Hyena asked, "What is it my son?" Kalulu the Hare giggled and said, "Should I go and get it?" "Sure," remarked Hyena. Kalulu ran straight to a nearby village and stole a goatskin which had been left lying outside the house. He then ran back to the swamp and gave the skin to Hyena, who thanked Kalulu the Hare and immediately started eating the skin, forgetting his task. Kalulu the Hare stole from the water. He drank and enjoyed himself swimming. He then urinated and defecated besides the pool and ran off happily home.

The following day, when the animals came to drink some water, they saw Kalulu the Hare's feaces and that's how they knew right away that Kalulu the Hare had come to drink the water, so Hyena was proved irresponsible. Lion then chose the Bear to be the guard over night. At night Kalulu appeared. When the Bear saw Kalulu, he wanted to catch Kalulu but Kalulu dodged. He then spoke sweetly to the Bear that he had brought him a present. Bear asked to see the present. Kalulu gave him a tin of honey. Bear thanked Kalulu and forgot about the water to be guarded against animals like Kalulu the Hare. Kalulu took this opportunity to drink, wash and defecated by the water and ran off well to his home. Animal after animal tried to catch Kalulu the Hare but none succeeded to withstand his tricks. One day Tortoise volunteered to guard the water. He told other animals to cover him with mud and be left by the pool. Seeing no one on guard Kalulu went to drink, wash and defecate by the water. When going he went towards tortoise as he took him to be a mound of soil. When he came very close to Tortoise, Tortoise quickly caught Kalulu. The next day all animals were called to King Lion's home to see Kalulu killed. Kalulu told the Lion that if they threw him hard on a rock he wouldn't die, but if thrown lightly on a heap of ash he would surely die. So Lion ordered the Elephant to throw Kalulu the Hare lightly on ash. To their surprise Kalulu the Hare, immediately after falling, woke up and ran straight to the deep forest and thus fooled all the animals.[28]

Rabbit, Tortoise, and the Well (Sena) (Variant 3)

One day when Rabbit was smoking out bees, Tortoise passed by and said, "What are you doing there, my friend?" Rabbit replied, "I am smoking out bees to get some honey. My wife has already got several potsful." Tortoise said, "I am looking for water." Tortoise wandered this way and that until he came to a *Mutinje* tree, which seemed to contain water, but being so small, and having nobody to help him, he had to return empty-handed ... The drought continued and a meeting was called for all the animals. Elephant presided in his capacity as chief. He rose and said, "The first one who finds a tree containing water can become chief in my place." Tortoise said, "All of us must look for a *Mutinje* tree, for its kind is certain to yield water." The elephant, thanking him, said, "In order to remember the name of that tree I order everyone to repeat it whenever he stumbles." So they all set off, each one eager to be the first to find a *Mutinje* tree and thus gain the chieftaincy. They ran themselves into a sweat, and whenever they stumbled they repeated the name of the tree. Soon, however, they began to get confused, naming other trees, and many arguments broke out. The hyenas were hacking away at one tree, the buffalos at another, and the lions at yet another. But none of them yielded water.

Meanwhile, the tortoise, who had been left behind, pursued his lonely journey. Having nobody to distract him, he remembered the tree's name perfectly, and whenever he stumbled he repeated the word correctly. Finally, he saw a *Mutinje* tree. Being a fellow of dwarfish stature, however, he needed help to cut it down.

No one really believed him when he announced his discovery; but having no success with the other trees, they decided to give it a chance. Thus they were all amazed when the tree was cut down and water gushed from its trunk forming a well. They all drank to their heart's content, the tortoise last of all, as he feared being trampled by the others. Sadly, however, the animals declared that it was the elephant and not the tortoise who had remembered the name correctly, and so elephants remained chiefs.

Now they had a well. But when the animals went there to fetch some water for drinking or cooking, they always found it empty. Someone had been here before them, taking all the water and leaving not a drop for the others. Another meeting was held under the chairmanship of the elephant. "My people," he said, "the task before us now is to protect the well.

---

[28] Steve Chimombo, *Malawian Oral Literature*, pp. 288-290.

Someone is taking more than his share and leaving nothing for the others. We need a strong guard. Are there any volunteers?" The hyena was the first to offer his services and was accepted at once. After the meeting he armed himself with club and spear and took up his post. People came and went with their pots and pans and there was no disturbance.

Now early one morning, before sunrise, the rabbit came with his large family carrying as many pots as they could, enough indeed to empty the well. The hyena stationed himself in front of the well, saying that each family was allowed no more than one or two pots for he could not let one family use all the water. The rabbit said, "Don't worry, there will still be enough, even if my family takes a drop more than its share. Moreover, knowing that you have gone without food since yesterday, we thought of bringing you some." Saying this, he lifted from his wife's head a pot of honey and gave a calabashful to the hyena, who emptied it in one gulp. "Give me some more," hyena said.

"I will," said the rabbit, "if you allow us to tie up your arms and legs." Overcome with greed, the hyena consented, and so they tied him up and gave him some more honey—after which he fell sound asleep. The rabbit family emptied the well and no one else could find any water. When the animals saw this, they grabbed sticks, flogged the hyena, and took him to the chief. Other guards were appointed and so it continued for many days. The lion was chosen, and the buffalo and a number of other animals. But all were deceived in the same way.

The animals went thirsty and the culprit remained unknown and unpunished. In the end the Tortoise was the only one who had not yet stood guard. "If you agree," he said, "I'll try my luck." As a matter of fact he had spent his time thinking, and had come up with a clever plan. He said to the chief, "Pour sticky resin all over my shield." And this was done. Then he said, "Put your wife's beads around my neck and carry me to the well." The chief carried him to the well and the tortoise said, "Drop me into the water and let nobody come near." Early next morning, the rabbit came again followed by his large family carrying pots.

To his surprise, he found that there was no guard this time; but looking down he saw something with lovely beads around it floating in the water. "Hey," he said, "those are pretty and will surely buy me a sack of salt." He took off his clothes and slipped into the water, anxious to grab the beads. But his paw stuck firmly to the Tortoise on account of the resin. He tried his other front paw but that stuck too. He kicked at the tortoise, which made his hind legs stick also. And so it came about that the rabbit was caught.

The chief and his people came and the death sentence was pronounced. The rabbit would have to die under the axe. The clever creature now said, "I know I deserve my fate, but please allow me one favour. Let me not die here as my blood would foul the well, let me die on the legs of the chief's wife, who is the mother of us all." They agreed to grant him this one last favour, and so they all went to the village meeting place, where the chief's wife positioned herself under a tree, her legs outstretched and the rabbit on top of them. Silence fell. But just as the executioner swung his axe, the rabbit darted off, and the chief's wife was mortally wounded. She died a few days later and the chief soon followed her, overcome with grief. Thus, it was that the wisdom of the Tortoise twice saved his neighbours. But they ultimately perished because they continued to despise him.

The three stories can be represented in a chart as below:

Tonga	Chewa	Sena
There was a great drought	There was a great famine in the whole world	The drought continued
		Rabbit was smoking out bees and met Tortoise
Lion summoned a number of animals Animals that attended were Baboon, Leopard Hyena, Jackal, Hare and Tortoise	Lion called all the animals All the animals gathered at Lion's house except Kalulu the hare.	A meeting was called and Elephant presided Elephant was made Chief of other animals
They agreed to scrape a hole to catch the rain.	They agree to dig a pool of water.	They all set off to find a *Mutinje* tree which would provide water.
Hare did not help	Kalulu the Hare and Tortoise did not come. The small animals and bigger animals squeezed the water out of dry swamps. But nothing came out and they were exhausted.	Animals ran around searching and forgot the name of the tree.
When the hole was ready the rains fell.	Hare and Tortoise came and Tortoise jumped into the pool and water came up.	Finally Tortoise finished. They saw a *Mutinje* tree. When they cut it down, water gushed from its trunk.

189

		They had a well. Animals went to fetch water. They found the well empty.
Hare was the first to come and drink the water and swam in the waterhole making it muddy.	At night Hare came back to the swamp to drink some water.	
Lion ordered Baboon to guard the water.		Elephant called the animals. Hyena volunteered to be the first guard to protect the well.
Hare came to the well carrying some honey. Baboon asked for some (deception)	Hare came to the well and brought a goatskin to Hyena (deception)	Rabbit lifted from his wife's head a pot of honey and gave it to Hyena (deception).
Hare drank the water and swam in front of Baboon, leaving Baboon tied up	Kalulu the Hare stored the water and drank it and enjoyed himself swimming and defacating besides the pool	The Rabbit family emptied the water, leaving Hyena tied up. Urinating
Lion severely punished Baboon.	So Hyena was proved irresponsible.	The animals came and flogged Hyena for being deceived by Rabbit.
	Bear offered to be the guard and he too was deceived by Kalulu the Hare.	Lion, Buffalo and other animals were likewise deceived.
Tortoise offered to be the guard and begged that his body be spread with a coat of bees' wax resin.	Tortoise offered to be the guard.	Tortoise offered to try his luck as a last guard.
Tortoise hid himself in order for Hare to step on him. Hare came and stepped on Tortoise, thinking he was stuck on account of the resin.	Kalulu the Hare went towards Tortoise thinking it was a mound of soil and immediately Tortoise caught him.	Tortoise put on beads and Rabbit slipped into the water to grab the beads, but the paw stuck firmly to Tortoise on account of the resin.
Lion and Hyena were to execute the sentence	Kalulu pleaded that he should be thrown on a	The Chief and his people pronounced for

and Hare pleaded for mercy asking that his tail be shaved and greased.	heap of ash and not on a stone.	the Rabbit that he would be under the axe, but Rabbit pleaded to die on the leg of the Chief's wife.
Hyena caught Hare to throw him on a stone, but Hare slipped away for his life.	Elephant threw Kalulu on the ash, and Kalulu woke up and ran to the deep forest for his life.	Rabbit's plea was granted and the Chief's wife offered her legs. As the axe was swung, Rabbit darted away leaving Chief's wife mortally wounded.

The Tonga and the Chewa stories have the same basic plots which can be set down briefly here:

- A time of drought
- A meeting of the animals to dig the well
- The Hare's (Kalulu) non-participation
- Deception of each of the guards at the well
- The Hare's capture
- The vain attempt to punish Hare.

There is a certain amount of repetition in the stories. Such structural repetition is observable in many folktales. However, some of the details differ from that of the Sena text, although Rabbit and Tortoise appear in all stories. The chief animal is Elephant whereas in the Tonga and Chewa stories Lion is the Chief. The cause of deception in the Chewa story is both a goat's skin and honey, while in Tonga and Sena it is honey and nothing else. In all the stories Hare or Rabbit (*Kalulu*) and Tortoise symbolically suggest that often the small and weak in society, exploited and tricked by the mighty, carry within them the means of a society's regeneration or survival, if only the powerful would realise it. Thus, when all animals fail Tortoise, who had hitherto been absent, appears and succeeds to provide water (Chewa), and it is the Tortoise that finds the *Mutinje* tree when the great ones ask, "Do you think you can do better than us?" Again it is Tortoise that catches the culprit.

Even though the characters are animals, we seem to be familiar with their behaviours, actions, values, and situations. We have Hare's eating vegetable matter, Hyena eating animal skins and the animals digging the well with their hooves. In times of crises like war, pestilence or drought, people meet together to deliberate and decide on the required course of action. This is seen in all the three stories. The animals have homes to go to after work. If these are recognizable to the audience, it stands to reason that the narrator is recreating a world he knows, in this case his own and the audience's, and along with it the patterns of the life, beliefs, customs and aesthetics of this society. This is true of the Tonga ecology. The narrator here uses the characters of animals around him, and recalls some of the drought seasons when people have been at crisis.

Furthermore, we can see what kind of interpersonal relationships exist between individuals, and what binds them to the society as a whole. In times of crisis the society acts together as an organic whole. We also see Hare (*Kalulu*), to our dislike, manipulating the other characters; although the animals find a solution to their problem, they still face difficulties in guarding the water from Hare. Symbolically this means that the society lays emphasis on respect and intelligence. There is a certain amount of greed, exploitation, and corruption in these stories. For example, Hare exploits Hyena's greed and stupidity.

Justice is also miscarried when the cunning Hare persuades the animals to kill him on the legs of the wife of the chief as in the Sena version. It is only when someone is cunning or mischievous that he/she is able to avoid the unpleasant consequences of disobedience. Without going too much into symbolism, there is also the theme, age-old and central to the drama of human living, of greed and selfishness of those who, turning their back on the community, insist on unfair shares for themselves and their own. Thus, in these texts Hare draws all the water from the well, or makes it muddy so that others should not have any share.[29]

(9) The Three Brothers

There were once three boys who set out for Harare to look for employment. They walked till they safely reached their destination. Fortunately, they all got employment within their first week of arrival in Harare

Two of the three, Juwaki and Juwawo, were spendthrifts and spent their money recklessly, but their friend, Yaledi, was a frugal man, careful with his money and the way it was spent. For three years the three boys worked,

---

[29] Matthew Schoffeleers and A.A. Roscoe, *Land of Fire, pp. 88-91.*

the two boys banking nothing while Yaledi accumulated his savings and bought all the things he would need at home. After their fourth year of work, they all decided to go back home.

As they left Harare, It was found that Juwaki and Juwawo had nothing but their empty boxes and money for the train fare. Their clothes were torn and shabby. All their wealth had been spent on beer drinking and girls. Yaledi, on the other hand, had two big boxes of clothes and a lot of money from his savings. The three boys travelled back home.

When they came to a certain place, Yaledi left his friends and his luggage for a short time. As soon as he had gone away, his two worthless friends conspired to kill him in order to share his belongings between themselves. This they did as soon as he returned, and they divided up all he had between them. But a bird saw what they did. Rich with what they had stolen from their friend, they started on their way home again. After walking for some distance they heard the voice of a bird singing from far away. As they listened the voice seemed to approach them and the words of the song were these:

Wanthu awa mbaheni	These men are bad
Abaya mubwezi wawu	They have killed their friend
Zina lake Yaledi	His name is Yaledi
Wanguvwala suti yifipa ndi skapato	He wore a black suit and shoes
Ndi chisoti chaki chifipa ku mutu	With a black hat on his head
Wenga ndi chuma chinande	Yaledi's wealth was much
Aba chose chuma chaki	They have stolen it all
Wanthu awa mbaheni	These men are bad
Anguza ndi kanthu cha.	They came with nothing.

The voice was that of Yaledi's bird. As Juwaki and Juwawo went on, the bird preceded them and sang of their deeds. They made many attempts to kill it, but they failed. At last, they felt tired. When they reached home and were admitted to a house, the bird was also on top of that house and sang about what they had done. People asked them where they had left Yaledi, and they tried to lie by saying that they had left him in Harare. But soon the whole attention of the village was drawn to the singing bird. When they had grasped all the words that were sung, the people were thrown into a raging fury and seized the two men and killed them under the Chief's command. All their belongings and what they had robbed were given to Yaledi's parents.[30]

Comments on "The Three Brothers"

This story examines family relationships. The Tonga tale can be paralleled to two Chewa tales. The three stories as variants show the Malawian oral tradition reflecting and didactically attending to the problems that arise between siblings in a family. Like in the story of the "Orphaned Millipede" (Tale 6 - Tonga), and "Kaumphawi the Orphan" (Chewa), they address democratic concerns for the weak in the family or in the society.

(a) Sikusinja and Gwenembe (Chewa I)

Once upon a time there were two brothers, Sikusinja and Gwenembe, who went to work abroad. After working for two years, they decided to return. The younger brother, Gwenembe, had saved more money and clothes than the elder brother who murdered him before they reached home. Gwenembe's blood turned into a bird which, when Sikusinja arrived home, landed in a nearby tree and began to sing:

Sikusinja, Sikusinja	Sikusinja, Sikusinja
Gwenembeee, Gwenembeee	Gwenembeee, Gwenembeee
Sikusinja, Sikusinja	Sikusinja, Sikusinja
Gwenembeee, Gwenembeee	Gwenembeee, Gwenembeee
Anapha m'bale wache	Killed his brother
Gwenembeee, Gwenembeee	Gwenembeee, Gwenembeee
Anapha m'bale wache	Killed his brother
Gwenembeee, Gwenembeee	Gwenembeee, Gwenembeee
Sikusinja, Sikusinja	Sikusinja, Sikusinja
Gwenembeee, Gwenembeee	Gwenembeee, Gwenembeee

The elders of the village understood the song and organized a hunting party during which Sikusinja was speared to death.[31]

---

[30] Source: This story was narrated to me by Gordon Nyirenda, at his home, Gondoli, October 9, 1994.

[31] Linus M. Magreta, "Recollections of Gogo Tuwalese's World" in *Kalulu Bulletin of Malawian Oral Literature and Cultural Studies*. vol. 1., no. 1. Jack Mapanje (editor), Zomba, 1976, pp. 74-78.

(b) The Three Men (Chewa II)

Three men set out to seek work. One, a cripple, saved a lot of money from his job of feeding chickens, whilst the other two squandered all their money. Eventually they all decided to return, but on their way home the two killed the cripple and took all his wealth. The blood of the cripple fell on a leaf and this turned into a bird which sang his fate in pitiful tones. When the two men arrived home, the bird landed on the hut of the dead cripple and began to sing:

Tii ti ti ti ndine timba	Tii ti ti ti I am a sparrow
Tii ti ti ti	Tii ti ti ti
Tii ti ti ti ndine timba	Tii ti ti ti I am a sparrow
Tii ti ti ti	Tii ti ti ti
Abale angawa	These relatives of mine
Tii ti ti ti	Tii ti ti ti
Chifukwa cha chuma	Because of my wealth
Tii ti ti ti	Tii ti ti ti
Ndine timba	I am a sparrow
Tii ti ti ti	Tii ti ti ti

From the song the village elders got the message and hanged the two murderers.[32]

In these three narratives the similarities are so striking that some kind of relationship has to be assumed. The similarities and differences can be displayed as shown in the chart below.

Tonga	Chewa (I)	Chewa (II)
Three brothers set out to work in a foreign country (*Juwaki, Juwawo and Yaledi*).	Two brothers went to work in a country, (*Sikusinja* and *Gwenembe*).	Three men set out to seek for work in foreign country (names not given).
Yaledi was careful with his money and accumulated his. The other two boys banked nothing.	The younger brother, *Gwenembe*, saved more money.	The cripple saved a lot of his money. The other two squandered their money.

32 Ibid., p. 74.

195

After four years of work they decided to return.	After two years they decided to return home	Eventually they decided to return home.
The two worthless brothers conspired to kill their brother. This they did, and shared his clothes and money.	*Sikusinja*, the elder brother, killed his brother *Gwenembe* and took his money and clothes.	The two men killed the crippled man and took all his wealth.
A bird saw what they did.	*Gwenembe's* blood turned into a bird	The blood of the one killed fell on a leaf that turned into a bird.
As they were approaching the home of *Yaledi*, the bird sang of his death		As they were approaching home, the bird sang his fate in pitiful tones.
When they arrived home they were admitted into a house. The bird sat on top of that house and sang about what they had done.	When *Sikusinja* arrived home, a bird sat on a nearby tree and began to sing about what they had done	When the two men arrived, the bird landed on the top of the house and began to sing what they had done.
When they grasped all the words from the bird's song, they seized the two boys and killed them under the chief's command. All their belongings and what they had robbed were given to *Yaledi's* parents.	The elders of the village understood the song and organized a hunting party during which *Sikusinja* was speared to death	From the bird's song the village elders got the message and hanged the two men.

The similarities and differences are quite obvious in these three stories. The Tonga text is more detailed than the two abridged Chewa texts.

All these stories show that the brothers went to work in a far country. The Tonga specifically mentions "Harare." The Tonga people have a long history of travelling and working in Zimbabwe and South Africa. Some took white collar-jobs and many others worked in the mines. In the Tonga text the boys worked for four years while in the first Chewa text it is only two years. There is no specific time given in the second Chewa version.

The extravagance of the boys in the Tonga text is seen in the way they were spending their money. *Yaledi* is symbolically a responsible boy, just as *Gwenembe* and the Cripple in the Chewa texts. All tales imply that they killed their brother because of jealousy. Envy is a common attitude which is condemned in Tonga society. It can be assumed that the three men in the second Chewa episode represent family brother relationships. However, the Cripple should be symbolically seen as representing the weak in the family or in society as in the stories about the "Orphaned Millipede" and "Kaumphawi the Orphan" (See Tale 6). This is also true with *Sikusinja* taking advantage of killing his younger brother. In a veiled way the story attacks the exploitation of the younger by the older generation, though this may not be very clear in the Tonga episode.

In all the three stories the blood of the murdered brother turns into a bird, which reveals the evils and injustices the brothers had done in secret. This is a common belief among the Tonga that some human beings reincarnate in animals or birds. When injustices are unbearable, the penalty is death or similar punishment. When you are cruel to a friend or brother/sister, he/she will also be cruel to you later. This is analogous to the Old Testament saying, "An Eye for an Eye" (Tale 21). The three stories also teach that justice must prevail in a community. The defenceless must be protected in a society. This is expressed in the Tonga proverb, *"Cho chawona munyako chaluta mawa che pako"* ("What your neighbour has seen is gone, tomorrow it will be you"). The morality behind the stories is that if the infirm, lame, crippled, orphans or well-to do persons are ill-treated in family or society, then somehow some human or supernatural power will take revenge on their behalf against those who inflict such ill-treatment.

(10) The Blind and the Hunchback

Long time ago a chief and his people were troubled by lions which ate many people. His land was almost left desolate. The chief decided to build a strong hut (*nthanganene)* for the maidens in the forest in order to attract the lions. Everyday lions spent much time around this hut trying to break it but failed.

Now, in another country, there were two men, one was blind and the other a hunchback. All the inhabitants of their land perished and only these two survived. The two set out for this chief's village. One day they came to a certain place and the hunchback saw a gun and told his friend, "There is a loaded gun here! Perhaps the hunters forgot it here, because there is also a shelter." And the blind man said, "Pick it up for me." And he did so. From

197

there they walked and walked till they came to another place, and found an elephant that had died there. And hunchback again said, "An elephant has died here. Its tusk is quite long. Perhaps it escaped after the hunters had shot it and died here." Blind man felt it and said, "Friend, pick this also for me." This time the hunchback refused, but his companion said, "Just pick it up for me," and he did so.

And they went somewhere else and found that a porcupine had died there. Hunchback said, "There is a porcupine here. The porcupine quills are very long." Blind man felt the quills and said, "Friend! Pick these also for me." Hunchback again complained that his companion did not care for his hump. And he picked the porcupine quills. They came to another place and found that a roan antelope had died there. Hunchback said, "There is a horn of an antelope here. It seems a lion had killed it." Blind man again felt the horn. He said, "Friend, pick this horn also for me." Hunchback bitterly complained and when Blind man forced him, he quietly picked up the horn.

The two of them went on and at last came to a maidens' hut (*nthanganene*). They said, "Darkness has overtaken us, and we need somewhere to sleep." But the maidens refused them a place to sleep, saying, "You cannot sleep here. As for us, our chief built us this hut so that, when the lions come, they can eat us." But the two men would not listen, and said, "This is where we are going to sleep."

While they were talking, the lions came roaring in and were disturbed when they heard men's voices. They said, "Who is talking in the hut? Let us eat them all together." Blind man said, "You cannot eat us. We only came here to find sleeping room." The leading lion said, "I am going to throw one of my hairs at you, and see if that won't frighten you!" Whereupon the maidens all fainted, but not Blind man and Hunchback. And then the lion threw a hair, and Blind man felt it with his hand, and said, "That tiny little thing! See, I am going to cast it into the fire."

And when he did so, it gave a crack, and he said, "Now I am going to throw you my hair." And he got out the porcupine's quill and threw it. The lion picked it up, looked at it, and said to himself, "Ah! Yes, he has long hair." But aloud he said, "No, I am not afraid. Now I am going to throw a tooth of mine for you to see." And he pulled out one tooth, saying, "There it is, I have thrown it for you to see." And Blind man felt about for it, and said, "Is that what I am to fear? Look at this."

And Hunchback took the tusk of an elephant and threw it at the lion. The lion gave a jump, saying to himself, "Ha! Yes, indeed, the fellow has a fearsome tooth." But aloud he said, "Now I am going to let you hear my voice," and he gave a tremendous roar. And Blind man told the Hunchback to bring him the horn of the roan antelope which he blew so hard. The lions trembled. Now the lions wanted to see how this was done. Then both lions came up close, and Blind man said, "Where are you?" and they said, "We are here." And he said, "Lay your heads and legs together so that you can hear my voice clearly."

Then Hunchback took the gun and pointed it in their direction. Blind man said, "Now listen, I am going to speak my words." Hunchback fired the gun and killed both of them. He asked, "Have you heard my words?" But he found that all was silent. Then he roused his maidens who had fainted, saying, "Get up, I have killed those wild beasts." And they argued with him, saying, "You are deceiving us." Hunchback and Blind man said, "You people, get up. You must open the door for us so that we can go and see for ourselves." And they did so, and they went and Blind man felt around and said, "This is the male and this the female. Come outside and see for yourselves." The maidens cried with great joy. The people came to find out what had happened. They saw two strangers sitting on the dead lions.

The maidens brought Blind Man and Hunchback to the chief, and explained how the men had killed the wild beasts. And the chief asked if that was indeed true and they said, "May we be struck down dead if it is not." And the chief was surprised to hear the shouts of joy from his people. He believed that the two men had really killed the lions.

Then the chief held discussion with his people, saying, "Well, those people killed the wild beasts, what are we to do about them?" and they said, "You must give them these maidens in marriage." So he gave Blind man his, and Hunchback his, and gave them wealth to share. And as they went along the road, they shared the wealth between them. And Blind man said, "Oh no, you are cheating me. Did the chief not say we should have equal share?"

Then Hunchback stood up and hit him in the eyes, and straightway Blind man found his eyes were opened. And Blind man also hit his companion on the back, and Hunchback found his back straightened. And thereupon they shook hands as a token of friendship. Thus, the chief honoured them after rendering the vital service of killing the lions.[33]

Wachiburumutiya ndi Wagonyo (Tonga version)

Mwaka kwenga fumu yeniyo wanthu wake ndi yenecho pamoza angususgika ndi Nkharamu zenizo zingupasuwa charu chake. Anthu anandi angumara kuliwe. Fumu yingukhoma fundu ya kuzenga nyumba ya

---

[33] Source: From *Nthanu za Chitonga*, by Filemon K. Chirwa, 1932, pp. 65-71 [translation mine].

Nthanganene ya wamwali ku dondo alinga Nkharamu zizimutuniyamu. Nyumba ya nthanganenen anguyikhozga ukongwa ndi kuserezgamo wamwali. Zua ndi zua Nkharamu zatangwamikanga pa nyumba yeniyi, ndikweni zatondekanga kupasuwa nyumba chingana zinguziwa kuti arangamo amwali pe.

Wachiburumutiya ndi Wagonyo, yawa wawi nau angapanyuka, kwau anthu ose angumara kunguja yiwo pe. Sono yawa angukhoma fundu yakuti, "Ife tawawi viyo tito lwendo tiyengenge mcharu vinu tamubulika ko kukuzenga wanthu tikajenge nau." Anguti ayana mu fundu yawo angusoka, Wagonyo wanguti, "Pano pe futi yakusoperasopera akhumba vikuruwapo viwinda chifukwa msasa nau we penipano." Wachiburumutiya wanguti, "Nganya ato yeniyi futi ndiyiwone." Wagonyo wanguto ndi kuyipaska ku Wachiburumutiya, ndipo wanguti wayiparapaska wanguti, "Abwezi pingani futi yeniyi mwaziwa uli ko tita kuurongo." Angutuwa pa angwendapo mtunda angubulika pa malo po pangufwiya Njobu, Wagonyo wanguti, "Abwezi, pano pe jinu la Njovu, Bama! Utali nalo, akhumba viwindi vyayilasa yinguthawa ndi kuwawala." Wachiburumutiya wanguti, "Abwezi anyamuwani dniyiwone nani." Wati wayimika ndi kuyitompho Wachiburumutiya wanguyiparapaska ndi wanguti, "Abwezi pingani Njovu yeniyi. Wangonyo wangukana ndikuti, "Abwezi pingani Njobu yeniyi. Wangonyo wangukana ndikuti, "Awa iwe wamunyangu ukhumba kundibaya uziwa kuti msana ndiwo upinga mtolo, uziwa ndi iwe kuti gonyo lenili likufyo, ndinguziwa viyo mphanyi ndingukana kusoka nawe." Wachiburumutiya wanguti, "Nganya uziwa ndi iwe kuti gonyo lenili likufyo kali msana, sono utiti ndinyekezgepo so uzitu uwu wa futi ndi wa Njobvu, ndinguziwa viyo mphanyi ndingukana kusoka nawe." Wachiburumutiya wanguti, "Nganya uziwa ndi iwe kuti ndichitiya dara cha, asani ndenga ndi maso ngendiwe mphanyi ndapinga ndine Chonde pingani viyo chingana muulevi msana wanthazi." Wagonyo wangunyamuwa jino liya la Njovu kupapika pachanya pa futi.

Angwenda mtunda unyake anguwona minungu ya Chunungu, Wagonyo wanguti, "Pano pangufwiya Chinungu, minungu yake njitali ndi njikuru so." Wachiburumutiya wali, "Aka ndiyione abwezi," ndipo wati wayiparapaska wanguti, "Abwezi yeniyi nayo yikhumbikwa kupingapo." Wagonyo wanguti, "Abwezi ndimwe wakusuzga mbwenu, yiku mupingenge ndimwe, ine cha. Iwe wamunyangu utenda waka penipo ndamunyako ndapinga mphingu ndikweni ko wakwaska utiti ndipingenge ndine kuti uziwa so cha kuti Katundu wafyo wakuyerekapo aka ndi aka." Wachiburumutiya wati wakokomezgapo Wagonyo wanguvviya ndi wanguto munngu wanguipinga. Angusoka pa anguza pa mtunda unyake anguwoa sengwe za ngoma, Wagonyo wanguti, "Abwezi pano pakufwiya ngoma manyi yikuliwa ndi

200

Nkharamu kaya." Wachiburumutiya wanguti, "Nganya ato ndiwone sengwe yeniyi." Wachiburumutiya" Wati wayiparapaska wanguti, "Pingani abwezi, musanjike pa Katundu yo mwapinga." Wagonyo wangufya mtima ndi kudinginika kuti, "Nganya ndiwe mulwani ukhumba kundibaya ndi mphingu, wawona po iwe utonya waka wambura kupinga kannthu." Wachiburumutiya wanguti wkoserezgapo ndi kumuweyere, Wagonyo wangupinga waka chisisi.

Kundondo wawi viyo angubulika pa nyumba ya nthanganenen, mwenimo fumu yinguwika wamwali wakuti Nkharamu zizimutuniyamu, ndi wati wawode wamwali anguziswa kuvwa mazu gha wanthulumi ndi anguti, "Ifwe tikana kumujuliyani kuti msere muno, chifukwa fumu yikutizenge kuno mwakuti Nkharamu zituniyengemo, ndi zileke kwamko wanthu ku muzi. Vinyo tikuchejezgani murutiyenge ku muzi wa fumu; mu nyumba yinu mwazamfwiyamo." Wachiburumutiya ndi Wagonyo wangukana kuya ku muzi. Amwali wati agowoka angujura chisasa walendo yawa wangusere mu nyumba.

Kwati kwafipa ena andale wanthu, Nkharamu zingubulika ndipo zati zaza pafupi zinguvwa mazu gha anthulumi kuhihita mu nyumba. Zingurwita ndi zingufumba kuti, "Mbayani yawa ahihita amu mu nyumba, le mwafwa; kuti muziwa so cha kuti mizi yose tayipankuwa ndifwe, sono napo taziya kupanyuwa nyumba yeniyi mulimo kuti tabaye wamwali wose wo wemo." Wachibumutiya ndi wangwamuka, "A nkharamu, muziwe kuti le muno mu nyumba tilimu ta nthulumi wanyinu, wenewo mko mbakupusa nazulo ghano takumana ta nthulumi pe." Nkharamu zinguti, "Kumbi ukhumba kukurongo weya widu mo uliri utali, ulinga muwuwone ndi muziwe kuti te wakali ukongwa munu mu charuchise?" Ndiopo zinguti zakuchuwa weya zinguuporoska pa dangazi ndi kurongo mu nyumba.

Wagonyo wauti wawuwona wanguti, "Weya winu ngumana ndi ngufupi posiposi napo ngwakorowa so, khazgani muwone weya wangu." Wanguto munungu wanguuporoska ndi wanguti, "Ehe, eangu weya mo ulira." Nkharamu zauti zawuwona ndi zingukhweruwa jinu ndi zinguti, "Weya tauwona kweni sono tikurongo jinu lo uliwone lenilo tilumiya nalo wanthu." Zati zaliporoska Wagonyo wanguti, "Kumbi ili ndi jinu lenilo lingatenthemeska ifwe, tatinge kwali ndi jinu lakuti di? Akani tikurongoni lidu muliwone ukuru wake mo liri." Wachiburumutiya wangunene Wangonyo kuti, "Nthole kuno jinu lo la Njovu leka kopa ndikoreyeko ndi uporoske penipo pa dangazi." Ndi wanguti waliporoska wangulitutuzgiya ku bwalo. Nkharamu zati zaliwona zingujangalika patali ndi zinguti, "Jinu tiliwona sono muvwe mazu ghidu ghenigho titofye wanthy tichokoroma," ndipo zingubangura. Wachiburumutiya wnaguti, "Sono muvwe mazi ghangu." Wangunene Wagonyo kuto sengwe ya Ngoma ndi kudiramo maji,

201

ndipo wati wachita viyo wanguyipaska ku Wachiburutiya mweniyuwa wati watukumuwa matama wanguyimba kwa nthazi, Nkharamu zose zinguchiruka ndi kujangalikiya patali ndi chitenthe. Wachiburutiya wanguti, "Kumbi imwe a Nkharamu mwaghavwa mazu ghangu? Nkharamu zinguzomera kuti, "Inya taghavwa kewni tikhumba kuwona mo umbiya." Wachiburumutiya wanguti, "Gonyo sono nthole futi yo, chere limu." Ndi wati wayichera, wachiburumutiya wangunene Nkharamu ziya kundere kufupi ku chisasa ndi wanguti, "Pakuma mitu muyane marudi nagho viyo, asani mwama viyo mazu ghangu mughavwenge umapha ndi ine nani mundiwonenge urusu mo ndimbiya." Zati zama viyo Wagonyo futi wangudunjika mbaramatutu; Wachiburumutiya wanufumba Wagonyo kuti, "Asi futi warunjika mbaramakutu?" Wali, "Inya," Wati waponya mporoporo zinguzotomu makutu, ndipo zose ziiwi zinguwa pasi zakufwa.

Wamwali weniwa angufwa chipoyo angufwerefwetuka ndi kubabanyukiya kubwalo ndi tumphundu ndi kukondwa kukuru. Anthu anguzizwa ndi tumphundu twenito anguvwa, ndipo wati waza anguwona Nkharamu ziwi zakufwa, pachanya paja wanthu wawi walendo, ndipo wati wafumba wamwali wa wanguwakonkome makani ghose mo ghangwende ndimo alwndo angubayiya Nkharamu. Anthu angutole makani gha ku Fumu, nayo yati yachivwa yingukondwa ndi yingutuma zinduna kwachiwatole ku muzi wake keachiwawona. Fumu yingurumba ukongwa nfi kuwawonga, yinguwapaska ndumbi ndi wamwali wa kuti akagawane, ndi wamwali kwachiwa wawoli wau.

Pakugawana vyuma Wagonyo wangupusika Wachiburumutiya. Uyu wati waziwa kuti m'nyake wamupaska chimana chuma wangudinginyikiya. Wagonyo ndipo wati wafya mtima Wangonyo wangujenyeska khofe ku maso gha Wachiburumutiya waka maso banu! Wachiburumutiya nayo knhonyu zuku pa gonyo—wala msana nyorunyoru! Charu chati chagona viyo Fumu yinguwachitiya ulemu ukuru chifukwa cha mlimo ukuru weniwo anguuchita wakubaya Nkharamu ziya.

Mlimo wamampha ndi wakukondweska we ndi marumbu ghakusa-ngaruska.[34]

Comments on the "Blind Man and the Hunchback"

This is a unique story, because it is one of the examples of a rogue genre in Tonga oral literature. For the sake of comparison, in the Chewa text the version is a literal translation by R.S. Rattray, which has here been

---

[34] Ibid., pp. 65-67.

reproduced by J.M. Schoffeleers and A.A. Roscoe.[35] The same Chewa text has also been paraphrased by Alice Werner. She suggests that it is one of those stories which have travelled.[36] The Tonga and Chewa texts are so similar that some sort of connection must be assumed.

The Tonga text is a literal translation of Filemon K. Chirwa, author of *Nthanu za Chitonga*. Filemon Chirwa served Livingstonia Mission as a Zonal Inspector of Mission Schools. His zone included schools in Kasungu district. It is most likely that Chirwa collected some stories from Chewa sages, and one of such unique stories was this one. The story can validate how the Tonga people have been interacting with the neighbouring Chewa people to the South of Tongaland, from the early 18th century to the early part of the 19th century.

I have deliberately included both Tonga and English versions. The English translation is mine. The inclusion of a Tonga version is a tribute to Chirwa's resourcefulness and creativity. He was a great Tonga sage, whose Tonga oral literature was withdrawn from schools in Tongaland in the early 1960s. Chirwa also composed Tonga hymns. The full Chewa text is not given here. However, an outline below will still give the reader an idea of the Chewa text as translated by Werner and Schoffeleers. The most important point to note is that the sequence of similar events is not in the same order.

---

[35] Reproduced in Matthew Schoffeleers and A.A. Roscoe, *Land of Fire*, pp. 137-140.

[36] Reproduced by Alice Werner in *Myths and Legends of the Bantu*, London: Frank Cass, 1968, pp. 308-310.

Tonga	Chewa
Lions caused in Chief's land a desolation eating the people	Lions came to eat the people
	Chief opens negotiations with the lions
	The lions ask the Chief to give them his two daughters.
Chief built a strong hut in the bush for the maidens in order to attract the lions. The lions could not break the hut	The Chief took his two children and went and made a rough grass hut for them on the hill.
From another country there set out two men, Blind man and Hunchback, whose country was also desolate and they went out to seek refuge.	From another country there set out two men, one blind and the other a hunchback
Hunchback saw a gun and told his friends, "There is a gun here"	The Hunchback saw a tortoise and told his comrade, "Here is a tortoise."
Blind man said, "Pick it up for me."	Blind eyes said, "Pick it up for me." He refused, but later on he did so.
And they went somewhere and Hunchback again said, "There is an Elephant tusk here, and it is very long"	And so they walked and walked and came to another place and found a porcupine had died there. Hunch-back, said "Here is a porcupine."
And his companion said, "Friend! pick it up for me. Well, pick it up for me."	And his companion said, "Well, pick it up for me," and he did so.
Hunchback refused, fearing that his friend would kill him. But his friend said, "Just pick it up for me," and he did.	
They walked and walked and came to a place and found a Porcupine that had died here with its long quills.	And went somewhere else and found that an elephant had died there.
	And Hunchback again said, "An elephant has died here and the hunter and his gun are at the same spot."
Blind man again said, "Friend! These too pick for me." After refusing bitterly, he picked them.	And his companion said, "Pick up the gun and one tusk." So he did.
They went further and the Hunchback saw the horn of an antelope.	

	His friend said, "pick it up for me."
The two men arrived at a maidens' hut (*nthanganene*) and asked the maidens for a place to sleep.	At sunset Hunchback climbed a hill and saw smoke rising. So they went on and found two maidens in a grass hut and asked for a place to sleep.
The maidens refused to give them room, fearing that the lions would eat them.	The two maidens refused to give them room, fearing lions would eat them.
The two men took no heed. The maidens gave them room	The two men took no heed. The two maidens gave them room.
As they were talking, lions came roaring and asked, "who is talking in the hut? Let us eat them."	As they were talking, lions came roaring and asked, "Who is talking in the hut? Let us eat them."

Both episodes have similar elements, but the sequence of events is different. Werner's translation is very close to that of Schoffeleers. Blind man and Hunchback perform the same feat by means of a series of highly imaginative ruses. The story does not exploit much symbolism. The two men are disadvantaged, yet they do not try to win our sympathy for them. The Chewa version begins by saying that a certain village was plagued by a pair of man-eating lions, and the chief, on the advice of his people, opened negotiations with the lions: "Why are you seizing people everyday?" the lions answered, "we say, you give us your two daughters whom you love and we will not come to seize people."

The emphasis on humour and didacticism is deliberately under-played. Instead of being restored to physical normality in the sacred flow at the end of the tale, these men are cured amidst a scene of knock about force, clearly designed for the entertainment of the audience. The different narrative key can also be noticed in the way these rogues traverse a forest, and in the narrator's decision not to exploit the potential symbolic change of the porcupine quill, elephant tusk, the roan antelope horn, and the gun. The story is fashioned by traditional Tonga society and involves the manipulation of the literary convention, to teach, to warn and to concur without causing strife, without risking social chaos. It also depicts an initiation practice which girls and boys undergo. The strong hut symbolizes the existence of *nthanganene* (girls dormitory), where maidens stay till their coming of age.

Finally, rogue tales do not necessarily contradict the validity of the truths propounded in the more moralistic and religious kind of tales. Rather they relativize their supposed importance by suggesting that cunning and a sense of honour are also commendable and useful qualities, when it comes to surviving in this life. In a single sentence, Chirwa closes the Tonga text with a moral injunction; *Mlimo wamampha ndi wakukondweska wendi marumbu ghakusangaruska* (A good and admirable work deserves commendable rewards). This moral exhortation is based on the motif that the two underprivileged suitors acquired wives of high rank and were given much wealth and land after rendering a vital service to the community.

(11) Why Monkeys Live in Trees

Once upon a time, Bush Cat (*Zumbwi*) had been hunting all day and had got nothing. She was tired. She went to sit down and rest, but the fleas wouldn't give her any peace. She saw Monkey passing. She called to him, "Monkey, please come and deflea me." Monkey agreed, and while he was picking out the fleas, the Bush Cat fell asleep. Then Monkey took the tail of Bush Cat, tied it to a tree, and ran away.

Bush Cat awoke. She wanted to get up and leave, but found her tail tied to the tree. She struggled to get free, but she could not do it, so she remained there panting. Snail came along, "please unfasten my tail," cried Bush Cat when she saw him. "You will not kill me if I untie you," asked Snail.

"No, I will do nothing to you," answered Bush Cat. So Snail untied her.

Bush Cat went home. Then she said to all animals, "On the fifth day from now, announce that I am dead, and that you are going to bury me." The animals said, "Very well." On the fifth day, Bush Cat lay down flat, pretending to be dead. And all the animals came, and all danced round her. They danced. Bush Cat sprang up all at once. She leaped to catch Monkey. But Monkey had already jumped into a tree. He escaped. This is why Monkey lives in the tree, and will not stay on the ground. He is too much afraid of Bush Cat.[37]

Moral Lesson: The tale is told to warn the young people against doing evil to other people, because the same evil will be done to them.

(12) Why Hyena does not Look at Wild Cat

Once upon a time, Hyena had a little one, and it died. Wild Cat also had a little one, and it died too. Wild Cat took a dislike to its country; and so did Hyena. Therefore, each went to seek a better place.

---

[37] Source: Narrated by Maria Manda, a standard 8 school girl at Bandawe F.P. School: Dictated on 5th October, 1994.

When it arrived at a spot it liked, Hyena said, "This will do. Tomorrow, at daybreak, I will come and pull up the grass." Wild Cat chanced upon the same place and it pleased him too. He pulled up the grass and went away to sleep.

Next morning Hyena returned. "Oh!" he cried, "what a good place! I was going to pull up the grass, and the grass already pulled itself up." He took possession, swept the grounds, and went away. Wild Cat came back in his turn. "Oh" he said, "What a good country! I was going to sweep, and the ground has swept itself." He cut down some trees to use as house poles, left them on the ground, and went away.

Hyena returned, fixed the poles in the ground, and went away to sleep. Then Wild Cat came. "The poles," he said, "have planted themselves," and he cut some bamboos and put them on the ground. Hyena came and fastened the bamboos to the poles. Then Wild Cat took the grass and thatched the house. "How is this?" said Hyena when he came again. "The roof is made."

He divided the house into two parts, keeping one room for himself and leaving the other for his wife. Then Wild Cat returned. "Good!" he said. "The house has divided itself into two. This part I shall keep for myself, and that I shall give to my wife. In five days I will bring my property here, and settle down." Hyena, too, arranged to move in at that time.

When the fifth day arrived, Wild Cat took his property and came with his wife. Hyena did the same. Hyena went into one room, and Wild Cat into the other. Each believed that there was nobody else in the house. Then at the same moment, each one broke something, and each one said, "Who is breaking something in the next room?" And each one ran away.

They ran each in his direction, and then at last they met. "What are you doing, oh, Hyena?" asked Wild Cat. "I had built a house," said Hyena, "and something drove me out. I don't know what." "The same thing happened to me," said Wild Cat." I cut down trees, and the poles planted themselves." Hyena said, "I found a place that I like, and I was going to pull the grass, but when I went to do it, the grass had pulled itself up!"

Then Wild Cat and Hyena began running again. They have never been able to look at each other since.[38]

Occasion: The tale is told to advise the young people not to hate other people. They might have similar interests to their own.

---

[38]   Source: Narrated by Jane Nyaphiri of Msundu village on October 6, 1994.

(13) The Dumb Maiden

Long ago, there was a very beaultiful girl, but dumb. Many young men admired her, but couldn't marry her because of her impediment. Many people said, "She is beaultiful for nothing; because once you marry her, you will lack someone to talk to since she can't speak."

One day, there came a stranger to that village, who was a friend to the owner of the village. He inquired if there was any girl to marry, "There is one who can't get married because she is dumb." His friend replied. "I will still marry her, despite her dumbness." His friend tried to discourage him, but the visitor insisted that he would be prepared to take her as his wife.

A few days had passed, and the stranger sent a messenger to the girl's father pronouncing the man's intention to marry the girl. The father said, "We are reluctant to let our daughter get married, lest the man divorces her within a short time." The parents' girl and brother (*nkhoswe)* expressed their doubt of the seriousness of the man who had sent the messenger.

"We have already discussed that. The man vowed to look after her well all the days they shall be together," said the messenger. "If he promises to take care of her and even to work for her, then we have accepted the marriage. But, we will not take any *chilowola* (bridewealth)."

After two days, his father-in-law showed him a field to cultivate. He rose up early in the morning to make ridges. At noon, his wife brought him some food: *sima,* sweet-beer (*mtibi*) in a jug and water in a cup. She placed these under a shade, and made signs to her husband to come and eat. Her husband came with a hoe and placed it against a tree. He washed his hands in sweet beer and cleaned his teeth with it, then he took the hoe, crushed the *sima* with it and rushed it against a stone, and on a log. He threw the hoe away. He then took a small piece of *sima*, soaked it in sweet-beer and mixed it with soil and then ate. He did this again and again till the hoe got crushed. He ate *sima* mixed with soil.

His dumb wife got angry when she saw this. She rose up and started speaking, "Had I known that you are foolish and a mad person, I wouldn't have got married to you. Why have you spoilt my father's hoe? Did you pretend to marry me? What good thing has my father received from you, which should stop me from divorcing you? Who among our forefathers ate *sima* after mixing it with soil? I have divorced you. As soon as you return home, proceed to your home." Saying this, she wept continuously. Immediately, with great anger, she left for her home. Her husband followed behind hearing her muttering something and weeping throughout the way. Many people, who heard her speak, wondered, knowing that she had been dumb.

Upon reaching home, she explained everything her husband had done at the field. Finally she said, "My father and brothers, this man is stupid. Since you didn't know how he was, you accepted that I should be married to him. Now, in the presence of all of you, I divorce him. He should go back to his home."

Her parents, brothers, and all the elders commended the man for whatever he did which resulted in the healing of their daughter. His father-in-law gave him a lot of wealth for making her speak again. This is how the dumb people, long ago, were made to speak.[39]

Occasion: The tale is used to advise young people to be responsible and care for their wives. They are to share happiness. The story also shows how loose informal marriages can be among the Tonga, where no *chilowola* (bride worth) is paid. The story is the only one I came across which depicts psychological healing.

(14) Why the Hyena has Ugly Spots

Once upon a time, there lived Hyena and Tortoise. Now Tortoise was particularly fond of mushrooms and he would go walking along the stream looking for his favourite food.

One day when Tortoise was out searching for the mushrooms, he met Hyena. As soon as Hyena saw Tortoise he started insulted him and the timid Tortoise was afraid to answer back. Hyena decided to pick up Tortoise and went to a place where the trees grew big and tall. He chose the biggest and tallest tree of them all and put tortoise high up in the branches. Tortoise begged for mercy, but Hyena just mocked and laughed at him.

"We are told you are clever, Tortoise, get yourself down," he said laughing over and over again, and he went away.

Finding himself in such a frightening situation, Tortoise started shouting for help and a passing Leopard heard his cries. He looked around to see where they were coming from and eventually saw Tortoise high up in a big tree. Leopard wondered at the sight and asked Tortoise how he came to be in so tall a tree. So Tortoise told him the whole story.

Now Leopard was a very kind animal and he climbed the tree and brought Tortoise with great difficulty to the ground. Tortoise was extremely grateful and told Leopard that he would do anything he asked.

---

[39] Source: Translated by me from Filemon Chirwa, *Nthanu za Chitonga*, pp. 36-38.

Leopard thought for a while and then said he would like to be painted bright colours. Tortoise was astonished at the request, but he agreed willingly. So he collected all his painting tools and set to work. When he had finished, Leopard had a bright colourful coat and went away happily after thanking Tortoise.

Now, on his way home, Leopard met Hyena who eyed his new coat enviously. He asked Leopard how he had come to be so beautiful, and the Leopard told him about Tortoise. Hyena was amazed when he heard that it was Tortoise who did such tremendous work. "This small animal must have magic powers," he said to himself. Wishing to acquire a beaultiful coat like Leopard he went to Tortoise's house. He ran as fast as he could, afraid that Tortoise would not be at home, but when he arrived, he found him sitting near the fire talking to himself about the events of the day.

On arrival, he ordered Tortoise to paint him and the timid creature agreed unwillingly, but without a word. He took a rope and tied Hyena's front legs together, high up in the branches of a nearby tree. It was funny to see a big animal like Hyena swing his hind legs in the air. Tortoise then brought out his painting tools, but instead of using the paints he had used for Leopard, he melted some wax. Then he began to paint spots on Hyena with the hot wax and it burnt into the animal's skin. Hyena, however, was so sure he was going to be painted like Leopard that he pretended not to feel the pain and let Tortoise continue his work without a word. Now Tortoise had finished and pulled Hyena down from the tree.

Hyena asked Tortoise if Leopard had been hurt so much when he had been painted and Tortoise replied, "Yes." So Hyena went away thinking all was well. But when he tried to walk he found it was difficult because his front legs had stretched while he had been hanging from the tree. Even today you can see that his front legs are longer than his hind legs and he doesn't walk properly but limps. Moreover, the Hyena also has ugly spots which are not really spots at all but the scars of the burns from hot wax.[40]

Occasion: the tale is used when advising young people not to be attracted by habits which can lead them to death.

(15) The Wild Cat and the Rooster

Wild Cat and Rooster were great friends. One day, Wild Cat invited his friend to have a meal in his home. When Rooster came, Wild Cat took a huge and tall basket and placed the dish inside it. He himself also sat inside. He then advised his friend, "Since you have a long neck, stay outside the

---

[40] Source: Narrated by J.C. Manda 10th October, 1994, at Kachere F.P. School.

basket and eat from there while standing." Rooster wandered and tried to stretch his neck to eat the food in the basket from outside, but he failed. Wild Cat ate all the food alone.

Rooster returned to his home, grieved at heart because of the mockery he had received from his friend, "Well, should it be the way my friend should treat me? He invited me just to fool me with his food."

A few days passed, Rooster also invited his friend to his home for a meal. He advised his wife to prepare a delicious meal—a lot of *sima* in a huge plate, with very nice relish—then placed it on top of a filled rubbish pit. Rooster assured his friend Wild Cat, "My friend, we don't take a meal inside a house, but on top of a filled rubbish pit. Therefore, wash your hands beforehand, then walk up to the rubbish pit to eat the food." When they had walked up to where the food was, Rooster told his friend that he had to go back to wash the hands since they had been soiled. While Wild Cat was gone, Rooster began eating food. Upon arrival, his hands were dirty again, and so Rooster sent him back again to wash them. Disappointingly, when he returned he found that Rooster had consumed all that delicious food.

In anger and frustration, Wild Cat returned home and conspired against his friend Rooster, and the rest of the chickens, "My friendship with Rooster has been severed. He is very cruel. From now onwards, all of us should be catching all roosters and chicken which come our way."[41]

Occasion: The tale is used to warn young people against being greedy. It is for this tale that the Tonga elders say, *Mwawahurwa ndi mwawa-sungwana, ususi nguheni, wezi ndiwo* (Boys and girls, do not be greedy but be generous). The story also teaches that if you do evil to someone, the same evil might be done to you.

(16) Courage

There were once two young men who were courting the same girl, and each man had two spears. One day, on their way home with her, they passed through the bush, and a Lion waylaid them. The girl fell down saying that her stomach was paining her. The Lion leapt at them, and the first youth threw his spear, but the Lion dodged and the spear fell to the ground. The youth threw his second spear also, and that, too, fell to the ground.

---

[41] Source: Translated by me from Filemon Chirwa, *Nthanu za Chitonga*, pp. 36-38.

In his turn, the other young fellow stepped forward and he too threw a spear, but like the rest it just fell to the ground. Then he threw his second spear, but again he missed the Lion. So all their spears were used up and still the beast hadn't been hit.

Then one of the two youths said to the other, "Hurry, and run home. In my mother's hut, at the head of the bed, you'll find some spears. Bring them, and some water in a calabash." At once the boy ran off to do these things. Meanwhile, the other young fellow leapt at the Lion, and after a struggle, threw him, and taking his knife cut his throat. Then he lifted the Lion into a squatting position, and the girl came over and lay down beside the lion. The youth got behind the mane and hid.

Soon the one who had left returned with the spears, the water, and the potash, but he couldn't find the other youth and the girl. A little further on, he bumped into the Lion crouching there, with the girl lying in front of him, but he didn't recognize her. He said to himself, "So that was the trick, was it? The two went off and ran away, and left the lion to kill someone else's child! Well, then, I can't let the Lion live to do that again." And tossing away his spears and his little calabash of water, he threw himself at the Lion. He grappled with it, and the Lion, of course, fell right over. The girl and the other boy got up laughing.

Well then - which of the two, the boy who killed the Lion, or the other boy who went and fetched the spears and the little calabash of water - which of the two showed greater courage? [42]

Occasion: The tale is used to encourage young people to be courageous when they undertake responsibilities. The story illustrates heroic acts.

(17) Who had performed the best?

Long time ago an old man had three children, all boys. When they had grown up to manhood, he called them together and told them that now he was very old and no longer able to provide, even for himself. He ordered them to go out and bring him food and clothing.

The three brothers set out, and after a very long while they came to a large river. As they had gone on together for such a time, they decided that once they got across they would separate. The eldest told the youngest to take the middle road, and the second to go to the right, while he himself would go to the left. Then, in a year's time, they would come back to the same spot.

---

[42] Source: Narrated by W. Yakota Phiri of Malenga-Sanga village, on October 13, 1994.

So they parted, and at the end of a year, as agreed, they found their way back to the riverside. The eldest asked the youngest what he had found during his travels, and the boy replied; "I have nothing but a mirror, but it has wonderful power. If you look into it, you can see all over the country, no matter how far away." When asked in turn what he had obtained, the second brother replied: "Only a pair of sandals that are so full of power, that if one puts them on one can walk at once to any place in the country in one step." Then, the eldest himself said: "I, too, have obtained but little, a small calabash of medicine, that is all. But let us look in the mirror and see how father fares."

The youngest produced his mirror, and they all looked into it and saw that their father was already dead and that even the funeral custom was finished. Then the elder said: "Let us hasten home and see what we can do." So the second brought out his sandals, and all three placed their feet inside them and, immediately, they were home to their father's grave. Then the eldest shook the medicine out of his bag, and poured it over the grave. At once their father arose, as if nothing had been the matter with him. Now which of these three sons had performed the best?[43]

Occasion: The tale is used to advise the children to be responsible for their parents. The Bible also teaches that children are like arrows in a soldier's hand (Ps 127:4). The boys showed a high sense of responsibility over their father's welfare. Here, too, is the theme of cooperation.

(18) The Five Helpers

Once upon a time there was a beautiful girl, the daughter of a Chief. She was finer to look upon than any other girl that men could see. But there was no one whom she would agree to marry. Men came from all countries, but she would not have them. And all the land heard the news of this beautiful girl that, though she was of marriageable age, she would take no one. There was also a snake, a large Python who dwelt in a vast lake, near the river. When he heard about this girl, he decided that he would marry her. So he changed himself into a man and came to the village.

As soon as the maiden saw the young man she was delighted, and said she would marry him at once. Everyone was pleased, and that night they took the young man and the girl to their house, and there they left them. Now, during the night, the snake licked the girl all over and swallowed her, and changing again into his snake form, he made off to the great lake.

---

[43] Source: Narrated and dictated to me by 'Chiŵiŵi Kanyama Mwasi on October 10, 1994.

Next morning people came to the house and called to the girl and her man to come out. There was no answer, and the Chief told the people to go in and see what was the matter. This they did, and reported that both the girl and the man were missing.

The Chief was very angry, and at once ordered all the people to follow the girl and her lover. But they could find no tracks. So they called for a man who could smell everything. He at once smelled the trail of the girl and followed it down to the great water. There he could go no further. The people, urged on by the anger of the Chief, then called on a man famous through all the country for his thirst. They told him to drink up the lake. This he did. But still there was no sign of the man or the girl. Then the people called a man famous for his capacity for work and told him to take out all the mud from the lake. This he did, and thereby revealed a hole. But it was so deep that no one could reach the bottom. Then they remembered that there was a man with an arm that could stretch over the entire island. They told him to put his arm in the hole and pull. Out came the great Python, which was immediately killed. And when they had cut open its stomach, they found the girl inside, but she was dead. Then the people remembered a man who had the power of medicine and was able to raise the dead. He came at once and restored the girl to life. Now which of these five men did best?[44]

Occasion: The tale is used to advise young people to share their various skills for the community to benefit. It also encourages young people to develop a spirit of cooperation.

(19) The Three Wives

There was once a man who had three wives. It happened that they were all about to bear him children, and they asked him for permission to return to their homes. He agreed to this, and on the appointed day set out with them to lead them on their way.

Presently, they came to a place where the road branched in three directions. The man turned to his women, and said: "Here I will leave you, as here it is that you will each take your different roads." As he said this, he fell dead.

Then the women began to make a great ado. The first woman said that she would not leave her husband like that, but would follow him, and then she went and hanged herself. The second woman said she could not leave her husband's body for the vultures and hyenas to devour, and she sat down by

---

[44] Source: Narrated by D.M. Manda, teacher from Chipayika, October 6, 1994.

the corpse and kept everything away from it. The third ran into bush bewailing her man's death, and there she saw a man who asked her what was the matter. When he heard, he said that he would help, and went back with the woman to the crossroads. There he took his magic cow's tail, and tapping the dead woman and the man, raised them both from the dead and gave them back their life. Now which of those women is the best?[45]

Occasion: The tale is used to encourage young wives to take full responsibilities for their husbands.

(20) Breaking the Promise

Long, long ago a man went hunting in the far bush. He took with him his wife. But one day he left her by a big tree and did not return, and the woman could not find her way home to their village. She therefore built herself a shelter near the tree, where not long after she gave birth to a boy child.

Now, a Lioness lived quite close to the tree, and she gave birth to a male cub at the same time as the woman: but she was unaware that the woman was nearby. Every day the Lioness went into the bush to look for meat, and the woman also wandered away in search of roots and fruits. While they were absent, the two children, the man-child and the Lion cub, met and played together, and became the fastest of friends, without either parent's knowledge.

One day, however, the Lioness lay in wait near the big tree, sprang on the woman as she was returning home, killed her, and brought the body back to share with her cub. The man-child missed his mother at midday, but even so went out in the evening to play with the Lion cub. The cub, however, would not play, and kept looking at the friend, who at last said: "Lion, what is the matter?" And the Lion replied: "Man, I have had no food today; I have bad trouble for you. Follow me."

So the man-child went with the Lion cub back to the latter's home, and there he saw his mother lying dead on the ground. He began to cry, but the Lion cub said: "Stop! I have sworn a big oath today that as my mother has killed your mother, I shall be your faithful friend until I die. I will revenge you, and until then I shall care for you." Having said this, he took the man-child back home.

Each day, for many months after that, the Lion cub brought a large share of the meat his mother gave him to the man-child. They grew together, playing and becoming more and more friendly, and every morning the Lion

---

45 Source: Narrated by Evans Kaunda, at Kachere F.P. School on October 5, 1994.

cub called the man-child, and, placing his paw in the paw-mark of his mother, said: "Soon, very soon, I shall be strong enough."

At last there came the day when the two fitted exactly, the foot printing of the cub and of its mother. Then the cub went out with its mother and said: "Teach me how to catch meat."

After a few lessons, the cub thought he was strong enough, and he told the man-child that the next day he would avenge the slaying of his mother. The following morning, the cub killed the Lioness, his mother, and showed the corpse to his friend, saying: "Now, I have kept the first part of my oath."

For a long time the two lived quite happily together, but one evening the Lion cub said to his friend, "It is time for you to return to your brothers, marry, and live in the village. I have seen a very fine girl, the daughter of a Chief; she must be your wife. Now listen to my plan. Go to the village. I will hide myself near the watering place and, when I see this girl, I will catch her, but I won't harm her. Everyone else will run away scared, so if you go to the Chief and ask him for his daughter, he will agree if you can save her. Then follow me and I will give her up to you. I will come to see you every Friday evening, and you must meet me here in the bush alone. But remember this, never take a second wife or trouble will surely come."

The man-child followed the Lion's instructions, and rescued and married the Chief's daughter. The people built him a house outside the village, but every Friday he sent his wife to spend the night with her family, while he and the Lion played together and exchanged their news.

A long time passed in this way, when one day there came to the village a woman of great wealth and power. She had refused every man's offer of marriage and having decided to choose for herself, was traveling everywhere throughout the land in search of a suitable husband. She saw the man-child, fell in love, and asked him to marry her. But, mindful of the Lion cub's words, he refused her. She insisted, so he compromised, and took her into household.

Every Friday, however, he sent her to the village with his wife. The Lion foretold trouble, but the man-child said that there would be no problem because he had not married the woman; she was merely his friend. But unlike his wife, this woman had a curiosity, which she couldn't contain - and one Friday, instead of leaving, she hid herself and saw the Lion coming to meet his friend. She went to tell a hunter and that night, while the two friends had their usual fun, he hid himself in the Lion's path. When the Lion left in the morning, the hunter shot him - and then immediately went back to tell the people. On hearing the news, the man-child ran to his friend's corpse and, seizing the arrow that had killed him, he stabbed himself with it and died. When his wife arrived and saw the body of her husband and his friend, she went straight back to the house, found a rope, and hanged herself.

"Now which of the three, Lion, Man, or Wife, do you think was the most virtuous?"[46]

Occasion: The tale is told to advise young people to take heed of the advice of others. The story also teaches young people to keep promises they make.

(21) An Eye for an Eye

Once upon a time, the son of a Chief heard a tale of the beautiful daughter of another Chief and set off to visit her. And as he travelled, he met a young fellow. He said, "Young man, I'd like you to come with me, for I'm off to seek a wife." "Oh, no," said the other, "for I have a father who had nothing, neither gown nor trousers nor loincloth; and this leather loincloth that you see me wearing is all that we have between us, my father and I. If my father is going out from our hole in the tree, then he takes it and puts it on; and I do the same when I'm going out." "Where is your father?" asked the Chief's son. "Over there, in the hole of a tree." And the Chief's son asked to be taken to him.

And off they went. When the boy got to the hole in the tree, he said, "Daddy, look: I was out walking, I met the son of a Chief who said he wanted me to go with him to seek a wife. But I answered that I must come and tell you first and hear whatever you had to say about it." "By all means, go along with him," answered his father. And the Chief's son said. "Take the leather loincloth off and give it to your father." And the Chief's son had a travelling bag, he opened it and took out a gown and trousers, and a cup, and a bow and arrows, and all these together were given to the other.

And so they took the road and travelled till they reached the other village. When word was brought to the Chief's daughter that she had visitors, they were taken to the house. She had food prepared for them - three goats were slaughtered, and chickens, too. Soon the Chief's daughter rose and came to them. But when she got there, her heart went out to the servant of the Chief's son, he whose father lived in the hole of the tree. And she spoke and said that he was the one she loved. "No, no!" he said, "I wouldn't dare. See, here's my master." "No," she answered, "you're the one I love." But again he protested that he and his father had nothing but lived in a

---

[46]   Source: Dictated to me by Rev W. Manda at Kang'ongo, at his home on October 12, 1994.

hole of a tree, and added, "Even the clothes that I'm wearing were given by the Chief's son here." "Oh," she replied, "is that all?"

She sent to her father's home, asking for two carrying bags, full of beautiful clothes. All her wishes were conveyed to her father, who got together everything she had asked for, and handed it over to her. Then she said, "Take those things off, and return them to him. Take these and put them on." "Very well," he answered, and did as she had said. He collected the Chief's son's clothes and returned them to him.

So the Chief's son set off home alone, leaving the son of the man with the leather loincloth. For the Chief's daughter had decided it was he whom she loved. Then she went and told her father, saying, "Father, today I want to be married." "Very well," he said, and so they were married.

Time passed and her father died. His large estate was duly divided and she inherited it all as he had no sons or other daughters. Her mother left the Chief's village and had a separate village built for her. Then the girl said to her husband, "Where is your father? Let someone go and fetch him, and let him and my mother be married." And he answered, "He's back there in the hole of a tree." They went and fetched him, and when they returned, the marriage duly took place. And so they lived for some time.

But after a while there came a time when the elder couple had a quarrel and the father of the girl's husband knocked his wife down, striking out one of her eyes. The girl then said, angrily, "Your father has quarreled with my mother and knocked her eye out. If you value our marriage, you'll go and put out one of your father's eyes. If you don't, take your leather loincloth, and you and your father can go back to your hole in the tree. But if you do, then let our marriage continue." Well, here was a nice problem! He had been quite destitute. If he put out his own father's eye, he might continue to live with his wife; but if he didn't then he must go back with his father to the hole in the tree, where they had come from.[47]

Occasion: The tale is told to advise the young to respect those who are responsible for their lives, and not look in contempt on them. It can also be used as a caution to those who believe in vengeance, which is illustrated in Jesus' teaching on retribution, "An eye for an eye" (Mt 6:28-29).

(22) Rich Man and Poor Man

Long time ago in a certain village there were two men who lived as neighbours. One was rich, and the other was poor, but they were friends.

---

[47] Source: Narrated by T/A Malanda of Mkundi village, on October 10, 1994.

The poor man worked for the rich man, helping him. Now a famine came to the land. And when the suffering became very severe, the rich man forgot the poor man, and the poor man, used to eat at his friend's house, now had to beg from him. Finally, the rich man chased him away altogether, because a rich man cannot remain a friend of a poor person for too long, and he felt that even the scraps he now gave his poor neighbour were just too much.

One day this poor man was walking about in the village begging something to eat. A man who took pity on him gave him cassava, and he took it home to his wife, and she cooked it. But they had no meat with which to make it into soup; nor did they have salt with which to season it. So the man said, "I will go to see if my rich friend is having a good soup tonight." He went and found that the meal cooking there gave out a nice sweet smell. So he returned back to his house, got the cooked cassava and brought it back to the rich man's house, where he sat against the wall and ate it, breathing in the smell that came from the rich man's meal. When he had eaten, he returned to his own home.

Another day the poor man saw the rich man and went up to him and said, "I came a few days ago, while you were eating your food, and I sat by the wall and ate my food together with the delicious smell that came from your food."

The rich man was furious, and he said, "So that's why my food was completely tasteless that day! It was you who ate the good taste from my food, and you must pay me for it! I'm taking you to the judge to file a case against you." And he did that, and the poor man was told to pay one goat to the rich man for eating the sweet smell from his food. But the poor man could not afford even one goat, and he broke down and cried as he went back to his house.

On his way home he met a wise man and speechmaker, and he told him what had happened. The wise man gave him a goat, and told him to keep that goat until he came back. Now, the judge had appointed a certain day when the poor man was to pay the rich man; and on that day many people came together to witness the payment. The wise man came also, and when he saw the people talking, he asked, "Why are you making so much fuss here?" The judge said, "This poor man is supposed to pay this rich man a goat, for the smell he breathed from the rich man's food." The wise man asked his first question again, and he was given the same answer. So the wise man said, "Will you let me give another judgment on this case?" The people said, "Yes, if you are a good judge!" So he went on to say, "A man who steals must give back only as much as he has taken, no more, no less."

When the people asked him how he could pay back just the smell of good food, the wise man replied, "I will show you!" Then he turned to the rich man, and said to him, "Rich man, I am going to hit this goat, and when it bleats, I want you to take its bleating sound! You are not to touch this poor man's goat, unless he touched your food." Then he said again to the people, "Listen now, while I pay back the rich man." So he beat the goat, and it bleated, and he said to the rich man, "Take the sound as payment for the smell of your good food!"[48]

Occasion: The story is used to advise young people to help the poor, marginalized and disadvantaged who are always around them.

(23) Finders Keepers

There was once a time of great famine, and Tortoise, like everyone else, was busy seeking food for his children. He bought much maize from his friend, Hawk *(Mnkhokoko)* and made up a good load. On his way home, as he was pulling his bag, he met Baboons.

One Baboon saw the bag behind Tortoise, and he said, "Well, look what I have found." Tortoise looked back and said, "That's mine - look at this string tied round my neck. I am pulling my load as I am walking." Baboon replied, "I don't know about that; all I know is that I picked it up. Finders keepers, losers weepers." Tortoise said, "Let us go to the elders and have them judge what to do."

When they came to the elders, Tortoise explained what happened: "I came from gathering food and there on the way as I was pulling my bag of maize I met Baboon who claimed that the bag was his." The elders said to Tortoise, "You know that the finder of such things is permitted to keep them. That is our rule." So Tortoise went his way, and Baboon took up what he had "found" and carried it to his children.

Now it happened one day that Tortoise and his companions went hunting, and they made a fire to lure prey into their trap. In the grass that they had set on fire Baboon was sleeping. Baboon woke up and ran here and there and found a small hole in which to hide, but his tail stuck out of it. Tortoise seeing Baboon's tail exposed, put out his hand and seized it saying, "Finders Keepers, Losers Weepers."

Baboon said, "You have got hold of my tail, my friend, let me alone." Tortoise said, "I did not touch your tail, I have found something to which I am entitled." Baboon begged, "My friend, this is my tail, you cannot claim

[48] Source: Dictated to me by Sheikh Shaffee K. Perela, Chinthenche Islamic Centre, on October 13, 1994.

it as spoil." Tortoise said to him, "Let us go to the elders." When they arrived, Baboon said, "I was running away from a fire and I entered a small hole, but my tail was outside, then this person came along and said, "This tail is mine," and I said, 'It is my tail,' but he would not listen."

Tortoise said, "Today you are surprised. Lately you took my food-gathering, and you thought nothing of it." The elders said, "Remember what you recently did to your friend." Baboon said, "It was only food that day. Wait my friend, and I will fetch what I took." Tortoise said, "Today is today." The elders said to Baboon, "Give your companion his tail," and the tail was cut off. Tortoise said, "Cut it high up, that I may have a good handle." So Baboon's tail was cut off and given to Tortoise, and half way home he threw it away, saying, "I only wanted to be even with him."[49]

Occasion: It is for this tale that we use to tell young people the following words of moral advice: *Mwawahurwa ndi mwasungwana sambirani umampha nthanu yeniyi, mweniyo wakwamphuwa kamunyake, kake nako kakwamphurikenge kwambura lisungu.* (Boys and girls, remember that if a person does harm to another, he/she should remember what might happen to him/her another day). Again this is implied in the Bible as: "An eye for an eye, and a tooth for a tooth" (Mt 6:28). Tale 21 has the same idea.

(24) Kindness Pays

There was a certain hunter who used to go out with his dog for game to bring back to his wife and children. One day he said: "I'm going deep into the bush, because game has become very scarce these days." He set off with his bow, arrows, spears, and dog. When he had gone some way, he heard a voice saying, "Oh, you, hunter, help me over the crossroads, and I will help you another day." He looked round without seeing who had spoken to him, then stopped, and said, "Who is it who's talking? Speak again, so that I can see what you are."

Then he heard again: "Oh, sir, help me over the crossroads and I'll help you some other time - I, a Muskrat" (*Mfusi*). The man looked down and saw the animal and said, "I would help you across the road only you stink so much and will make me smell likewise." The Muskrat replied, "Oh no, sir, just help me across the road, because if I don't get over I shall die. If you do help me, I will save you one day." The man said, "What! You who are so small will save me who I am so big? Whatever could beat me that you

---

49 Source: Translated by me from *Nthanu za Chitonga*, by F.K. Chirwa, pp. 86-94. An abridged similar story is recorded in *Mcapu wa Chitonga*, p. 18. Here the characters are Tortoise and Hare.

would be able to cope with? You are lying, you little animal!" The Muskrat replied, "Oh, no sir, just lift me with your bow if you are afraid I will make you stink, and throw me so that I fall on the other side of the path, and one day I will rescue you from a great trouble!"

The gentleman took his bow and lifted Muskrat over the path, dropping him on the other side. "Thank you very much for having pity on me," said Muskrat. Then both went their separate ways. That was all that happened on that day.

In the evening, the man returned home and told his wife about his encounter with Muskrat and what it had told him. His wife said scornfully, "What nonsense! How could a rat help you!" The husband replied, "Well, I thought that, too, when he said he would save me one day, but that's what he promised." And the man slept until morning. That day he stayed in the village, saying that the next day he would go hunting in the bush. When darkness returned, he slept again.

Came the morning, he said to his wife, "Oh, wife, prepare some food so that I can eat, because today I am going farther than I have ever gone before." His wife heated some relish, grilled some flour, and prepared cassava porridge. Her husband ate and was satisfied. Then he took his customary hunting equipment, called his dog, and set out. He kept going until he had covered a great distance. It was the wet season, at that time, and the sky was heavy with rain, with vast clouds obscuring the view. He said to himself, "Yes, today I'm going to get soaked, but what can I do?" Just before the rains poured he killed three guinea fowls.

He thought, "Just let me find somewhere to shelter" (the man would have died for sure, if he hadn't exerted himself). He kept going and then, luckily, he noticed a cave and got inside with his dog, just as the rain began pelting down. Well, there hidden in the darkness was the Muskrat, too.

Now, it happened that a certain Lion, who had also been hunting, was himself seeking shelter from the rain, and he came to that very cave. The man glanced up and saw the Lion had come in. Fear gripped him, and his dog began to bark, but the man silenced him by holding his muzzle. Then he said, "Yes, O Lion, you may eat me, but I want to say that I am not a thief, I have not stolen people's goods, nor taken from their granaries, neither have I ever killed anyone. I am just a man of the bush, a poor man with wife and children, and like you, I was looking for food, and the rain has brought you here, so now you can eat me."

Lion began to roar, until the tears fell from the man's eyes, plop, plop, plop. He gripped his weapons with manly courage, but Lion set to roaring even more, until the cave shook and seemed about to collapse. Then Lion said to

222

the man, "Oh, sir, give your dog those guinea fowls there, and when he has eaten, you can eat the dog, and finally I'll eat you. What do you say?" The gentleman, whose insides had by this time turned to water, said, "Yes, today I'm going to die, because of this hunting business of mine!"

Lion told him again, "You sir, give your dog the guinea fowls, and when he has eaten, then you eat the dog, and then I'll eat you. How about it?" At that moment, they heard a voice coming from somewhere in the cave, saying, "Yes, sir, give the dog those guinea fowls, and when he has eaten, you can eat the dog, and Mr. Lion can eat you, and when he has eaten, I'll eat him." When the Muskrat had finished saying this, he added, "Well, my boys, of the royal bodyguard, what do you say?" And the termites in the cave wall replied, "Waaa, Waaa." At this, Lion and the man were amazed, wondering who was speaking in there. Then they heard again, "You sir, give the dog the guinea fowls, and you eat the dog, and Lion will eat you, and then I will eat Lion. All right, men of the royal bodyguard?" The termites again replied, "Waaa; Waaa; Waa-aa!"

Lion was thinking more about being eaten than about eating anyone else, and the man said to him, "Hold up the cave so it doesn't collapse, and I'll go and cut some timber so we can hold it up." Lion agreed. The man then left, with the Lion still holding up the cave, thinking it would fall. The man hurried off as fast as he could go, and his dog likewise, and they didn't stop until they reached home.

One day he met the Muskrat again, and the rat said, "Did you know who was speaking in the cave, saying, "Oh, sir, give the dog the guinea fowls and you eat the dog and Lion can eat you, then I'll eat Lion. Did I not say I would save you when you helped me across the path? And indeed I scared Lion and rescued you." The man thanked him very much, then went home and told his wife, and they were all happy.[50]

Occasion: This tale is used to reprimand young people not to underrate other people who are weaker than they, because next time the same weak people will come to their rescue when they fall in trouble. This story supports the Biblical principle, "Do for others what you want them to do for you" (Mt 7:12).

(25) Friendship

Once upon a time there was a rich and famous King, who made friendship with someone who led a prayerful life. He also had a younger brother and a

---

[50]   Source: Dictated to me by T.C. Katenga Kaunda – on October 9, 1994 at Chifira, his home.

cousin, whom he did not love despite their love towards him and lending him a hand in his daily duties. Throughout his life he didn't look after them. All his wealth and power lay in the hands of his friends. He despised them like a dog because his heart was after his friend. His counsellors tried to advise him that he should take care of his brother and his cousin in their poverty, but the King could not concede this. His sisters also voiced their concern, because even they were neglected, but the King would not take heed of their complaints.

After many days had passed, one day the King thought to himself, "All my people together with my sisters (*mbumba zangu*) and my counsellors contend against me, because I have neglected my relatives, but turned to love the friend after my own heart. One day I will do something which must prove to me who loves me the most."

One day, the King instructed his wife, "My dear wife, you know that I have bestowed you and all my wealth on my friend after my own heart. He even partakes in my power over the people. I have neglected all my relatives, though they complain about it. Now, call one counsellor for me that I may assign him a little job." At evening time, the counsellor was called, and he was told to bring before the King a he-goat. The counsellor went back to his home, not knowing anything about the intentions of the King. Thereafter, the King slaughtered the goat, and placed it on his bed, and covered it with his sheets.

Four days elapsed, before they could know the secret, the King advised his wife to inform his counsellors that he was ill, so they should invite his friend.

The King afterwards instructed his wife that she should show his friend the bed on which the dead goat was lying, and tell him that it was the King who was lying there dead, while he himself was hiding in the other room. When his friend came, he smelled the stink, and inquired of how the illness began. He believed that the King was indeed dead and now the body was going bad, he said angrily, "Why didn't you invite me to see him when he was still ill? I would have invited a medicine man. I will not bury him, but his relatives." Before he even finished speaking, he was already on the way to his home.

Then the king beckoned his wife and instructed her to invite his brother and his cousin to find out if they would behave the same way as his heart-felt friend. His wife informed the King's brother and cousin. When they had arrived, she said, "I have called you because the King is dead. While he was ill he prevented me from informing you. This should not be strange, considering how he would stay with you. He told me that if he dies, I should call his friend to come and bury him. His friend has refused, but has left for his home in anger."

His younger brothers and cousin said, "We can't revenge the ills he did to us though we were relatives. We can't behave the way his beloved friend has done. We shall call people to assist us in burying him." The King immediately got out from his hiding room and confessed, "Truly, friendship doesn't count much, but kindred." From then onwards he loved his relatives and disregarded the friendship.

Occasion: The tale is used to warn young people against the danger of forsaking their kinsmen at the expense of friendship, which can only be on temporal basis. It also reflects the motif on "friendship" among Tonga people. We should be careful when choosing friends, because some of them can not be trusted. It is for this tale that the elders say, "*Ubali umara cha, ubwezi umara ndi uziwa kukorana ndi munyake* (Brotherhood can not end, but friendship can; you can easily find another friend).

(26) Friends for a time

Long time ago, a certain hunter no longer wanted to live in his own village, but decided to make a little home for himself in the far bush. He searched for a nice place and there built a small hut and made a little farm of yams and cassava.

One day he returned to his hut and found there a young Lion, who said to him: "My friend, I have come to see you. This is my country, but I like you and we two will share this hut." The man did not mind at all and agreed that Lion should live with him. Now, every day the man went out and looked at his farm and watched the crop growing, while Lion went away into the bush and killed meat, which he brought back and shared with the man. Thus they became fast friends.

But one day the Lion said to his friend: "You told me you were a hunter, and yet all this time that we have been together it is I, not you, who has killed our meat." Then the man told the Lion that men killed their meat with guns, and the Lion said nothing. However, he set forth and came near the dwelling place of man. One day he saw a band of men come out to a farm, and all began to hoe the field together. First, though, they had set their guns against a tree. So the Lion rose up and went to the tree and took away one of the guns with all the little bags of powder and medicine attached to it. These he carried home and gave them to his friend, the man.

225

The hunter went out every day and killed meat until they were both tired of it. Then the man said that it was now time for him to leave the bush and return to the villages of men. The Lion said he was sorry, but that the man knew best, and that he, the Lion, would never forget him and would remain his friend so long as he never told other men that he had Lion as a friend. The man promised and left the bush and settled in a village where he married and had many children.

One day the Lion, remembering his friend, decided to visit him to find out if the man was still faithful to their friendship. He came down to the man's farm and hid himself near some rocks, pretending that he was asleep. When one of the man's youngest children found the Lion, he told his father to come quick and kill it. Then the man went to see, and when he looked, he remembered, and said: "Maybe it is my friend. I will not take its skin." The Lion got up and thanked his friend, and said that now he knew that the man was his friend and would go back to the bush happy.

Not long afterwards, the Lion again wished to visit his friend to show him his eldest son. So he took the cub with him to the farm and again hid himself, pretending to be asleep. But this time he did so in a different place. The cub was told to keep away, but to watch how his father's friend was a good man.

When the man and his children came to the farm, one of the boys saw the Lion and told his father that there was meat lying there. The man took his gun and went to the spot, and thinking that the Lion was not his friend - since he had chosen a different place to hide himself in - shot the Lion and killed it.

Then he saw that it was his friend and he began to weep. But the Lion's child, who had watched his father killed, was angry. He swore that from that day onward, he and all other lions would never again look on the face of hunters with pleasure, and that they would kill them whenever they had the chance. That is why, since that day, hunters and lions hate each other.[51]

Occasion: The tale is told to advise young people to keep secrets. They should also honour promises they make. The tale also depicts how things were in the past, how harmony was lost.

(27) An Old Woman who did not Heed Advice

There was once an old woman who had no husband and no relations, no money and no food. One day she took her axe and went to the forest to cut a little firewood to sell, so that she could buy something to eat. She went

---

[51] Source: Dictated by V/H Mnchindwi on October 12, 1994 at his new home.

very far, right into the heart of the bush, and she came to a large tree covered with flowers, and the tree was called *Musolo*. The woman took her axe and began to fell the tree. The tree said to her, "Why are you cutting me? What have I done to you?" The woman said to the tree, "I am cutting you down to make some firewood to sell, so that I can get some money, so that I can buy food to keep me from starving for I am very poor and have no husband or relations." The tree said to her, "Let me give you some children to be your own children to help you in your work, but you must not beat them, nor are you to scold them. If you scold them you will see the consequences." The woman said, "All right, I won't scold them." Then the flowers of the tree turned into many boys and girls. The woman took them and brought them home.

Each child had its own work - some tilled, others hunted bush bucks and still others fished. There were girls, who had the work of cutting firewood, and girls who had the work of collecting vegetables, and girls who pounded flour and cooked it. The old woman didn't have to work any more, for now she was blessed.

Among the girls there was one smaller than all the rest. The others said to the woman, "This little girl must not work. When she is hungry and cries for food, give it to her and don't be angry at her for all of this." The woman said to them, "All right, my children, whatever you tell me I will do."

In this way they lived together for some time. The woman didn't have to work, except to feed the smallest child when it wanted to eat. One day the child said to the woman, "I am very hungry. Give me some food to eat." The woman scolded the child. Saying, "How you pester me, you children of the bush! Get it out of the pot yourself."

The child cried and cried because the woman had scolded her. Some of her brothers and sisters came, and asked her what was the matter. She told them, "When I said I was hungry and asked for food, our mother said to me, 'How I am worried by these bush children!' Then the boys and girls waited until those who had gone hunting returned, and they told them how the matter stood. So they said to the woman, "So you said we are children of the bush. We'll just go back to our mother, Musolo, and you can dwell alone." The woman pleaded with them in every way, but they wouldn't stay. They all returned to the tree and became flowers again, as it was before, and all the people laughed at her. She dwelt in poverty till she died, because she did not heed the instruction given to her by the tree.[52]

---

[52] Source: Dictated by Margaret F. Nyaphiri at her 'Kande Bank' home on October 15, 1994.

Occasion: This tale is told to advise young people not to misuse blessings. A mother should treat her children with love and care. It is also important to heed advice from others. It also warns us against destroying our ecology.

(28) The Lion and the Sparrow

Long time ago Lion came to Sparrow to tell him what lay buried in his heart. "I have seen that you are the smallest bird in this whole land. You eat the tiniest things. The parts of your body like lungs and legs are very, very small. As a result, you lack a lot of things. I would like to enthrone you so that you should also be King, you should be eating delicious things, which I eat. If you obey what I shall instruct you, you shall be as strong as I am and shall be able to kill any animal as I do. You will be roaring as I do. This is how you should be singing, 'Not mine! Not mine! Not mine!' (*Waweni! Waweni*). Once I hear such, I will then know that you have killed an animal. I will come to partake of it, though I might have been very far away." Sparrow agreed to this. On the same day, he received the authority and power to rule and kill animals.

One day Sparrow went into the bush to look for animals. He met some, and killed one. Before he cleaved it, he sang aloud the song he had been taught by Lion, "Not mine! Not mine! Not mine! Not mine!" Lion heard this from where he was. He came to Sparrow and found the animal lying still. "If you do this all the days, and remember the rule I gave you, you shall eat meat all the time." Lion was quite happy because of the song Sparrow had sung. Lion returned to his place after staying with Sparrow for a few days, partaking of the meat. Sparrow continued killing a lot of animals as long as he abode by Lion's instructions. The other birds coveted Sparrow. Unfortunately, when he got used to it, he boasted in his heart, "Who else is like Lion in killing animals except me? He gave me the kingship and the authority to kill animals for good. Lion recognized only me in the whole land. All other birds are useless. Therefore, I can do anything I want to do."

Sometime later he went into the bush and killed an animal. He then sang, "It's mine! It's mine! It's mine! It's mine! (*Wakundamwene-wakunda-mwene*). Upon hearing this, Lion left for Sparrow's place in anger and rebuked him, "Since you have exalted yourself, I have taken away the kingship and the power from you." Immediately, Sparrow was humbled and reduced to what he was in the beginning.[53]

Occasion: The tale is used to warn young people against becoming self-conceited. It is for this tale the elders say, "*Ahurwa ndi asungwana,*

---

[53] Source: Translated by me from *Nthanu za Chitonga* by F.K. Chirwa, pp. 52-54.

kumbukani sambiro ili laku Mtiti mweniyo wangujitutumuwa pa ulemu weniwo ungumuwiya. Mweneko wa ulemu wangukwatapuwa, Mtiti wanguwayuka." (Boys and girls should learn from the Sparrow's downfall, who usurped somebody's authority because of being self-conceited, in the end the owner of authority got it back and the Sparrow was humiliated).

(29) Tupa and his Children

Long time ago the people of a certain village lived in terror of a large snake, which lived in a big pool. Now, in the village was a man called *Tupa*, who had two children and a wife. Like all other parents in the village, *Tupa* was worried about the safety of his children. Whenever they had to go away on a trip, they would leave the children plenty of food, and tell them to stay inside the house.

Tupa was also aware of the Honey-bird (Soro) which sometimes, if his children were not careful, would invite them to danger. It was not always that the Honey-bird would invite someone to plenty bee-hives. One day Tupa and his wife had to go to a distant place. Before they set out on their journey they warned the two children to be very careful. They said, "Children, while we are away, don't follow the Honey-bird, if it comes around. It will lead you where there is danger. In this village there is a pool where a big snake lives."

But the children were irresponsible and they did not listen to their parents' warning. One day the Honey-bird came singing, Che! che! che! It flew all over around the house. As soon as they heard the sound of the Honey-bird, the children ran after it. The Honey-bird flew fast towards the direction where there was the big pool. The children continued to follow it until they arrived at the pool, and never saw the Honey-bird again. All the children saw was a vast pool and a fig tree, which grew besides it.

The children felt very hungry and went up the tree to pick some figs. Some of the figs fell into the water. The noise provoked the snake. It appeared on the water surface with a big splash, and asked, "Who is picking my figs?" The children said, "We are the children of Tupa." The snake said, "If you are the children of Tupa, swell now, so that I can believe." (for 'Tupa' means 'swell'). The children were unable to swell. So the snake came and swallowed them alive.

When the parents came back they found that the children were not at home. They looked for them all around the village and they could not find them. Tupa realized that the children had been misled by the Honey-bird, and that the snake of the pool ate them. Tupa went to the pool and saw nothing except the fig tree. Tupa was tired and hungry. So, he went up a fig tree to pick some figs. Some of the figs fell into the water. At hearing this the snake rose up to the surface of the water. The snake asked, "Who is picking my figs?" "I am Tupa," answered Tupa. The snake said, "If you are Tupa, swell now, so that I can believe it." Now, Tupa began to expand. He became so large that in the end he drank all the water from the pool, leaving the snake on bare ground.

Tupa began to swallow the snake starting from the tail. Now, the snake began to vomit out the two children who came out alive. After that Tupa swallowed the whole snake, and went back with his children. From that day on, they all lived happily. The children never disobeyed their parents again.[54]

Occasion: It is for this tale that children are advised to take heed of the parents' advice which says: *"Mwawana lekani kujumpha chichinyiya cha wapapi winu asani mujumphiya dara muthemwenge uli ndimo anguchitiya yawa wana.* (Children, take head of your parents' advice, lest you fall into trouble as it happened to these children). Children must follow the advice of their parents in order to acquire good behaviour.

(30) The Roan Antelope and the Lion

Long, long ago Antelopes gathered by midday along a river to rest. Unexpectedly, a Lion came out of a bush and came to where the Antelopes had gathered. Antelopes were shaken with fear. Lion said, "Don't fear me because I have come as a friend, not as an enemy. I would like to make friendship with one of you. Once he concedes with this, we should go home together, carrying me on his back because I have been quite ill for some few days. When he returns his reward will be prosperity and great riches, and I will install him as the Chief among you, because I will give him authority over you." Most of the Antelopes were reluctant to agree with the Lion and said, "We all know for sure that we are always destroyed by you, the Lions. Your words are very enticing."

Surprisingly enough, one Antelope agreed with the Lion's words, "Since none of you is willing to be a friend to the Lion, I will be his friend and I will carry him on my back to his home." The Lion became very grateful to this Antelope, which carried him to his home. While on the Antelope's back, the Lion assured the rest of the Antelopes, "You will admire him when he returns with riches and power." Then he turned to his friend Antelope, "My

---

[54] Source: Translated by me from *Nthanu za Chitonga* by F.K. Chirwa, pp. 113-116.

home is very far; move very fast so that we should reach home when it is still light."

The rest of the Antelopes stood in awe. Hare came to where they were and inquired, "Friends, what has transpired so that you should look so gloomy?" Explained one Antelope, "Lion came here and asked us to be friends with him, promising us riches and power. All of us refused, only one of us accepted, so he has left with the Lion on his back for his home. Only he has been persistent. We have tried to discourage him, but he would not pay heed to our advice. There he goes now with the Lion on his back." Hare remarked, "This is the only stupid animal I have seen. It has carried death for itself on its back. I will follow them and cause it to come back."

Hare left immediately with confidence and approached Antelope with Lion on his back and shouted, "Antelope, what have you carried on your back?" The Antelope replied, "It's my friend the Lion whom I am escorting home because he is ill." The Hare alerted the Antelope, "You are very unwise. Don't you know that the Lions are the animals that destroy you? Can't you hear the trumpets blown by the people, which they make from your horns? None of the animals dares to make friendship with the Lion. Look! You have carried 'death' for yourself on your back. You will be destroyed when you reach your destiny." When the Lion heard this, he advised the Antelope to answer, "That's jealous, the Hare! Leave it."

Now the Antelope shouted back in obedience to the Lion. The Hare became very persistent, "Antelope, don't you feel the deathly grip around your thighs and the blood coming out, though you say that I am saying this out of jealousy? Is such a wise friendship? I have never seen such a stupid person who makes friendship with an enemy. You fear people hiding away from them, but the Lions, which devour you, you even carry on your back? Before you reach the destination, the Lion will have devoured you. Better pay heed to this advice." The Lion also was persistent, he advised the Antelope to answer the way he had done at first. Hare then realized that what Antelope was answering came from Lion. "Now I know that you are just being fed what to say by Lion."

Hare then kept quite. Then Antelope realized that he was indeed carrying 'death' on his back. He threw Lion down and escaped to where Hare was. Hare commended Antelope, "You have done a wise thing. Now, get into the water of this river, leaving your horns in sight as though they were branches of a tree." Lion in desperation followed Antelope but couldn't catch it because Lion was exhausted and very thirsty. When he reached the river, he desired to drink water. There was no proper place to step on so as to drink the water, except the horns of Antelope, which appeared like two branches of a tree for support.

So, Lion stepped on these and drank the water. He returned to his home very disgusted, "It's Hare who has made me be stricken with hunger today. I will sleep on an empty stomach. Because of this, Hare has a case to answer. I will go for him." So Lion went home, planning to avenge on Hare. When he was gone, Hare got Antelope out of the water. Antelope expressed his gratitude to him because of saving him from death.[55]

Occasion: This tale is used when advising young people to take heed to what others say about one's life. It is for this tale that the elders say; "*Mwa wahurwa ndi mwa wasungwana lekani kumizizriya ndi kunchakatiya; lusu lenilo ndi rwani kweni kulijowo ndiku kupaska umoyo pakuvwiya mazu ghakucheweska*" (Boys and girls! Do not cling to habits, which will lead you to death, but stop them in order to save your life).

(31) Dishonesty

Long time ago there was a very important chief of a village who had three wives. All the three wives were living in one house. This Chief used to eat dog meat. One day he killed a dog and gave it to the senior wife and said, "Cook this for me." After she had cooked it, she came back and ate it. When the Chief had arrived, he asked his junior wife, "My senior wife has cooked dog meat, who has eaten it? The junior answered, "I haven't eaten it." He then asked the second wife and she also replied, "I haven't eaten it."

He asked the senior wife and she answered, "Are you asking me purposely? Have you forgotten that your junior wife steals whatever relish has been cooked? Who do you think steals all the relish I cook? Is it not your favourite wife? Ask her well, she is surely the one who has eaten all your dog meat. I had fried it very well for you to eat it with good appetite, but she came and ate it all when your junior wife and I had gone to draw water."

The Chief was very angry and said, "She who has eaten my meat will soon be known. When I kill a wild cat someone comes and eats it. When I kill a fox someone comes and eats it too. And now, my fatty dog meat has been eaten also. You women will be in trouble one day."

He made a string and tied it to both sides of the river and said, "You women start one by one crossing the river using the string. The junior wife should cross first, since you say that she is the one who has eaten my meat. As soon as she reaches the middle of the river the string will break if she has indeed eaten my meat. She will fall into the river and die."

---

55 Source: Translated by me from *Nthanu za Chitonga*, by F.K. Chirwa, pp. 76-79.

So it was the junior wife who began to cross the river for she was suspected of having eaten the meat of the Chief. She cried and sang the following song:

Njani warya nyama yabwana?	Who has eaten Chief's meat?
Nye, nye, mulumbeni nyeni	Praise her! Praise her!
Walowoki wakawi pasirya	Let her walk through the string safely
Ndi muole wafumu yo warya nyama	The senior wife ate the dog meat
Nye, nye mulumbeni nye!	Praise her! Praise her!

His junior wife caught hold of the string and swung over until the middle of the river, and finally crossed the river successfully. Then came the second wife—she caught hold of the string and tried to swing over the river. She also sang the same song—she reached the middle of the river. A storm grew and tried to sweep her away, but she withstood it and reached the other side.

Lots of people stood there and waited to know whoever ate the Chief's meat. Then came the turn of the senior wife. She started to cross the river and she too cried and sang the song:

Njani warya nyama yabwana?	Who has eaten Chief's meat?
Nye, nye, mulumbeni nyeni	Praise her! Praise her!
Walowoki wakawi pasirya	Let her walk through the string safely
Ndi muole wafumu yo warya nyama	The senior wife ate the dog meat
Nye, nye mulumbeni nye!	Praise her! Praise her!

The senior wife caught hold of the string and swung over and swung over, and swung over the river up to the middle. A storm came and pushed her this side and that side, this way and that way. She wept bitterly and the string just broke, and there she went deep into the river and died. Then the people were all surprised and said, "Was she just insisting that the junior wife had eaten the meat while it was herself who had eaten it?"

They made merry and said, "You daughters, whenever you have cooked dog meat, give it to the Chief to divide it alone."[56]

Occasion: This tale is used to advise young people to be honest and trustworthy.

(32) The Beautiful Proud Girl

In a certain village there was a very beautiful girl, as beautiful as the moon. All the men sighed over her beauty. But her parents told her to marry no

---

[56] Source: Narrated by Mariya Banda at Kande F.P. School on October 9, 1994.

one but a rich and handsome man. Many men tried to win her love but failed.

One day Hyena heard about this beautiful girl and decided to try his luck. But his friends laughed at him. "Do you think you can win her to love you? What about your tail? She is bound to hate it." But Hyena said. "If you lend me a good suit I will hide my tail in the trousers, she won't know I am Hyena."

Now his friends asked, "What will happen when you go to bed, are you not going to take off your clothes?"

Hyena assured them that he would not dare take off his clothes.

Thus someone lent him a good suit and he looked really prosperous and handsome. No one could guess he was Hyena. As soon as the girl saw him approaching, she ran to her mother to tell her that that was the man of her dreams. Hyena was well received and his marriage proposal was accepted. After the marriage the wife was surprised to see that her husband never took off his clothes, even in bed. "Why don't you take off your clothes?" She asked one day. "I was born with them," was the reply. Hyena refused to bathe in hot water, he preferred the river.

One day, while bathing in the river naked and free, his brother-in-law saw him accidentally. He quickly ran home and told the people to come and see. When the villagers came, they saw that their in-law was Hyena. Hyena was so ashamed that he ran away naked crying, "Huwi-i-i." That was the end of the marriage. The girl felt very humiliated.[57]

Occasion: The tale is used to warn young people against being hypocrites.

(33) Someday someone may be better than you

This story is about four girls, Ngoza, Zione, Tilekeni and Kasiwa. The four girls heard a report of a certain youth who was very handsome, but the son of an evil spirit. They all rose up, and then they set off.

As they were going, Kasiwa dragged behind the others, who drove her still further off, telling her she stank. But she crouched down and hid until they had gone on, and then she kept following them. When they reached a certain stream, they came across an old woman who was bathing. She thought they would rub down her back if she asked, but one said, "May *Chiuta* save me that I should lift my hand to touch an old woman's back." The old woman did not say anything, and the five passed on.

---

[57] Source: Narrated by Jelasi Mduzi of Chalaundi Village on October 10, 1994.

Soon Kasiwa came along, encountered the old woman washing, and greeted her. She answered, and said, "Maiden, where are you going?" Kasiwa replied, "I am going to find a certain youth." And the old woman asked her, too, to rub her back, and unlike the others, Kasiwa agreed. After she had rubbed her back well, the old woman said, "May *Chiuta* bless you." And she said, too "This young man to whom you are all going, do you know his name?" Kasiwa said, "No, we do not know his name." Then the old woman told her, "He is my son, his name is Kamzunguzeni, but you must not tell the others," then she fell silent.

Kasiwa continued to follow far behind the others till they got to the place where the young man lived. They were about to go in when he called out to them, "Go back, and enter one at a time," which they did.

Ngoza came forward first and was about to enter, when the voice asked, "Who is there?" "It is I," she replied, "I Ngoza, who is the most beautiful of all the girls on earth." He said, "What is my name?" She said, "I do not know your name! I do not know your name." Then he told her, "Go back, young lady, go back," and she did.

Next Ziona came forward. When she was about to enter, she too, was asked, "Who are you?" She answered, "My name is Zione, many people come to see my beauty." And he said, "What is my name?" But she did not know, either, and so he said, "Turn back, little girl, turn back."

Then Tilekeni rose up and came forward, she was about to enter when she was asked, "Who is this, young lady, who is this?" She said, "It is I who greet you, young man, it is I who greet you." "What is your name, young girl, what is your name?" My name is Tilekeni, who is the most beautiful of the girls. "I have your name, young woman, I have heard your name. Speak mine." She said, "I do not know your name, little boy, I do not know your name." "Turn back, young lady, turn back." So she turned back and sat down.

Now only Kasiwa was left. When the others asked her if she was going in, she said, "Can I enter the house where such good people as you have gone and been driven away? Would not they the sooner drive out one who stinks?" They said, "Rise up and go in," for they wanted Kasiwa, too, to fail.

So she got up and went in there. When the voice asked her who she was, she said, "My name is Kasiwa, little boy, my name is Kasiwa." He said, "I have heard your name. There remains my name to be told." She said, "Kamzunguzeni, young man, Kamzunguzeni." And he said, "Enter." A rug was spread for her, clothes were given to her and slippers of gold. And then of Ngoza, Zione, and Tilekeni, who before had despised her, one said, "I will always sweep for you," another, "I will pound for you," another, "I will draw water for you." They all became her handmaidens.[58]

Occasion: This tale is used when advising young people to be kind to old people, the poor and the needy in society. You do not know that someday they may be better than you. It is why the elders say, "*Kudanjiya nkhufika cha*," (Being ahead of others does not mean to arrive first). This is affirmed by the Biblical teaching which says, "If anyone wants to be first, he must be the very last, and the servant of all" (Mk 9:35 NIV). Here too, a good service rendered deserves a good reward.

(34) The Wisdom of the Spider

Hare and Spider were once great friends and used to visit each other. One day, Spider decided he wanted to marry. His fiancé lived in one of the heavenly bodies and he asked his friend Hare to accompany him on a trip to see his future parents-in-law. Hare accepted, without knowing that the journey was to the heavens.

At the appointed time, Hare dressed up and went to the home of Spider, who then revealed their destination. Hare told Spider that he could not go, after all, because he was unable to fly. It had always been Hare's habit to say that he could do whatever Spider did, and in many cases he succeeded by cunning. This time, however, he had to admit defeat, and Spider was very pleased to learn that at last his clever friend had to recognize his own great intelligence. He told Hare that he would devise a means for him to go, knowing that Hare would never rest until he found out how it was done. He, therefore, prepared food for Hare, and while Hare was eating, Spider said that he was going to have a bath. He then spun a web reaching to the heavenly body, and as soon as he had done this, he went into the bath so that Hare might not suspect him.

When Spider had bathed, and Hare had eaten, they set off. Spider tied Hare on his back and started climbing the narrow cobweb he had made. Hare was amazed and he greatly praised the cleverness of Spider, trying all the time to induce him to reveal his secret. This Spider refused to do. Hare then began to play his usual tricks. He told Spider that since they were respectable visitors, they ought to make a vow not to interfere with each other. When Spider asked him what he meant by this, Hare said that they should agree that whatever was given them in the name of the 'Son-in-law' should automatically belong to Spider—and Hare must not touch it—and

[58] Source: Narrated by Maira Banda and recorded on October 8, 1994 at Kande F.P. School.

whatever was given them in the name of the 'Visitor' should belong to Hare—and Spider must not touch it. Spider, not knowing that it was contrary to tradition on the heavenly body to use the name 'Son-in-law,' accepted this quite happily. He thought that Hare was on the losing side.

When they arrived, they were welcomed warmly, and the mother-in-law of Spider called on her daughter to bring chairs for the visitors. Hare then said to Spider, "Have you not heard that the chairs are for the visitors? They must then be mine." Spider conceded. This went on for most of their stay—Spider didn't even get anything to eat. Finally he became annoyed with his friend. He told Hare that he wanted to go outside to have a confidential talk with his girl friend. Hare accepted this and remained in the house. Outside, Spider told his girl friend that Hare was not a good person, and he told her also how he had been starving. She explained this to her parents, and from then on they only used 'Son-in-law.'

And so it went on for a considerable time. Hare, however, couldn't keep up his end of the bargain and broke his promise eventually, not to interfere. He made many unpleasant remarks about Spider. He remarked of his table manners, that it was the first time he had seen a greedy person who used his feet as well as his hands when eating. Hare said this in the presence of his fiancé in order to embarrass Spider, so Spider decided to punish his friend by leaving him behind. When, at last, his girl friend had become his wife, and was free to go with him, the three of them set off to the place where he and Hare had originally landed, but only Spider knew where it was. On the way Spider asked Hare to go on ahead since he and his wife had family matters to discuss, and when Spider was out of sight, they went in the opposite direction, for that was where the web between earth and the heavenly body really was.

Hare was now in a dilemma. He could neither live in that world nor leave it. He tried everything, but in vain. Then he decided to jump down. When he landed, he was unconscious. A woman and her son came by. Thinking he was dead she picked him up and put him in her basket, in which she had some food for her son and the boy's shoes. As they walked, the boy, lagging behind, noticed that Hare was eating his food. But when he told his mother she said not to be so silly for "How can a dead thing eat?" The boy kept quiet and so did Hare, who was pretending to be dead. But by and by the boy saw Hare wearing his shoes, and again told his mother. The woman grew suspicious and put the basket down in order to check. Hare immediately jumped out and ran away wearing the boy's shoes. The mother lamented this sorely.

Continuing on, Hare met Elephant, who asked him where he had bought the shoes. He said he had made them. Elephant asked Hare to make some for him, but he refused, saying that as Elephant's feet were so big, the shoes would be very difficult to make, and it would take a long time. But Elephant was persistent, so Hare finally agreed and asked him to go and dig holes deep enough to stand in, and gather four piles of firewood. Elephant did this at once and then called Hare to start to make the shoes. Hare came and told Elephant to stand in the holes. He arranged the firewood around Elephant's feet and set fire to it. Elephant endured the heat for a while and then started to complain that he was burning. Hare told him to have courage.

"You are bigger and stronger than I am and yet you complain when one shoe is made. Your great size is useless. It is mere flesh without energy and resistance. You lack determination." Elephant persevered a little, but it was too late. His feet had burnt, and when Hare told him to come out, he simply fell down and died. Hare then rejoiced and said, "You pretend to be big and clever for nothing. I will now be able to enjoy your meat."[59]

Occasion: It is for this tale that young people are warned against doing evil to others because the same evil will return to them.

(35) The Fox who Cost the Life of his Wife

A long time ago, Fox and Hare befriended each other. Just after that had happened, they found that they had no food to eat. They asked each other what they were to do to save the situation. Hare was the first to answer.

"My friend, don't worry. Now that we're almost starving, I'll go into the garden of the Elephant." Indeed, he went there, and found plenty of elephants, all cultivating the huge garden. On one of the edges of this garden there was an Elephant calf which kept on wailing. Hare talked to these elephants.

"Why is this youngster wailing in that way?"

"Oh, he is like that always," one of the elephants answered.

"Can't you give me this baby so that I can nurse him myself?" Hare asked.

"Sure - if you don't mind."

One of the elephants came over and instructed Hare on how to nurse the young creature. But Hare had his own pans. From time to time he pinched the baby's bottom and so caused him to cry the more. The elephants got alarmed and angrily asked,

"Why is the young one crying again?"

---

[59] Source: Dictated by B. Zgawowa Mphande on October 8, 1994 at his home, Mgodi.

"Oh - he would like to have some bananas." Hare answered.

The same Elephant that had previously come to give instructions came again with a lot of bananas. After she had left, Hare ate everything. Hare slapped the young one. As it was crying, the mother Elephant asked once again what was wrong this time. Hare replied that the baby needed some green maize. Some fresh cobs of maize were brought and Hare repeated, after the departure of the mother Elephant, what he had done previously. For the third time, he made the baby cry by knocking him over. This time, realizing that he had eaten enough bananas and maize, he decided to be frank with the big elephants. The mother Elephant inquired again what was wrong this time and Hare boldly answered, "I have beaten him."

She became so infuriated that she decided to come and tear Hare to pieces. The chase then began. The Elephant never got discouraged despite her clumsiness in running. Hare, however, had set a trap in the forest and he decided to go and pass near it. Elephant saw nothing. Just as she was trying to get through, she stepped over the trap and was caught by the legs quite firmly. Hare, seeing his success, stopped running. He came back to where the Elephant was and noting that Elephant could hardly move any limb, started milking her. Finding that there was a lot of milk coming, he brought from his hiding place all the jugs and pots he had. After filling all of them, he called his friend, Fox, "Hey Fox! Come over here and see this big thing that's caught in my trap."

Fox, seeing that it was a female Elephant, also brought with him all the pots he had. But before he started milking into his pots, he began by sucking the breasts. Hare then said, "Hey boy! That's enough."

"Oh no - just one minute more please," Fox pleaded.

"No, no my friend. You've had enough."

"Oh please no - just a second, my friend!"

"Ok!" Hare consented - but with mischief brewing in his mind. He took away all his jugs and pots, and hid them in the bush where he started singing:

Chiwana changu khwapuka	My trap break!
Khwapuka-khwapuka	Break! break!
Chiwana changu khwapuka	My trap break!
Khwapuka-khwapuka	Break! break

Fox, who was eyes-dropping while at the same time enjoying himself under the Elephant, got alarmed and asked; "Hey - what are you trying to say?"

"Oh nothing. I'm merely humming a tune I learnt a few years ago - so that I don't feel the weight of these jugs as I'm arranging them in good order," Hare answered cunningly.

Fox, satisfied with the answer, went on milking Elephant. Hare, noticing this, once again sang his song;

Chiwana changu khwapuka	My trap break!
Khwapuka-khwapuka	Break! break!
Chiwana changu khwapuka	My trap break!
Khwapuka-khwapuka	Break! break!

Before he started the third line of his song, the trap disentangled itself. Panic-stricken, he tried to run away - but Elephant in the heat of war chased him with all malice.

Luck was with Fox, he rushed into his cave where he found the rest of the members of his family quite excited as they had all this time been waiting for the milk too. Seeing Fox coming in panting, they were perplexed. Elephant, very annoyed at this disappointment, uprooted a piece of bush and with it closed the cave. Then she went back to her own home.

Fox, on seeing the dairy object at the entrance, thought elephant was still waiting for his re-appearance. So, for a number of days the Fox family went without any food or drink. Fox and his wife began killing their own children and eating them. Finally, there was nobody else except the two heads of the family. They began discussing what their next move had to be since Elephant was still waiting for Fox just outside. So they compromised on fighting each other and whoever fell down to his knees first was to be the victim to be eaten by the other.

The fight started, very vigorously. A minute only - and Mr. Fox was down.

"Well my dear, I have to eat you," the wife of Fox announced.

"Oh! No - please - you know if you kill me - you won't have anyone to keep you company."

"I know very well. Ok! Let's forget about it."

But no sooner had his wife turned away than Mr. Fox attacked her so vehemently that she fell down. Mr. Fox showed no mercy. The wife tried to plead in just the same way her husband had done - but in vain.

"I'll find another," he savagely replied as he tore open his wife and began eating her. So hungry was he that he ate her up all at one go. Yet still he was feeling empty. So he decided to eat some of his own parts. He ate up his tail - about half of it, and also both his ears, and some of his fingers.

Hare, who all this time could not understand this long absence of his 'friend', started to hunt for him. He came over to the cave and removed the stump of grass from the entrance and started calling:

Kwambwe -yooo!	*Hey Fox!*
Kwambwe - yooo!	*Hey Fox!*

Fox, peeping out, saw that the dark object was no longer there. After all he could even hear his own friend's voice. Concluding that there was no more danger, he came out lame as he was.

They went to Hare's place where Fox dressed, indeed, very well. They arrived at their destination where they found plenty of lovely girls dancing. They joined them. So attractive was fox that all the beauties flocked to him. Hare, whose hopes were so thwarted, decided to play another trick on Fox. Hare asked the dancers that he should beat the drums himself and they were given to him. He beat them so well that Fox got very involved in the dance. While he was dancing, Hare was humming his own tunes:

My clothes, come on, come off
My clothes, came on, come off
Keteketekete (the sound of drums).

Not a minute passed before Fox's clothes fell to the group and the girls at seeing the ugliness of Fox jeered at him so much that he ran away to hide himself. The girls came to Hare and tried to make him as happy as possible.[60]

Occasion: This tale is told to advise young people not to be greedy.

(36) The Lions and the Hare

There once lived a Chief whose people were caught by a Lion. Lions terrorized the people both day and night. The Chief, his counsellors and ministers, tried to devise ways and means of killing the lions, but failed since they were very cunning and wild. As a result, many people died, and many villages were deserted.

The Chief called his ministers. When they had gathered, he said to them, "My people, you know how dangerous these lions are. Villages are deserted, and many people are still being caught. Today I offer my daughter as a reward to anyone who will prove to be brave by killing these lions, and I will give him the authority to rule over my territory with me." The elders heard this, but none had the courage to do so, because the lions were very wild.

---

[60] Source: Narrated by Jelasi Mkhuzi, Chalaundi village, October 10, 1994.

During this gathering, there came Hare in their midst. When Hare heard all what the Chief had said, he felt the drive within himself to fulfil it. Hare stood up bravely, amidst jeering, and said to the Chief, "I vow before the people to kill the lions on my own, so that I should marry your daughter, and rule with you in your kingdom, as you have said. If I fail to kill them, I will just drive them to a distant place so that your people should live in peace."

The Chief grated permission to Hare to go on with his plan. When all the people had gone to their homes, Hare went straight to the thicket where the lions were, and discovered where they had kept their cubs. After finding this, he took an axe, obtained a bark from a tree, and brought it where the cubs were. He told the cubs to report to their parents that Hare had left that bark so that they should make a bark-cloth for him. He will come and get it after two days. If they refused to do so, Hare would come and kill one of them. This time Hare killed one of the cubs, and went back to his home.

Upon return, the lions found a dead cub. They knew that it was Hare who had killed their cub. In trying to save the life of the remaining cubs, the lions tried to make the bark-cloth by chewing the bark and clutch it with their teeth. But the bark was so hard, only blood dripped from their gums and their teeth started falling out, because the bark was too tough to soften it. Secretly they went away to a distant place.

The next day, Hare came to where the cubs were, but found none. He knew that the lions had failed to make cloth, and had now run away so as to save the cub's life. Hare continued to follow them with his bark. He found the place where they left the cub. He left threatening words to the cub for its parents as he did before. He came to the Chief's village and inquired if the lions were a threat again. To their joy, the people said, "We have received no complaints this month, as we used to in the past. People are at peace, working in their fields without any fear of being captured by lions."

After talking to the Chief, Hare returned to his home. The next day, in the morning, he left for the place he left his bark with the cub. He found that the lions had tried to work at the bark but failed, so they took their cub and sneaked again to a more distant place. He tried to pursue them, but he didn't find them. People knew it was Hare who had chased the lions.

The Chief kept his promise and gave Hare his daughter, wealth and the power to rule with the Chief in his area. The Chief was really pleased with Hare, because he had saved his people from danger.[61]

Occasion: This tale is cited to advise young people to ask for help from those who can deal with a problem they cannot solve on their own. It is for this tale that the elders say, *Mwawahurwa asani ulwani utikwindika ndipo titondeka taweni kuugoda, tikumbe anyidu weniwo angaziwa kutifyanka-nyuwa andi kutijalika pa usenguli.* (Boys! if you see danger surrounding you, and you fail to overcome it, you should ask your friends to come to come to your rescue).

(37) Evil Returns to the One who Does it

A man once hoed his garden and planted it with beans, but when the crop grew, the animals from the forest came and damaged it, so he set a snare.

One day, Leopard came that way and got his leg caught in the trap. He lay there unable to move, and after a time, he spied Bushbuck with his mate and four young ones, whom he called to come and help him. When Bushbuck saw Leopard in the trap, he took pity on him, unfastened the rope and set him free. Said Leopard, "I have been here three days and am famished. You have been very kind to me. Will you extend your kindness and take me to your home and give me food? I am very much indebted to you, and to show my gratitude, I will remain with you." So Bushbuck agreed and led him to his home, where beans were cooked and put before Leopard. But Leopard refused them, saying that he did not eat beans, and made his host kill and give him some fowls to eat.

Everyday, after that, he was given fowls to eat, until none were left; soon the same thing happened with the goats. Finally, when there was no more meat to feed Leopard, he offered him beans again, at which Leopard repeated his indebtedness to his benefactor, Bushbuck, and said he would like to show his gratitude by staying with him, but he really could not eat beans. Then he asked Bushbuck to give him one of his children. Not wishing to offend his guest, he killed one of his little ones, and Leopard ate him. Next day, Leopard asked for and received another child, and so on, until all had been sacrificed and only Bushbuck and his wife remained. Leopard demanded the wife and the poor Bushbuck, not knowing how to get out of it, had to give Leopard his own wife to be eaten. When Leopard again felt hunger, he said to Bushbuck, "Well, now, you have been very kind to me

---

[61] Source: Translated by me from *Nthanu za Chitonga* by F.K. Chirwa, pp. 102-106.

243

and given me all you have, but you still remain. I think I will have to eat you, too." Bushbuck, now really frightened, made off into the forest, chased by Leopard.

After running for three days, Bushbuck met Buffalo who asked him what he was running from. Bushbuck told him and asked his advice, and Buffalo answered, "Well, I don't think that you can do anything except continue your kindness and give yourself up to Leopard." But Bushbuck ran on, and soon met Elephant who, when he heard the story, offered advice identical with that of Buffalo. All the animals of the forest said the same, except Hare who, after listening to Bushbuck's story, offered to act as judge in the case.

When Leopard came up, Hare told him he would like to see how the whole thing had come about, from the moment he got caught in the trap. All then returned to the place where it had happened. "Now," said Hare, setting the trap, "will you just show me how you got caught? Of course if you are trapped, I will free you again." So Leopard stepped on the snare and was immediately caught by the leg. "Ah," said Hare, "that is the way it happened, is it?" Saying that, he went off, taking Bushbuck with him. Man soon found Leopard in the snare and killed him.[62]

Occasion: The story is used when advising young people to help those in trouble. It is also used to warn those who do evil to those who have helped them, because next time the same evil will be done to them. Also the young can be of help to solve a problem in the society.

(38) The Greedy Hyena

Long time ago, Elephant had cultivated millet. He had placed Hare as a watchman in the millet field. Hare prepared his supper after Elephant had left for his home, and took it, but he never got satisfied. "Since the millet is ready on one part of the field, I will be removing one ear every day, taking it as part of my super. In so doing Elephant won't know that it's me who is eating the millet." Hare conceived this in his heart.

One day, Elephant came around the field to inspect it, whereupon he discovered that all the millet, which was to be ready, was no longer there. Elephant asked Hare, "What animal eats my millet which is in season? What a watchman are you since my crop is being consumed?" Hare said, "I don't know the animal." Elephant returned to his home. While at his home, Elephant devised a plan of how to catch the one who was eating his millet. As it was his habit, after taking his super, Hare went for the ripe millet

---

62 Source: Narrated by Rev Try Manda of Kauta village, Fuka-Mapiri, 9.10.1994.

again, not knowing that Elephant was keeping watch. Elephant caught Hare and asked him, "Is it you who is finishing my millet? Tomorrow, I will burn you!"

"Please, please, my friend; before you burn me, wrap me in a bundle of grass while naked, and leave me on a road just over night. Tomorrow you will just light the grass to burn me," Hare pleaded with Elephant. Then Elephant agreed to this and did as Hare assured him.

When Elephant was gone, Hare started singing a song, "Something rotten! Something rotten!" He repeated this over and over, till dawn. Hyena heard the song from a distance. Moved with greed, he ran to where Hare was and said, "The voice is that of you, Hare. Why are you in a bundle of grass, and what kind of a song are you singing?"

"Elephant wrapped me naked in here and left me on the road, promising to bring to me rotten meat very early in the morning. I am worried because I am not used to eating such unclean meat," said Hare. "What a foolish complaint you make! Don't you know that rotten meat is what I delight in eating! Please, please, let me unwrap you, then wrap me therein, so that I should receive the rotten meat," said Hyena.

Hare said, "Since you say that rotten meat is good, then leave me so that I may test it and see if I won't vomit it." Hyena protested persistently, "I am already used to rotten meat. Just wrap me there instead of you." When Hare realized that Hyena was already salivating, he gave in. Hyena unwrapped Hare, and lay in it, whereupon Hare tied him tightly. He was taught the same song so that he should sing throughout the night, till Elephant came.

Very early in the morning, Elephant came with a glowing firewood. As he came near, he was surprised to hear Hyena's voice coming from the bundle instead of Hare's voice. "Is this Hare's voice?" Elephant inquired.

"No, my friend, Elephant. It's me, Hyena. Hare has assured me that you have promised him rotten meat which he doesn't eat. Since he expressed his concern, I offered to be wrapped in his stead since I am used to eating such meat. He had also taught me this song," said Hyena.

"I know it's you, greedy Hyena. Hare escaped because of your greed." Elephant lit the bundle of grass, and Hyena got burnt because of his greed.[63]

Occasion: The tale is told when advising young people against being selfish. It is this tale that the elders warn their children with these words:

---

[63] Source: Translated by me from *Nthanu za Chitonga*, by F.K. Chirwa, pp. 33-36.

"Mwawahurwa nda mwasungwana mbuna njiheni yitaya mwaku ndawona." (Boys and girls, do not be selfish, it can lead you into great trouble).

(39) The Warning that Went Unheeded

Long, long ago, Hare and Deer were friends. Deer lived happily in a garden all by itself; it ate, played and slept without bothering about anything, and it is not surprising that it gained a lot of weight in a month! But about two kilometres away there lived Hare - the only friend of Deer which, for some peculiar reason, came to see Deer but never lived together with it.

One day, Deer asked his friend Hare to show him what Tragedy was like. Hare, with eyes protruding like the Chameleon's, and moustache that told of old age, cleared his throat, licked his dry lips and said, "Ah! A good story in one sense. Now if you're sure that you want to experience "Tragedy," then simply come to my house tomorrow morning and we make some arrangements, don't look so skeptical, because what I can tell you is that you will really see how people escape from danger. The next day the two friend met and arranged to go to a pool.

As it happened, Hare told Dear to climb up a tree. The shadow of Deer reflected on the water. Deer was told to be silent up the tree. Hare then ran towards the bush and found Leopard who looked very hungry and tired. Leopard asked Hare if he had seen some of the prey. Hare told Leopard that he saw Deer hiding in a pool. "Come I'll show you," said Hare. The two went to the pool. As Leopard saw the shadow of Deer on the water, Leopard jumped into the water angrily. But alas! Leopard could not catch Deer. The shadow disappeared because the water was dirty and disturbed. When the water became clean the shadow appeared again.

This continued for a number of occasions, Leopard tried repeatedly for a long time and it was all in vain. Leopard became so doubtful that it thought the hunt was meaningless to continue. Leopard got tired and got angry against Hare for cheating him. That day Leopard went away hungry. Hare came back to Deer and said, "My deer friend, this was the end of your life today, had I not hidden you up the tree. You should not ask for this silly thing again." But Deer said, "My friend, never have I known any danger. You had better stop this, my dear friend. We can't call each other friends, unless I see what Tragedy is."

When Hare emphasized that the warning was meant to preserve Deer's life, Deer simply trotted away and shook his ears to make sure that next time he really saw Tragedy. Deer still insisted that he really wanted to see what Tragedy was like. That evening, on the third day, Hare came to Deer's house and arranged for a place for Deer to see his fate. This time Hare met a team of hunters and told them where he saw Deer hiding. The hunters, too happy not to miss this chance, cast their nets around the bush. When Deer saw that it was in great danger, it ran into the net and was killed.[64]

Occasion: The tale is used to ridicule young people against making demands which can lead them into problems. It is for this tale elder people say, "*Soka lo wakhumbanga ndenili*" (This is the tragedy you wanted to see).

(40) The Two Hunters

Once upon a time there was a hunter in the village of a well-known Chief. This man had established himself as the ablest hunter in the village. He was always the subject of women's talk. Even men envied and feared his superiority in hunting.

Lately, the man had not been doing as well as he usually did. Often his traps yielded no game and his bows and clubs brought nothing to his wife's pots. In the light of this, his wife called him one morning and said, "I have called you, my husband, to tell you my feelings. Not long ago, you were the marvel of the village; everyone respected you for your superiority in hunting. Meat was not a problem here at our home, and no visitor complained of having gone home hungry. Now it appears that this is no longer the case. Yesterday, I cooked the last leg of that cane-rat we had and there is no more meat left." She paused, and without waiting for an answer she added, "If you do not pray to the ancestors to give you any kill today, you must not complain when I cook you the vegetables (*mayani*) you dislike for supper."

The husband then promised to hunt unceasingly that day so that he should succeed in killing an animal however small it might be. He took his weapons and headed for the jungle. He spent a hard time chasing this Kalulu (Hare) and that wild pig, but his efforts were not rewarded. He hunted until just before mid-day, the time to return home. And remembering that half a loaf is better than no bread, he killed two rabbits which he tied to the end of a club and set off for home.

On the way he met a Lion, which was carrying a girl on its back. He threw his arrows and clubs down, and puffing and panting ran for his life in his flight from the fearsome animal. The Lion, contented with the girl it was carrying, called to the gasping hunter, "Stop my friend for we are both hunters. While you were hunting at my home and killing those two rabbits, I was hunting in your village where I seized the Chief's daughter."

---

[64] Source: Translated by me from *Nthanu za Chitonga* by F.K. Chirwa, pp. 71-74.

247

The Lion looked at the dead rabbits. "You have killed two members of our community, while I have had only one from yours. Therefore, you have won. I mean no harm to you: but listen. All I ask you to do is to go home and mind your own business."

The hunter did not wait any longer but ran hot-toot home. There he was greeted by the sound of wailing and lamentation for the loss of the Chief's only daughter. He learned that a group of men had set off to hunt the Lion. He followed the men and told them where he had met the Lion and which way it was heading. He then went into his house, put his rabbits in a corner and went to join the search party.

While this was going on, the Lion had followed the man at a distance and had hidden among some tall-branched trees. When the man was describing his meeting with the Lion, this animal had overheard everything. In its fury it took the dead girl and entered the hunter's house. There it replaced the rabbits with the dead girl and left.

The search party returned without success and sat down to arrange the funeral proceedings. Every family was to contribute food for the funeral and the hunter instructed his wife to bring the two rabbits from the house. The woman, upon reaching the house, was amazed to see the buzzing of houseflies in the corner in the house. She went to look, only to find that it was the Chief's daughter. But she was long dead. She drew back. As she was with two other women who followed her, they were startled to see her recoil from the house. Asked what lay in the house, she only shook her head to show her surprise, and she went to reproach her husband. The two women entered the house, but they too were speechless and came out again.

They rushed to break the news to the Chief. When the mourners at the funeral heard what had happened, they all rushed to the scene to prove the women's tale. They too were horrified to find the dead girl there.

Before the Chief could order his men to arrest the hunter for the murder of his daughter, the innocent victim had fled along the same way he had come. The Lion had not gone home yet. He stood waiting for the man some distance from the Chief's house. As the fleeing hunter approached this spot, the Lion leapt on him and caught him and said, "Now man, what did I tell you? Look at what has happened to you. Now that you are being chased, I might as well eat you." With these words the Lion strangled the hunter and ate him leaving his head in the middle of the road.[65]

---

[65] Source: Dictated by T.H. Chirwa of Kauta village, Fukamapiri, on 9.10.1994.

Occasion: It is for this tale that elders say, *"Uchiwinda ukamba wako wamunyako cha"* (You should talk about your own hunting experiences, not other people's) meaning, one should mind his own/her own business. In other words a person should be self-disciplined and keep secrets.

General Comments on Tonga Myths and Folktales

Indeed, many folktales in Tonga perform this specialized function: the characters and events contained in them are fundamentally symbols illustrating various moral and philosophical issues relating to people. In many cases a specific message is given at the end of the story, which confirms that the various elements operating in the tale have simply been used as symbols to illustrate that message. Other tales do not necessarily spell out their messages, but the audience is expected to derive meaning from the events narrated. Since most of these tales are set in the fantasy world of animals and spirits, the events contained in them can only have meanings for us if we treat them as symbols illustrating certain aspects of life and its problems in the real world of human beings.

As in written literature, therefore, symbols are widely employed in various forms of Tonga oral literature for probing deep philosophical, moral, and spiritual matters. They are a mark of high artistic sophistication in oral culture. In some aspects the literature promotes an obsession which underplays the literary or aesthetic merits of oral literature.

The texts studied here, which have parallels with those found in Chewa, Sena, Yao, Lomwe and Tumbuka ethnic groups, indicate that the Tonga society is not isolated from cultural practices of other societies in Malawi. They reveal the interaction of the peoples of Malawi and their neighbourliness. It has been shown that some of these tales have travelled.

Therefore, reading through these stories, it can be observed that the Tonga employ patterns of symbolic references for analyzing issues brought for consultation, serving as highly symbolic language to explain problems of existence. For instance, the myth about the "Origin of Death" (Tale 2) shows the Tonga concept of God, transcendent from man. The Chameleon is clearly intended as a symbolic manifestation of the divine. It has been shown that it is associated with the supernatural.

While diverse in content and style, the texts in this anthology share many common elements: some feature animal characters (Tale 2, 3, 11 and 12), others are examples of the rogue genre (Tales 10 and 13). There are also

249

stories about people and their environment, or stories which show animals associated with man in some special way. The satirical use of animals seems to play a supportive role, alongside human characters, in order to reflect actual experience. This is clear in the case of the Blackbird, the Hare, the Lion and the Elephant. What seems clear, however, is that from the analysis made of some of these stories, is that their narrators display towards the beasts an attitude of moral tolerance or neutrality, for much indulgence is shown towards creatures whose destructive powers make them a threat to man. The Hyena, for example, who comes closest in oral literature to complete moral proscription as his greed is a deadly example for human society, is sometimes seen as a hard-working character concerned about truth, justice, and cooperation (Tale 8).

Folktales address various themes which include: conflict; drought; defence-lessness, friendship; marriage; obedience and disobedience; good and evil; unity; and so on. On conflict, stories about misunderstanding among members of one clan have brought in chaos and enmity as opposed to the harmony which was at the beginning (Tales 11-15). The story of the three brothers (Tale 9) also illustrates this point. When the elders of the village got the message from the song of the bird, they killed the other two boys. Therefore, wrongdoers should be punished accordingly for their offence. On the theme of drought, for example, Hare manipulates other characters. Although the animals find a solution to their problem, they still face difficulties in guarding the water from Hare (Tale 8). Nothing stains the communal feeling in this story. When people are faced with a challenging situation, the animals cooperate in an attempt to end the drought.

The defenceless such as travelers and orphans, the aging and the needy should always be treated kindly. The able or rich ones in the community should not look with contempt on the poor or the weak. This is portrayed in the stories "Kindness Pays" (Tale 24), and the "Orphaned Millipede" (Tale 6). It is these despised people who achieve the impossible. The orphan shows this progress from tragedy to comedy in a more subtle way. He is on a pilgrimage of triumph over oppression.

The themes of friendship and justice overlap. When you are cruel to a friend, he will also be cruel to you later. This is analogous to the Old Testament saying "An eye for an eye." The stories about "An Eye for an Eye" (Tale 21), and "Friends for a Time" (Tale 26), illustrate these two themes. The theme of marriage has also been reflected in several stories. Of these, in

Chimutu (Tale 7), the inevitable misfortune of a handicap makes the girls refuse marriage. When a humble girl accepts him, she discovers that she is married to a man worth admiring. The moral of the story is that appearance should not be a criterion in choosing a marriage partner. Closely related to appearance is how wealth determines certain marriages.

The theme of reward for obedience or the penalty for disobedience is also a feature noted in these tales. Disobedience to advice brings punishment. Only the cunning or mischievous are able to avoid the unpleasant consequences of disobedience as shown the "Old Woman who did not Heed Advice" (Tale 27). The old woman later on lived in poverty till she died. In the story about "Lion and Sparrow" (Tale 28), Sparrow was humiliated because Lion took back his authority. The theme of unity is illustrated in several tales. The story about "Hare and the Well" (Tale 8) is a good example. Those showing no concern for the misfortune of a neighbour do not value fellow human beings. The list of themes is long as seen in the folktales. Enough to say that the sample of the folktales shows features which are of general interest to modern life. They are profoundly homocentric, yet theocentric as well (Tales 2 and 9 etc).

CHAPTER SEVEN

AN ANTHOLOGY OF TONGA PROVERBS

While the previous chapter has given an anthology of the different Tonga myths and tales, this chapter provides an anthology of another major genre of oral literature, the proverbs and sayings. Here again a selection had to be made.[1] This chapter has three aims. The first is to present the proverbs and to translate and explain them. The second is to investigate the moral applications and the third aims is to directly relate tem to Christian moral teaching.

Sources and Authority of Proverbs

Tonga proverbs are like Old Testament proverbs and those of the people of other cultures, and they can indeed be used for evangelization. Therefore, in this section the term proverb will include Tonga proverbs as well as the written proverb, both Biblical and literary; the latter type has come to us mainly in the form of collections of proverbs.

According to George R. Hamilton, written proverbs should perhaps be called not proverbs but "aphorisms or maxims, of which the maxim has the narrower meaning of a principle by which the author would guide himself or seek to guide others."[2] By that standard, many of Christ's statements are maxims, i.e., guidelines for a good life, moral principles and daily rules. Hamilton continues:

> A proverb is an aphorism (often of extreme brevity and the easier to remember) which has passed into wide currency and become a byword... These compact sayings can only contain a fragment of the whole truth. Yet, as flashes of insight coming from the author's experience, they derive value from a silent context ... aphorism is a timeless and international mode of expression.[3]

---

[1]   For additional proverbs see the appendix.

[2]   George R. Hamilton in *Cassell's Encylopaedia of World Literature I*, London, 1973, p. 35.

[3]   Ibid., p. 36.

George B. Milner is perhaps the first to ask the question: Should not a proverb be defined in terms of its forms of proverbs in French, English or Polynesian languages? He classifies proverbs generally into sixteen formal categories, based on their syntax.[4] The student of traditional proverbs, when interpreting the contents of proverbs of a given ethnic group, will take into account and explain the beliefs of that group in so far as they are relevant for the proverbs. These beliefs are usually not his own.

Students of Biblical proverbs, on the other hand, especially of the numerous maxims in the New Testament, usually have a different approach: if they are believers, the truth of all the Biblical proverbs is taken for granted, including such as: "God has made man upright" (Eccl 7:29), a statement which some people might wish to challenge. However, the true meaning of a proverb is often only implied, not explicitly stated, and in this Biblical proverb, I think the implied meaning is: "Try and be what God intended you to be, an upright man." Proverbs are exhortations, not dogmas.

This exhortative function of the proverb is closely connected with its conservative survival in the oral tradition. The proverb is the last living genre in the oral traditions of urbanized, modernized peoples. Stories can be read, songs are taped or put on disk, but the proverb remains oral and personal. In this chapter I shall make a few suggestions to help readers engage in some further study of and reflection on Tonga proverbs and the Christian message in preaching and teaching.

In Tonga society, proverbs are never ascribed to any particular individual, but collectively to the ancestors, the wise men and women of old, and it is not known who composed a particular proverb, and all proverbs are credited to the elders. In many African societies, when a proverb is cited, it is preceded with a statement like, "so said the elders..." This formula may be a way of stating a proverbs' authority. It is also a way of saying that all the people own the proverbs, and that they contain experience, wisdom, and valid counsel, which are to be acknowledged by all. Thus collective values and beliefs of the Tonga people can be discerned from their proverbs.

These proverbs touch on all conditions of life: wealth and poverty, health and sickness, joy and sorrow, occupations, farming, hunting, fishing, walking, sleeping, marriage, childbearing, upbringing. They are proverbs

---

4   G.B. Milner, "What is a Proverb?" in *New Society* no 332, London: SPCK, p. 199.

which speak about and to all manner of people: chiefs and subjects, rich and poor, women and men, children and adults.

In their present form, the bulk of Biblical proverbs and parables have been ascribed to specific individuals; namely, King Solomon (Prov 1:1), Agur (Prov 30:1), the mother of King Lemuel (Prov 31:1), and Jesus Christ (Mt 13:1-3). In Biblical times, proverbs were composed by wise men and were widely used in Israelite society and among other ancient peoples. King Solomon, for example, acclaimed to be wiser than the wise men of the East and Egypt—indeed, acclaimed to be the wisest of all men. He is said to have composed three thousand proverbs (1 Kings 4:29-33, Eccl 1:1; 12:9).

Solomon and the other composers of proverbs formulated their proverbs from life's experiences. These experiences were based on their observation of human life and behaviour, animals, birds, reptiles, and fish (1 Kings 4:33). Solomon is said to have been given his unusual wisdom and insight by God himself (1 Kings 4:29).

In the Gospels Jesus uses proverbs as guidelines for a good life, moral principles and daily rules. They are exhortations, not dogmas. For instance, when Jesus wanted to teach the people on "God's Kingdom," he used parables. Thus, on many occasions, Jesus used proverbs. Here are a few sources and some example from the Bible:

Observations from the world of nature: for example, the parable of the sower (Mk 4:1-9); the parable of the seed growing secretly (Mk 4:26-29)

Knowledge of familiar customs of everyday life and events: the parable of the yeast (Mt 13:33); the parable of the ten virgins (Mt 25:1-13).

From well-known events in recent history: e.g., the parable of the high-ranking man about to be made king but who was not liked by some of the citizens, and who gave gold coins to servants to trade with (Lk 19:12-27). Some historians have identified this person to be Archelaus, son of Herod.

From normal events: as in the parables of the labourers in the vineyard (Mt 20:1-16); the prodigal son (Lk 15:11-32), and the unjust judge (Lk 18:2-8).

On the theme of the 'Kingdom of God' Jesus says, "Many are invited but few are chosen" (Mt 22:14) and "No one can break into a strong-man's house and take away his belongings unless he first ties up the strong man then he can plunder his house" (Mt 12:29).

On 'hypocrisy', he says, "They are blind leaders of the blind and when one blind man leads another, both fall into a ditch" (Mt 15:14).

On the theme of 'responsibility', Jesus says, "To have good fruit you must have a healthy tree" (Mt 12:33).

On 'justice' and 'reconciliation' the Bible says, "Eye for an Eye and a tooth for a tooth" (Mt 5:38).

On 'showing respect', Jesus says. "A prophet is never welcomed in his hometown" (Lk 4:25).

On 'humility', Jesus says, "Whoever wants to be first must place himself last of all and be the servant of all" (Mk 9:35) and "For everyone who makes himself great will be humbled, and everyone who humbles himself will be made great" (Lk 14:11).

On taking 'self-initiative', Jesus says, "People who are well do not need a doctor, but only those who are sick" (Lk 5:32).

On the theme of 'repentance', Jesus warns: "No one tears a piece of a new coat to patch up an old coat. If he does, he will have torn the new coat, and the piece of new cloth will not match. Nor does anyone pour new wine into used wineskins, because the new wine will pour out, and the skins will be ruined" (Lk 5:36).

On 'making decisions', Jesus says, "Foxes have holes and birds have nests, but the Son of Man has no place to lie down and rest" (Lk 9:58).

On 'making choices', Jesus says, "No servant can be the slave of two masters" (Mt 6:24).

On 'perseverance', Jesus says, "anyone who starts to plow and then keeps looking back is of no use for the Kingdom of God" (Lk 9:62).

On 'trust', Jesus says, "A person's true life is not made up of the things he owns, no matter how rich he may be" (Lk 12:15).

On 'disobedience', Jesus says, "Anyone who does evil things hates the light" (John 3:20).

On 'obedience', the Bible says, "The one who gathered much did not have too much, and one who gathered little did not have too little" (2 Cor 8:15, cf. Ex 16:18).

On 'faith', Jesus says, "Whoever eats my flesh and drinks my blood lives in me and I live in him" (John 6:56).

On 'trust', Jesus says, "People will look at him whom they pierced" (John 19:37, cf. Zechariah 12:10).

On 'responsibility', the Bible says, "The parents ate the sour grapes but the children got the sour taste" (Jer 31:29).

Jesus saw that God's word with its message of salvation would be more meaningful and better understood if he used proverbs, parables or riddles. Likewise the word of God can become more meaningful in the Tonga culture, if preachers can use proverbs. There are many values that are conveyed through Tonga proverbs, which the Gospel affirms.

In this chapter, 114 Tonga annotated proverbs are presented as a case study, showing the possible integration of Tonga proverbs into the teaching of the Christian church.

Each of them has notes written on it, in five sections, as follows: First comes the common version of the proverb in Tonga with an English translation. Under *Explanation,* a literal explanation of the proverb is given. In a few cases, the story of the origin of the proverbs is given. But the explanation is limited to the image used, the actual life situation depicted, custom or history referred to. Under *Meaning,* the deeper or real meaning and moral lesson of the proverb is given. Under *Occasion,* the actual or probable occasions in which the proverb is used in Tonga traditional society are stated. Possible occasions or purposes for which the proverb can be used in Christian preaching and teaching are also suggested.

Finally, under *Related Biblical Themes and Stories* a number of Bible passages, themes or stories are cited. Preachers and teachers are encouraged to use these proverbs.

AN ANTHOLOGY OF TONGA PROVERBS

1 Abaya chiwanda

They have killed a spirit

Explanation: The Tonga believe that certain creatures, e.g. snakes, have human spirits. Thus killing such a 'snake', e.g., *Mlinga* (a short, stubby, blackish non-poisonous snake) means killing the spirit of someone and is believed to lead to the death of that person who kills it.

Meaning: Cutting off the spirit's chance of visiting its former haunts by killing the form it made use of.

Occasion: The proverb is used when warning people against killing certain creatures which are believed to be human spirits in animal form. Usually people are advised not to kill any creature that comes around at a funeral.

Related Biblical Themes and Stories

There was a large herd of pigs nearby, feeding on the hillside, so the spirits begged Jesus, 'Send us to the pigs and let us go into them (Mk 5:11-12).

2 Abaya soro cha

You don't kill a honey-bird

Explanation: There is a legend that the Tonga people call the honey-bird, Soro, because it has power to draw people after it and to show them something important. In most cases it leads them to where there is a beehive with plenty of honey.

Meaning: You should not reject or despise a person who has the virtue of looking after the people on whom his/her influence is directed.

Occasion: The proverb is used when advising people to respect those who care for them in their families or community and not despise them. Preachers have cited it to decry how the Jews killed Jesus, who was the source of their salvation.

Related Biblical Themes and Stories

We should never leave the Lord to serve other gods! The Lord our God brought our fathers and us out of slavery in Egypt and we saw the miracles that he performed. He kept us safe wherever we went among all the nations through which we passed (Joshua 24:16-17).

Peter and John condemned the Jews for killing Jesus, because of Him the scripture says, "The stone that you builders despised, turned out to be the most important of all. Salvation is found through him alone; in all the world there is no one else whom God has given who can save us" (Acts 4:11-12).

3 Amunkhwele asekana viphata

Baboons laugh at each others' hind parts

Explanation: People often talk about things that involve others and not those involving themselves.

Meaning: A person should mind his/her own business.

Occasion: The proverb is cited for those people who are hypocrites. They condemn others, while they too are equally condemned. In other words, people should not despise others.

Related Biblical Themes and Stories

David became very angry with the rich man and said, "I swear by the living Lord that the man who did this ought to die. For having done such a cruel thing he must pay back four times as much as he took." "You are that man," Nathan said to David (2 Sam 12:5-7).

You hypocrite! First take the log out of your own eye, and then you will see clearly to take the speck out of your brother's eye (Mt 7:5).

4 Boza liwele mweneko

A lie returns to the one who tells it

Explanation: Usually liars are exposed in the community.

Meaning: You should not tell lies about people in their absence, since lies are bound to be exposed and you will get ashamed of yourself.

Occasion: The proverb is often cited in courts where the accused persons bear false witness to each other. It is used to advise someone to stop telling lies. Preachers use it to warn people who tell lies.

Related Biblical Themes and Stories

One of the seven things that the Lord hates and cannot tolerate is "a witness who tells one lie after another" (Prov 6:19).

Isaiah deplored the people of Judah for depending on lies and deceit to keep them safe (Is 28:15).

The Lord said that hailstorms would sweep away all the lies they depend on and floods would destroy their security (Is 28:17). That is, God will expose their lies and they will be humiliated.

In the story of Ananias and Saphira, Peter exposed their lies and they were humiliated: Peter said to him, "Ananias, why did you let Satan take control of you and make you lie to the Holy Spirit by keeping part of the money you received for the property?" (Acts 5:3)

5 Changa epa wamko ku mchira wataya

If you hold a changa (squirrel) by the tail, you lose it.

Explanation: If one wants to catch a squirrel, one should avoid aiming at its tail. It can slip away by leaving parts of its tail behind.

Meaning: There are certain things which are short-lived; therefore, one must be careful in making decisions.

Occasion: The proverb is used to warn a person against clinging to something which is short-lived. For instance, one should seek a permanent job. The proverb is also cited when people want to deal with a culprit involved in a particular case. To catch such a person one must be careful.

Related Biblical Themes and Stories

Do not store riches for yourselves here on earth, where moths and rust destroy, and robbers break in and steal. Instead, store up riches for yourselves in heaven (Mt 6:19-20).

Judas agreed to it and started looking for a good chance to hand Jesus over to them (Mk 14:11).

6 Charu mbanthu

The world is people

Explanation: The world cannot be enjoyable without people.

Meaning: A person should be careful with his/her life.

Occasion: The proverb is cited when advising young people not to be careless with their lives, because they are the next generation. Sometimes it is used in times of epidemics as a lament when many people are dying. Hence it is used as a caution to those living to be careful, because they will make the world of tomorrow.

Does a person gain anything if he wins the whole world but loses his life? (Mk 8:36)

He was in the world, and the world was made through him, yet the world knew him not (John 1:10).

I have given them thy word, and the world has hated them because they are not of the world, even as I am not of the world (John 17:14).

7 Chigau ndi ku mupozwa

Cassava is a young plant

A good harvest of cassava is determined by young growing cuttings.

Explanation: The society should take care of the youth, and the youth should work hard in order to acquire the skills and knowledge employed in adult life. The Tonga look at the young cassava seedlings in forecasting a bumper yield. The proverb is metaphorically used.

Meaning: Today's youths are the future nation.

Occasion: The proverb is cited at funerals when a young person dies. The implication is that the society loses future leaders. Sometimes it is used in circumstances where someone is being reproached for mistreating a young person or when reprimanding a young person for his/her lack of knowledge. The implication is that the youth are warned against indulging in habits which can bring early deaths upon their lives, e.g. to avoid sex outside marriage. Preachers apply this proverb during catechetical teaching of the youth. The implication is that socialization of the youth to be future leaders depends on the elders.

Related Biblical Themes and Stories

Never forget these commands that I am giving today. Teach them to your children (Dt 6:6-7 and Ps 78:5-7).

The proverb can be related to Jesus' regard for the children, when he said, "Let the children come to me and do not stop them, because the Kingdom of God belongs to such as these" (Lk 18:16).

8 Chikumbu chimoza chituswa nyinda cha

One thumb cannot crush a louse

Explanation: The problems requiring a people's collective efforts always exist. It is difficult for one thumb to destroy a louse without the help of another finger - just as it is equally difficult for one person to solve a problem. This is equivalent to "No man is an island."

Meaning: Unity is strength. We rely on each other.

Occasion: It is cited when advising young people on the need for unity in the house, the village, the community. Politicians use it when they campaign for their parties in order to win in the elections. Preachers use the proverbs to help people understand Church unity.

9 Chingana nyoko wawi ndi nyivu ndi nyoko mbwenu

Even though your mother has gray hair, she is still your mother

Explanation: Elderly parents with gray hair are sometimes despised. Young people should love their parents, although they are getting old and may not appear attractive or firm.

Meaning: Don't disown your parents just because they happen to be poor, of low social status, or old.

Occasion: It is used when advising young people who exhibit such deplorable attitudes to their parents. Preachers use it as an exhortation for young people to respect their parents and elders.

Related Biblical Themes and Stories

The proverb addresses the theme of respect as reflected in the fifth commandment which says: "Respect your father and your mother, so that you may live a long time in the land that I am giving you" (Ex 20:12).

A wise son makes his father proud of him; a foolish one brings his mother grief (Prov 10:1).

When your mother is old, show her your appreciation (Prov 23:22).

Anyone who makes fun of his father or despises his mother in their old age ought to be eaten by vultures or have his eyes picked out by wild ravens (Prov 30:17).

10 Chiuta wamto

God has taken him/her

Explanation: This expresses the belief that death originates from God, or that God wills that one should die and live with Him.

Meaning: A person receives life from God (Chiuta). Therefore, death is the call of Chiuta (God) who will take care of the dead.

Occasion: The proverb is cited during a funeral to give hope and courage to the bereaved that the one who is dead is a child of God who has called him/her to himself, that is, God will take care. It is also used in preaching to refer to God as the Creator, who takes back life to Himself.

Related Biblical Themes and Stories

Moses, the Lord's servant, died in the land of Moab as the Lord had said he would. The Lord buried him in a valley in Moab, opposite the town of Beth-peor, but to this day no one knows the exact place of his burial (Dt 34:5-6).

God will take care of me (Ps 27:10).

But God will rescue me, he will save me from the power of death (Ps 49:15).

11 Chiwele vuli chingubaya Tungwa

Returning killed the Antelope

Explanation: The proverb refers from a folktale where Antelope went back postponing his journey. On his way back he met Leopard who killed him.

Meaning: A person should be steady in making decisions. In other words, a decision taken should be adhered to.

Occasion: The proverb is cited to warn people against making hurried decisions so that they don't mess up things. People should live by principles about their lives.

Related Biblical Themes and Stories

But Lot's wife looked back and was turned into a pillar of salt (Gen 19:26).

12 Cho chingukwezga Pusi, chingukwezga Munkhwere

What made the monkey to climb a tree made the baboon also to climb a tree

Explanation: A person should not rejoice when others are ill-treated.

Meaning: It is unwise for a person to laugh at a colleague or a relative in difficulty, since he too may one day experience a similar situation.

Occasion: The proverb is used to advise a person to sympathize with or even help others involved in a problem, rather than rejoice over it. The teaching is worth noting by people in various walks of life like classmates who may see one of their number mistreated by their teachers, or workers who may see some colleagues unfairly treated by a cruel master, or even citizens who may see the rights of some fellow nationals infringed upon by a dictatorial leader. It is also used to warn young people against neglecting their peers who fall into trouble. Preachers use it to exhort people to care for others.

Related Biblical Themes and Stories

You are my friend! Take pity on me! The hand of God has struck me down (Job 19:21).

Let not those rejoice over me who are wrongfully my foes, and let not those wink the eye who hate me without cause (Ps 35:19).

Don't be glad when your enemy meets disaster, and don't rejoice when he stumbles. The Lord will know if you are gloating and he will not like it, and then maybe he won't punish him (Prov 24:17-18).

13 Cho chituza chitumba ng'oma cha

That which comes does not beat a drum

A certain thing that comes does not beat a drum .to announce itself.

Explanation: Certain things come to us by surprise. Therefore we should always be ready, otherwise we are taken by surprise.

Meaning: An urgent thing must be given prompt attention.

Occasion: The Proverb is used when advising a person to attend to a problem promptly in order to prevent it from worsening. Sometimes in a job situation, young people are advised to complete their tasks for they do not know when the boss will need the final report. In order to safeguard the job one needs to complete the task in good time. Otherwise we are taken up by some unexpected events. For instance, a watchman is warned not to sleep in the night, daring thieves might rob the property he guards. Preachers warn Christians to be ready for Christ's second coming.

I lie awake; I am like a lonely bird on a housetop (Ps 102:7).

I will climb my watchtower and wait to see what the Lord will tell me to say and what answer he will give to my complaint (Habakkuk 2:1).

Keep watch and pray that you will not fall into temptation (Mt 26:41).

Our Lord Jesus Christ constantly warned his hearers to keep watch. "Watch then, because you do not know when the master of the house is coming—it might be in the evening or midnight or before dawn or at sunrise. If he comes suddenly, he must not find you asleep. What I say to you then I say to all: "Watch!" (Mk 13:35-36).

The end of all things is near. You must be self-controlled and alert, to be able to pray (1 Peter 4:7).

14 Cho utanja ndichu chipunduwa

A habit that you like destroys you

Explanation: A person should not over-indulge in silly habits.

Meaning: Excessive indulgence in a thing is harmful.

Occasion: The proverb is used when advising people who do not stop their bad behaviour, e.g. over-drinking, fighting, smoking, sexuality, etc.

Related Biblical Themes and Stories

Don't spend all your energy on sex and all your money on women; they have destroyed kings (Prov 31:3).

Jesus warned those who had sinned but had been forgiven, lest something worse would happen to them (John 5:14).

15 Garu yiruma mbuyake

A dog bites its master

Explanation: A hungry dog, if provoked, can bite even its master.

Meaning: A person should be careful in the way he/she handles things.

Occasion: The proverb is used when warning people against being careless with their lives. Sometimes it is used as a warning against being self-conceited or proud. Preachers warn people against provoking God, their master.

The Israelites turned against their God and made Him angry: when Israel was a child, I loved him and called him out of Egypt as my son. But the more I called to him, the more he turned away from me (Hosea 11:1-2).

God resists the proud but shows favour to the humble (Prov 3:34; 1 Peter 5:5).

16 Jenda-yija wangukukurwa ndi maji

A lone traveller was swept away by a stream

Explanation: The proverb is based on legends that lone travellers have disappeared without any trace. It was common for Tonga people in the old days to travel to South Africa alone and never come back. It was thought that either wild beasts, which were prevalent at the time, or slave traders had captured them. The equivalent English proverb is: "Two is a company, one is none."

Meaning: There is danger in travelling alone. We need to make fellowship with other people.

Occasion: The proverb is used when reminding travellers of the importance of company for purposes of security. It can also be applied to urban dwellers who like to walk at night for beer parties or for other purposes. Young people should choose good company with good moral habits. Preachers use it to exhort people to walk with God, protector of their lives.

Related Biblical Themes and Stories

Enoch walked with God (Gen 5:22-23). He spent his life in fellowship with God who protected his life, and he lived a long life of 365 years.

Two are better than one, because together they can work more effectively. If one falls down, the other can help him up. But if someone is alone and falls, it's just too bad because there is no one to help him (Eccl 4:9-12).

Jesus sent two of his disciples ahead to find a colt in the village of Bethany (Mk 11:1-2). This was to ensure that there was security between them.

17 Juwani lapa mchenga nkhwambiya pamoza

A race in the sand should be started together

Explanation: Part of Tongaland is along the lakeside. Its beautiful beaches cover a vast landmass with heaps of sand. It is difficult to run in the sand, so that no matter how good one is at running, if he or she is left behind, they cannot catch up with others.

Meaning: It is better to start your work early to yields good results.

Occasion: This proverb is cited to advise young people to be vigilant, diligent and hard working, especially those who are at school. They are advised to work hard from early classes since knowledge accumulates. Pupils trained in running races are advised not to look behind when they compete with others. Farmers are advised to clear their lands early so that they may have better harvests. Thus, to do well in certain activities, one is advised to start at the same time with others.

Related Biblical Themes and Stories

It comes out in the morning like a happy bridegroom, like an athlete eager to run a race (Ps 19:5).

Jeremiah, if you get tired racing against men, how can you race against horses? (Jer 12:5)

Surely you know that runners take part in a race, but only one of them wins the prize. Run then in such a way as to win the prize. Every athlete in training submits to strict discipline in order to be crowned with a wreath that will not last; but we do it for one that will last forever. That is why I run straight for the finishing-line (1 Cor 9:24-27).

Since we are surrounded by such a great cloud of witnesses, let us throw off everything that hinders and the sin that so easily entangles, and let us run with perseverance the race marked out for us (Hebrew 12:1).

18 Kanda apa nani ndi kandepo

Where you step I shall also step

Explanation: The proverb shows how true friendship should be. Friends should be kind to each other. The equivalent English proverb is "A David and a Jonathan."

Meaning: People who are great friends.

Occasion: The proverb is cited when referring to young people whose friendship appears so bound up that no one can separate them. Preachers often use the proverb with the story about the friendship of David and Jonathan as role models of true friendship.

Related Biblical Themes and Stories

Jonathan swore eternal friendship with David because of his deep affection for him. He took off the robe he was wearing and gave it to David, together with his armour and also his sword, bow and belt (1 Sam 18:3-4). Both David and Jonathan were crying as they kissed each other (1 Sam 20:41).

Jesus said that the greatest love a person can have for his friends is to give his life for them (John 15:13-14).

19 Kanthu kekose kendi nyengo yaki

Everything has its own time

Explanation: Things happen according to their own time.

Meaning: A person should not force something to happen.

Occasion: This proverb is cited to advise people to wait patiently for things to happen at the right time. In other words, people are warned against being too anxious over things. Preachers constantly use this proverb to refer to specific events in the society, like sudden deaths and disasters caused by floods etc and thereby console people.

Related Biblical Themes and Stories

For everything there is a season, and a time for every matter under heaven (Eccl 3:1).

The time is coming when I will make a new covenant with the people of Israel and with the people of Judah (Jer 31:31-34).

Put it in writing because it is not yet time for it to come true. But the time is coming quickly, and what I show you will come true. It may seem slow in coming, but wait for it; it will not be delayed (Habakkuk 2:3).

But the time is coming and is already here, when by the power of God's Spirit people will worship the Father as he really is, offering him the true worship that he wants (John 4:23).

20 Kayuni ko kaja pauta kalasika cha

A bird on your bow cannot be shot

Explanation: A person seeks the assistance of another person when he/she is in difficulty. The equivalent English proverb is, "Blood is thicker than water." In Tonga society parents can decide on matters of the marriage of their daughter. It is the aunt who handles such issues.

Meaning: It is not easy for a judge to pass judgement against a relative.

Occasion: The setting of the proverb is at the court, or at the elders' council, when a person objects to having his case tried by someone related to the other party in the conflict; or when a judge declines to settle a case involving a relative. Sometimes it is used to show one's failure to solve a problem which involves one directly, like a medicine man failing to cure himself. It is also used to advise children to ask others to help them when they are in trouble.

Related Biblical Themes and Stories

"Doctor, heal yourself." You will also tell me to do here in my home town the same thing you heard were done in Capernaum (Lk 4:23).

21 Kufumba nkhuwona nthowa

To ask is the desire to know the way

Explanation: There is no reason to be self-conceited when in actual sense you know very little.

Meaning: It is always helpful to ask for advice before one does things that one is not sure about.

Occasion: The proverb is cited when reproaching a person who has made a serious mistake, or has done something wrongly because of his failure to seek advice in the first place. Pupils in a school setting should ask their teacher to show them how to do things correctly.

Related Biblical Themes and Stories

Ask, and you will receive; seek, and you will find; knock, and the door will be opened to you (Mt 7:7).

The gate to life is narrow and the way that leads to it is hard, and there are few people who find it (Mt 7:14).

Thomas said to him, "Lord, we do not know where you are going, how can we know the way?" Jesus answered him, "I am the way, the truth, and the life. No one goes to the Father except through me (John 14:5-6).

22 Kujikama uryengi kanthu ndi wala, kusoka uwengi waka

Kneeling you eat with elders, keep standing you eat nothing

Explanation: One of the etiquettes practised by young people in order to show respect to their elders is that of kneeling down.

Meaning: You learn a lot of things from elders when you are humble, but not when you are rude.

Occasion: This proverb is cited when advising a young person to be good to elders in order to win their love and open their storehouse of knowledge and wisdom. Sometimes humble young people in the society are used as role models for their acquisition of an unusually large amount of wisdom or wealth for their age. Those who have a stupid outlook are examples of those who have behaved badly to the elders.

Related Biblical Themes and Stories

It is better to be humble and stay poor than to be one of the arrogant and get a share of their loot (Prov 16:19).

I have sinned against you. I am no longer fit to be called your son (Lk 15:21).

God exalted Jesus because he was humble (Phil 2:1-11). "And all will openly proclaim that Jesus Christ is Lord to the glory of God the father" (v. 11).

23 Kukana kwa mutu wa garu

To refuse like a dog's head

Explanation: A dog's head is very hard to break, even if it is run over by a vehicle. The proverb is used metaphorically.

Meaning: A person who is hard-hearted, or who has no sympathy for others.

Occasion: This proverb is used to reprimand a person who is hard-hearted, or a person who shows no sympathy for others. Sometimes it is used to caution young people who refuse to go on errands, if sent by elders.

Related Biblical Themes and Stories

Jonah refused to go to Nineveh and set out in the opposite direction in order to get away from the Lord (Jonah 1:1-10).

The story about Peter's denial of Jesus can be illustrated by this proverb. When one of the servant girls saw him sitting there at the fire, she looked straight at him and said, "This man too was with Jesus." But Peter denied it, "Woman, I don't even know him" (Lk 22:56-60).

24 Kukanda pa moto

To step on fire

Explanation: People should examine their position carefully before involving themselves in incidents that may have serious consequences. This is equivalent to the English proverb: Let sleeping dogs lie.

Meaning: People should not provoke situations because they happen to be in a group. They will each face the consequences of their actions alone.

Occasion: The proverb is cited to warn people against deliberately provoking a situation. Especially it warns on the dangers of mob action.

Related Biblical Themes and Stories

They provoked the Lord to anger with their doing, and a plague broke out among them (Ps 106:29).

As he went away from there, the scribes and the Pharisees began to press him hard and to provoke him to speak of many things, lying in wait for him, to catch him at something he might say (Lk 11:53-54).

When the people of Israel provoked the Lord in the wilderness for forty years, they perished (Heb 3:17).

25 Kakuza kija kasikuwa

What comes on its own is a bad omen

Explanation: The proverb is based on the Tonga principle that you cannot have something good without sweating for it.

Meaning: Nothing good can come without working for it.

Occasion: The proverb is told when advising young people to work hard in their fields in order to have abundant food. Students are advised to work hard at school so that they can pass exams and prepare themselves for a bright fortune.

Related Biblical Themes and Stories

Cursed is the ground because of you, in toil you shall eat of it all the days of your life (Gen 3:17).

When Jacob learned that there was grain in Egypt, he said to his sons, "why do you look at one another? Behold, I have heard that there is grain in Egypt, go down and buy grain for us there that we may live and not die!" (Gen 42:1-2)

See, the place where we dwell under your charge is too small for us. Let us go to the Jordan and each of us get there a log and let us make a place for us to dwell there (2 Kings 6:1-2).

Keep on working with fear and trembling to complete your salvation (Phil 2:12).

26 Kulinda malinda-linda

To wait for trouble

Explanation: A person should try to take initiative instead of just sitting idle.

Meaning: One should not wait indefinitely for a good job or a better deal, lest the period of much waiting leads one into suffering and misery.

Occasion: It is cited when encouraging people to do whatever is available to earn their living, instead of waiting for good jobs or deals that may not be forthcoming. Sometimes it is used to warn those who always rely on others to do things for them without themselves taking the lead. It is also used to advise farmers not to wait for too long before they plant their crops during the first rains. Preachers use it to exhort people to respond to the gospel immediately.

Related Biblical Themes and Stories

The right time has come, and the Kingdom is near, turn away from your sins and believe the Good News (Mk 1:14).

Go and sell all you have and give the money to the poor and you will have riches in heaven. Then come and follow me (Mk 10:21).

The angel said, "There will be no more delay!" (Rev 10:6)

27 Kumuzi waku ndi kumuzi waku

Your home is your home

Explanation: The people should maintain good relations with their kinsmen (relatives). In the colonial period, many Tonga people used to go to work in South Africa for many years, even forgetting their own homes and families. To them life was sweet in their early years there, but when they were faced with problems, they were forced to come back, even empty-handed. Some even died there.

Meaning: People should not despise their own relatives (or original home), because time may come when circumstances may force them to go back.

Occasion: The proverb is used when we advise young people who despise their homes or relatives. When they come back we may reproach them before we receive them back. It is also an article given at a funeral, if the people had received their dead relative, who never thought of home during his lifetime. Preachers use it to exhort people to prepare to go to heaven, which is their permanent home. So they should not despise God.

Related Biblical Themes and Stories

I want to be buried where my fathers are; carry me out of Egypt and bury me where they are buried (Gen 47:30).

The story of the prodigal son is a good example. He despised living with his father and elder brother at home. When he went to a far away country, trouble came. He squandered all his money, and in the end became helpless. Life was unbearable. He could not stand the problems he faced in the foreign land. He almost died of hunger. He then thought of going home to his father, where he was kindly received back (Lk 15:11-32).

There is no permanent city for us for us here on earth (Heb 13:14).

28 Kupaska nkhusunga

To give is to keep

Explanation: This proverb reflects the Tonga belief in the importance of interdependence as opposed to individualism as a way of life.

Meaning: Giving is a way of saving, because the people you give things to, or the people you help, will come to your aid in time of your need.

Occasion: It is normally used when praising someone for having given something to someone in need or when approving his/her intention to do so. Young people are taught to share things with others. Preachers exhort people to offer gifts to God, who is the keeper of their lives. This is used as an encouragement for stewardship.

Related Biblical Themes and Stories

Do not store up riches for yourselves here on earth, where moths and rust destroy, and robbers break in and steal. Instead store up riches for yourselves in heaven where moths and rust cannot destroy. For your heart will always be where your riches are (Mt 6:19-21).

If you only know what God gives and who it is that is asking for a drink, you would ask him, and he would give you life-giving water (John 4:10).

It is more blessed to give than to receive (Acts 20:35).

Each one should give then as he had decided, not with regret or out of a sense of duty; for God loves the one who gives gladly. And God is able to give you more than you need (2 Cor 9:7-8).

29 Kusewe ndi chirwani mbuzereza

To play with danger is foolishness

Explanation: This is from a tale that a person tamed a leopard. When it grew up it killed all his goats, and even the master himself.

Meaning: A person should be careful with what he/she does.

Occasion: The proverb is cited to warn people against imitating silly habits, which may end up ruining their lives. It is also a warning against apostasy. Elders cite it to warn young people not to play with danger or anything that can ruin their lives. Preachers use it to warn people against the wrath of God if they continue sinning.

Related Biblical Themes and Stories

They are saying that this is their god, who led them out of Egypt. I know how stubborn these people are. Now, don't try to stop me. I am angry with them, and I am going to destroy them (Ex 32:7-10).

Let sinners bear their own punishment; let them feel the wrath of Almighty God (Job 21:20).

30 Kusewe ndi lezara la uyi kosekose

Playing with a double-edged blade

Explanation: A person should avoid taking for granted people they do not know well, since in their hearts may lay evil intention.

Meaning: A hypocrite or a liar.

Occasion: The proverb is used to advise a person to be careful in his/her dealings with someone known to be a liar. Sometimes the proverb is used to warn people against associating themselves with people believed to be witches in the community.

Related Biblical Themes and Stories

In that day the Lord will shave with a razor which is hired beyond the river with the King of Assyria—the head and the hair of the feet, and will sweep away the beard also (Is 8:20).

Behold, you are relying on Egypt, that splintered reed of a staff, which will pierce the hand of the man who leans on it (Is 36:6).

31 Kuwezga janja or, Kase ruta kase weku

To return a hand

Explanation: This is similar to the English saying, "One good turn deserves another." We should do what we expect others to do for us. Tonga life is interdependent.

Meaning: Do something good to a person who did something good for you.

Occasion: The proverb is used to advise people not to keep on seeking for favours but think of ways of assisting others. Young people should learn the principle of reciprocity. Preachers use the proverb when teaching on generosity and reciprocity.

Related Biblical Themes and Stories

Do for others what you want them to do for you (Mt 7:12).

32 Kuyambiriya nkhugona pakati

Be early, you will sleep in the middle

Explanation: The English equivalent is "An early bird catches the worm." Thus, if you want a big share, you should be early.

Meaning: Begin eradicating a problem before it gets worse. For instance, you treat a wound before it gets worse.

Occasion: The proverb is used to advise young people to plan for their future early in their lives. Also in order to avoid contracting epidemic diseases, people are advised to take preventive measures. Likewise, school children are advised to be punctual, so that they do not miss their lessons. Preachers advise Christians that their duty is to watch, especially when things seem to be uncertain to them.

Related Biblical Themes and Stories

The five foolish virgins were not fully prepared. When they later on arrived, they found the door already closed, and the five clever virgins had already been welcomed by the bridegroom (Mt 25:1-13).

The people who were late to come and listen to Jesus' message were kept out, for there were so many people who came together that there was no room left, not even out in front of the door (Mk 2:2).

Jesus was born in a manger because there was no room for his parents to stay in. Obviously Mary and Joseph arrived late in Bethlehem, they could perhaps have been given a room (Lk 2:7).

33 Kwambiriya maji gheche mugongono

You should cross a stream when the water is at your knees

Explanation: The analogy is drawn from a stream that rises gradually on a rainy day, and if one is late to cross, one can be carried away by the floods. The English equivalent is, "A stitch in time saves nine."

Meaning: One is to start solving a problem before it becomes serious. That is, a problem should be attended to in its initial stages.

Occasion: The proverb addresses the theme of decision-making. It is used to advise young people to effect some remedy before a thing gets worse. For instance, students should set their right choices from the early stages of their education, such as in choosing subjects for their future career. Sometimes the proverb is cited to warn young people against acquiring habits that can undermine their future, e.g. smoking and drinking. If these habits cannot be controlled at the early stage, it will be very difficult to eradicate them when they are rooted in a person. It is also used in advising a person to promptly attend to a problem (e.g. that of disciplin-ing his/her children), which the advisor fears may grow out of proportion and thus become impossible, if left unattended to longer. Preachers use it to stress the urgency of the gospel, just as Jesus warns us that there is no time to spare for burying the dead or for saying good-bye to the family.

Related Biblical Themes and Stories

The prophet Isaiah says, "Seek the Lord while you can find him. Call upon him now while he is near" (Is 55:6).

Jesus said, "Anyone who starts to plow and then keeps looking back is of no use for the Kingdom of God" (Lk 9:57-62).

34 Kwawiyako Chiuta

God has fallen on them there

Explanation: In Tonga tradition lightning and other terrifying phenomena in nature are associated with the nature of God. Thus disease is frequently so spoken of. God is seen as punishing people by inflicting diseases on them for the sins they have done.

Meaning: An epidemic disease has wiped out the inhabitants of a place.

Occasion: The proverb is cited to acknowledge the presence of God. It is used to warn people against committing evil, because God will visit them by sending plagues. Preachers use this proverb when they refer to the outbreak of diseases as God's way to punish sinners.

Related Biblical Themes and Stories

The proverb reflects the situation of Israel when God inflicted the Egyptians with boils that became open sores on people and animals (Ex 9:8-10).

If I had raised my hand to strike you and your people with disease, you would have been completely destroyed (Ex 9:15).

An angel of the Lord went to the Assyrian camp and killed 185,000 soldiers. At dawn the next day, there they lay all dead (Is 37:36).

Does disaster strike a city unless the Lord sends it? (Amos 3:6)

There will be terrible earthquakes, famines, and plagues everywhere, there will be strange and terrifying things coming from the sky (Lk 21:11).

35 Kwe karakato

There is one risen

Explanation: There is a belief in Tonga society that some people can rise from the dead in another form, e.g. as a lion or a leopard.

Meaning: A person who overcomes death.

Occasion: The proverb is cited during situations when a strange wild animal such as a lion or leopard roars within the vicinity of a village. People feel this can be a risen person who is reincarnated in that particular animal. Preachers cite it to refer to the resurrection of Jesus.

Related Biblical Themes and Stories

Jesus has authority over death. This is seen in the story of raising Lazarus from the dead. Jesus called out in a loud voice, "Lazarus come out." He came out, his hands and feet wrapped in grave clothes, and with a cloth around his face. "Untie him, and let him go" (John 11:43-44).

Jesus' resurrection story can be illustrated by this proverb. Jesus is the one who conquers death (John 20:1-10).

36 Likhwechu lamunyako payika, mawamle pako

A whip used on someone else should be kept away because tomorrow the same whip will be used to whip you

Explanation: The same judgement you give to others will also be passed on you. The proverb is used symbolically.

Meaning: We should not rejoice at the fate of others.

Occasion: The proverb is cited when judging cases at the court. The acquitted should not look with contempt on the one who has lost the case, because next time it will be himself/herself. Again young people should not rejoice over the fate of others.

Related Biblical Themes and Stories

Jesus said, "Do not judge others, so that God will not judge you, for God will judge you in the same way you judge others, and he will apply to you the same rules you apply to others" (Mt 7:1).

Never take revenge, my friends, but instead I will take revenge. I will pay back, says the Lord (Rom 12:19).

37 Lilime lenge moto

The tongue is like fire

Explanation: The tongue is here used metaphorically to indicate that little things sometimes become uncontrollable.

Meaning: A person should be careful in handling small things.

Occasion: It is used to advise people to control their temper in order to reach a harmonious decision. Preachers have used this proverb to condemn divisions in their congregations.

Related Biblical Themes and Stories

Behold, the name of the Lord comes from far, burning with his anger, and in thick rising smoke; his lips are full of indignation, and his tongue is like a devouring fire (Is 30:27).

Like fire they eat up the plants. In front of them the land is like the Garden of Eden, but behind them it is a barren desert (Joel 2:3).

So it is with the tongue, small as it is, it can boast about great things (James 3:5).

38 Limphezi liweliyamo cha mu chimiti

Lightning does not strike the same tree twice

Explanation: There are things that happen only once in a lifetime.

Meaning: Chance does not repeat itself.

Occasion: The proverb addresses the theme of "responsibility." It is used to advise young people to take care of things they have, or chances they have. If they have acquired wealth, they should not be extravagant.

Related Biblical Themes and Stories

Do those things that will show that you have turned from your sins. The axe is ready to cut down the trees at the roots; every tree that does not bear good fruit will be cut down and thrown into the fire (Mt 3:8-12).

The parable of the prodigal son can affirm this proverb. When the son had spent all the wealth he received from his father, he ended up being helpless. He lost all his chances and ended up starving (Lk 15:11-21).

Therefore, we should hold fast with what we have, lest one takes it away (Rev 3:11).

39 Maliro nkhuliyana

A funeral is to mourn one another

Explanation: In Tonga society no person is an island. The people are interdependent.

Meaning: People should help one another in times of trouble.

Occasion: The proverb is cited to urge people who stay aloof when others get into trouble or are bereaved. They can offer charitable services to those who mourn, like burying the dead or helping others in times of disaster. The participation is important because next time one would need similar help when facing a problem. Young people should learn to offer help at a funeral, like digging the grave or running errands. Preachers exhort people to participate in church fellowships.

Related Biblical Themes and Stories

In the Sermon on the Mount, Jesus said, "Whatever you wish that men would do to you, do so to them" (Mt 7:12).

A related story is that of Jesus raising Lazarus from the dead (John 11:1-4). Verses 31-34 present a similar picture of the neighbouring Jews coming to console and weep with Mary and Martha for the death of Lazarus.

Paul, in his letter to the Thessalonians, advises them to comfort one another (I Thess 4:18).

40 Malo gho utanja kusambapo ndigho patachikukole mng'ona

The bathing place you like best brings a crocodile bite

Explanation: We should be careful with our lives lest we are taken up by events.

Meaning: Danger may exist where you least expect it.

Occasion: The proverb is used to warn people against carelessness, or against taking things for granted. Thus young people should be responsible enough and be sensitive to situations. They should avoid to frequent places that attract them, yet danger is there, like drinking places. Preachers warn people against doing things that can ruin their faith.

An evil spirit from God suddenly took control of Saul and he raved in his house like a madman. David was playing the harp as he did every day and Saul was holding a spear. "I'll pin him to the wall," Saul said to himself, and he threw the spear at him twice; but David dodged each time (1 Sam 18:11).

41 Manda ghawole pa khomo

The manda mushroom grows near the house

Explanation: 'Manda' is a type of mushroom that usually grows around houses. In most cases people do not know that there is this mushroom within the vicinity until it gets rotten: that it is when they discover it.

Meaning: A person should not take for granted that things are always as they seem. Danger is inevitable in any place.

Occasion: The proverb is used to discourage people from taking chances without thinking. For instance, one should not take chances by walking alone at night just because there is light in the area, or leaving the door of one's house open because there are no wild animals or thieves etc. It is also used to warn young people against travelling alone in the dark or against frequenting places where there can be danger.

Related Biblical Themes and Stories

Be on watch, be alert, for you do not know when the time will come (Mk 13:32-36).

In the parable of the rich fool, we are warned that when things go well with us we should also know that death is near us. "You fool, this very night you will have go give up your life" (Lk 12:20).

42 Mata gha mula ghatuwa pasi cha

An old person's saliva cannot fall to the ground

Explanation: What an old person has said will one day come true. The old person's saying in Tonga society is supposed to be taken seriously. The proverb originates from a tale about young people who killed all the old people. One young man hid his old father in a cave. One day trouble came upon their young chief. As he woke up from sleep he saw a snake that rolled round his neck. The young people needed a solution to save their chief. It was the old man who gave a wise advice and the chief's life was spared (see Tale 4, in Chapter 6).

Meaning: The old are the wise.

Occasion: The proverb is related to the theme "obedience." It is told to induce the young to respect the views of their elders, or to reprimand those who find themselves in trouble after ignoring their elders' advice. Preachers use the proverb to stress the need to obey God. God is depicted as ancient and wise. His words do not fail. What is spoken from the mouth of the Lord shall come to pass.

Related Biblical Themes and Stories

Eli's warning to his two sons came true. Hophni and Phinehas were both killed just as Eli had told his sons (1 Sam 4:11 and 2:25).

God's word through the angel Gabriel to Marry can be referred to here: "For there is nothing that God cannot do" (Lk 1:37).

43 Matako ghawi ghaleka cha ku kwenthana

Two buttocks cannot avoid friction

Explanation: People should learn to live together in spite of any problems they might have.

Meaning: Misunderstandings are unavoidable where there are two or more people living together.

Occasion: The setting of the proverb is in court when elders try to reconcile people who have either quarrelled or fought each other, e.g. a husband and wife or two villages in friction. Children in a family are advised to live together despite disagreements which might occur. Preachers use the proverb to encourage unity in the church.

Related Biblical Themes and Stories

The proverb can be related to the story about Abraham (Abram) and Lot quarrelling over land. Lot also had sheep, goats, and cattle, as well as his own family and servants. And so there was not enough pastureland for the two of them to stay together, because they had too many animals. So quarrels broke out between Abraham's herdsmen and those who took care of Lot's animals (Gen 13:5-7).

An argument broke out among the disciples as to which one of them should be thought of as the greatest (Lk 22:24).

There arose a sharp argument that led to the separation between Paul and Barnabas. It is reported that Barnabas wanted to take John Mark with them, but Paul did not think it was right to take him because he had not stayed with them to the end of their mission in Pamphylia. There was a sharp argument between them and they separated. Barnabas took Mark and Paul chose Silas and they left (Acts 15:39f).

44 Maungu tikumwa, matali tikurya, kwajanji so?

We have supped the marrows, and eaten the mushroom! And what is remaining now?

Explanation: It is a form of thanks-giving prayer to God for fruits and fungi growing wild in the woods, which Atonga are very fond of. They see them as planted by God.

Meaning: A person should consider himself/herself safe having eaten the gifts of heaven with thankfulness.

Occasion: The proverb is used during Tonga traditional worship as a thanks-giving prayer to God, the Giver of rain and to him alone this *Chiwi* or rain-prayer' should be offered, with hope for the new life. Preachers use it in their prayers of thanks-giving to God for giving them the first rains or good rains.

Related Biblical Themes and Stories

This proverb is affirmed by a passage on harvest offerings: "My ancestor was a wandering Aramean who took his family to Egypt to live ... The Egyptians treated us harshly and forced us to work as slaves ... He brought us out of Egypt and gave us this rich fertile land. And behold now I bring the first of the fruit of the ground which the Lord has given me" (Dt 26:5-10).

Behold I have given you every plant yielding seed which is upon the face of all the earth and every tree with seed in its fruits; you shall have them for food (Gen 1:29).

45 Mawala ghatuswa vyaka

Over eagerness breaks hoe handles

Explanation: Hoe handles are delicate to make, because they are made from wood. One should be skillful in using them lest one breaks them. The English equivalent is "Pride goes before a fall."

Meaning: An eager person can prove to be foolish when he/she spoils other people's things.

282

Occasion: The proverb addresses the theme of modesty. It is cited to warn young people who have good intentions before they can actually acquire the skills of doing things properly. If the advice is not heeded, they end up destroying things or other people's lives.

Related Biblical Themes and Stories

Who are proud will soon be disgraced. It is wiser to be modest (Prov 11:2).

Pride goes before destruction, a haughty spirit before a fall (Prov 16:18).

Your pride has deceived you (Jer 49:16).

46 Mazua ghasintha

Days always change

Explanation: People should learn to be interdependent as opposed to living independent lives. Since there are many days in one's life which alternate, one should not do bad things to others thinking that there will be no time when one should need their help.

Meaning: Life cannot be consistent. There are ups and downs in life, just as days also can change.

Occasion: This saying is used to urge people who are privileged to help the un-privileged ones, since they may one day require the services of these same people when fortunes change. Politicians use it in their campaigning for change and warn the electorate against future consequences when the pendulum swings to the opposition side. Young people should be sensitive to the changes of the time they live in. Preachers use the proverb to give hope for better days in the future through God's grace.

Related Biblical Themes and Stories

Never boast about tomorrow, you don't know what will happen between now and then (Prov 27:1).

Jerusalem will be restored in the later days (Is 4:2-6).

Many prophets who rose in Israel believed that days would not always be the same. Amos proclaimed that the "Day of the Lord" shall come and it would be a fearful one (Amos 5:16-20). And then "A day is coming when I will restore the Kingdom of David which is a house fallen into ruins" (Amos 9:11). Isaiah also talks about times of chaos in Jerusalem (Is 3:1-6).

47 Mazua nganande, weya wang'ombe ngumana

Days are more than a cow's hair

Explanation: There is need to desist from disappointing others through showing them harshness on matters that can be solved, because you will still meet somewhere one day so long as you live, and you will be ashamed of yourself.

Meaning: It is not good to disappoint someone, since you are also bound to get into trouble one day and fail to get his sympathy or assistance.

Occasion: The proverb is recited when someone has done evil to another. It is an advice to let a person know that others will revenge some day. Preachers use the proverb to exhort people to forgive one another, because the wrong done to you, at another time, you yourself may be doing it.

Related Biblical Themes and Stories

Jesus said, 'If you are about to offer your gift to God at the altar and there you remember that your brother has something against you, leave your gift there in front of the altar, go at once and reconcile with your brother and then come back and offer your gift to God (Mt 5:23-24).

My brothers, if someone is caught in any kind of wrong doing, those of you who are spiritual, should set him right; but you must do it in a gentle way. And keep an eye on yourselves, so that you will not be tempted (Gal 6:1).

48 Mbawa kume masengwe nkhuwambala lisito

For a deer to grow longer horns is to go round the 'lisito' fence

Explanation: If one wants to live longer, one must be careful with one's steps. The traditional Tonga way to kill game was to dig game-pits. If the animal does not avoid the hedge, then it will fall into the pit.

Meaning: People who are careful with their lives usually live longer.

Meaning: If one wants to live longer one must be careful. Thus, people who are cautious usually avoid unnecessary danger.

Occasion: The proverb is often used in situations when students blindly or ignorantly find themselves participating in ill-conceived boycotts or violence. In the end they are expelled from school. It is also cited to warn young people to be careful in the way they move in company with their peers, so that they should not ruin their lives. Preachers warn people against being careless with their lives, lest the devil carries them away.

Wisdom will add years to your life (Prov 9:11).

Have reverence for the Lord and you will live longer. The wicked die before their time (Prov 10:27).

If you love your life, stay away from the traps that catch the wicked along the way (Prov 22:5).

49 Mlamba ndiyo watunga

The mudfish is what you have on your carrying stick

Explanation: The mudfish is very slippery while in the water. Once it is caught one must hold it tight. Hence one should not be deceived by the fish wriggling in water. What is yours is what you have in your hands. The English equivalent is: "All that glitters is not gold."

Meaning: A person should concentrate on what he/she is supposed to do. You should not dispense with an old thing or relationship, or abandon your job, just because you hope to or have acquired a seemingly more attractive one. You must care for something you already have in your possession.

Occasion: The proverb is used to caution young people who act in an envious manner, at the time their hopes fail to materialize, or when the newly acquired things or relationships prove worthless. In marital life young people tend to despise their wives when they look at young girls and feel like divorcing their old wives. It is also a warning to young people who are greedy. A person should be satisfied with what one has. Students are advised not to divert from their main function of learning.

Related Biblical Themes and Stories

One of the Ten Commandments affirms this proverb: "Do not desire another man's house; do not desire his wife, his slave, his cattle, his donkey or anything else that he owns" (Ex 20:17).

In Rev 3:11, we are advised to "keep safe what you have, so that no one will rob you of your victory prize."

50 Mlendo ndi dungwi

A stranger is like dew

Explanation: There are certain things in life, which are short-lived and temporal. There is a Tonga folktale about an old man and three boys. The one who welcomed the visitor received blessings. Those who rejected him died of hunger.

Meaning: A stranger is a blessing and stays for a short time, so we should not bother.

Occasion: The proverb is cited when advising young people, who are hostile to strangers to welcome and treat them well. They are with us for a short time. A stranger is not a bother. At a later day the same stranger might receive you in an unexpected place. Preachers use the proverb to exhort Christians to receive Jesus during the Christmas season.

Related Biblical Themes and Stories

When Abraham saw the three visitors coming to him, he ran to meet them. Bowing down with his face touching the ground he said, "Sirs, please do not pass by my home without stopping, I am here to serve you" (Gen 18:2-15). The three strangers later brought good news to Abraham and Sarah about the promised son. The visitors were not a bother, but rather a blessing.

The visitors to Sodom and Gomorrah were welcomed by Lot. The two men said to Lot, "If you have anyone else here—sons, daughters, son-in-law, or any other relatives living in the city—get them out of here, because we are going to destroy this place (Gen 19:12-13).

Remember to welcome strangers in your homes. There were some who did that and welcomed angels without knowing it (Hebrew 12:3).

51 Mlendo ndiyo wabaya njoka

A stranger is the one who killed the snake

Explanation: There is a story in Tonga society referring to Hare and Leopard. While the council of the elders was in a deadlock to judge a case, Hare from the bush came in and helped to pass the judgement. The visitor can be more diplomatic.

Meaning: A visitor or traveller can sometimes make a better discernment and judgement when there is a critical issue.

286

Occasion: This proverb is used to ask a visitor to help solve a problem, when the local men seem to be entangled in a riddle. Young people should develop the spirit of being kind to strangers. However, they should know who the stranger is, because some can be dangerous.

Related Biblical Themes and Stories

The prophet Elijah, a visitor at the time of the great famine, helped the woman to have enough food after he had performed a miracle. At first the woman thought that, by offering to the stranger her last meal, things would be worse for her son; but we see that the visitor became a blessing, giving a solution to her problem—more food was found in her jar (1 Kings 17:8-15).

Elijah also restored the widow's son to life (1 Kings 17:23).

Joshua then told the two men who served as spies, "Go into the prostitute's house and bring her and her family out, as you promised her (Joshua 6:22-23). Here, Rahab and her family were protected because of receiving the two visitors (spies) in Jericho.

52 Mnthenkhu waryiya pa chipando

Mnthenkhu bird eats while sitting on a stump

Explanation: *Mnthenkhu* is a small black-bird. The Tonga people have observed that it can fly for a long time without perching, but when it has caught something to eat, it perches on a tree stump.

Meaning: A person should respect himself/herself.

Occasion: The proverb is cited when advising young people to cultivate good manners or etiquette. For instance, children like to eat while walking around or standing, which is contrary to the norms of Tonga society. The proverb is used to imply that we need friends or relatives to help us in times of trouble, just as the *mnthenkhu* perches on a tree stump. Preachers urge Christians to be friends of Jesus, who can help them in times of trouble.

Related Biblical Themes and Stories

Do not let wine tempt you, even though it is rich red, though it sparkles in the cup, and it goes down smoothly (Prov 23:31).

Jesus said to him, 'Foxes have holes and birds have nests, but the Son of Man has no place to lie down and rest (Lk 9:58).

Paul advised the Corinthians to respect themselves when he said, "If any one is hungry he should eat at home, so that you will not come under God's judgement as you meet together" (1 Cor 11:34).

53 Moto walimbuni utocha lisuwa likuru

A small fire destroys a big forest

Explanation: We should be careful with little things because they can be dangerous and magnify.

Meaning: Small things can cause great damage.

Occasion: This proverb is used to advise people to take care of small inconveniences or embarrassments caused to others, since such provocations can cause bigger trouble or even disaster. Young married couples are advised to take care of little issues that may lead to the breaking up of families. A person who inconveniences or embarrasses another over a minor issue is bound to find himself/herself in much bigger trouble. Preachers advise people not to be liars as that can lead to confusion in the church.

Related Biblical Themes and Stories

The proverb can be related to several texts in the book of James.

When we put bits into the mouths of horses to make them obey us, we can turn the whole animal (James 3:3).

A ship, big as it is and driven by such strong winds, it can be steered by a very small rudder, and it goes wherever the pilot wants it to go (James 3:4).

The tongue is like fire. It is a world of wrong occupying its place in our bodies and spreading evil through our whole being (James 3:3-10).

54 Mtiti ungamugolore cha pa mazila ghake

A sparrow is never small on its eggs

Explanation: The sparrow is one of the smallest birds in the world, but when it wants to protect its eggs, it becomes so angry that even bigger birds cannot fly around.

Meaning: A person should be respected on his/her own right, without looking at position, race or sex.

Occasion: It is used when cautioning a person who despises those who are under him/her just because he/she is in a higher position. The proverb is also used to warn people against taking other people's property just because they cannot defend themselves, forgetting that the owner has the right to his/her property.

Related Biblical Themes and Stories

Hammer the points of your plows into swords and your pruning knives into spears. Even the weak must fight (Joel 3:10).

God chose what the world considers weak in order to shame the powerful (1 Cor 1:27).

King David was condemned because he planned Uriah's death in order to take his wife (2 Sam 12:1-50).

55 Mtonga nchigumbuli

A Tonga person is a Chingumbuli fish

Explanation: The proverb is used metaphorically. The metaphor is drawn from a small spotted fish called *Chigumbuli*, which is very cunning. It can easily adapt itself to different situations. When danger comes it can disguise itself or buries itself in the sand.

Meaning: A person should not deliberately be exposed to danger.

Occasion: This proverb is used to encourage Tonga young people to be intelligent, but also to adapt to certain situations in life, e.g., to live peacefully even in hostile situations. In other words the Tonga should liken themselves to this fish.

Related Biblical Themes and Stories

They had to be youths without blemish, handsome and skillful in all wisdom, endowed with knowledge, understanding and learning (Dan 1:4).

So that we may no longer be children tossed back and forth (Eph 4:14).

Listen! I am sending you out just like sheep in the midst of wolves; so be wise as snakes and innocent as doves (Mt 10:16).

56 Mu moyo ndi sitolo

The womb is a store

Explanation: The proverb is used to show that children born from one mother cannot be the same. Their attitudes, behaviour and even appearance will be different.

Meaning: In every family there is a bad person and hence no family should be condemned wholesale because of the existence of one bad individual.

Occasion: It is used to advise those who condemn whole families or communities for breeding different members of the society, forgetting that people differ in many ways. It is important to accept such differences.

Related Biblical Themes and Stories

The four sons of Jesse i.e. Eliab, Abinadab, Shammah and David were totally different in the eyes of God, because God pays no attention to how tall and handsome a man is. God looks at the heart of a person (1 Sam 16:6-13).

It is one of the twelve disciples, Judas, who betrayed Jesus, yet he was one in the circle (Mk 14:45-46).

The two sons of Jacob, Esau and Jacob, were totally different. Esau was a very skilled hunter, a man who loved the out-door life, but Jacob was a quiet man who stayed at home (Gen 25:27).

57 Mukucha nkhazunguliyanga chulu

Another day I will be wandering round an anthill

Explanation: The Tonga believe that the corpse turns into a heap (*chulu*), i.e. the old grave would become a heap.

Meaning: A person will go beyond and out of sight, as in death.

Occasion: The proverb is used to warn a child to mind his/her behaviour. It is used to make one's advice the more impressive. When an elder dies, he or she goes with all the wisdom.

Related Biblical Themes and Stories

Do not let such a woman (prostitute) win your heart; do not go wandering after her. If you go to her house, you are on the way to the world of the dead (Prov 7:25, 27).

When Jesus predicted his death he said, 'A little while and you will see me no more, again a little while and you will see me' (John 16:16).

In speaking about his death Jesus also said, "Do not forget what I am about to tell you! The Son of Man is going to be handed over to the power of men (Lk 9:44).

290

58 Munthu wambura kuvwa wabuchira mbavi ye mu mutu waki

A person who does not hear, learns when the axe is in his head

Explanation: A person should obey instructions without being forced.

Meaning: A person should take heed of instructions and advice in order to avoid troubles.

Occasion: It is used when warning disobedient and disrespectful children to stop their bad habits. The proverb addresses the theme of obedience.

Related Biblical Themes and Stories

The disobedient will miss God's Kingdom, because they will be thrown out into the darkness, where they will cry and gnash their teeth (Mt 8:12).

The message given to our ancestors by the angels was shown to be true, and anyone who did not follow it or obey it received the punishment he deserved (Heb 2:2).

59 Munthu wamtimba kuwi

A person with a double heart

Explanation: A person who goes to the other person and says something else and comes to another and again says something different.

Meaning: A liar or double dealer.

Occasion: The proverb is cited to warn a person against associating with someone known to be a liar. Thus, it teaches young people the need for caution, and to avoid taking people we do not know well for granted, since behind their broad and friendly smiles may lay evil intentions. Preachers use it to advise people not to associate themselves with liars.

Related Biblical Themes and Stories

All of them lie to one another, they deceive each other with flattery (Ps 12:2).

Then Judas Iscariot, one of the twelve disciples, went off to the chief priests in order to betray Jesus to them (Mk 14:10).

Church helpers must also have good character and be sincere (1 Tim 3:8).

A person like that, unable to make up his mind and undecided in all he does, must not think that he will receive anything from the Lord (Jas 1:8).

60 Munthukazi wakuja pa khonde watuba vyaweni, po anyaki alima yiyu cha

A lazy woman ends up stealing food if she just sits idle while others work in their gardens

Explanation: There is no way you can eat something good unless you work for it. Survival means working hard.

Meaning: People should work hard in order to lead good lives.

Occasion: The proverb is cited to advise young married couples to be responsible and strive to work hard for their lives.

Related Biblical Themes and Stories

Working hard will give you power, being lazy will make you a slave (Prov 12:24).

If you are lazy, you will never get what you are after, but if you work hard, you will get a fortune (Prov 12:37).

If you are lazy, you will meet difficulty everywhere, but if you are honest, you will have no trouble (Prov 15:19)

A lazy person is as bad as someone who is destructive (Prov 18:9).

Go ahead and be lazy. Sleep on, but you will go hungry (Prov 19:15).

The lazy man stays at home; he says a lion might get him if he goes outside (Prov 22:13).

61 Mwana kopa kazimu nkhumuluma

A child fears an insect if it bites him/her

Explanation: Children cannot judge what is good and bad until they gradually discover through experience.

Meaning: Experience is a good teacher. Through accumulation of knowledge we have a better insight into things.

Occasion: The proverb is used to encourage young people to endure difficult circumstances because they will confront them throughout their lives. On the other hand the proverb is cited to warn people to be careful in the way they handle their lives. They are advised to keep away from things that can ruin their lives. Again people are warned through experience not to do the same bad things.

62 Mwana mranda wasambira vyo wanthu wakamba pa mphara

An orphan child learns from what people say at the Mphara

Explanation: *Mphara* is an open place for men to meet, where boys can learn many things. There is the story of two millipedes, one of them an orphan (Tale no. 6). The mother excluded the orphaned millipede from her advice to her own child: "When the rainy season comes to an end, dig a hole so that you can hibernate therein during the dry season." Her own child did not do it and died, while the orphaned millipede had overheard her advice, followed it and survived.

Meaning: If you want to be wise, listen to what wise people say as they gather around, and try to make use of such wisdom. In other words a child should take heed even of advice directed to others.

Occasion: The advice is cited when a person draws the attention of his disobedient child to some good advice given to another child by its parents or guardians. The intention is to teach children to take note of any good advice from whomever it may come. Preachers advise people who attend church services to obey the word of God.

Related Biblical Themes and Stories

If young men listen to advice, they will grow wise. If they follow good instructions from elderly people they will live a long and happy life. If they cling to wisdom, it will protect them (Prov 14:1-6).

Teach a child how he should live and he will remember it all his life (Prov 22:6).

63 Mwana ndi chola

A child is a bag

Explanation: You cannot leave your own child who is supposed to help you.

Meaning: Parents do not reject their child, even if the child offends them.

Occasion: The proverb is used to warn against being excessively rough with an offending child. Fathers usually ask their children to accompany them on short trips, because children can help them in carrying things, taking messages and so on.

Abraham was asked to take his son Isaac to offer as a sacrifice at Moriah. There Abraham made Isaac carry the wood for the sacrifice (Gen 22:2-7).

Children are a gift from the Lord, they are a real blessing. The sons a man has when he is young are like arrows in a soldier's hand (Ps 127:3).

Parents, do not treat your children in such a way as to make them angry. Instead raise them with Christian discipline and instruction (Eph 6:4).

64 Mwana wakuti kaya kuti wachila cha

If one is pessimistic about a child, that child does not survive the sickness

Explanation: If one is pessimistic about the outcome of an affair, things may turn out badly, even if they would have turned out well had one been optimistic.

Meaning: Pessimism does not produce anything good.

Occasion: The proverb is used in cases of chronic illnesses, when people lose their hope. The people are cautioned not to lose hope. Elders say that we must never be pessimistic, because pessimism can bring bad luck. Young people are advised to have courage when life seems to be hopeless and frustrating.

Related Biblical Themes and Stories

Jesus said to Thomas, "Put your finger here and look at my hands, then reach out your hand and put it in my side. Stop your doubting and believe" (John 20:27).

But if he has doubts about what he eats, God condemns him when he eats it, because his action is not based on faith. And anything that is not based on faith is sin (Rom 14:23).

65 Mwana wambula kuvwa wangume masengwe ku masu

A stubborn child grew horns on the foreface

Explanation: There is a Tonga tale which says that a certain animal asked for horns to be on its forehead. When a drought came, this animal found it difficult to drink water from a deep well. The animal is supposed to have been a rhinoceros.

Meaning: He who does not follow other people's advice runs into trouble.

Occasion: The proverb is used to rebuke people when they get into problems as a result of their egocentric behaviour. The proverb is also cited in a court setting to reprimand lawbreakers. It is also used to reprimand disobedient children who are in a problem. Preachers cite it to exhort Christians to obey the word of God and not be hard-hearted.

Related Biblical Themes and Stories

By experience Laban knew that God had blessed him through Jacob (Gen 30:27).

Experience makes one far wiser than anyone (Eccl 1:16). Throughout the story of Israel, God reminded them to remember their past experience. Remember this and consider, recall it to mind, you transgressors, remember the former things of old. (Is 46:8).

Jesus warned: "No indeed! And I tell you that if you do not turn from your sins, I will come to you soon and fight against those people with the sword that comes out of my mouth (Rev 2:16).

66 Mwana wamunyako ndi samba m'manja, wako ndi ryangako

To somebody's child you say, "Wash your hands," to your child you say "Be eating"

Explanation: The treatment we give to our own children is often better than that given to other people's children, for example, while you tell the other child to wash his/her hands properly, you tell yours to start eating so that the other child is disadvantaged.

Meaning: It is not good to discriminate against other people's children who are under your care.

Occasion: The proverb is used to ridicule those who favour their own children in the home at the expense of those entrusted to them by relatives. It is therefore a warning to those who care for relatives.

Related Biblical Themes and Stories

This proverb has the same principle as stipulated in the second most important biblical commandment: "Love your neighbour as you love yourself" (Mk 12:31).

67 Mwana wangu wakana marangu yiku yimulange ndi Njovu

If the child refuses to obey advice, take it to the elephant to be punished

Explanation: Without following rules it is difficult for a child to acquire good moral standards, or to behave properly. The proverb is used metaphorically. The elephant is the most fearful and most powerful animal.

Meaning: Children should not despise rules given by their parents or elders.

Occasion: This proverb is cited to warn those children who do not want to heed the advice from parents or elders. Preachers warn people against disobedience to God's laws.

Related Biblical Themes and Stories

If the people disobey and do not faithfully keep God's rules and laws, many evil things will happen to them and God will curse them (Dt 28:15-19).

If you get more stubborn every time you are corrected, one day you will be crushed and never recover (Prov 29:1).

In the history of Israel, as God's people, when they disobeyed God's law, they were punished by other nations, from time to time. "In that day the Lord will whistle for the fly which is at the source of the streams of Egypt and for the bee which is in the land of Assyria" (Isa 7:18).

You will not escape; you will be captured and handed over to him. You will see him face to face and talk to him in person; then you will go to Babylon (Jer 34:3).

68 Mzimu ndirinde

Take my hand, my ancestral spirit

Explanation: The Tonga people believe that there are certain places which are inhabited by spirits: some good, others bad. Some of such places are river valleys, river gorges and mountains.

Meaning: A shadow of death.

Occasion: The proverb is used when a person is travelling through dangerous places believed to be inhabited by evil spirits, like when crossing river gorges, passing through slopes of mountains or hills, or passing through thick forests. It is also used to advise young people to take courage because there is a power that protects them. Preachers use it to give hope to people that they are always with God who protects them.

Related Biblical Themes and Stories

Even if I go through the deepest darkness I will not be afraid, Lord, for you are with me. Your shepherd's rod and staff protect me (Ps 23:4).

The danger of death was all around me; the horrors of the grave closed in on me; I was filled with fear and anxiety. Then I called to the Lord, "I beg you, Lord save me!" (Ps 116:3-4)

When you pass through deep waters, I will be with you ... When you pass through fire, you will not be burnt (Is 43:2).

Let gloom and deep darkness claim it. Let clouds dwell upon it; let the blackness of the day terrify it (Job 3:5).

69 Mzinda unyenga

A crowd deceives

Explanation: It is not always true that the majority is on the right track or makes correct decisions. The minority can have bright ideas.

Meaning: A person should be cautious of what is said at gatherings.

Occasion: The proverb is sometimes cited to warn newly married people from acquiring bad influences from their peer-groups that may spoil their marriages. It is also used by politicians when campaigning for their parties, perhaps challenging the views of the majority party which is currently ruling. Also young people are advised to be analytical in their treatment of all that they hear at meetings with their peers.

Related Biblical Themes and Stories

Don't be envious of evil people, and don't try to make friends with them. Causing trouble is all they ever think about; every time they open their mouth someone is going to be hurt (Prov 24:1).

The proverb can be related to the story of Paul sailing to Rome when a great storm came up. Paul advised: "Men, I see that our voyage from here on will be dangerous; there will be great loss to the cargo and to the ship, and to our own lives." But the captain and the owner of the ship (the majority) convinced the army officer not to follow Paul (Acts 27:10-11). Paul proved this afterwards when he stood before them (the majority) and said,

"Men, you should have listened to me and not have sailed from Crete; then we should have avoided all this damage and loss" (Acts 27:21) .

70 Mazu gha wala ghawe pawaka cha

Words of old people become fulfilled after a long time

Explanation: The Tonga believe that there are sages in their community, whose wisdom and advice should be adhered to. These wise people are the source of moral and spiritual wisdom.

Meaning: What the old people say always comes true in the end, although the young can despise the saying or the warning.

Occasion: The proverb is used when old people resign to young people's decisions and emphasize their advice or warnings on the matter at the same time. At judging cases the jury may utter such a proverb to fulfill some advice or warning that was given to the accused earlier. Preachers advise young people to listen to God, who is the source of knowledge.

Related Biblical Themes and Stories

The story of Eli and his two sons affirms this proverb. The warnings of Eli to his sons Hophni and Phinehas came to be true in the end (Sam 2:22-25 and Sam 4:10-11).

On many occasions prophets warned the people of Israel about impending dangers, yet the people did not believe that the prophecies would come true. For instance, Isa 8:16-18 relates that Isaiah had to give up when people refused to listen to his advice. But in the end Judea was devastated by the Assyrians. Isaiah's words were fulfilled (Isa 36:1-2).

Jesus also warned his disciples against the fate Jerusalem would suffer (Mk 13:1-2). This was fulfilled when Pompey destroyed Jerusalem in 70 AD. The word of God shall always come to pass.

71 Ndakana Chiuta mkali

I swear in the name of the angry God

Explanation: This is the Tonga way of frequently using the name of Chiuta (God) in swearing and cursing. God is associated with lightning. So He is seen as an angry God. The proverb is used metaphorically.

Meaning: An emphatic denial implying innocence and challenge to God to take vengeance on a person were he/she is in the wrong.

Occasion: The proverb is used when a person wants to defend him-self/herself in court, i.e. to prove his/her innocence in the alleged matter. It is commonly used in families. When something is stolen, those concerned use the proverb implying that God will prove them innocent.

Related Biblical Themes and Stories

Everyone will come and kneel before me and swear to be loyal to me (Isa 45:23).

Anyone in the land who asks for a blessing will ask to be blessed by the Faithful God. Whoever takes an oath will swear by the name of the Faithful God. The troubles of the past will be gone and forgotten (Isa 65:16).

72 Ndakukambiyanga kuti ndi nyanga cha kwene mheni ndi tiringanenge

I have been telling you that it was not witchcraft, but the witch is the one that says, 'Let us be equal'

Explanation: There are people who believe that suffering is caused by witchcraft only.

Meaning: The person you trust most is the one who can harm you.

Occasion: The proverb is cited to warn young people who join bad company. They put trust in some of their close friends, yet they forget that these very people can ruin their good behaviour, or even cause their perpetual suffering. It is cited to advise people who think that a person who warns them against danger has evil intention against them; but there are others who wish them bad luck.

Related Biblical Themes and Stories

Those who caused Paul's sufferings were his fellow Jews. While in Lystra some Jews came from Antioch in Pisidia and from Iconium, they won the crowd over to their side, stoned Paul and dragged him out of the town, thinking that he was dead (Acts 14:19-20).

The Jews were jealous and gathered some of the worthless loafers from the streets and formed a mob to attack Paul and Silas (Acts 17:5).

"Don't be envious of evil people, and don't try to make friends with them. Causing trouble is all they ever think about; every time they open their mouth, someone is going to be hurt (Prov 24:1-2).

But look! The one who betrays me is here at the table with me (Lk 22:21). Thus, the one who betrayed our Lord Jesus was one of his closest friends.

73 Ng'ombe yo yadanjiya yitumwa maji ghakutowa

The first cow drinks clean water

Explanation: The Tonga are known as adventurous in all walks of life. People should go into new ventures whose markets are still virtually untapped, rather than into ones where markets are flooded with goods. The English equivalent is: "The early bird catches the worm."

Meaning: A person who starts something early usually succeeds.

Occasion: This proverb is used to encourage young people who want to undertake something to do so before others do. Also when advising farmers that a bumper yields can only be realized if one starts planting in the early rains.

74 Njifwa ye pose

Death is everywhere

Explanation: We cannot escape from death

Meaning: Everyone and everything is susceptible to death.

Occasion: The proverb is cited to remind the people when a sudden death has occurred away from the home. The bereaved are advised to accept that death can occur anywhere. Preachers use the proverb at funerals.

Related Biblical Themes and Stories

Sin came into the world through one man, and his sin brought death with it. As a result, death has spread to the whole human race because everyone has sinned (Rom 5:12).

If we live, it is for the Lord that we live, and if we die, it is for the Lord that we die, so whether we live or die, we belong to the Lord (Rom 14:8).

75 Njovu yitufwa ndi mivwi yinande

An elephant dies because of many arrows

Explanation: The Tonga people believe in communal work, just as one would need many shots to kill an elephant. The English equivalent is, "Many hands make lighter work." The proverb is used metaphorically.

Meaning: A big task can only be accomplished by many people, and a big problem can only be solved by many.

Occasion: The proverb is used when advising a person to call upon others to come to his/her aid. Usually the proverb is used during harvest time when more labour is needed. Preachers use it to encourage people to work together when they want to carry out a church project.

Related Biblical Themes and Stories

Be brave, Philistines, fight like men, or we will become slaves to the Hebrews, just as they were our slaves. So fight like men (1 Sam 4:9).

Finally, build up your strength in unity with the Lord and by means of his mighty power. Put on all the armour that God gives you, so that you will be able to stand up against the Devil's evil tricks (Eph 6:10-20).

So Ruth went out to the fields and walked behind the workers, picking up the heads of grain which they left (Ruth 2:3).

Help to carry one another's burdens (Gal 4:2).

76 Nkhombo atamba kusuka mkati

A calabash is first cleaned from the inside

Explanation: The proverb is the equivalent of the English saying: "Charity begins at home." A person should put her/his house in order before she/he can tell others to do the same.

Meaning: We should not blame our friend before we check on ourselves.

Occasion: The proverb is related to the theme of judging others. It is told to show disregard for one's piece of advice, when the person giving such an advice is known to be contrary to one's statement. It also teaches young people to be honest with themselves.

Related Biblical Themes and Stories

Jesus advised his hearers not to judge others, so that God will not judge them. He said, "God will judge you in the same way you judge others, and he will apply to you the same rules you apply to others. Why, then, do you look at the speck in your brother's eye and pay no attention to the log in your own eyes? You hypocrite! First take the log out of your eye, and then you will be able to see clearly to take the speck out of your brother's eye" (Mt 7:1-5).

77 Nozga kapasi mwakuti kapachanya kasike

Take care of that which is down so that the one that is up should come down

Explanation: Things that are properly done or planned have good results. It is similar to the English proverb: "A good beginning makes a good ending." We should take care of little things which may bear implications on greater things.

Meaning: Doing things well earns one trust. The English proverb is: "Charity begins at home."

Occasion: The proverb is used when advising someone to manage his/her responsibilities properly in order to be trusted and possibly earn himself a promotion or many followers. In other words, one must take the initiative so that something better can be done. Often young people are advised to lay a good foundation for their bright future like concentrating on attending school. Preachers use the proverb to exhort people to prepare their lives in order to enter the Kingdom of God.

Related Biblical Themes and Stories

The lesson drawn from the proverb is that of a race or a competition, as Paul puts it to the Philippians: "Of course, my brothers, I really do not think that I have already won it; the one thing I do, however, is to forget what is behind me and do my best to reach what is ahead" (Phil 3:13).

Every morning each one gathered as much as he needed; and when the sun grew hot, what was left on the ground melted (Ex 16:21).

78 Nyoko ndi nyoko chingana wapunduki

Your mother is your mother even if she is disabled

Explanation: It is not possible to be born into the world without a mother.

Meaning: People should not disobey, disown or disregard their parents.

Occasion: This proverb is often used when reproaching children, who are rude and disobedient to their parents or elders, as well as those who are unkind and inconsiderate, even to disown their own parents. Preachers use the proverb to exhort children to honour their parents, so that they can receive blessings from God.

The Bible tells us to respect our fathers and mothers so that we may live a long time (Ex 20:12).

In Ephesians 6:3, children are advised to obey their parents, as part of their Christian duty, for it is the right thing to do.

In Dt 27:16, God's curse is on anyone who dishonours father or mother.

79 Nyoli yizirwa ndi mavungwa

A chicken is dignified by its feathers

Explanation: Tonga people believe that a person is more respected if he/she has children. The condition for a permanent marriage is the provision of children.

Meaning: An old person is respected because of his children.

Occasion: The proverb is cited when urging a young person whose wife or husband is believed to have failed to bear children to marry another one in the hope that this may help him/her bear children. Preachers use the proverb to exhort people to live a good religious life.

Related Biblical Themes and Stories

The proverb is related to what Jesus said to his disciples: A Christian can only be dignified if he/she is in Christ and only then can bear good fruit. Jesus says, "I am the real vine and my Father is the gardener... Remain united to me and I will remain united to you. A branch cannot bear fruit by itself; it can do so only if it remains in the vine. In the same way you can not bear fruit unless you remain in me" (John 15:1-5).

80 Palima mphamoyo

It is the stomach which farms

Explanation: The proverb is used metaphorically to state that a person who is hungry cannot work, but one who has eaten has the energy to work.

Meaning: Food gives energy to a person.

Occasion: The proverb is used when advising a wife to prepare food for the husband, because work is done better when one has eaten enough and never when one is hungry.

Related Biblical Themes and Stories

A worker should be given what he needs (Mt 10:10).

The disciples of Jesus saw that the crowd was hungry and could withstand no longer to hear the Word of God. The disciples asked Jesus to send them away in order to buy themselves something to eat. In the end Jesus fed the people (Mk 6:36-44).

The elders who do good work as leaders should be considered worthy of receiving double pay, especially those who work hard at preaching and teaching. For the Scripture says, "Do not muzzle an ox when you are using it to thresh corn" (1 Tim 5:17-18).

Since food gives energy, after healing Jairus' daughter, Jesus said, Give her something to eat (Mk 5:43).

81 Po pe josi pe moto

Where there is smoke, there is fire

Explanation: The equivalent English is, "There is no smoke without fire."

Meaning: There is some truth in anything that many constantly talk about. Rumours often come true.

Occasion: The proverb is used in a court setting to show the judge's feelings that a statement being denied by one of the parties has some truth in it, because many people testify to it. It is also used to advise young people to avoid places where old people think danger would be inevitable.

Related Biblical Themes and Stories

The proverb can be related to the story of King Solomon's judgement in the difficult case between the two women. He ordered the child to be cut into two halves so that each women would get an equal share. The real mother, out of her love for her son, said to the King, "Please, Your Majesty, don't kill the child! Give it to her!" This is how Solomon discerned who the real mother was (1 Kings 3:23-27).

82 Pundu waruwa cha po wangurya chiwanga

A hyena never forgets where he ate a bone

Explanation: A person does not forget one who renders help, that is the person making the request is appreciative of previous help rendered.

Meaning: One normally seeks help from one who assisted previously.

Occasion: The proverb is told by a person in need as an introduction to an intended request for further assistance from one who had previously

304

helped. It is also used to remind those who despise a person who at one time assisted them, when all is well with them, forgetting that one day they will go back to the same person when they need help. Young people are warned against despising the places or people who brought them up.

Related Biblical Themes and Stories

This proverb reflects the message of Hosea. Israel becomes an apostate but in the end returns to her God. The story of Gomer and Hosea illustrates this point (Hosea 3:6:1). Thus, Israel will come back to the Lord for protection: "My people will follow me when I roar like a lion at their enemies. They will hurry to me form the west. They will come from Egypt, as swiftly as birds, and from Assyria, like doves. I will bring them to their homes again" (Hosea 11:10-11).

What portions have we in David? We have no inheritance in the son of Jesse. To your tents, O Israel! Look now to your own house, David (I Kings 12:16). This picture of a divided Kingdom reflects the idea in the proverb that people do not forget places of peace and tranquillity.

By the waters of Babylon, there we sat down and wept, when we remembered Zion (Ps 137:1).

83 Pusi wakukota atimuliska wana wake

An old monkey is being fed by its children

Explanation: An old Monkey does not have the strength to find food for its living. It needs energy to jump from one branch of the tree to another. Therefore, its young ones feed it.

Meaning: People should look after their aged parents or relatives.

Occasion: The proverb addresses the theme of caring for others. It is cited to advise a carefree young person to take care of needy parents or relatives. In so doing they show their respect to them.

Related Biblical Themes and Stories

The story of Jacob and Esau reflects the point of the proverb. Isaac said, "You see that I am old and may die so soon. Take your bow and arrows, go out into the country and kill an animal for me, cook me some of that tasty food that I like and bring it to me. After I have eaten it, I will give you my final blessing before I die (Gen 27:2-4).

If anyone does not take care of his relatives, especially the members of his own family, he has denied the faith and is worse than an unbeliever (1 Tim 5:8).

84 Somba yakuvunda pamumphika yiziwa kuvundiska zonse

One rotten fish in the pot will make all the good fish rot as well

Explanation: A small mistake a person makes can affect not only himself or herself but others as well.

Meaning: One bad individual can spoil others.

Occasion: The proverb is cited when warning a person in bad company that could spoil good behaviour. It is also used as advice to people who are in charge of others to see that they do not employ confusionists who can mislead others at a working place. Preachers use it to caution Christians who go about with unbelievers so as not to compromise their faith.

Related Biblical Themes and Stories

Keep company with the wise and you will become wise. If you make friends with stupid people ,you will be harmed (Prov 13:20).

It is not right for you to be proud! You know the saying, "A little bit of yeast makes the whole batch of dough rise!" You must remove the old yeast of sin so that you will be entirely pure (1 Cor 5:6-7).

85 Sonu awiya ose pa msana pe, ndikuti manja pu! pu! Pepa, pepa!

Then they all fall over on to their backs assenting by clapping their hands and saying, be appeased, be appeased

Explanation: This is a proverbal prayer in Tonga traditional religion. It is a request being made that the spirit should go away to the spirit land and leave alone the living, or if interfering in their affairs, that it might work only for the good of its friends/relations, and provide them with an abundance of the desirable things of life.

Meaning: A person should not disappoint the spirits of the ancestors, because they can become angry with those living.

Occasion: The proverb is used at traditional worship, when offering sacrifices to the ancestors as one way of appeasing them or of seeking their favour.

Receive my prayer as incense, my uplifted hands as an evening sacrifice (Ps 141:2).

Make an altar of earth for me and on it sacrifice your sheep and your cattle as offerings to be completely burned and as peace offerings. In every place that I set aside for you to worship me, I will come to you and bless you (Ex 20:24).

86 Sunga khose mukanda wazamuvwara

Keep your neck, you will wear the beads

Explanation: There are good things that await a person's life, so be careful with it. If you want to enjoy good things you should not be impatient.

Meaning: A person should obey the rules given to him/her.

Occasion: This proverb is cited to advise young people who think they can have things before they are ready for them. For instance, students are advised to obey certain rules at school, follow study times, work hard, etc, in order to prepare for their successful future. Young people should also obey the rules given by their parents. Preachers use it to exhort people to be patient when trouble confronts them as God is on their side.

Related Biblical Themes and Stories

Poor and humble people will once again find the happiness which the Lord, the Holy God of Israel gives (Is 29:19).

Blessed are the meek, for they shall inherit the earth (Mt 5:5).

My sons, listen to what your father teaches you. Pay attention, and you will have understanding (Prov 4:1).

Son, do what your father tells you and never forget what your mother taught you. Their teaching will lead you when you travel, protect you at night (Prov 6:20-24).

87 Ubwezi wa mbavi wanbura kurumba mbuyaki

A friendship between an axe and its carrier

Explanation: The person you help can turn against you next time.

Meaning: A person who does not appreciate something good done for him/her.

Occasion: The proverb is used to reprimand people who return evil to those who have helped them. Such people have no appreciation whatsoever. Preachers use it in order to condemn people who do not thank God for what He does for them.

Related Biblical Themes and Stories

The story about David and Saul can be a good example here. At first Saul liked David (1 Sam 18:10-11). Later on Saul tried to kill him.

Jesus was still speaking, when a crowd arrived, led by Judas, one of the twelve disciples. He came up to Jesus to kiss him. But Jesus said, "Judas, is it with a kiss that you betray the Son of Man?" (Lk 22:47-48)

88 Uchiwinda ukamba wako

You should only talk of your own hunting skills

Explanation: There is a common folktale, when man and Lion became friends. Both were hunters. Lion warned man not to reveal his skills of hunting. Man eventually did not keep the secret. He revealed the activities of Lion, yet Lion heard this. Lion quickly ran home where he killed the Chief's daughter. The allegation was that man killed the Chief's daughter, which eventually led to his death. Because the man talked of Lion's activities, he endangered his life.

Meaning: Mind your own business.

Occasion: The proverb has to do with self-reliance and responsibility. It is used to advise a person not to involve himself/herself in other people's affairs. It is also cited to warn people to keep out of gossip. The proverb is also used to advise people to keep secrets and promises, so that they may be seen to be reliable and responsible.

Related Biblical Themes and Stories

Why then do you look at the speck in your brother's eye and pay no attention to the log in your own eye? How dare you say to your brother, 'Please, let me take that speck out of your eyes'. You hypocrite! First take the log out of your own eye and then you will be able to see clearly to take the speck out of your brother's eye (Mt 7:3-5).

Don't give evidence against someone else without good reason, or say misleading things about him (Prov 24:28).

89 Uku-vyanowa, uku-vyanowa, Pusi wanguwa chagada

This is sweet and that is also sweet! Monkey missed a branch and fell upside down

Explanation: One must choose one thing at a time. A Tonga tale depicts a hyena who burst his stomach because he would not choose which path to take, just because from both paths came such sweet smells.

Meaning: A person who usually does wrong things will one day be caught.

Occasion: It is used to advise young people to make wise decisions. Sometimes it is used when commenting on a person so caught; or when advising a person known to be indulging in some bad practices to stop, lest he/she falls into trouble. It is also an advice to people who are greedy and corrupt. They should not take everything to be theirs. Preachers use it to exhort their listeners to shun away form idol worship and worldly things and be faithful to Christ.

Related Biblical Themes and Stories

The proverb can be related to the advice Jesus gave in his teaching in the Sermon on the Mount. "No one can be a slave of two masters, he will hate one and love the other. You cannot serve both God and money" (Mt 6:24).

He who is greedy for unjust gain makes trouble for his household (Prov 15:27).

I do not want you to be partners with demons. You cannot drink from the Lord's cup and also from the cup of demons; you cannot eat at the Lord' table and also at the table of demons. Or do we want to make the Lord jealous? Do we think that we are stronger than he? (1 Cor 10:20-22).

90 Ulemu ubaya

Kindness kills

Explanation: The origin of the proverb is from a Tonga folktale which portrays kindness as a source of danger. When *Kalulu* (Hare) helped the snake to escape from a trap, the snake in turn wanted to bite Hare. Thus, the motif that 'the good are not spared' is depicted in this proverb.

Meaning: Some people are ungrateful and do not appreciate kindness.

Occasion: The proverb is negatively used when regretting a person's unbe-coming behaviour towards a friend, or a neighbour. It is a warning to people to be careful with those who pose as friends, since people can pre-

309

tend to be friendly, while they plan to do evil against them. Young people are warned against spending their time with unreliable friends.

Related Biblical Themes and Stories

The proverb is related to the kind deeds Jesus did. When he showed kindness to people, they plotted against his life. After raising Lazarus from the dead, the Jewish authorities planned to kill him (John 11:53).

In Lystra Paul was stoned because of healing a cripple (Acts 14:1-9).

In Philippi, Paul and Silas were arrested for healing a slave girl, who had an evil spirit that enabled her to predict the future. She earned a lot of money for her masters by telling fortunes (Acts 16:16-24).

91 Uyu ndi Chimbwi

This person is a Hyena

Explanation: The proverb is used symbolically to refer to a person who has knowledge of death and also has the courage to handle the corpse. The hyena is able to smell a dead animal from a long distance. People believe that a hyena dreams where its prey can be found. *Mzukuru* is a similar term, meaning a person who washes and dresses a corpse, or one who buries the dead.

Meaning: A person who has some special knowledge in certain things—in this case, one who first approaches a dead body.

Occasion: The proverb is cited when giving recognition to people in the community who have some special role to play at a funeral or to those who have special knowledge of detecting things.

Related Biblical Themes and Stories

Joseph of Arimathea went to Pilate and asked for the body of Jesus. Then he took it down and wrapped it in a linen shroud, and laid him in a rock-hewn tomb where no one had ever yet been laid (Lk 23:50-53).

Nicodemus, who at first had gone to see Jesus at night, went with Joseph, taking with him about one hundred pounds of spices, a mixture of myrrh and aloes. The two men took Jesus' body and wrapped it in linen cloth with the spices according to the Jewish custom of preparing a body for burial (John 19:39-40).

92 Vimiti vyo vyepamoza vileka cha kuchita ng'wema

Trees that are together brush against each other

Explanation: The analogy is taken from Tonga ecology. As one walks through the forest one hears a sound form trees causing a friction as they brush against each other.

Meaning: It is common for people living together to quarrel.

Occasion: The proverb is used to advise people who have quarrelled to reconcile and continue to live together. The proverb also has a court setting and is often cited at a council of elders where the accused are brought to be judged. Young people are advised to forgive each other if they have disagreed on certain issues.

Related Biblical Themes and Stories

The proverb can be affirmed by the story of Martha in Lk 10:38-41. Martha is full of good works and entirely free from the selfishness that seeks its own pleasure—a fault she detects in Mary. This causes friction: Martha was upset over all the work she had to do, so she came and said, "Lord, don't you care that my sister has left me to do all the work by myself? Tell her to come and help me" (Lk 10:40). But Martha earns a reproof from Jesus, because she has not yet learned that unselfishness, service and even sacrifice can be spoiled by self-concern and self-pity (v 41).

Bear with each other and forgive whatever grievances you may have against one another. Forgive as the Lord forgave you (Col 3:13).

93 Vitotoka vigona mu chikutu chimoza cha

Two cockerels cannot sleep in one cage

Explanation: People living in the same house or community cannot avoid friction.

Meaning: One community cannot be ruled by more than one leader.

Occasion: This proverb is used to disapprove one's unjustified challenge of the leader's authority in the same community. Sometimes, when there is strife in a family, the wife is advised to submit to the husband or the husband to submit to the wife.

Any country that divides itself into factions that fight each other will not last very long. And any town or family that divides itself into groups which fight each other will fall apart (Mt 12:25).

When a strong man, with all his weapons ready, guards his own house, all his belongings are safe. But when a stronger man attacks him and defeats him, he carries away all the weapons the owner was depending on and divides up what he stole (Lk 11:12-22).

Submit yourselves to one another because of your reverence for Christ (Eph 5:21).

94 Vya mzinga

She/he is surrounded (tied up)

Explanation: The analogy depicts a person who is surrounded by danger. *Maskawi* (spirit possession) is common among Tonga women and men. Once the victim is attacked, she/he appears as if she or he is bound up, especially when falling in convulsions.

Meaning: She/he is spirit-possessed.

Occasion: The proverb is cited when sympathizing with a person who is spirit-possessed. Some preachers relate it to the sprit-possessed people in the Bible. They bring up an analogy as to how sin binds a person.

Related Biblical Themes and Stories

The Lord Jesus said that if an evil spirit goes out of a person and brings seven other spirits even worse than itself, and they come and live there, that person is in a worse state than he was at the beginning (Lk 11:24-26).

He was some distance away, when he saw Jesus. He ran, fell on his knees before him, and screamed in a loud voice, "Jesus, Son of the Most High God! What do you want with me? For God's sake, I beg you, don't punish me" (Mk 5:6-8).

The next day an evil spirit from God suddenly took control of Saul, and he raved in his house like a madman (1 Sam 18:10).

95 Vyotikamba vya mng'ombe

We speak to the cattle

Explanation: Cattle are not easily controlled. A cow will not retreat on crossing a road, even if one sounds a hooter. Cattle turn a deaf ear.

Meaning: There are people who pay a deaf ear when others are advising them.

Occasion: The proverb is used to advise young people to be obedient to what the elders of the community say to change their bad character.

Related Biblical Themes and Stories

In the Temple vision, Isaiah saw that the people of Judah were constantly committing sin. So Isaiah brought the following message to the people: "No matter how much you listen, you will not understand. No matter how much you look, you will not know what is happening." Isaiah was to make the minds of the people dull, their ears deaf, and their eyes blind so that they cannot see, or hear, or understand. The people of Judah were so deaf that they could not even change their ways (Is 6:9-10).

In the parable of the sower those who turn a deaf ear on the word of God are like seeds that fall on the path, on a rock or under thorns (Lk 8:11-14).

96 Wabila pa chandi mutu uwoneka

You are drowned in a gourd, the head is seen

Explanation: A gourd is a traditional drinking vessel. It can contain a small quantity of water to quench one's thirst. A big object can easily be seen if it is in the water.

Meaning: We should not cover up our sufferings because they reveal our weaknesses.

Occasion: The proverb is cited to warn people not to cover up problems, because one day they will come into the open. Often the advice is given to a young woman, who is hiding her pregnancy, forgetting that one day everyone will see it. Thus sufferings can reveal our character. We also advise young people to accept suffering as a challenge to life. It is also cited when you know what a trickster is up to.

Related Biblical Themes and Stories

Paul says, "More than that, we rejoice in our sufferings, knowing that suffering produces endurance, and endurance produces character, and character produces hope, and hope does not disappoint us" (Rom 5:3-4).

Whatever is covered up will be uncovered ... Whatever you have said in the dark will be heard in broad daylight (Lk 12:2-3).

97 Wakozga kwa wiske

He/she is like the father

Explanation: A child who behaves exactly in the manner the father does.

Meaning: People inherit their parent's characteristics.

Occasion: The proverb is cited when discussing a person's peculiar behaviour or unique talents, like those of one's parents or direct relatives, e.g. hard-working habits, wisdom, courage, and so on.

Related Biblical Themes and Stories

He always had the nature of God, but he did not think that by force he should try to become equal with God (Phil 2:6).

Christ is the visible likeness of the invisible God. He is the first-born Son, superior to all created things (Col 1:15).

Whoever has seen me has seen the Father (John 14:9).

So that they may be one just as you and I are one (John 19:11).

98 Wakuya ku muzi ukuru

He/she went to the great village

Explanation: Death in Tonga society is seen as a journey to a great home where one is received by one's ancestors.

Meaning: He/she has joined the majority who have died.

Occasion: This proverb is used when someone has died. The people often speak of the dead as joining the ancestors. It is an advice that where the dead people go is even a safer place than we have in this life. Preachers often use it to console the bereaved implying that the dead person has been received in God's Kingdom.

Related Biblical Themes and Stories

Jesus said, "There are many rooms in my Father's house, and I am going to go and prepare a place for you. I will come back and take you to myself, so that you will bc whcrc I am" (John 14:2-3).

"And I saw the Holy City, the New Jerusalem, coming down out of heaven from God, prepared and ready, like a bride dressed to meet her husband" (Rev 21:2).

For Abraham was waiting for the city which God has designed and built, the city with permanent foundation (Heb 11:10).

But now that he is dead, why should I fast? I will some day go to where he is, but he can never come back to me (2 Sam 12:23).

99 Wamuchontha muguto

You have pricked him/her in the ear

Explanation: To make someone understand or to convince a person.

Meaning: To give a person enough evidence.

Occasion: The proverb is often cited in a court before a judge or jury or at a council of the elders (*mphara*), when one is defending himself/herself in order to convince the jury.

Related Biblical Themes and Stories

Jesus asked the chief priests and scribes and elders: "Tell me, where did John's authority to baptise came from, was it from God or from man?" (Mk 11:30).

100 Wavituta

He/she has possessed them

Explanation: This refers to a person who has been possessed by the spirits. The incident usually manifests itself in an alteration of the consciousness, the personality or the will of the individual.

Meaning: A form of trance in which the behaviour or actions of a person are interpreted as evidence of control by a spirit external to him/her.

Occasion: The proverb is cited normally when the spirit-possessed begin to mourn their loved ones. Preachers also use it to refer to demon-possessed people who were healed by Jesus. Spirit-possessed people

315

deter witches form coming around their homes; the proverb is used to refer to such events too.

Related Biblical Themes and Stories

When the seven sons of Sceva were spirit-possessed, they said, "I know Jesus, and I know about Paul, but you - who are you?" (Acts 19:14-15)

In the Synagogue was a man who had the spirit of an evil demon in him; he screamed out in a loud voice, "Ah! What do you want with us, Jesus of Nazareth? Are you here to destroy us? I know who you are: you are God's holy messenger!" Jesus ordered the spirit, "Be quiet and come out of the man!" (Lk 4:33-35)

In the story about the healing of a boy with an evil spirit: as soon as the spirit saw Jesus, it threw the boy into a fit, so that he fell on the ground and rolled round, foaming at the mouth (Mk 9:20).

101 Wawona masu gha chulu ghatema

You should not always expect mbulika (flying ants) to fly, just because you saw their holes opening on an anthill

Explanation: Flying ants fly out during the early rains. Some of these are edible. But they are unpredictable, even if they show signs of coming out. Yet people become impatient when they do not come out.

Meaning: Wait patiently as everything has its own time.

Occasion: The proverb addresses the theme of self-reliance and patience. It is cited to warn those people who are so anxious over things that they become impatient and frustrated. There is need to be patient and wait for the right time. Also, people should not rely too much on promises from others because they might not materialize. So it is important to be patient and self-reliant. The proverb is used by preachers to teach that everything that happens in this world happens at the time God chooses.

Related Biblical Themes and Stories

There is a time for everything (Eccl 3:1), as we live in a world of changes. In the wheel of nature sometimes one spoke is uppermost and then the other; it is a constant waxing and waning from one extreme to the other.

Let your hope keep you joyful, be patient in your troubles, and pray at all times (Rom 12:12).

102. Wazamukumana ndi aweya wa mujino, mumphunu ulimu kale

You will meet people with hairy teeth, while they already have hair in their nostrils

Explanation: There are more fierce people than we have ever known.

Meaning: People should not disobey or disregard their elders or parents

Occasion: The proverb is cited when warning unruly young people against despising others, because some day they will meet tougher people who will treat them harshly. It is a strong warning to those who feel that their malicious acts are not known by others. Sometimes the proverb is used to advise those who take things for granted and do not care. Preachers use it to exhort people to obey God who is Lord over their lives.

Related Biblical Themes and Stories

Eli always advised his sons to behave. But they always did what displeased God. The warnings that Eli gave did not mean anything to them: "Stop it, my sons! This is an awful thing the people of the Lord are talking about. If a man sins against another man, God can defend him, but who can defend a man who sins against the Lord?" (1 Sam 2:24-25)

Some boys made fun of Elisha, "Get out of here, baldy!" Elisha turned round, glared at them and cursed them in the name of the Lord. Then two she-bears came out of the woods and tore forty-two of the boys into pieces (2 Kings 2:23-24). This is what the proverb would imply.

103 Wendi jisu la nkwazi

He/she has a fish eagle's eye

Explanation: A fish eagle can see its prey from a long distance. The proverb is used as a simile.

Meaning: She/he has sharp eyes which are like an eagle's eye.

Occasion: The proverb is cited when a person recognizes others from a long distance, especially in a crowd. Sometimes it is used to praise one who finds a lost article that took someone a long time not to find.

Related Biblical Themes and Stories

She lights a lamp, sweeps her house and looks carefully everywhere until she finds it (Lk 15:8).

He was still a long way from home when his father saw him, his heart was filled with pity, and he ran, threw his arms round his son and kissed him (Lk 15:20).

104 Wendi mzimu uheni

He has a bad spirit

Explanation: The spirit which works against or torments a person.

Meaning: A restless spirit which is always blood thirsty.

Occasion: The proverb is cited when warning a person against associating with bad or murderous people. Sometimes it is used to refer to a person who is possessed by an evil spirit, such as a madman. It is also used to refer to a proud person. Some preachers use it to condemn those with bad behaviour.

Related Biblical Themes and Stories

The Lord's spirit left Saul, and an evil spirit sent by the Lord tormented him (1 Sam 16:14).

Pride goes before destruction, a haughty spirit before a fall (Prov 16:18).

Then Herod, when he saw that he had been tricked by the wise men, was in a furious rage, and he sent and killed all the male children in Bethlehem and in that region who were two years old or under (Mt 2:16).

105 Wendi mzimu wamampha

He/she has a good spirit

Explanation: It is the sense in which the Tonga speak of a living person having a guardian spirit.

Meaning: A person who has a good guardian spirit who looks after him/her.

Occasion: The proverb refers to those people who have a healthy life. In most cases it is used to refer to a person who has good luck, as the spirit of one's ancestor guards and guides the person in the right way, or when the spirit of his/her ancestor does not work against him/her. Preachers also use it to refer to role models of good Christian spirit in the community. They also preach that it is the spirit of God which guides people.

God asked Moses to choose seventy respected people as leaders and promised to take some of the good sprit God gave to Moses and give it to the people in order to assist Moses in some tasks (Num 11:17).

It is the spirit of Almighty God that comes to men and gives them wisdom (Job 32:8).

But my servant Caleb, because he has a different spirit and has followed me fully, I will bring him into the land into which he went, and his descendants shall possess it (Num 14:24).

106 Yo pamuko pa moyo ndiyo wajura kukhomo

The one who is purging is the one who should open the door

Explanation: The proverb is derived from a legend about conditions in the past, when owing to the roaming about of wild animals, it was expected that anyone who would go out from a shelter and be escorted in order to help himself/herself outside at night, would take the risk of opening the door himself.

Meaning: A person who has a problem should take the initiative towards solving the problem instead of asking others to help him or her.

Occasion: The proverb is used when encouraging a person to take initiative in doing something before asking someone else to assist. Do not wait for external assistance without putting your effort into it first. Sometimes it is used in a court setting. The one concerned should take the case to court. Young people should develop the spirit of taking initiative to solve their problems.

Related Biblical Themes and Stories

Jesus said, "People who are well do not need a doctor, but only those who are sick (Mk 2:17).

The Lord says, "Come everyone who is thirsty, here is water! Come, you that have no money—buy grain and eat! Come! Buy wine and milk—it will cost you nothing (Is 55:1).

Come to me all of you who are tired from carrying heavy loads, and I will give you rest (Mt 11:28).

I will get up and go to my father and say: "I am no longer worthy to be called your son; treat me as one of your hired workers" (Lk 15:18-19).

107 Yo waswela mviheni wariyengi

A person who delays doing the right thing will end up crying

Explanation: Similar to the English proverb: "A stitch in time saves nine."

Meaning: A person should not waste time in things that can ruin one's life.

Occasion: The proverb addresses the theme of decision-making. Sometimes it is used in preaching, admonishing those who do not make up their minds to repent of their sins. Such people find themselves overtaken by events, and lament. The proverb is also used to advise a person whose property needs to be attended to before it gets beyond repair.

Related Biblical Themes and Stories

Jesus warned some people to turn away from their sins, "But unless you repent, you will all perish "(Lk 13:3,5).

Again the theme of judgement in the story of the Ten Virgins illustrates this proverb. One must prepare and make a decision before it is too late. The five foolish virgins found the door closed. They cried out "Sir, let us in," the answer they received was, "Certainly not! I don't know you" (Mt 25: 1-13).

108 Yo watenda ndi mnkhungu nayo wawengi mnkhungu

The one who walks with a thief, will also become a thief

Explanation: If one person in a group is bad, then his/her bad behaviour will affect the others.

Meaning: Often our behaviour is affected by joining wrong peer groups.

Occasion: This proverb is used to advise young people not to join peer-groups of drunkards, drug abusers, smokers and so on, because it is easy to imitate what they do, only to find in the end that life has been ruined.

Related Biblical Themes and Stories

It may be that someone will not obey the message we send you in this letter. If so, take note of him and have nothing to do with him so that he will be ashamed (2 Thess 3:14).

Don't associate with people who drink too much wine or stuff themselves with meat, for drunkards and gluttons become poor, and drowsiness clothes them in rags (Prov 23:20-21).

"Come and join us and we'll all share what we steal." Don't go with people like that. Stay away from them (Prov 1:10-15).

Don't be envious of evil people, and don't try to make friends with them. Causing trouble is all they ever think about. Every time they open their mouth someone is going to be hurt (Prov 24:1-2).

Keep company with the wise and you will become wise. If you make friends with stupid people you will be ruined (Prov 13:20).

109 Yo watondo wasunga, yo wataya waliya

The one who finds, keeps; the one who loses, weeps

Explanation: People should keep account of what they find.

Meaning: A person should be responsible and not become extravagant.

Occasion: This proverb is used to ridicule people who do not keep their jobs or what they have, thinking that they can always have new chances. At the time their hopes fail to materialize, newly acquired things or relationship will prove useless and they lose everything.

Related Biblical Themes and Stories

So each of us shall give account of himself to God (Rom 14:12).

Now, take the money away from him and give it to the one who has ten thousand coins. For to every person who has something, even more will be given, and he will have more than enough; but the person who has nothing, even the little that he has will be taken away from him. As for this useless servant—throw him outside in the darkness; there he will cry and gnash his teeth (Mt 25:28-30).

110 Zeru yimoza yibayiska

One tactic will make you die

Explanation: One must have several tactics in solving problems and not only stick to one, even when he/she sees that it fails.

Meaning: It is better to mix with others in order to learn from their ideas and ways of life. We need to live in harmony with others.

Occasion: The proverb is used when advising a young person who isolates himself/herself from others. It is also cited to warn a selfish person. When problems overtake you, others will not come to assist you, if you keep to yourself. A person needs another person to help in everything. Preachers exhort people to pray to God for help.

In the 'High Priestly Prayer', Jesus prays for the disciples, "that they may be one" (John 17:21).

Here too the idea of 'unity is strength' comes out very clearly. The picture we see is common. Those who believed "were together and had all things in common; and sold their possessions and goods and distributed them to all who had need" (Acts 2:44-47).

111 Zeru zakuwija zibayiska

Self-conceit can kill a person

Explanation: Individualism and self-conceit are discouraged in the Tonga community.

Meaning: It is better to mix with others in order to learn from their ideas and ways of life. We need to live in harmony with others.

Occasion: The proverb is used when advising a young person who isolates himself/herself from others; or to warn a selfish person. When problems overtake you, others will not come to assist you.

112 Ziulikanga zikumpoka mahomwa[1]

Negligence was defeated by havoc

Explanation: In a battle one needs to make quick decisions.

Meaning: Those who are late will find themselves taken up by events or miss blessings.

Occasion: The proverb is cited when people do not heed advice, especially when young people are not fully prepared to withstand certain circumstances with readiness, awareness and alertness. Preachers use the proverb to exhort people to accept Jesus as their saviour before it is too late.

Related Biblical Themes and Stories

In the parable of the ten virgins our Lord Jesus warns us not to be late in making the decision to enter the Kingdom, i.e. to accept His word. It will be too late if we wait until we are in trouble (Mt 25:1-13). We are therefore to keep watching.

---

[1] Boston J. Soko, "A Collection of Tonga Proverbs" (Zomba, Chancellor College, 1985), p. 18. This collection is not published.

Likewise in Mk 13:32-37, Jesus warns us to be ready all the time for we do not know when that day or hour will come, neither do the angels in heaven nor the son, only the Father knows. We have to watch because we do not know when the master of the house is coming. If he comes suddenly, he must not find us asleep.

Isaac began to tremble and shake all over, and he asked, "Who was it, then, who killed an animal and brought it to me? I ate it just before you came, I gave him my final blessing, and so it is his forever (Gen 27:33).

113 Zua limoza kuti liwozga nyama ya Njovu cha

One day cannot make an elephant rot

Explanation: The elephant is a very big animal, and it cannot rot within a day once it is killed.

Meaning: It is not harmful to postpone one's work to the next day. We should not fear to postpone other jobs when we need to attend to the most urgent one.

Occasion: The proverb is cited when persuading a person to put off what he/she is doing for some time in order to facilitate their involvement in some other pressing duties or issues. For instance, students should learn to prioritize their study schedules. Preachers use the proverb to encourage people to worship God, first and foremost.

Related Biblical Themes and Stories

God is going to judge the righteous and the evil alike because every thing and every action will happen at its own set time (Eccl 3:17).

Jesus said, "what if one of you has a sheep and it falls into a deep hole on the Sabbath. Will he not take hold of it and lift it out?" (Mt 12:11)

As long as it is day, we must keep on doing the work of him who sent me; night is coming, when no one can work (John 9:4).

114 Zunguliyane, ine ndizunguliyengi uku tikumanenge kurweka

If you go round this side, I'll go round the other and so we will meet beyond

Explanation: The Tonga have a hope that, although people die at different times, one day they will meet again.

Meaning: Death is not the end of everything.

Occasion: The proverb is used to give hope to people that death is not the end of life, because they shall meet their loved ones one day. So the proverb is cited during funerals. It is also cited when one is prepared to suffer for others. Preachers cite the proverb to give hope to the bereaved so that one day, if they believe in God, they will meet their beloved ones.

Related Biblical Themes and Stories

Then Jesus went with his disciples to a place called Gethsemane and he said to them, "sit here while I go over there and pray" (Mt 26:26).

"So that you will not be sad, as are those who have no hope … Those who have died believing in Christ will rise to life first; then we who are living at that time will be gathered up along with them in the clouds to meet the Lord in the air. And so we will always be with the Lord" (1 Thess 4:13-17).

CONCLUSION

I am aware that, for various reasons, not all who will read this book may like the idea of using proverbs in preaching the Christian message. First, objectors may contend that since Tonga proverbs are part of African traditional culture, Christians must not go back to them. Secondly, they may be reluctant to use African proverbs because of fear that they may overshadow Bible texts or themes, since some of the proverbs are so vivid that they may be more easily remembered than the Bible texts. Thirdly, some religious people may be uncomfortable with the traditional proverbs, for the reason that some of the teachings they contain conflict with the teachings of the Bible. These possible objections to the use of indigenous Tonga proverbs in the Church are quite strong. For my part, I think that there are responses to them that are equally strong and worthy of careful and sympathetic consideration.

It is true that some aspects of traditional culture must be left behind when one becomes a Christian; for example, calling up the spirit of the dead, or cursing people who have wronged us. The Bible forbids such practices. (See, for example, Deut 18:9-13; Lk 6:27-36; Rom. 12:17-21). But this does not mean that all aspects of African culture are unchristian.

It is good to remember, too, that culture is very broad. It includes (1) *the beliefs* of a people, e.g. about God or the nature of humans; (2) *their values,* e.g. what they regard as good or bad, right or wrong and, therefore, ought or ought not be done; or what they consider to be true, or beautiful; (3) *their customs,* e.g. how they behave, relate to others, talk, greet, dress, eat or build houses; and (4) *the institutions* that help them express the above, such as the social structure, the institution of chieftaincy, the family, system of government, courts, markets, clubs and associations. It is this system of beliefs, values, customs and institutions that binds a people together and gives them a sense of identity, dignity, security and continuity.

As can be seen, no part of a people's life falls outside their culture. There-fore, it will never be possible to reject the whole of a culture; to try to do so would mean to refuse to live in this world. One must remember also that many aspects of African understanding of the family, community, empathy, respect for elders, awareness of the supernatural and belief in God are expressed through their culture.

On the second issue, it is true that there can be a real danger, if proverbs are not used well. The solution is that preachers should not build their sermons around proverbs. They must use Bible passages for sermons, and use the proverbs to explain, illustrate or reinforce the biblical truths with concrete examples. This must be done to help make it easier for their hearers to understand the message of the Bible. Proverbs that teach what is in opposition to what the Bible teaches should not be used, but one may cite them, if the intention is to show a better way through biblical revelation. Jesus did a similar thing when He declared: "You have been told of old ... You heard that .... But now I tell you ..." (Mt 5:21-28). For the Christian, the Bible as the revealed word of God must remain the highest authority, when it comes to considering which religious claims to accept.

As a solution to the third problem of the possibility of a proverb teaching something that is opposed to biblical teaching, we would suggest the following. In the selection of proverbs for use in preaching, the preacher must ask and answer some questions related to those proverbs, if they are really affirmed in the Bible, or if they are popular to the people, and so on.

African proverbs can be extremely useful and effective for all the things they can be for, particularly as a tool for teaching spiritual, moral and social values, and how to conduct oneself successfully in the business of life. They are short and easy to remember. They are also popular for their humour. Moreover, they provoke vivid images in the mind, such that things that are otherwise abstract and difficult to grasp become easier to understand.

At this point in Africa's history, when there are cries everywhere for moral and social reform, the use of proverbs in moral education is urgent. The many positive features of African proverbs, as shown above, are useful instruments of teaching. The Church should use African proverbs even more earnestly, especially in preaching and teaching. Their use will help immensely to teach the truths of many biblical themes and stories, and to affect the moral, social and spiritual lives of the people for the better; for when a proverb is used correctly, it speaks to the intellect, the soul and the heart—that is, to the understanding, the feelings and the will. Over the centuries, African proverbs have successfully done this. They can thus be used to great advantage in Christian preaching and teaching.

RECOMMENDATIONS FOR APPLICATION

On the Use of Folklore in the School Curriculum

For the purpose of instilling morals in the youth, it is imperative to use the folklore of the people, such as legends, myths, folktales, and proverbs more effectively. The student of traditional folklore, when interpreting its content, should take into account and explain the norms or beliefs of that ethnic group as they are relevant for that oral literature. The exhortative function of the folklore of the people is closely connected with its conservative survival in oral tradition. The corpus of the folktales and proverbs is their only literary thesaurus of didactic character. They are the last living moral vehicles in the oral tradition of even urbanized or modernized peoples. It is therefore desirable to include Moral Education in the school curriculum, as a separate subject from Religious Education. The justification for this is found in the philosophy of the curriculum based on Phenix 'Realms of Meaning,' and 'Forms of Knowledge'. [1] Hirst and Phenix argue that the total curriculum should cover various areas and involve the use of various modes of experience and forms of knowledge which are fundamentally different in character and employ distinctive concepts. Among these areas are aesthetics, the sciences, religion and ethics.

Creation of Tales and Proverbs

If folktales and proverbs are promising methods to influence not only a people's thought and motivations, but also their customs and daily behaviour, then there is a need to add hundreds of them to their language. In order to anchor them in the minds and memories of the people, there should be constant creation and recreation; telling and retelling of the tales and proverbs. If these stories and proverbs have the right form, they will stick in the minds of the youth and the sheer weight of their numbers, their euphoniousness, and their lucid composition, might tip the balance in the people's minds in favour of the new lore.

I am suggesting that mother tongue speakers and especially poets and narrators should create new stories and proverbs. They should be rephrased according to the rules of prosody that can be formulated on the

---

[1] P.H. Phenix, *Realms of Meaning*, London: McGraw-Hill, 1964, p. 57.

basis of an analysis of the existing tales or proverbs in the Tonga language. A wonderful example of just what I mean is the rich heritage, which is coming through the Radio under programmes like *Nzeru Nkupangwa, Pabwalo, Pamajiga and Wakusina Khutu ndi Mnansi.* This is one way of preserving Malawian culture. Poets should endeavour to write story lines for the artists to act them.

In line with this recommendation, the Government should form a Folklore commission, to gather up the fragments of the tales and proverbs that remain, so that nothing can be lost. Those concerned with education of the youth have a responsibility to gather up these fragments and must instil into the youth an enthusiasm for "elders' wisdom" (*Zeru za wala-wala*). The words of Ocitti can confirm this point. He points out that old people and parents used them in their dealings with children to convey precise moral lessons, warning and advice, since they made a greater impact than ordinary words.[2]

Status of Tonga Oral Literature in School

This book recommends restoring Tonga oral literature in schools. There was a time when the schools in Tongaland used some literature such as *Kanthini-kanthini* (Little by little), *Mkwele* (Go up), *Kumuzi* (At home), *Mchapu* (Walk faster), *Nthanu za Chitonga* (Tonga Fables) and *Chiswamsanga* (Opener of the way), which were withdrawn from schools. This type of literature can be revised or improved and be reprinted. This will be one of the teaching methods in which children will be fully involved, in order to make meaningful learning, sustain learner's motivation, and strengthen their power of concentration. It will also help the Tonga youth to gradually assimilate their cultural heritage embedded in the Tonga oral literature. As such, folklorists and linguists should explore new venues of writing more literature on issues related to morality, such as sexuality, marriage, respect for life, coexistence, respect for other peoples' views, tolerance, and so on. These themes can be transmitted through stories and proverbs.

---

[2]   J.P. Ocitti, *African Indigenous Education*, Nairobi, Kampala, Dar es Salaam: East African Literature Bureau, 1973, p.7.

Story-telling and its Alternatives

In speaking about effective use of story-telling and retelling, teachers should understand that young people love story time and like to hear a favourite story again and again. Often these stories employ metaphor, symbol, fantasy and drama to express and interpret the intangible. Folktales and fairy tales can be seen as childish or mildly amusing, yet they can shed light on our past and present experience and say something about the real world. Most of the stories in this study represent such a picture.

Story-telling provides listeners with time to picture the events as they occur and then, in later discussion, to share reactions and points of interests as represented in dilemma stories. All good stories and proverbs have layers and depths of meaning that do not appear immediately, but need to be reflected upon. Therefore, story-telling should have alternatives, which provide a lot of activities for pupils to understand the depths of a story and see in it their own interests and concerns.

These alternatives include, for example, miming, dramatizing, role-playing, discussing pictures related to the story, singing, using models or puppets, using work-cards and related objects, questioning and answering, and so on. Working in this way can reveal the process in which a hearer or reader moves from being aware of simple allegory to perceive much deeper and paradoxical meanings.

The conditions one chooses to adopt will depend on the ability, mood and maturity of the pupils as well as on the kind of story one uses. The groups need to be comfortable and able to hear clearly the story being told to them. Establishing a relaxed and receptive mood is therefore important. The audience or class should sit comfortably.

The pupils can brainstorm possible titles for a story and select the best three. Groups of pupils can compose questions they would like to ask about the story. Proverbs and proverbial sayings appropriate to a particular story can be suggested or investigated. It is also important to provide non-verbal means of expression. Pupils' responses can be given in paint, clay, collage or mime. In this way a mood or shades of meaning can be explored which might not be caught in words. This can be expressed by picturing a scene or sequence, or adopting a more symbolic form of image, or acting the story out to develop a ritual. The teacher should also discover ways of intergrating story-telling or proverbial sayings with other subjects such as Languages, History or Religious Education.

Recreation of Venues for Moral Instruction

Now as a result of the failure of families in instilling moral values, perhaps because the old ways are questioned, or because the old venues which used to be sources of moral instruction like the *mphara* have declined, it should be recommended that those venues which still appear should be encouraged. For instance, *Paduli* (Pounding place) is a communicative event within which conversational interchange takes place. Within the small group setting, women tell each other individual social experiences through song as a means of transmitting information. They gossip through ordinary conversation. In this social network of individuals, who know each other, the gossip and the stories they tell each other bind them together.

The focus on the dynamics of small group interaction is a strategy for stylized communication and for achievement of one's goals. Such factors as individual choice, persuasion, negotiation and manipulation of linguistic and cultural rules and norms in the accomplishment of social action are to be important, because verbal behaviour is purposeful.[3]

On this strategy, Timpunza Mvula looks at Maseko Ngoni women's pounding songs, which are a form of conversation.[4] Women's gossip, which is performed in this case through the medium of song, cannot be glossed over as mere chitchat as it provides a means to maintain unity, morals and values of a social group. Through being discussed, people are made to adhere to social values and behave well, for they know that if they don't, they risk being verbally condemned and ridiculed.[5]

If the *Mphara* setting cannot be recaptured in some Malawian communities, the Government should create institutions for preserving ethnic culture. These will provide venues where art and drama can be performed. Elders will be appointed to train youth in moral behaviour, using some traditional strategies by way of employing folklore of the Malawian ethnic groups. The elders are custodians of culture for the youth. Today, British Broadcasting Corporation (BBC) airs at least one African proverb every

---

[3] I. Basgoz, "The Tale Singer and his Audience," In Dan Ben-Amos and Kenneth S. Goldstein (eds), *Folklore: Performance and Communication*, The Hague: Mouton, 1974, pp. 143-203.

[4] Timpunza Mvula, "Strategy in Ngoni Women's Oral Poetry" in *Critical Arts in Journal for Cultural Studies*, vol. 5, no. 3, (1991).

[5] Ibid., p. 5.

morning. The Malawi Broadcasting Corporation (MBC) or Television Malawi (TVM), could introduce a similar programme. Documentation of oral literature is an urgent issue today, because most of our proverbs and stories are endangered. Therefore it is strongly recommended that proverbs, tales and other related genres of oral tradition should be collected to be printed for both transmission and posterity. Politicians and other intellectuals should safe-guard against the erosion of our cultural heritage in order to resist the forces of modernization, which may in the end totally ruin the moral behaviour of our youth.

Inculturation of the Gospel

The annotated proverbs for preaching and teaching discussed in this chapter prompt me to recommend that religious leaders should make policies to accommodate inculturation for the Gospel. Both Old and New Testament affirm the use of folktales and proverbs in the propagation of the word of God. Some European missionaries have been Christians for so long that they do not realize that the very traditional language they use in preaching is soaked in Biblical expressions, even though they have ignored it. Between the proverb and the long hymns that are sung in Church, there is the neglected genre of folk poetry of great beauty, the religious folk songs. As discussed in Chapter Seven, the Gospel, for example, affirms Tonga proverbs about the idea of God and Christian ethics.

For instance, on the theme of good and evil, God punishes His people if they continue to do wrong things. In Proverbs, *Kwawiyako Chiuta* (God has fallen on them there) shows how God is believed to punish sinful people. The Proverb *Mlendo ndi dungwi* (a visitor is like dew) is affirmed by the concept of hospitality in the Old Testament as in the story of Abraham and Sarah receiving visitors (Gen 18:1-9). A visitor is the one who kills the snake (*Mlendo ndiyo wabaya njoka),* or brings good things. The Proverb, *Moto walimbuni utocha lisuwa likuru* (A small fire destroys a big forest), can be affirmed by the use of a 'tongue', as an analogy described in James 3:1-12.

I am therefore recommending that missionaries in the language area where they work make new proverbs on the basis of the Biblical proverbs, especially of the New Testament. Mother tongue speakers and especially poets should be invited to give Biblical proverbs or stories a native appearance. Translation will be seen as the art of representing another culture in a way that makes it accessible to our own people. Another example is that of the Tanzania poet Maliasi Mnyampala (died in 1969), a

Catholic from Dodoma, who wrote a long poem of about 5,000 lines about the life of Jesus *Utenzi wa Enjili Takatifu,*[6] the 'Epic of the Holy Gospel,' giving speakers of Swahili an almost inexhaustible source for the study of the Gospels in an African appearance.

An Ancestral Religion

Enough reference has been made to Ancestral religion in this book. Hence, I also recommend the use of rituals offered to ancestors, because they are the custodians of morality. Ancestral religion is an enacted religious experience. The ritual action should attract the analytical attention of theologians. Good ideas and logical teachings are not enough. They must be incorporated into theology, catechesis and liturgy. There could be some Christian significance of certain traditional rituals for the natural recognition of the priestly and the elders' roles. Theologians must strive for the liturgical realization of that vital participation of which ancestral religion is such a vivid expression. Rituals which have to do with its purity are of great significance in morality and these must be explored. Some of these rituals are directly affirmed in the Old Testament, like that a person, who has touched a corpse, was believed to be impure. Of course, rituals and taboos that are discriminating should be revised, or revisited.

Most of the foregoing recommendations urge us to learn from those who have already walked the path. A person of experience can be of great value to someone setting forth on a particular path. The wealth of insight and knowledge carried by the older people of any community is indispensable to the community. However, this also applies to any person with knowledge and experience. Therefore, on occasion an older person may even learn from a younger person. A wider concept is that a nation evolves through the passing on of knowledge and skills. An individual's knowledge broadens both through personal experiences and incorporating the knowledge and skills of those around them, especially older people. Successive generations thereby acquire knowledge and skills with which a better life and a strong nation can be built.

---

6 Cited by Jan Knappert in "The Use of Proverbs for Evangelisation of Africa," Symposium on the *African Proverb in the 21st Century*, UNISA, 2.-6.10, p. 7.

ADDITIONAL TONGA PROVERBS FOR STUDY AND REFLECTION

1	Afwiti mbanasi	Wizards are relatives
2	Akufwa apaska nchitu	The dead give a job
3	Akwanjana asiyana	Even those who love each other do part
4	Amtekwa	A disabled person
5	Amwenda natu	Liar mongers
6	Anyamata azomphe	To let young people take messages quickly
7	Asani kunthazi nkhwamampha kuvuli nkhwamampha, yikamba ndi nyezi	It is a fly that indicates whether your destiny is safe
8	Azamsaniya nchalanga chitenje bu!	They will find you dead!
9	Boza litaska	A lie saves
10	Boza lilivi mweneko	Lie has no owner
11	Changa chaka Gamphani	The fame of Mr Gamphani, he planted
	chakupandiya zobala anyau achipanda malalanji	lemons while others planted oranges
12	Chanju che mu manja	Love is in the hands
13	Chakuziwanizga chingulinda chirwane	That which was late waited for danger
14	Chawa mu maso ghaki	Any one who has seen a lost thing
15	Chimeza mankhawa	A gluttonous person
16	Chimukira angumudina ndi musu pa duli	The intervener was hit with a pestle at the pounding place
17	Chiruwa chilivi munkhwara	Forgetfulness has no medicine
18	Chiwere vuli chingubaya Tungwa	Returning back killed the antelope
19	Chiruwa chakuruwa mbavi pa phewa	Forgetfulness is like one forgetting his axe on the shoulder
20	Cho chawona ine charutapo mawa che paku iwe	That which has seen me is gone, tomorrow it will see you
21	Cho walutapo nchako cha	That which passed is not yours
22	Dele laku lenduka	As slippery as ochra

23 Dolora nkhali	One who breaks a pot because of greed
24 Epa napo abikanga mtama kwene le ukume mchira	A neighbour was sick but he/she is now healed
25 Fukunyuwane makutu ghachiri nja	To reveal the news so that ears can be fed
26 Fumbanani mungabayana waka	To reason together in order to avoid quarrels
27 Fu wangujiwone bachi	A tortoise found a jacket for itself
28 Garu walondo kweniko atimupong'e viwanga	A dog likes to go where it receives some bones
29 Gonani ndikubayeni we patali cha	Spend a night and I will kill you is not a difficult thing
30 Guri wanowe nthenderu	A dance becomes sweeter with *nthenderu* relish
31 Jisu likuntha nyoli cha	An eye does not pluck feathers from chicken
32 Kachepa nkhakuvwala kakurya agawana	It is a cloth which does not suffice, food can be shared
33 Kakumaliya kawawa	The last trick is the most painful
34 Kakuziya maze	That which comes unexpectedly
35 Kakuza kija kasikuwa	What comes on its own is a bad omen
36 Kamuzunguzeni wanguji guziya nyifwa	'Kamzunguzeni' brought death upon himself
37 Kanyele kangutuma Njovu	An ant sent an elephant
38 Kayuni karyarya kawira mlomu	A clever bird is caught by its mouth
39 Kugomore thusi mphamulenji lenji	To make ridges is to start very early
40 Khungulikutu ngwe chimphara tukumu	Very early in the morning
41 Kidu ndi kangu vipambana	'Ours' and 'mine' are two different things
42 Koka bira boza kabuka	That which is light does not sink
43 Ko yikuwa kayuzi	Famine that whistles/great famine
44 Kuchelera nkhuvwa tambala	To be early is to hear a cock-crow
45 Kuja nge mba pusi mbwenu	To sit like hungry monkeys

	waka tafu-tafu	which chew their tongues
46	Kuja kauru ka unkhaka	To meet as a council of elders
47	Kujumpha chichinyiya chawapapi nkhujidaniya soka	To disobey parent's advice invites misfortune'
48	Kukamba chiuvwa-uvwa	To babble/to speak nonsense
49	Kulauska munthurumi ndi chivivivi	To feed a husband is to give him an early meal
50	Kumba nkhuyana mazu	To sing well is to have the same voice
51	Kumwana nkhumakolelo	A child is a scapegoat
52	Kunyeta nge maji ghanyeta pa chipopomo	As slippery as a water-fall
53	Kupambana kwa munkhwele ndi mbulika	A miss like that between a baboon and *mbulika* flying ants
54	Kupangandiya minyu nkhuziwani zga kwa mpapi	For a child to get his/her teeth twisted is due to parents' negligence
55	Kurya kwa mteki-teki	To eat extravagantly
56	Kurya pusi ndi mutu waki	To eat a monkey and its head
57	Kusele pambula kupupa	To disappear suddenly
58	Kutama watama mtiti, simbu wamtema phululu wa mutu ukuru	It is the sparrow which fell sick but *simbu* (incisions) were cut on an owl which has a big head
59	Kutali nkuchanya	It is only heaven which is far
60	Kutiryiya masuku pa mutu	To eat fruits (*masuku*) on the head
61	Kutondo nkhuba cha	Picking up something is not stealing
62	Kutuzga kadonthu pa msana	To pick a dot on one's back
63	Kuvuli ndi bamba lapamsana	Where you are coming from is a scar at the back
64	Kuyenda mchapu	To hurry
65	Kuvwiya mu kayuni	To hear from a bird
66	Kuweka ndi mantha	Blocking a blow is done out of fear
67	kuwe ndi chirewa	To come back with a crown
68	Kuwonana nge nkhu tulo	To see each other as in a dream
69	Kwadumuwanje tafipa ntima	That which has passed concerns us
70	Kwenda chakudumuka mutu	To walk as if one's head is cut off
71	Kwende pa msana	To walk by the back
72	Liwawu la munthu ndi	A man's body is an elephant,

njovu, uyu watuza wagwazamu	whoever comes, stabs it
73 Liwavu ndi muwela	The flesh is returnable
74 Makani ghatenda ghija, munyinu watimungumuliyani magumu-gumu	The case that is well presented
75 Maji asani ghadika ghayoleka cha	When water is split it is never recollected
76 Maji ghamunkhombu ndighu ghabaya	It is water in a drinking gourd which kills
77 Makutu ghachiri nja	Ears should be fed
78 Mawa ndi mawa lose	Tomorrow is forever
79 Masozi ngayoyokenge	Tears should be fed
80 Mtenda ghakuchita kung'anamurizga	A person who is critically ill
81 Mazua ghamwawi nganande lasoka ndimoza	For many days one is lucky, but there is only one day when one is unlucky
82 Mbavi yifwiya mu lumono	An axe can be broken by a soft wood
83 Mbewa yasoni yingufwiya kuzenji	A shy mouse died whilst in a hole
84 Mbiri yamampha yijumpha chuma	Good reputation surpasses wealth
85 Mbunu njiheni yitaya mwakundawona	Greed is bad because it leads a person in great trouble
86 Mbuzi yambura masengwe	A goat without horns
87 Mbuzi yisangaluka asane malonda ghepafupi	A goat becomes happy when it is about to be sold
88 Mlandu atata kweni thumba ndilu lisowa	A case is started but money for paying the fine is scarce
89 Mlanga ndi mheni cha, kweni mheni ndi tiringanenge	An instructor is not a bad person, but one who says, "Let us be equal"
90 Mlendo ndi nyoli yituwa	A stranger is a white chicken
91 Mlomu wa wala ndi ula	Elders' words are a prophecy
92 Mlomu ndi mphingu cha	The mouth is not a burden
93 Mlomu ndi fwiti	The mouth is a wizard
94 Motu ukuwa ndi kuphutiriya	Fire grows as one blows it

95	Muchuwa wanguzizwa mu maji	A frog was astonished while in its own
	muchiwa mwaki	water
96	Mu maji mukukana mchuwa	A frog failed in water
97	Mumphika wakuchichizga usweka	You force a pot, it will break
98	Munkhuwi wachirya maka	When *Munkhuwi,* a jar, eats charcoal
	Watijithemba usani pakhosi	trusts its big gullet
99	Mutinge ndikamwanda foja	Tobacco alone upsets the stomach
	pe wazinduwa	without anything else
100	Mtiti wangujitukumuwa	A Sparrow misused someone's
	pa ulemu wo wanguronde	authority
101	Mtiti wanguwele ku umtiti wake	A Sparrow went back to its sparrowness
102	Mwana kopa kazimu	For a child to fear an insect it must
	nkhumuruma	bite him/her first
103	Mwa wakukunhuzgika	A rolling stone gathers no moss
	kunkhuzgika wendi ndeli cha	
104	Muduzi wagalu ngumoza	A dog has one shade
105	Nchinkhu tyeku, ndi ng'o	Better eat a little than nothing
106	Ndachita nge ndalota	It seems I am dreaming
107	Ndifwiya kubala	I suffer because of bearing children
108	Ndalama zingubaya Yesu	Money killed Jesus
109	Ndali yenge vyamba	Politics is like *chamba* (Indian hemp)
110	Ndopa ku ndopa	Blood for blood
111	Nja yemu jino	Hunger is in the teeth
112	Ndimba ya maji gha moto	A depth of very hot water
113	Nthowa yimoza yibizga	One way leads a person to
	mu mathawali	*mathawali* water
114	Ntchakuziwaziwa garu	It is a well-known thing, Kalulu's dog
	yaku kalulu	
115	Nyaliwezga wawezga	Dusk sends a person back home
116	Nyamakazi yafyo msana	Rheumatism has broken the back
117	Nyama yaliuma, *chipemberi*	A stubborn animal, a rhinoceros, grew
	yingume masengwi pamasu	horns on the forehead

337

118	Nyifwa yilivi ku maji,	Death does not choose, it takes elders
	mla yito, mumana yito	as well as young people
119	Odi! Odi! Odi! Potateke pano tiryepo	Listen to the announcement for us to be fed
120	Pa mphunu ndipa mlomo	From nose to mouth
121	Pewanthu wo nawo nditenere kuti ndiwalereske	To feed information to people
122	Saza limaliya ku ndeu	A play ends in a fight
123	Saza lisazga bweka	Play includes everything
124	Skapato yimoza avwala anthu wawi cha	One pair of shoes is never worn by two people
125	Somba ndi maji	Fish is water
126	Soni zingubaya nkhwali	Pity killed the fracolin
127	Thenga abaya cha	A messenger should never be killed
128	Tione angumronda nkhanga	"Let us look at it," was deprived of a guinea fowl
129	Tireke kudumbizga anyidu weniwo suzgu yawakwindika,	A person should not rejoice over another's suffering because tomorrow
	chifukwa mawaliya ye paku iwe	it will be on you
130	Tiyeni-tiyeni wasokeka cha	If people just say: "Let's go," they never leave
131	Tiziwa kuwa ndi malusu ghakuzizikiya anyake ndikweni ghazamukutizizika taweni pavuli	You can trick others but some tricks can trick you
132	Uchembele nkhuryiyana	Kinship is to share food with others
133	Ufumu nchuma	Wealth is kingship
134	Unandi ngwamampha kweni unangiya kumala dendi pambali	It is good to be many, but being many finishes relish in the plate
135	Uranda ulaka waka njoka, wakwende malunga	The pitiful sight of a snake which moves on its belly
136	Wala-wala apemphe masu	Elders use eyes to beg
137	Wana nchuma	Children are wealth
138	Wamunthazi wakoleka cha	You cannot catch up with someone who is ahead of you

139	Yo wachiona ndiyu wathawa	He who has seen it is the one who runs away
140	Zina litufwa cha	A name does not die
141	Zuma ndizu ateghe mani, mbulika cha	*Zuma* is what can be caught by using leaves and not *mbulika*

BIBLIOGRAPHY

Banda, Tito, *Old Nyaviyuyi in Performance. Seven Tales from Northern Malawi as Told by a Master Performer of the Oral Narrative* (Musical notation by Mjura Mkandaŵire and Andrea Matthews), Mzuzu: Mzuni Press, 2006.

Basgoz, I., "The Tale Singer and His Audience," in Amos Dan and Kenneth Goldstein (eds), *Folklore Performance and Communication*, The Hague: Mouton, 1974, pp. 143-203.

Bone, David (ed), *Malawi's Muslims. Historical Perspectives*, Blantyre: CLAIM-Kachere, 2002.

Bourguignon, E. (ed), *Religion, Altered States of Consciousness and Social Change*; Columbus: Ohio State University Press, 1973.

Bultmann, Rudolf, *Jesus Christ and Mythology*, New York: Charles Scribner's, 1958.

Chakanza, J.C., "Some Chewa Concepts of God," *Religion in Malawi*, 1987, pp. 4-8.

Chakanza, J.C., Voices of Preachers in Protest. The Ministry of Two Malawian Prophets: Elliot Kamwana and Wilfred Gudu, Blantyre: CLAIM-Kachere, 1998.

Chakanza, J.C., *Wisdom of the People. 2000 Chinyanja Proverbs*, Blantyre: CLAIM-Kachere, 2000.

Chakanza: J.C., "Religious Independency in Southern Malawi Sectarianism in Joseph Booth's Mission Foundations 1925-1965, and the Response of the Mainstream Churches," in *Ministry of Missions to African Independent Churches* (1987), edited by David A. Shank, Mennonite Board of Missions, pp. 134-151.

Chimombo, Steve, "Oral Literature Research in Malawi: A Survey and Bibliography 1870-1986," in Bernth Lindfors (ed), *Research in African Literature*, 1987.

Chimombo, Steve, *Malawian Oral Literature*: The Aesthetic of Indigenous Arts, Zomba: Centre for Social Research/Domasi: Malawi Institute of Education, 1988.

Chimombo, Steve, *Malawian Oral Literature*: The Aesthetics of Indigenous Arts, Domasi: Malawi Institute of Education, 1988.

Chirwa, Devlin, The History of the African Methodist Church in Malawi, Zomba: Kachere Documents, 2003.

Chirwa, Filemon Kamunkhwara, *Nthanu Za Chitonga*, Published by the Livingstonia Mission and printed at the Mission Press, Blantyre, Nyasaland, 1933.

Chirwa, Filemon Kamunkhwara, *Nthanu za Chitonga*, Zomba: Kachere, 2007.

Cox, H. Machell, "A Debasing Influence," *Central Africa*, vol. 27, no. 313, 1909, p. 96.

Cox, James L., Expressing the Sacred: An Introduction to the Phenomenology of Religion, Harare: University of Zimbabwe, 1992.

Culley, Robert C., *Studies in the Structure of Hebrew Narrative*. Philadelphia: Fortress Press, 1976.

DeGabriele, Joe, "When Pills don't Work—African Illnesses, Misfortune and Mdulo," *Religion in Malawi*, 1999, pp. 9-28.

D'egh, Linda, Folktales and Society: Story-telling in a Hungarian Peasant Community: Bloomington: Indiana University Press, 1969.

D'egh, Linda, *Folktales of the World*. (ed Richard M. Dorson), Chicago: The University of Chicago Press, 1965, p. 78.

Dicks, Ian, "It Takes an Initiation to Make a Yawo Chief, " *Religion in Malawi* no. 16 (2011), pp. 3-11.

Dicks, Ian, *An African Worldview. The Muslim Amachinga Yawo of Southern Malawi*, Zomba: Kachere, 2012.

Dicks, Ian, *Wisdom of the Yawo People. Under the Elephant's Belly, you can't Pass Twice*, (*Lunda lwa Ŵandu ŵa Ciyawo. Kusi kwa Lutumbo kwa Ndembo, Kwangapita Kawiri*), Zomba: Kachere, 2006.

Dundes, Alan, *Morphology of North American Indian Folktales*, Helsinki: Folklore Fellows Communications no. 195, (1964), pp. 52-60.

Eliade, Mircea, *The Sacred and the Profane*, New York: Harcourt Brace, 1959.

Elmslie, W.A., *Among the Wild Ngoni: Being some Chapters in the History of the Livingstonia Mission in British Central Africa*, with an Introduction by the Right Honourable Lord Overton, Edinburgh: Oliphant, Anderson and Ferrier, 1899.

Fiedler, Klaus, *The Making of a Maverick Missionary. Joseph Booth in Australasia*, Zomba: Kachere, 2008.

Fiedler, Rachel NyaGondwe, *Coming of Age. A Christianized Initiation among Women in Southern Malawi*, Zomba: Kachere, 2005.

Fikilini, Esha, Umwali Initiation among the Tonga in Kasitu in Nkhotakota District, Mzuni Press, 2013 (Mzuni Documents no 48) [BA, Mzuzu University, 2012].

Finnegan, Ruth, *Limba Stories and Story-telling*, London: Clarendon Press, 1967.

Finnegan, Ruth, *Oral Literature in Africa*, London: Clarendon Press, 1967.

Fontenrose, J., *The Ritual Theory of Myth*, Berkeley: Univ. of California Press, 1966.

Frankfort, H.A. and H. (eds), "Myth and Duality" in *Before Philosophy*, Baltimore: Penguin, 1966.

Frazer, James G., *The Golden Bough*, vol 1., London: MacMillan, 1911.

Gray, Ernest, "Some Proverbs of the Nyanja," *African Studies 3*, (1944), pp. 101-128.

Jeffrey, Edward, The Impact of Jando Initiation on its Initiates in the Area of Kasamba Village in Nkhotakota, Mzuzu: Mzuni Documents no. 49, 2012 [BA, Mzuzu University, 2012].

Johnston, Harry, *British Central Africa: An Attempt to Give Some Account of a Portion of the Territories under the British Influence North of Zambezi*, London: Methuen, 1897.

Joseph, Booth, "Africa for the African" (Lynchburg 1897), reprinted as Laura Perry (ed), Joseph Booth, *Africa for the African*, Zomba: Kachere, 2008.

Jung, Carl, *Memories, Dreams, Reflections*, New York: Vintage Book, 1963.

Kalinga, O., *A History of the Ngonde Kingdom of Malawi*, Berlin: Mouton, 1985.

Kapito, Macduff, The Impact of Yao Traditional Initiation Teachings on Women: A Case Study of Traditional Authority Malemia, Zomba District, BA, Mzuzu University, 2010.

Kern, Sam, 'Man and Myth': 'A Conversation with Joseph Campbell," *Psychology Today*, (1971), p. 35-40.

Kumakanga, Stevenson, *Nzeru za Kale*, Blantyre: Dzuka, 1934.

Langworthy, Harry, "*Africa for the African." The Life of Joseph Booth*, Blantyre : CLAIM-Kachere, 1996.

Levi-Strauss, Claude, *Structural Anthropology*, vol. 1, London: Allen, 1968.

Lord, Albert B., "A Comparative Analysis," in Merlin Ennis (compiler and translator), *Embugu: Folktales from Angola*, Boston: Beacon Press, 1962.

Lord, Albert B., *Singer of Tales*. Harvard Studies in Comparative Literature 24, Cambridge: Harvard University Press, 1960.

Luka, Dennis, Christian Boys' Initiation Rites at Sitima Catholic Parish in Zomba, Mzuzu: Mzuni Documents no. 88, 2012.

MacAlpine, Alexander G., "Tonga Religious Beliefs and Customs," *The Aurora*, (Published by Livingstonia Mission), 1905.

MacDonald, Duff, *Africana or the Heart of Heathen Africa*, London: Dawson, 1882.

Magreta, Linus, "Recollections of Gogo Tuwalese's World," *Kalulu, Bulletin Malawian Oral and Cultural Studies*, Vol. 1, Jack Mapanje (ed), Zomba 1976.

Malinowski, Bronislaw, *Myth in Primitive Psychology*, New York: Norton, 1926.

Manda, Griffin K.M., "Funeral Conduct in Nkatha Bay," *The Society of Malawi Journal*, 18, (2), (1965), pp. 30-35.

Matemba, Yonah, Aspects of the Centenary History of Malamulo Seventh-day Adventist Mission, Makwasa, Malawi, 1902-2002, Zomba: Kachere, 2008 (Kachere Documents no. 53).

Matiki, Alfred J., "Problems of Islamic Education in Malawi," *Religion in Malawi* 1994, pp. 18-22.

Mbiti, John S., *African Religions and Philosophy*, London: Heinemann, 1974.

McCracken, John, *Politics and Christianity in Malawi 1875-1940*, London: Longman, 1977.

McCracken, John, *Politics and Christianity in Malawi 1875-1940. The Impact of the Livingstonia Mission in the Northern Province*, Zomba: Kachere, [2]2008.

McMinn, 'The First Wave of Ethiopianism in Central Africa', in *Livingstonia News*, August 1909, pp. 56-59.

Mdoka, Harold, The Impact of Jando and Msondo on Boys and Girls: A Case Study of Ntaja, Machinga, Mzuzu: Mzuni Documents no. 137, 2012.

Mitchell, J. Clyde, *The Yao Village*, Manchester, 1956, pp. 25, 138.

Mphande, David, *Nthanthi za Chitonga za Kusambizgiya ndi Kutauliya*, Blantyre: CLAIM-Kachere, 2000.

Mphande, David, *Tonga Proverbs for Preaching and Teaching*, Zomba: Kachere, 2006.

Murry, A. (ed), "The Possible Nature of a Mythology to Come," *Myth and Myth Making*, Boston: Beacon Press, 1968, pp. 300-353.

Mvula, Enock Timpunza, "Chewa Folk Narrative Performance," *Kalulu* 3 (1982), pp. 32-36.

Mvula, Enock Timpunza, "Some Chewa Folkstories from Central Malawi," MA, University of Leeds, 1978, pp. 22-24.

Mvula, Timpunza, "Strategy in Ngoni Women's Oral Poetry" in *Critical Arts in Journal for Cultural Studies*, Vol. 5., no. 3, (1991), pp. 1-36.

Mwasi, Yesaya Zerenji, "My Essential and Paramount Reasons for Working Independently 1933," in Kenneth R. Ross (ed), *Christianity in Malawi: A Source Book*, Gweru: Mambo-Kachere, 1996.

Mwasi, Yesaya Zerenji, *My Essential and Paramount Reasons for Working Independently*, Sanga, Chintheche: West Nyasa, 12th July 1933 (unpublished).

Mwasi, Yesaya Zerenji, *My Essential and Paramount Reasons for Working Independently*, Blantyre: CLAIM-Kachere, 1999.

Ncozana, Silas, Spirit Possession and Tumbuka Christians, PhD, Aberdeen University, 1985.

Ncozana, Silas, *The Spirit Dimension in African Christianity. A Pastoral Study among the Tumbuka People of Northern Malawi*, Blantyre: CLAIM-Kachere, 2002.

Nkhoma, Howard M. and Moira Kirwan, "Social Change and Widowhood: the Experience of the Tonga People of Northern Malawi," *Religion in Malawi* no. 7 (1997), pp. 13-18.

Ocitti, J.P., *African Indegenous Education*, Nairobi, Kampala, Dar es Salaam: East African Literature Bureau, 1973, p.7.

Okpewho, Isidore, *African Oral Literature*, Bloomington: Indiana Univ. Press, 1992.

Okpewho, Isidore, *Myth in Africa*, Cambridge: Cambridge University Press, 1983.

Okpewho, Isodore, "Rethinking Myth," *African Literature Today*, no 11: *Myth and History*, Eldred D. Jones (ed), London: Heinemann, 1990.

Olausson Jessica, Jarhall, *A Look at Changes in Primary Religious Education*, Linköping: Linköping University Electronic Press, 2001. Also available on the web under swepub:oai:DiVA.org:liv-62973 for free download.

Pachai, Bridglal, *Malawi: The History of the Nation*, London: Longman, 1971.

Parrinder, E.G., *African Traditional Religion*. London: SPCK, 1968.

Petersen, J., "Lessons from the Indian Soul. A Conversation with Frank Waters," *Psychology Today*, vol. 6. no. 2., New York, 1973.

Phenix, P.H., *Realms of Meaning*, London: McGraw-Hill, 1964, p. 57.

Phiri, Bentley Martin Ndonde, Independent African Churches in Nkhata Bay, History Seminar Paper, 1969/70, Soche Hill College.

Phiri, D.D., *Let us Fight for Africa*, Zomba: Kachere, 2007.

Phiri, Kings M., "Oral Historical Research in Malawi: A Review of Contemporary Methodology and Projects," *Kalulu: Bulletin of Malawian Oral Literature and Culture Studies*, vol. 1, no. 1, (June 1976), pp. 86-93.

Ranger, Terence O., *Dance and Society in East Africa*, London: Heinemann, 1975.

Rattray, R.S., *Some Folklore Stories and Songs in Chinyanja*, London: SPCK, 1907.

Scheub, Harold, "Parallel Image Sets of African Oral Narrative Performances," *Review of National Literature*, 2, 1969.

Scheub, Harold, "The Ntsomi: A Xhosa Performing Art," PhD, University of Wisconsin, 1969.

Schoffeleers, Matthew (ed), *Guardians of the Land*, Gweru: Mambo Press, 1979.

Schoffeleers, Matthew and A.A. Roscoe, *Land of Fire: Oral Literature from Malawi*, Limbe: Montfort Press, 1985.

Schoffeleers, Matthew, "Myths and Legends of Creation," *Vision of Malawi*, vol 3, no 4. (1972).

Schoffeleers, Matthew, "Twins and Unilateral Figures in Central and Southern Africa: Symmetry and Asymmetry in the Symbolization of the Sacred," *Journal of Religion in Africa*, Vol. 21 (1991), pp. 345-372.

Schoffeleers, Matthew, *River of Blood: The Genesis of a Martyr Cult in Southern Malawi* c. AD 1600, Madison: University of Wisconsin Press, 1992.

Shepperson George, and Thomas Price, *Independent African*, Edinburgh University Press, 1958.

Shepperson, George, "The Jumbe of Kota-kota" in I.M. Lewis (ed), *Islam in Tropical Africa*, London, Oxford: Oxford University Press, 1966.

Shorter, Aylward, "Religious Values in the Kimbu Historical Charter," *Africa*, 39, (1969), 227-237.

Sinclair, Margaret, *Salt and Light. The Letters of Jack and Mamie Martin in Malawi 1921-28*, Blantyre: CLAIM-Kachere, 2002.

Smart, Ninian, *The Phenomenon of Religion*, New York: Seabury, 1973.

Soko, Boston and Brian Shaŵa, *Tumbuka Folk Tales. Moral and Didactic Lessons from Malaŵi*, Mzuzu: Mzuni Press, 2007.

343

Soko, Boston J., "A Collection of Tonga Proverbs," Zomba: Chancellor College, 1985.

Soko, Boston, "The Vimbuza Possession Cult: The Onset of the Disease," in *Religion in Malawi*, Nov. 1987, no. 2, p. 14.

Soko, Boston, *Vimbuza. The Healing Dance*, Zomba: Imabili, 2014.

Thompson, Jack, "Xhosa Missionaries in Late Nineteenth Century Malawi: Strangers or Fellow Countrymen?" *Religion in Malawi*, 2008, pp. 8-16.

Thompson, Jack, *Ngoni, Xhosa and Scott. Religious and Cultural Interaction in Malawi*, Zomba: Kachere, 2007.

Thompson, Jack, *Touching the Heart. Xhosa Missionaries to Malawi, 1876-1888*, Pretoria: UNISA, 2000.

Turner, Victor W., *The Ritual Process*, Ithaca, New York: Cornell Paperbacks, 1977.

Turner, Victor W., *The Forest of Symbols: Aspects of Ndembu Ritual*, Ithaka: Cornell UP, 1987.

Tutuola, Amos, *The Palm-Wine Drunkard*, New York: Grove Press, 1953.

Vail, Leroy (ed), *The Creation of Tribalism in Southern Africa*, Berkeley/Los Angeles: University of California Press, 1989.

Vail, Leroy and Landeg White, "Tribalism in the Political History of Malawi," in Leroy Vail (ed), *The Creation of Tribalism in Southern Africa*, London: Currey, 1989.

Vail, Leroy and Landeg White, *Power and the Praise Poem: South African Voices in History*, London/Charlottesville: James Currey/University Press of Virginia, 1991.

Vail, Leroy, "Review of 1970, Republication of Notes on History," *African Studies* 30:67f (1971),

Velsen, Jan van, "Notes on the History of the Lakeside Tonga of Nyasaland," *African Studies*, 18, (1959), pp. 105-111.

Velsen, Jan van, "The Missionary Factor among the Lakeside Tonga of Nyasaland," *Rhodes-Livingstone Journal 26*, (1960), pp. 1-22.

Velsen, Jan van, *The Politics of Kinship: A Study in Social Manipulation among the Lakeside Tonga of Nyasaland*, Manchester University Press, 1964.

Werner Alice, in *Myths and Legends of the Bantu*, London: Frank Cass, 1968.

Willis, R.G., "Traditional History and Social Structure in *Ufipa*," *Africa* 34, (1964).

Young, Cullen and Hastings Kamuzu Banda, *Our African Way of Life*, London: Lutterworth, 1946.

Young, Cullen, "Notes on the Customs and Folklore of the Tumbuka-Nkhamanga Peoples of the Northern Province in Nyasaland (Livingstonia)," *Africa* 4 (1931).

Young, Cullen, "*Notes on the Speech and History of the Tumbuka-Henga Peoples,*" Livingstonia: Mission Press, 1923, p. 223.

Young, Cullen, *Some Proverbs of the Tumbuka-Nkamanga People of Northern Province in Nyasaland*, Livingstonia: The Mission Press, 1931.

Young, Cullen, "Some Proverbs of the Tumbuka-Nkhamanga Peoples of the Northern Province in Nyasaland," *Africa* 4 (1931), pp. 345-351.
Young, Cullen, "The Idea of God in Northern Nyasaland," in E.W. Smith (ed)., *African Ideas of God. A Symposium*, London: Edinburgh House Press, 1950.
Young, Cullen, *Notes on the Customs and Folklore of the Tumbuka-Kamanga People*, Livingstonia: The Mission Press, 1931.